K

My Heart

Also By Allie Everhart

The Haydon Falls Series:

1. *Keep My Heart*
2. *Break My Heart*
3. *Take My Heart*
4. *Protect My Heart*

Keep My Heart

Allie Everhart

embla books

First published in the UK in 2025 by

embla books

An imprint of Bonnier Books UK
5th Floor, HYLO, 105 Bunhill Row,
London, EC1Y 8LZ

Originally published as 'Be With Me' by Allie Everhart in 2022

A CIP catalogue record for this book is available from the British Library.

ISBN: 9781471420825

Also available as an ebook and an audiobook

1

Typeset by IDSUK (Data Connection) Ltd
Printed and bound in Great Britain by Clays Ltd, Elcograf S.p.A.

MIX
Paper | Supporting responsible forestry
FSC
www.fsc.org
FSC® C018072

The authorised representative in the EEA is Bonnier Books UK (Ireland) Limited.
Registered office address: Floor 3, Block 3, Miesian Plaza, Dublin 2, D02 Y754, Ireland
compliance@bonnierbooks.ie
www.bonnierbooks.co.uk

Chapter 1

Lyndsay

'Hey, I'm here,' I say, searching the airport terminal. 'I don't see you.'

'I'm running late,' Diane says. 'Had to go home and get Leah's soccer shoes. I just dropped her off. I'm on my way. I'll text you when I get there.'

'Okay. See you soon!'

Going to a bench by the window, I take a seat and scroll through my phone.

'Mind if I sit here?' someone asks.

I look over and see a guy pointing to the seat beside me. He's cute—average height, stocky build, short blond hair.

'Go ahead.' I scoot over, giving him room.

'I'm just waiting for a friend,' he says. 'His plane's here, but they haven't let them off yet.'

I nod and look back at my phone.

'You waiting for someone too?' he asks.

'I'm waiting to be picked up.' I look up from my phone. 'I just got into town.'

'Oh, yeah? Where are you from?'

'Los Angeles. I'm just here for a few days.'

'You got family here?'

I nod. 'My mom.'

The guy turns to me. 'What's her name?'

'Patty Davis.' I glance behind me out the window to check for Diane's minivan.

'Wait.' The guy turns more as he stares at me. 'Lyndsay?'

I stare back at him, realizing I recognize him. 'Matt?'

His eyes widen and he smiles. 'Holy shit. Lyndsay Davis. Or I guess you go by Sommers now. I haven't seen you since high school.'

'Yeah, I guess that was the last time, wasn't it?'

'You missed our ten-year reunion. I thought for sure you and Chris would be there.'

'We couldn't make it,' I say, looking away. I don't want to talk about Chris. I came here to get my mind off him, but now that I'm back, I'm realizing this town is just a reminder of him. It's where we met and where we fell in love. Coming back here was probably a mistake, but I needed to see Diane. This is a time in my life when I need my best friend.

'So where is he?' Matt asks, looking around. 'Where's Chris?'

'Oh, um, he couldn't make it.'

'He had to work?'

'Yeah.' I should just tell him the truth. Why would I keep it a secret? In a town this small, it won't be long before everyone knows. I'm surprised they don't already. The way my mom gossips, I can't believe she hasn't told the whole town. I'm guessing it's because she thinks Chris and I still have a chance. We've broken up and gotten back together so many times, she probably thinks this is just a temporary separation. But it's not. Yesterday the divorce was made final. My marriage to Chris is officially over.

'Actually, that's not the reason,' I say.

'What was that?' Matt asks, glancing over at me.

'The reason Chris isn't here. It's not because of work. It's because we um . . .' It's hard to say this. I don't know why. It should be easy, especially since I'm the one who filed for the divorce. 'Chris and I are divorced,' I blurt out.

'Oh, shit. I'm sorry.' He pulls me in for a hug. I haven't seen this guy since high school and he's acting like we're best friends. But that's Matt. He was a nice guy back then and obviously still is, the way he's acting so concerned for me. He was on the football team with Chris, but they weren't really friends. Chris was a cocky jerk whose friends were other cocky jerks. He only cared about himself, and still does.

'It's fine,' I say, pulling away. 'We'd talked about it for a long time. We just took forever to actually do it.'

'And it just happened? Like this week?'

'It was final as of yesterday. My lawyer called and let me know. I assume Chris knows. I haven't talked to him. He's in Vegas with a friend.'

'I'm really sorry it didn't work out.' Matt scoots back a little, giving me a genuine look of concern. Why didn't I marry someone like him? A nice guy who would've treated me well. 'Anything I can do to help?'

'No, but thanks for offering.' I smile and glance down at his hand, noticing the wedding band. Of course he's married. He's a great guy. Some girl probably scooped him up years ago. 'So what's new with you? What have you been up to since high school?'

He shrugs. 'Got married. Had a couple kids.'

'How old are the kids?'

'Mia is three and Bella is six. How about you? Any kids?'

'No,' I say, trying to hide my disappointment with a smile. 'We decided kids weren't for us.'

'Really?' He eyes me, his head tilting to the side. 'For some reason I always pictured you having kids.'

'We thought about it, but Chris wanted to focus on work.'

'What's he doing for work?'

'A little of everything,' I say with a laugh, but it's not funny. Chris has practically bankrupted us with all of his businesses, none of which took off. 'I'd rather not talk about it, or him.'

'Yeah, of course. Sorry about that.'

'It's okay.'

He checks his phone for the time.

'So who are you waiting for?' I ask.

'Nick.' Matt looks up from his phone. 'You remember him, right? From high school?'

'Nick Kanfield?' My pulse ticks up just saying his name. I had a small crush on him back in high school, which is odd because he wasn't at all my type back then. He was one of the smart people who got all A's and took the hardest classes. I, on the other hand, took the easiest classes and still struggled.

'Didn't Nick used to tutor you?' Matt asks.

'Yeah, that's right, he did,' I say, as if I just remembered that. But the truth is, I've thought about those tutoring sessions more than I should've the past 15 years. Nick was so patient and kind. He never made me feel stupid when I didn't understand something. Those tutoring sessions are what made me fall for Nick, although I never told anyone that. I tried to convince myself it wasn't true. How could it be? I had a boyfriend. A guy I loved. Nick was just a friend.

'Looks like he's finally off the plane,' Matt says as he looks at his phone. 'He should be here in a few minutes.'

'Where's Nick living now?'

'New York City.' Matt shakes his head. 'I don't know how he does it. That place stresses me out. I've only been there a couple times to visit him and I couldn't wait to leave. So much noise and traffic and all those people.' He laughs. 'Guess I'm just a small-town type of guy.'

My phone rings and I see Diane's name on the screen. 'Hey,' I answer. 'Are you here?'

'I'm at the airport, but I'm stuck behind a line of cars. I should be there in a minute or two.'

'Okay, I'll wait outside.' I get up from the bench.

'Is your mom picking you up?' Matt asks as I put my phone away.

'No.' I smile. 'She doesn't like driving in the big city anymore.'

He laughs. 'She calls Madison big?'

'Compared to Haydon Falls, yes. If it's big enough to have an airport, it's too big.' I pull the handle up on my suitcase. 'Well, it was good seeing you again.'

'Yeah.' Matt gets up. 'Hey, if you have time, maybe we could all get together and have a beer. You could meet my wife. Nick could come over. It'd be a good chance to catch up.'

'Thanks, but I don't think I'll have time.' It's not true. I have plenty of time, but I'd rather not spend it with people from high school. They'll want to talk about Chris, and this trip was supposed to get my mind off him and the divorce.

'Over here!' Matt yells, waving at someone.

I turn and see a tall, extremely handsome man in a suit coming this way. His eyes dart to me, then back to Matt, before going back to me.

Wait, that's not Nick, is it? It couldn't be. Nick was skinny and wore glasses and had longer hair that curled up on the sides.

'Hey, man, welcome back,' Matt says, giving him a hug.

'Thanks.' He pulls back, his eyes going to me.

'Look who I ran into,' Matt says. 'Remember Lyndsay? Chris' girl?'

Chris' girl. That's what people called me back in high school. Chris and I were a total cliché. I was head cheerleader and Chris was quarterback of the football team, the guy all the girls wanted. If I'd known back then how he'd turn out, I would've let some other girl have him.

'Hey, Lyndsay,' Nick says in a deep, strong voice that's nothing like the timid voice he had back in high school.

'Hey,' I say, sounding breathless. I glance at Matt. 'I need to get going. Diane's probably out there by now.'

'Diane Ellis?' he says.

'Yeah. She's picking me up.'

He nods. 'My wife used to take yoga with her. I didn't know you two were still friends.'

'Yeah. So anyway, good seeing you both.' I glance at Nick as I leave. His head is down and he's checking his phone.

He looks up. 'See ya, Lyndsay.' He gives me a smile and my insides do some kind of nervous flip-flop thing. What is wrong with me? I didn't react this way around him back in high school. Then again, in high school, he didn't look like this.

When I get outside, I see Diane's red minivan pulling up to the curb. She stops and jumps out, meeting me at the back of the van.

'Welcome home!' She hugs me. It's not home anymore, but I get what she means. She pulls back and looks at me. 'How do you never age?'

I smile. 'Believe me, I've aged about ten years through the stress of this divorce. If you can't tell, it must be my makeup. I have a friend who's a makeup artist. She taught me everything I know.'

'You'll have to teach me,' Diane says, grabbing my suitcase and flinging it in the back of the van.

'You look great!' I say, noticing she seems thinner than the last time I saw her. 'I like the pants.'

She has on yoga pants in an orange and white pattern that looks like a flame.

'Thanks! I just got them.' She winks at me. 'Tom loves them, if you know what I mean.'

She met her husband, Tom, back in college. They've been married for ten years and still flirt with each other and hold hands and kiss in public. I love that she found someone like that, a guy that's still crazy about her after all these years.

'Was that it?' she asks, looking around me.

'Yeah. I'm only here for ten days.'

'I wish you'd stay longer.'

'I can't. Ten days with my mom is long enough.'

She laughs as she goes to get in the van. Diane and I have been friends since ninth grade. She knows my mom and knows her constant advice-giving and questioning of my decisions drives me crazy. I almost didn't come here, knowing my mom would offer up her comments about the divorce, but I really needed to get away and I didn't know where else to go.

'Thanks for picking me up,' I say as Diane pulls away from the curb.

'I was happy to! It's a pretty drive.'

The scenery is one of the things I missed most when I moved away. Haydon Falls is a small town in a part of Wisconsin that's lined with rolling hills, dense forests, and winding roads. Along the river are the falls. You have to hike on a trail to get there, but it's worth the walk. The falls are beautiful, especially in autumn when they're surrounded by pops of orange, yellow, and red from the turning leaves.

'Sorry I was late,' Diane says. 'Hopefully you weren't waiting too long.'

'No, not at all. And while I was waiting, I ran into Matt.'

She glances at me. 'Matt Jennings?'

'Yeah. Isn't that weird? I haven't seen Matt since high school.'

'I see him around town. I used to take a yoga class with his wife but she got busy with the kids and stopped going.'

'Who's his wife? Anyone I know?'

'No. Tessa's not from around here. She's from Indiana. Matt met her in college. She's adorable. Tiny little blonde with big blue eyes. Her daughters look just like her.' She turns onto the highway. 'So what'd he say? He must've been shocked to see you.'

'We didn't talk long.' I pause. 'He asked about Chris.'

'Oh, Lyndsay, I'm sorry,' she says, reaching over to put her hand on my arm.

'It's fine. Being back here, I knew people would ask.'

'Did you tell him about the divorce?'

'Yeah. He didn't seem surprised, or maybe I just interpreted it that way.'

She sighs and puts her hand back on the steering wheel. 'Maybe this wasn't the best idea.'

'What?'

'You coming back here the week of your divorce. I thought it would help to have friends and family around, but it might just make things harder, with all the memories.'

'It's still better than being back in LA, living in that apartment and seeing all of Chris' stuff.'

'He still hasn't cleaned out his stuff?'

'Not yet. He promised me he'd get everything out next week, before I got back.'

'What's taking so long? He's had months to move out.'

'I don't know. I didn't ask. I'm trying not to talk to Chris.'

'Did Matt say anything else? Besides asking about Chris?'

'Not really.'

'Why was he there? Was he picking someone up?'

'Yeah.' I pause. 'Nick.'

'Nick Kanfield?'

'Yeah. You remember him, right? Smart. Kind of quiet.'

She laughs. 'Of course I remember him. Everyone knows Nick.'

It's because of his family. If you say the name Kanfield around here, everyone knows who you mean. Nick's parents own an apple orchard that's huge and draws in tourists from all over the area, even surrounding states.

'Is he here for the reunion?' Diane asks.

'I don't know. He didn't say.'

'I'd be surprised if he went. He doesn't seem like someone who'd like that kind of thing. Maybe he's just here visiting his family.' She glances at me. 'Didn't he used to tutor you in math?'

'Yeah. He's the reason I passed algebra.'

'So how did he look?'

'Good,' I say with a shrug.

'Does he still wear those big glasses?'

'No, he must've got contacts. He looked, um . . . different.'

'Different how?'

'Just different. Like bigger, more muscular.'

She smiles at me. 'You saw his muscles?'

'Well, no, but I could tell by the way his suit fit. His shoulders were broad, his chest was bigger. He looked like he'd put on some muscle.'

'I don't know when he'd have time to go to the gym. Being a lawyer, he probably spends all his time at work. Did he say if he's married?'

'No, but I didn't see a ring.'

Her brows rise. 'You checked for a ring?'

'I was just curious. I assumed he'd be married.'

'Maybe he is and just doesn't wear a ring.'

'If he was, you'd think he'd bring his wife with him.'

'Maybe she had to work.'

'Yeah, maybe.'

'He was kind of a nerd back in high school, but like one of those sexy nerds.' She glances at me. 'You know what I mean?'

I know exactly what she means. Nick was one of those guys who had a way about him that seemed sexy even though he didn't fit the traditional definition of the word. It was the way he carried himself—confident, yet serious. He was one of those quiet types that you imagine having a wild side he doesn't let come out very often. And by wild, I mean in the bedroom, or that's how I imagined him being in the few, but detailed, fantasies I had of my math tutor.

'So you said he's hot now?' Diane asks in a teasing tone.

'I didn't say that.'

She looks over at me, smiling. 'You didn't have to. I can tell just by looking at you.'

'What do you mean?'

'You're all flushed, like Nick got to you.'

I roll my eyes, laughing. 'I spent like a minute with the guy and we barely said two words to each other.'

'Sometimes that's all it takes.'

'Yeah, well, I'm not interested in Nick, or anyone else. I just got divorced. Dating is the last thing on my mind. It'll be a long time before I even consider dating again.'

'You wouldn't have to date him,' she says, smiling. 'Sometimes a night or two with someone else helps you get over an ex a lot faster than endless nights of crying and eating ice cream.'

'I'm not doing that. Eating ice cream or hooking up with a guy. The crying part? Yes, but not for much longer. I need to get over this and move on with my life.'

'I don't think it'll be that easy,' she says, frowning as she reaches over to squeeze my hand.

'I know, but being here is a start, right? Getting away from Chris, and the apartment, and LA?'

'For now, but then you'll have to go back.'

I look down. 'It'll be different when I'm back. I'm officially divorced now. Chris and I are over.'

It hurts to think about that. As much as I wanted to end things with Chris, knowing my marriage is over still hurts. I thought Chris and I would be together forever. When I imagined my future, it was always with him. Now that he's gone, I'm not sure what to do with my life, where I'll go from here, and if I'll ever trust a man enough again to give him my heart.

Chapter 2

Nick

'How's it feel to be home?' Matt asks as we get in his car.

'Same as it always does. I need a day or two to get used to the slow pace. It's such a huge change from the city.'

'I don't know how you live in New York. I'm there a few minutes and want to leave. Too many people. Makes me anxious.' He drives up to the parking lot gate.

'You get used to it.' I take a twenty from my wallet and hand it to him. 'Here.'

'I got it,' he says, swiping his credit card.

'Matt, what the hell? I told you I'd pay.' I drop the twenty in the cupholder. 'Use that to pay for the gas.'

He laughs. 'We're not in high school anymore. I can afford to pay for gas and parking.'

It's true, he can, but I make way more money than him and I'm single. He has a family to support. I don't want him spending his money on me, but I'm not going to argue about it. He's just being a friend.

'I can't believe we ran into Lyndsay,' he says as he drives away from the airport. 'She looked really good.'

'Yeah,' I say, trying to sound like I'm just casually agreeing with him. But damn, she looked more than good. She looked hot, even hotter than she did in high school. Back then, she wore a ton of makeup, had long blonde hair that ended at her waist, and was really skinny. Today her makeup had a more natural look and her hair was more brown than blonde and cut to just below her shoulders. She's still thin, but her breasts are bigger than they were in high school and her hips and ass are more filled out. When she was leaving, I couldn't help but watch her walk away, that round little ass keeping my attention from whatever Matt was saying.

'I had such a crush on her in high school,' Matt says with a laugh.

'Every guy did. She was hot and the head cheerleader.'

'You didn't.' He glances at me. 'Did you?'

'No,' I say, shaking my head. 'I knew I didn't have a chance with her so I didn't let my mind even go there.'

That's a lie. My mind definitely went there. I had more than a few late night fantasies starring Lyndsay. It made it difficult to tutor her.

'Can I ask you something?' Matt asks, checking the mirror before changing lanes.

'What?'

'It's personal, so you don't have to answer if you don't want to.'

'What is it?'

'Did you graduate a virgin? No judgment if you did. I'm only asking because I can't remember you dating much in high school.'

Matt and I weren't really friends back then. We didn't become friends until the summer after we graduated. He got a job at my parents' apple orchard and we worked together every day in the fields. I'd always assumed we wouldn't get along since he was a jock and I was more of an academic, but once we got to know each other, we got along great. We've been friends ever since.

'You don't have to give me an answer,' he says when I don't respond.

'I was kind of a late bloomer. And a nerd, so yeah, I didn't do it in high school.'

'You weren't a nerd,' he insists. 'You were just focused on school instead of girls.'

'It wasn't just that. I didn't want to get involved with someone and have people talking about it at school or in town. You know how people around here gossip. That's one thing I don't miss about living here. In New York, nobody cares.'

'So when did you finally do it?'

I smile. 'First week of college.'

'Was she older?' He laughs. 'Did she teach you stuff?'

'I didn't need someone to teach me. I figured it out on my own. And she wasn't older. She was my age.'

'Did you guys date?'

'Only for a few weeks, then we each met someone else.' I look over at him. 'I more than made up for what I missed out on in high school.'

Maybe I shouldn't admit that, but it's not like Matt would judge me for it. He was with a ton of girls before he finally settled down.

'Did you get serious with any of these girls?' he asks.

'No. You know how I am. I don't get serious with someone if it's not going to last. I knew I was going to law school after college and didn't want a girl thinking she had to go with me.'

'But aren't you still doing that?'

'What?'

'Keeping things casual. You've dated girls in New York but it never goes anywhere.'

'Because I haven't met the right girl. You'd think it'd be easy to find someone in a city that big but it's actually not.'

'What about that girl you dated last year? The doctor. You were totally into her, talked about her all the time. Why'd you guys end it?'

'We were both too into our careers. Two workaholics aren't good in a relationship.'

'One isn't either. You can't work all the time and expect the other person to stick around.'

'I don't really have a choice. I'm trying to make partner, and that won't happen if I don't work all the time.'

'So you're just going to keep dating without it going anywhere?'

'It's either that or stop dating until work slows down.'

He shakes his head.

'What? You don't agree with this plan?'

'You can do what you want. I'm just saying, you're not getting any younger. You're 33. At this rate, you'll be in your forties before you settle down, and 50 before you have kids. You know how much energy kids take? I can barely keep up with them in my thirties. There's no way I could do it in my fifties.'

'I won't be having kids in my fifties. I'm not even sure I'll have kids.'

'Really?' he says, sounding surprised. 'I thought you wanted kids.'

'I did, but lately I've been thinking about it and thinking it might be better if I didn't. I wouldn't want my kids growing up in the city. Kids need to be able to run around outside and play, like we did. You can't really do that in Manhattan.'

'So move back.'

'Yeah, that's not happening. My life's in New York.'

'Doesn't mean you can't move back. We don't have everything New York has, but we have fresh air, beautiful scenery, and this really great apple orchard that has this awesome fall festival every year.'

'My parents got you doing their public relations now?' I kid.

'No, but I could. I love that place. Everyone does.' He pauses. 'You really never considered taking it over someday?'

'Hell no.' I laugh. 'I got enough of that place growing up there. I couldn't wait to leave.'

'What about your brothers? Any of them talk about taking over when your dad retires?'

'No. Sawyer just opened the brewery, so he's committed to that. Jason isn't giving up teaching and being a coach. And Brody's lawn care and snow removal business is really taking off. I guess out of the four of us, I could see Brody doing it since he likes being outdoors, but he hasn't said he wants it.'

'So your dad will just have to sell it?'

'Probably, but it won't be anytime soon. He just turned 60. He's not retiring for a long time. I could see him working into his eighties.'

'It's too bad it can't stay in the family.'

'My dad never planned on us taking it over. The orchard was what *he* wanted. He didn't expect us to want the same thing.'

'Well, when he's ready to sell, I know a real estate guy who could handle the sale,' Matt jokes, referring to himself.

'You know he'll give you the business. You became like a son to him that summer you worked there.'

'What's your mom think about selling the orchard?'

'She's more sentimental than Dad. To her, the orchard is full of memories of the four of us growing up. She'll be sad to see it go.'

I feel a pang of guilt as I say that. There's a part of me that feels like I'm the reason my parents will have to sell the orchard someday. As the oldest son, I feel like I'm setting an example for my brothers, and by choosing a different career over the family business, I gave them permission to do the same. Maybe I'm giving myself more credit than I should, but I know my brothers look up to me and I know at least one of them would've considered working at the orchard if I'd gone down that path. It's just not what I wanted to do. But I don't like thinking about it being sold. I don't even let my mind go there. My parents don't either. They've never once brought up selling the place.

'So changing topics,' Matt says. 'Any chance you'd reconsider going to the reunion?'

'I won't be here. I'm leaving on Monday.'

'You could stick around. You haven't had a vacation in what . . . five years?'

'It hasn't been that long. And going to our high school reunion would not be a vacation.'

'Maybe not, but at least you'd get some time off. You could hang out with your family, your best friend.' He smiles at me.

'You'll be working next week.'

'I could find some time to hang out. I only have a few showings next week and a couple of closings.'

'You're selling two houses next week?' I ask, impressed because in a town this size, two is a lot.

'One's about 20 miles from here. I've expanded my area to get more business.'

'That's great.'

'Yeah, well, I got a family to support. I gotta hustle if I want to pay the bills. Going back to the reunion, just think about it. It'd be a good chance to catch up with people.'

'People I have no desire to see again,' I say, checking my phone. I see a message from one of my clients and text him back.

'Why wouldn't you want to see them? You're a big success.'

'I'm not going there to brag. And I really don't want to go back and relive high school. Once was enough.'

'It's not reliving high school. Everyone's old now, or 15 years older than they were back then.'

'Yeah, and they'll go back to how they used to be. That's what happens at reunions. Everyone goes back to their old roles. The cool kids are still cool. The smart people are still nerds. The jocks are still jocks, or pretend to be.' I reply to another message, feeling my stress level rise as I see how behind I am at work after just a few hours of being gone.

'I wonder if that's why Lyndsay is here.'

When I hear her name, I look up from my phone. 'What was that?'

'Lyndsay. She didn't say why she was in town. I wonder if it's because of the reunion.'

'Probably. I'm sure Chris insisted on it. It wouldn't be a reunion without the quarterback and the cheerleader,' I say, fighting an eye roll. I still can't believe Lyndsay married that jerk. I look back at my phone and finish the text I was about to send.

'They're divorced.'

I stop typing and look over at Matt. 'Who's divorced?'

'Lyndsay and Chris. She said it's official as of yesterday.'

Lyndsay and Chris are divorced? I shouldn't be surprised. I'm sure Chris cheated on her, but he cheated on her in high school and she still stayed with him.

'She told you that?' I ask.

'Yeah, when I was waiting for you. I'm surprised they made it that long. It's gotta be like, what . . . ten years they were married?'

'I don't know. I lost track of her after high school.'

But I always wondered what happened to her. I could've looked her up online, but I didn't want to see pictures of her with Chris. It's not like he bullied me or anything. He was just a pompous jerk who thought he ruled the school and everyone in it. And senior year, he snuck into the orchard one night and took an axe to ten of our trees. He claimed he didn't do it, but I know it was him. He did it to send a message to Sawyer, my younger brother, who Chris claimed was hitting on Lyndsay. Sawyer had a girlfriend at the time. He had no interest in Lyndsay. He just gave her a ride home one day after school when her car wouldn't start. But Chris, being the jealous prick that he was, decided Sawyer helping her out meant he wanted to date her and so he hacked up our trees.

'I don't know why you were friends with that guy,' I say.

'You know how I am. I'm friends with everyone. And I was on the team with him. I had to at least pretend to be friends with him.'

'What'd he end up doing? Do you know?'

'Not sure. Last I heard, he was trying to start some kind of rock-climbing business in LA.'

'I can't see Chris running a business. The guy couldn't stay focused except on the football field. I can't imagine him trying to run a business.'

'I'm sure it didn't last. You'll have to ask Lyndsay what he's up to these days, although I don't think she wants to talk about him.'

'When am I going to see Lyndsay? Those couple minutes at the airport will probably be it.'

'You could go to her mom's house. I'm sure she's staying there.' He pulls off at the road that goes into town. 'You know what's funny?'

'What?'

'I used to think you and her would be good together.'

'Me and who?'

'Lyndsay.'

'Yeah, because I'm totally her type,' I say with a laugh.

'Maybe you are. It's the opposites attract thing. You're all serious and by the book, and she's more of a free spirit.'

'By the book? What's that supposed to mean?'

'You follow the rules. You're a lawyer. Your whole job is about abiding by the law.'

'It's about *interpreting* the law in favor of our clients. Totally different thing.'

'Whatever. I'm just saying, you two complement each other.'

'Why are we talking about this? I'm not even going to see Lyndsay again.'

He pulls into his driveway. 'You ready for this?'

'Ready for what?'

He laughs. 'My kids. They can be a little loud.'

'I think I can handle it.'

We get out of the car and walk up to his house. It's a simple white two-story that cost less than a parking spot in New York City. I'm not kidding. My boss paid more for a reserved parking spot in Manhattan than Matt's house cost.

'Dad!' Bella runs up to him the minute we get through the door. She looks small for six, but what do I know? I'm never around kids. I don't know what six-year-olds look like.

Matt picks her up and kisses her cheek. 'Remember Nick?'

She shakes her head.

'It's been over a year since she saw me,' I say. 'I didn't think she'd remember me.'

He sets her down. 'Where's your mom?'

'In the kitchen,' she says.

We go down a hallway to the kitchen. Tessa, Matt's wife, smiles at me as we walk in. 'Nick, it's good to see you again.' She comes over and gives me a hug. I feel like I'm hugging a kid. She's barely five feet and I'm six three.

'Good seeing you too,' I say. 'Thanks for the dinner invite.'

'It's nothing fancy. Just grilled steaks and some sides. Nothing like the food you're used to in New York.' She laughs. 'I was worried about what to make, knowing you eat at all those great restaurants.'

'I'm actually looking forward to this. It gets old going out all the time.'

'I keep telling her to stop worrying,' Matt says. 'Just because you live in New York doesn't mean you forgot where you grew up.' Matt looks over at Tessa as she takes a jar of mayonnaise from the fridge. 'Nick's family used to have cookouts all the time over at the orchard. I'd work late just so his mom would invite me to dinner.'

I smile. 'And here I thought you were just a hard worker.'

'I love your parents' orchard,' Tessa says. 'It's so beautiful up on that hill with views of the river and the trees. They could host weddings there.'

'I'm not sure there's much demand for that,' I say, smiling, 'but I could mention it to them.'

'Want a beer?' Matt asks, going over to the fridge.

'Maybe later. I'll take some water for now.'

He takes a glass from the cupboard and fills it at the sink. I'm so used to drinking bottled water that it seems strange to see someone get water from the sink.

'Are you staying for the reunion?' Tessa asks as Matt hands me the water.

'No. I need to head back on Monday. I'm already behind on work.'

'Oh, that reminds me,' Matt says, going over to Tessa. 'We ran into someone from high school at the airport.'

'Do I know her?' Tessa asks, spooning mayonnaise into a bowl.

'You haven't met her, but you know her mom. Lyndsay is Patty's daughter.'

'From daycare?'

'Yeah.' Matt looks over at me. 'Lyndsay's mom used to work part-time at the daycare we took Bella to when she was younger.'

'I didn't know you went to school with her daughter,' Tessa says to Matt.

'I told you. You probably just forgot. I went to school with her husband too. Played football with him.' Matt takes a drink of his beer. 'I should probably say ex-husband. They just got divorced.'

'That's too bad,' Tessa says.

It's actually not. I'm glad Lyndsay divorced him. She deserves so much better than Chris.

'Did you invite her over?' Tessa asks Matt.

'No, I wasn't sure if I should without checking with you first. I didn't know if we had enough food.'

'We have plenty,' Tessa says, opening the fridge. 'You should call her up, see if she'd like to come. And invite her mom. Bella would love to see Patty again.'

'I would, but I don't have her number.' Matt smiles at me. 'We could send Nick over there. He knows where she lives. He used to tutor Lyndsay back in high school.'

He's giving me a look like he wants me to ask her out. What the hell is he thinking? She just got divorced. She doesn't want to date me. Even if she did, we live on opposite coasts.

'I'm sure she's busy,' I say. 'She just got into town.'

'Wouldn't hurt to ask,' Matt says, still giving me that look.

I ignore him and drink my water.

Would I like to see Lyndsay again? Sure, but I'm not going to go knock on her door. I'm here to see my family, and I'm leaving on Monday. Seeing Lyndsay would just bring up old feelings, something I don't need. I've moved on from that part of my life. High school. This town. It's my past, and I need to be focused on my future.

Chapter 3

Nick

'So when's your mom's party?' Tessa asks, setting a watermelon on the counter.

'Tomorrow at four,' I say. 'But my dad wants us over there early to help get the barn decorated.'

'That's so sweet of him to throw her a surprise party.' Tessa looks at Matt. 'You should do that for me someday. Gather up all the kids and throw me a party.'

'*All* the kids?' He gives her a funny look. 'We only have two.'

'So far,' she says with a devious smile before turning back to the fridge.

'Wait—what are you saying?' He holds onto her arm before she opens the fridge door. 'We're having more kids?'

'Maybe,' she says with a shrug and a smile.

He sighs. 'I'm gonna have to get another job.'

She laughs as he walks back to the counter to get his beer.

'Maybe it'll be a boy next time,' I kid.

'Yeah, maybe,' Matt says, looking over at Tessa and smiling. He's always saying they're done having kids but I think he secretly wants another one.

'Do you think your mom knows about the party?' Tessa asks me as she searches for something in the fridge.

'I don't think so. My dad's pretty good at keeping secrets. He's kept her out of the barn all week by telling her there's a family of rats living there. He told her he sprayed the place with chemicals and that it'll take a week for it to take effect.'

'Eww, rats,' Tessa says. 'That'd keep me away too. The party's in the new barn, right? The one they built a few years ago?'

'Yeah, he'd never have a party in the old barn. It's in rough shape. It's just used to store equipment.'

A few years ago my parents built a barn next to the house that's more like a regular building that was made to look like a barn from the outside. The inside has concrete floors, a beamed ceiling, and a large open space where we can set up tables to sell our products. There's a room in the back that was made into a kitchen so Mom could make the apple pies, donuts, and other apple desserts we sell.

Tessa glances at Matt. 'Honey, you got the marinade, right?'

'What marinade?'

She sighs as she shuts the fridge door. 'When you went to the store last night I asked you to get the marinade for the steaks.'

'Shit, I forgot. I'll go back and get it.'

'Mommy!' Bella yells as she runs into the kitchen. 'Mia hurt her finger!'

We hear wailing coming from upstairs.

'I'll go check on her,' Matt says, racing out of the kitchen.

'What'd she do to her finger?' Tessa asks Bella.

'She was wearing your shoes and fell down.'

Tessa leans down to her. 'Bella, I told you to stop playing dress-up with my high heels. They're for mommies, not little girls.'

'But they're pretty.'

'Go upstairs and be with your sister. See if Daddy needs help.'

She nods and runs off.

'It's always something with those two,' Tessa says, laughing.

'Yeah, I'm not sure I could handle that, although you and Matt make it look easy.'

'Trust me, it's not easy.' She rolls her eyes, smiling. 'Not even close. But we love it.' She opens the fridge. 'I can't believe he forgot the marinade. Maybe I could just make one.'

'If you want, I could go to the store.'

She turns back. 'Would you? I hate to ask, but Matt's probably going to be up there awhile and—'

'I'm happy to do it. Just tell me what you need.'

She gets out her phone. 'I'll text it to you.' She sends the text. 'Let me get you some money.'

'Forget it. It's on me. Need anything else while I'm there?'

'No, just the marinade. You can take Matt's car.' She grabs the keys from the drawer and hands them to me.

'I'll be back in a few minutes. Call if you think of anything else.'

'I will. Thanks, Nick!'

As I go out to Matt's car, I call up Sawyer.

'You in town yet?' he answers.

'Yeah, just got here. I'm at Matt's house, or actually I'm running to the store, but I'll be going back there when I'm done. Did you leave me a key?'

'Yeah, but I'm not sure I'm going out now. I think my date might've ghosted me.'

'Is this the girl you met online?'

'Yeah, and I haven't heard from her in two days. I've called her and texted her to see if we're still on for tonight but haven't heard back.'

'I'd say it's not happening. You could come over to Matt's house for dinner. His wife said there's plenty of food.'

'Thanks, but I think I'll stay here. I've been working on a new brew and think I almost have it figured out.'

'Working on a Friday night? You sound like you're turning into me,' I kid.

'I'm not that bad yet, but I could be. I just really like what I'm doing. It doesn't even feel like work, you know?'

Actually, I don't. My job definitely feels like work. Sometimes I'm not even sure I want to keep doing it. The long hours, the stress, and the demanding clients make me not want to be a lawyer, but after all the money and time I spent on school, I feel like I can't go back and change my mind. Even if I could, I don't know what else I'd do.

'What time you think you'll be here?' Sawyer asks.

'Not sure. Maybe around eight? Matt's gotta get the kids to bed. He probably doesn't want me there too late.'

'Just let me know. If my date falls through, I'll let you in. You can still take the key if you want to come over to get some time away from Mom and Dad.'

'I'm only here a few days. That's not long enough to need a break from them.'

'It might be if Mom starts in with the marriage talk,' he says with a laugh. 'She's been laying it on pretty heavy with me lately. You're the oldest, so she'll be even worse with you.'

'She knows I'm too busy to date right now. Her efforts are better spent on you.'

'Yeah, well, it's not happening.'

'I'm at the store. I should go. I'll text you later to let you know when I'm coming over.'

'Sounds good. See ya.'

I'm staying with Sawyer tonight because Mom doesn't know I'm home. If she knew, she'd ask why, ruining my dad's surprise. I could tell her I'm home for her birthday, but I don't usually come home for that, which would make her think something's up.

Sawyer lives in the space above the brewery. It was meant to be an office, but he turned it into an apartment by having a kitchen put in and hanging a curtain to divide his bedroom from the rest of the living area. I'll be sleeping on his couch tonight.

Going into the grocery store, I get out my phone and look for Tessa's text. I find it and see the name of the marinade. I look up at the signs above the aisles, not sure where to find bottled marinade. Living in New York, I rarely shop for groceries. I eat out or get takeout.

'Excuse me,' I say, stopping one of the employees as he walks by. He's a kid, maybe 16, with braces and a huge zit on his forehead.

I'm so glad to be done with the teen years. It's such a shitty time of life with the raging hormones and braces and zits popping up on your face at the absolute worst times. I had that happen right before one of my tutoring sessions with Lyndsay. I swear the thing wasn't there when I got home from school, but an hour later it looked like a crater had formed between my eyebrows. Lyndsay kept looking at it. I almost told her I was sick so she'd leave, but I didn't want her to go. Our tutoring sessions were the only time I had alone with her and I wasn't giving that up.

'You looking for something?' the kid asks.

'Yeah. Where do you have marinades?'

'By the salad dressings. Aisle four.' He smiles and I immediately see the resemblance to Mr. Petro, my high school English teacher.

'Hey, are you Petro's kid?' I ask.

'Yeah. Why?'

'I had your dad for English.'

He looks confused. 'When?'

'Like 15 years ago. Is he still teaching?'

'Yeah, but not here. He got married and moved to Eau Claire. I stayed here with my mom.'

Mr. Petro was married when he was my teacher, which means he got divorced and remarried in the past 15 years. I haven't even had a serious relationship in 15 years, unless you count Mina, a girl I dated for over a year, but neither one of us wanted to get married. We talked about living together, but it never happened and eventually we broke up.

'Next time you see him, tell him Nick Kanfield says hi. Or just say Nick, the orchard kid. He'll know who you mean.'

Growing up, my brothers and I were known around town as the orchard kids. The apple orchard is a huge deal around here because it brings in a lot of tourists in the fall when people swarm the state to see the fall colors. We get tour buses, vacationers from all around the country, people from Chicago coming up for the weekend. The orchard brings a boost to the local economy, which is why my parents are like celebrities around here. That might be a stretch calling them that, but in a small town, it's kind of true. Everyone knows them and knows our name.

'Your parents own the orchard?' the kid says, sounding impressed.

'They do. You been there?'

'Yeah, of course. Everyone has. My parents took me there every year.' He smiles. 'I liked the pumpkin patch the most. One year I got this huge pumpkin that was so awesome. I'd never seen one that big.'

'My dad planted a new field of pumpkins last year. You should check it out this fall. Hey, I need to get going, but it was good meeting you.'

'Yeah, see ya.'

The orchard started with just apples, but my dad quickly realized pumpkins drew in even more people than apples, so when the fields next to his went up for sale, he bought them and planted pumpkins. He gets people coming from all over to pick pumpkins, especially families and school groups. It's kind of cool hearing that kid talk about it, like going there was something special. I've always just thought of the orchard as a business, but to some people it's more than that. It's a memory they'll never forget.

Continuing to aisle four, I get out my phone again to check the name of the marinade.

'Oh! I'm so sorry,' a woman says, bumping into me. 'Nick?'

I look up and see Lyndsay standing there, holding her phone, looking up at me with the same beautiful blue eyes that I used to gaze at as she asked me questions about her algebra homework.

'Hey.' I smile at her. 'We meet again.'

'Yeah.' She takes a step back. 'Sorry I bumped into you,' she says with a laugh. 'I was looking at my phone and didn't see you.'

'Same here.' I hold up my phone. 'Matt's wife sent me here to get something and I keep forgetting what the name is. She texted it to me.'

'You're staying with Matt?'

'I'm just having dinner there. I'm staying with Sawyer tonight.'

She smiles and I get those feelings again, the ones I felt for her in high school. I had such a huge crush on her. She was one of those girls who was gorgeous but didn't know it, or she did, but didn't let it go to her head. She was also really sweet. She didn't fit the stereotype you see in movies of the mean cheerleader. She wasn't mean to anyone. I remember the first day of our sophomore year, this girl who was new to the school was sitting alone at lunch and Lyndsay went over to her and invited her to sit at her table. How does a girl that nice end up with an asshole like Chris?

'I heard Sawyer opened a brewery,' Lyndsay says, bringing my attention back to the present.

'It's not really open yet. Well, it is, but not every night and he's not doing any promotion to let people know. This week is more of a soft opening so he can work out the kinks before he has the official opening.'

'I'll have to go check it out while I'm here. Maybe we could go together.' She seems nervous, her voice breathy, her eyes darting around. 'I mean, just as friends, since he's your brother and it's his place and—'

'I'd love to,' I say, trying to figure out what's going on here. Did she just ask me out? And why is she so nervous? It's like we've switched roles from back in high school and now she's the nervous, awkward one instead of me.

'You don't have to,' she rushes to say. 'I know you're busy and I don't want to take up your time.'

'You're not. I'll be there anyway. Sawyer's insisting I try all his beers. He's having a tasting on Sunday. You're welcome to join us.'

'Um, yeah, sure, Sunday works. Or tomorrow. Either one works.'

'I have a family thing tomorrow. My dad's having a surprise party for my mom's 60th birthday. That's why I'm here.'

'He's throwing her a party? That's so sweet.'

'Yeah, he's not really the romantic type, but now and then he does something like this and surprises us all. Anyway, the party's tomorrow night but he wants us all there early to help set up.'

'So when are you leaving?'

'Monday. I need to get back to work. I've only been gone a few hours and I'm already behind.'

'Diane said you're a lawyer,' Lyndsay says, glancing down at my suit. I was going to change into something more casual but didn't have time. I left for the airport from work and didn't want to change clothes in an airport bathroom.

'Yeah, I'm hoping to make partner one of these days.'

'I'm sure you will. You were always really smart.' She looks away, then back at me. 'So how do you like New York?'

'It's good.' I pause. 'How did you know I live in New York?'

'Diane told me.'

I smile, still confused what's going on here. 'You were asking Diane about me?'

'No,' she says, her cheeks turning a slightly deeper shade of pink. 'I mean, we talked about you, but only because I told her I saw you at the airport.' She looks at her phone, then at the row of salad dressings beside us. 'She's waiting for me in the car. I should probably get going.'

'Yeah, me too.'

We both turn toward the shelves and I search for the marinade.

'Oops!' Lyndsay says, dropping the bottle of dressing she was holding. She seems really flustered today.

I reach down to pick up the bottle. As I give it to her, our hands touch and I swear I feel a spark, or maybe I imagined it. My body's doing some strange shit right now. I'm not sure what the hell's happening. My heart's beating way too fast and I can't think straight. My mind keeps flashing back to high school, then returns to the present, looking at Lyndsay and wondering if she's really here or if this is all a dream.

Damn, she looks good. She's got on these sexy little jean shorts and a pink tank top with a cropped white hoodie over it. It's unzipped and my gaze keeps lowering to her breasts, then her tan legs, down to her painted pink toes peeking out of her flip-flops.

Lyndsay puts the bottle back on the shelf and continues to look for whatever she's here to get.

'Can I help?' I ask.

'I got it.' She takes a bottle of dressing from the shelf, then turns to me. 'How about you? Need some help?'

'Um, yeah, I'm looking for this.' I get out my phone and show her Tessa's message.

'Oh, I've used that one before. It's good.' She finds it on the shelf and hands it to me. 'Need anything else?'

'No, that was it.'

'Okay, well, I better get going. Good seeing you again.' She smiles at me, pausing a moment before going around me to leave.

Shit, I didn't get her number. We're supposed to meet on Sunday.

'Lyndsay!' I call after her.

She turns back. 'Yeah?'

'Would you want to come to dinner tonight? At Matt's house?'

What the hell? Did I seriously just say that? I was supposed to ask for her number, not invite her to dinner.

She walks back to me. 'I'd love to, but I already told Diane I'd have dinner with her and her family.'

'Yeah, of course.' I laugh a little. 'I wasn't thinking. But I do need to get your number for Sunday. I'm not sure what time I'll be there.'

We exchange numbers, then walk together to the self checkout.

'Have a good night,' I tell her as she leaves.

'You too!' She turns back and gives me a smile, and damn, I feel something again, those feelings from the past coming back.

When I get to Matt's house, I find all of them in the kitchen. Matt's holding Mia, the three-year-old, and Bella's on a stool by the sink, helping her mom wash potatoes.

They have such a different life than I do. I kind of envy Matt when I see him like this, looking so damn happy with his kids and his wife. It's not that I don't like my life, but going home to an empty apartment every night in a city full of strangers isn't exactly how I imagined my life at 33. I thought I'd at least be married by now.

'You're back,' Matt says, smiling at me. 'You pick up some beer while you were there?'

'No, sorry, I should have.' I set the marinade on the counter.

'He's kidding,' Tessa says, glancing back at me with a smile. 'We have plenty of beer, or wine if you prefer that.'

'Beer is for daddies,' Bella says as she washes the potatoes with her tiny hands. 'Wine is for mommies.'

Tessa laughs. 'That's not true for all mommies and daddies. Some mommies like beer.'

'Are we gonna go to your brother's brewery this weekend?' Matt asks, setting Mia down. She toddles over to her mom.

'We can. I'm planning on being there Sunday. Sawyer wants me to try the new brews he's planning for fall.'

'It's only June.'

'He's not serving them yet. He's just getting the recipes figured out.'

'Would he care if I joined you?'

'He'd actually like that. He's looking for more opinions than just my brothers and me.'

'I'm sure if he asked around town he'd get plenty of volunteers,' Matt says.

'I'm sure he would, but he doesn't want many people knowing what he's planning now that there's that other brewery opening up.'

'When's it opening? Do you know?'

'I'm not sure. I think later this summer.'

'And Sawyer still doesn't know who the owner is?'

'Not yet. Isn't that something you could find out? You see all the real estate sales.'

'It wasn't a sale. The person inherited the building.'

'That's right. I forgot about that.'

'I'm sure they'll both do well,' Tessa says. 'Plenty of people in town like beer, and tourists love going to breweries.' She takes the marinade from the counter. 'Thanks for going to get this.'

'Sure. Anything to get Matt out of the doghouse.' I smile at him.

'She's used to it,' he says. 'I forget shit all the time.'

'Daddy said a bad word,' Bella says, pointing at Matt.

'I said *mint*,' he tells her. 'I forget *mint* all the time. Your mom uses it in recipes.'

Bella folds her arms over her chest and eyes him like she doesn't believe him.

He looks back at me. 'You see anyone you know there?'

'Just Lyndsay,' I casually say.

'You ran into Lyndsay?' he says, like he can't believe it. 'Again?'

'Yeah. She was in there getting salad dressing. It's next to the marinade. I went down the aisle and there she was.'

'No shit? That's crazy.'

'Mommy, he did it again,' Bella says. 'Daddy said a bad word.'

Tessa looks over at Matt. 'Why don't you guys go out back and talk? I cleaned off the patio furniture.'

'Yeah, okay.' He walks to the door that goes out back.

'I need to go change first,' I say. 'I need to get out of this suit.'

'In a minute.' Matt opens the door. 'Get out here.'

I follow him outside to the patio. 'What is it?'

He gets the same goofy grin on his face that he had in high school when he'd talk about girls. 'So what happened?'

'When? What are you talking about?'

'You and Lyndsay. What happened?'

'Nothing. We just got our stuff and left.'

'That's it? You didn't talk?'

I wasn't going to tell him this, but now I want to. I need to get another opinion about what happened because I still have no idea.

'We talked.' I look around, making sure his girls didn't sneak out here.

'And? What'd she say?'

I look back at Matt. 'I'm only telling you this because I need a second opinion. I think I'm reading meaning into something that was probably nothing.'

'Yeah, so what is it?'

'She was talking about Sawyer's brewery and asked if I'd go there with her.'

'Like on a date?'

'I don't know. That's what I'm trying to figure out.'

'What exactly did she say?'

'She said she wanted to go check it out and then said maybe we could go together.'

'Huh.' He rubs his chin. 'That kind of sounds like she was asking you out.'

'I know, right? But then she said we'd be going as friends, but she got all flustered when she said it. She kept talking and getting more flustered so I interrupted her and told her I'd do it. I'd meet her there on Sunday.'

He nods. 'She asked you out.'

'You think so? But she made it clear we'd be meeting up as friends, nothing more.'

'She said that, but it's not what she wants.'

I shake my head. 'I think the friend thing is what she wants. She just got divorced. She's not looking to date someone. And she knows I'm leaving on Monday.'

'Maybe she wants you for something else,' he says, giving me that goofy grin again.

'Yeah, that's not happening. Even if I was open to that, I wouldn't do it when she's fresh off a divorce.'

'Why the hell not? The marriage is over. She's free to do whatever she wants.'

'It's still not happening.'

'So did you agree to go out with her?'

'I told her I'd meet her at the brewery on Sunday, and now you'll be there too, so it's definitely not a date.'

'Make it one. Take her to dinner after we're done at the brewery.'

'I'm not taking her to dinner. I can't believe we're even talking about this. I'm leaving on Monday. Nothing's going to happen.'

'Did you say anything else to her?'

I hesitate, then just tell him. 'I might've mentioned dinner tonight.'

'Here?'

'Yeah, but only because you talked about inviting her. I threw it out there, but she already had plans. She's having dinner with Diane and her family. Maybe her mom will be there too. I'm not sure.'

He laughs. 'You invited her to dinner. But you're not interested in her.'

'I'm not. Are you saying I can't invite an old friend to dinner without it meaning something more?'

'Not when the old friend is a girl you have the hots for.'

I sigh. 'I'm going to go change out of this suit. And then I'm having a beer.' I walk back to the house.

'You're gonna need it,' Matt calls out, laughing, 'to calm your nerves before Lyndsay gets here.'

'She's not coming,' I yell back.

But I wish she was, because I really want to see her.

Chapter 4

Lyndsay

'I'm not going to Matt's,' I say to Diane as we go in her house. 'I already made plans to have dinner here.'

'Which you can do any other night this week,' she says, stopping when we get to the kitchen. She sets her purse and the sack of groceries on the counter and turns to me. 'Nick obviously wants to see you, and he's leaving on Monday. Call him and tell him you're coming over.'

'That's crazy! Why would I tell him I'll be there when I already told him I couldn't?'

'Tell him Leah is sick and I cancelled dinner to take care of her.'

'You want me to lie to him?'

'It's not a lie,' she says, waving her hand around. 'It's a story. One that isn't totally true.'

'It's a lie.'

'Fine. Then just tell him you changed your mind and want to come over.'

'I can't tell him that. He'll think I'm interested in him.'

'You are.'

'Diane, I just got divorced. I'm not dating someone a day after my divorce.'

'It's been more than a day. You filed almost a year ago. Yesterday just made it official. You and Chris haven't even been living together.'

'It still feels too soon.'

'Why? What are you waiting for?'

'I don't know. More time to pass?'

'How much time has to pass before you can date again?'

'More than a day.' I cover my face with my hands. 'Ugh. I can't believe I did that. I can't believe I asked him out.'

'You were nervous. It's easy to blurt stuff out when you're nervous.'

I drop my hands and slump down on the stool that's next to the center island. 'You should've heard me. I sounded like a complete idiot. I just kept talking and making no sense. Nick must've thought I was crazy.'

'You're being too hard on yourself,' she says, sitting next to me. 'The guy is good-looking. Rich. Successful. I totally get why you'd be flustered.'

'He looked so good in that suit,' I say, an image of him filling my head. 'I thought he was cute back in high school, but now he's this tall, muscular, handsome man that gets me all . . . tingly inside.'

Diane laughs. 'Oh God, you've got it bad.'

'What do you mean?'

'I remember feeling that way. It led to me marrying Tom, then getting pregnant, twice.'

I smile. 'You two were in love. This isn't love. It's just attraction making me feel this way. Nick is so handsome and smart and he has that deep voice that gets me all turned on.' I sigh. 'I can't believe I'm talking like this about some guy the day after my divorce.'

'Okay, listen.' Diane puts her hands on my shoulders and looks me in the eye. 'Your marriage is over. You and Chris are done. You two have been over for a long time and you're never going back to him.'

'It's still too soon to get involved with someone else. And Nick and I live thousands of miles apart. It's not like we'd ever actually date.'

'So have some fun with him.' She gets up and goes around the counter to unload the groceries. 'You have what . . . three nights until he leaves? Don't waste them.'

'I'm not sleeping with Nick.'

'Why not? And don't say it's because you still feel some kind of loyalty to Chris. You have every right to be with someone else. And let's not forget that Chris wasn't loyal to you when you guys were married.'

I look down. 'I try not to think about that.'

'I didn't want to bring it up, but I had to so you'd remember what a jerk he was and so you'd realize you don't have to keep being faithful to him. You were way too good to him for way too long. Now it's time for you to get out there and have some fun with a guy who would actually treat you well. And you and I both know Nick is that guy.'

'I can't do it. I don't even think Nick would want that.'

'Are you kidding? The guy had a huge crush on you back in high school.'

'He did not. He was just being nice to me.'

'He had a crush on you, and I bet he still does. You'll never know unless you go over there tonight. Just go as a friend. Nothing's going to happen with Matt and his family there.'

'I guess, but what about dinner? You already bought everything. I feel bad leaving.'

'We'll do it some other night.' Her phone rings and she answers. 'Hey, you're still picking up the kids, right?' She listens. 'Okay, yeah, I can do it. See you at home.' She ends the call. 'Well, there you go. I can't make dinner. I have to go get the kids. Tom's car got a flat and he can't pick them up.'

'We could order takeout,' I offer.

She goes to get her purse. 'This is a sign that you should be at Matt's house tonight, hanging out with Nick.'

'I don't know. I'd feel weird going over there. Matt and Chris were friends.'

'Matt was friends with everyone. It's just his personality. Now hurry up and call him. I'll drop you off there on my way to get the kids.'

I get out my phone and find Nick's number. My heart pounds as it rings.

'Hey, this is Nick,' he answers in his deep, sexy voice.

'Nick, it's Lyndsay. Any chance that dinner invite is still open?'

'Yeah, of course,' he says, a smile in his voice. 'Are you saying you're coming?'

'Um, yeah.' I look at Diane. 'What time should I come over?'

'Right now, if that's good for you. We're out back on the patio having drinks. Dinner will probably be in an hour or so. You need me to come get you?'

'No. Diane's dropping me off. I'll see you soon.'

'Looking forward to it.'

I end the call and set the phone on the counter, trying to catch my breath.

'Relax,' Diane says, laughing. 'It's just Nick.'

'I know. I don't know why I'm reacting like this, why I'm so nervous just talking to him.'

'Because you really like him.' She slings her purse over her shoulder. 'Let's go. I have to drop you off, then pick up Andy at his friend's house before I get Leah.'

I follow her out to the minivan.

'Wait! I can't wear this.' I point to my shorts and tank top.

'Why not?'

'It's not nice enough, and I wore it all day on the plane. I need to go change.'

'We don't have time.' She gets in the minivan.

I join her, sighing as I look down at my clothes. 'Nick definitely won't be interested in me when he sees me in this.'

'He already did, at the store, and he still invited you to dinner.'

'Okay, but I still should've changed.'

'What you're wearing is fine.' She glances at me. 'With a body like that, you look good in anything. How do you stay in such great shape?'

'Teaching yoga helps. And walking a lot. I used to walk on the beach for hours after Chris and I would fight. We fought a lot . . .' My voice drifts off as I remember those fights. Chris had a horrible temper. He'd yell and throw things. I didn't want to be around him when he was like that so I'd leave and go on a walk.

'Try not to think about him tonight,' Diane says. 'Focus on Nick and getting to know him again.'

'Diane, nothing's going to happen between us. I know you want me to find someone else, but it's too soon, and I'm not sure I even want that.'

'You don't want to get married again?'

'Not if it's going to be like it was with Chris. I don't want to be in that kind of relationship ever again. We didn't even like spending time together.'

'You were with the wrong guy. When you find the right one, everything will be different.'

As she stops at a light, my phone rings. It's my mom. I texted her when I got off the plane to let her know I was here. She's volunteering at her church tonight for a spaghetti dinner fundraising event. That's why I was planning to have dinner with Diane.

'Hey, Mom,' I answer. 'Are you at the church?'

'Yes, we just started serving. How was your trip?'

'Good. I slept through most of the flight.'

'Are you at Diane's house?'

'Um, yeah,' I lie, not wanting to tell her I'm going to Matt's house. She'd want to know why and I don't want to tell her. I love my mom, but she feels the need to give me advice about everything so it's best if I don't tell her stuff. 'We just started making dinner.'

'What time do you think you'll be home?'

'I'm not sure.' I glance at Diane. 'It might be kind of late. Diane and Tom want to play cards after the kids go to bed.'

'Okay, well, if it's after ten, just let yourself in.'

'I will. Bye, Mom!' I end the call and put my phone away.

'You might be out late?' Diane says, smiling at me. 'How late are we talking? Two, three in the morning? I'm guessing this means you and Nick are going out after dinner.'

I roll my eyes. 'That's not what I meant. I just didn't want her expecting me to be home early.'

'Why didn't you tell her you're having dinner with Nick?'

'Seriously? You know my mom. If she knew I was hanging out with a guy a day after my divorce she'd tell me it's too soon and that I should wait at least a year before dating again.'

'A year?' Diane says like I'm crazy. 'How are you supposed to give her grandkids if you wait a year to start dating again? You're not getting any younger.'

I laugh. 'Thanks. I didn't know 33 was that old.'

'It's not, but you know what I mean. By the time you meet someone, get engaged, and get married, you could be almost 40, especially if you wait a year to start dating.'

I'm dreading dating again, starting over from scratch. I'm not sure I even remember *how* to date. I was with

Chris since high school, except for a few months when we were 20 and not sure we wanted to get married. We both tried dating other people during those months and all I remember is that I didn't like it. The dates always felt awkward and I never felt any kind of connection with the guy. I think that's why I went back to Chris. He was my safe place, because he was familiar and reminded me of home. We were living in California and I missed my family and Haydon Falls. Chris was the closest thing I had to home without actually being there.

'I made so many mistakes,' I say.

'What do you mean?' Diane asks with concern.

'Marrying Chris. Moving to LA. Not going to college.'

'You went to college.'

'Community college, and I went when I was 26. I missed out on going to college when everyone else did and living on campus.'

'It wasn't that great. Just a lot of getting drunk at parties and feeling like crap the next day.'

I smile at her. 'You loved college. You met Tom there. But it's sweet of you to try to make it sound horrible for my sake.'

'I'm just saying, it's not as great as they make it look in the movies.' She slows down as we approach a sharp curve on a road that's surrounded by trees. It's such a beautiful area. Sometimes I really miss my hometown.

'Why don't you move back?' Diane asks, like she was reading my mind. 'Your mom's here. You have friends here. And there's no chance of you running into Chris now that his parents moved to Florida.'

'I don't want to move back here. What would I do for a job?'

'I'm sure you could find something. Oh! I have an even better idea! You could move to New York.'

'Why New York?'

'Because it's where a very handsome lawyer lives.'

I laugh. 'Yeah, I don't think so. I'm sure he already thinks I'm crazy for asking him out at the grocery store. He'd get a restraining order on me if he found out I'd moved to New York just to be with him.'

'Are you kidding? It'd be his dream come true. I'm telling you, Lyndsay, the guy totally wanted you back in high school.'

'I don't believe you, but even if he did have a crush on me, that was 15 years ago. He's changed. He's not the same person now. Neither am I.'

'All the more reason to get to know him again.' She pulls into the driveway of Matt's house and turns to me. 'Just go in there and be yourself. Don't try to impress him or pretend you're someone you're not. And relax. It's just Nick from high school. If it helps, imagine him like he used to look, the cute nerd with braces and glasses.'

I glance behind her, noticing someone coming out of Matt's house. 'Oh, shit, it's him. He's coming out here.'

Diane puts the minivan in park, leaving it running as she gets out. 'Hey, Nick, good to see you again.'

She gives him a hug as I get out of the minivan and meet up with them. 'Hey, Nick.'

'Hey.' He smiles and pulls me in for a hug. I wasn't expecting it and stand there with my arms at my sides, too flustered from the feel of his muscular arms around me and the intoxicating smell of his cologne, to hug him back.

'Well, I should get going,' Diane says as Nick lets me go. 'I've got to go pick up the kids.'

'How old are your kids?' Nick asks, smiling at Diane.

'Leah is seven and Adam is five.' She looks over at me. 'Just call me when you're ready to leave.'

'I can take her home,' Nick says.

'That'd be great!' Diane smiles at me. 'Have a good time!'

Why is she so insistent on playing matchmaker? Nick and I don't even live in the same state. We're on separate coasts. It would never work. Maybe he's not even interested in dating. Maybe all his focus is on his career.

Why am I doing this? I just got divorced. It's too soon to date. But this isn't a date. It's just dinner. Dinner with old friends. So why am I so nervous?

Chapter 5

Lyndsay

'Who'd she end up marrying?' Nick asks as we watch Diane drive away. 'Someone we went to school with?'

'No, she met Tom in college. He's from Illinois.'

'Should we go in?' Nick asks, nodding toward the house.

I turn to him. 'Are you sure this is okay? I feel like I'm crashing your dinner party.'

'You're not crashing it. I invited you, or actually Matt did. He wants you to meet his family.'

So it's Matt who wanted me here? Not Nick? I knew he wasn't interested in me. Why did I let my mind even go there?

'Hey, you made it!' Matt says as Nick and I go into the house. Matt's one of those guys who's always laughing and smiling and making you feel welcome. He gives me a hug. 'Drinks are out back, but first I want you to meet Tessa, my wife.'

I follow Matt to the kitchen, with Nick trailing behind. Now that I know he has no interest in me, I feel more relaxed.

'Babe, this is Lyndsay.' Matt leads me over to a tiny blonde woman who's standing at the counter, mixing a bowl of potato salad.

'It's nice to meet you,' she says, smiling at me as she wipes her hands on a dish towel. 'I'm glad you could join us for dinner. I've got beer and wine set up out back, or if you want something else, just let me know.'

'I'll have a glass of wine,' I say, thinking it'll help me relax even more. But just one glass. I don't want wine making me do something stupid with Nick, which is possible since I tend to lose my inhibitions when I'm tipsy.

'Follow me,' Nick says, going to a door at the far end of the kitchen.

I head over there, looking back at Matt and Tessa.

'I'll be out there in a minute,' Matt says, giving me a wave as Nick and I go out back.

'Red or white?' Nick asks, stopping in front of a metal bar cart stocked with beer and wine.

'White,' I tell him. 'But I can get it.'

'I've got it,' he says, taking the bottle from the bucket of ice and pouring the wine into a glass. He changed out of his suit into light-colored shorts and a fitted black t-shirt. My gaze goes to his muscular arms and shoulders. I still can't believe how much his body has changed since high school.

'Lyndsay?'

I force my eyes off his muscles and notice him holding the wine glass in front of me.

'Thanks,' I say, taking it from him.

'You're welcome.' He picks up a bottle of beer and takes a swig. 'So what changed your mind?'

'About what?'

'Coming here. I thought you'd already made plans.'

'Diane had something come up with the kids so we decided to do dinner another night.'

He smiles. 'I'm glad it worked out. It'll be good to catch up.'

'Yeah,' I say, feeling nervous again. He's so damn handsome, and he smells amazing. I take a big gulp of my wine, hoping it'll calm my nerves.

'So how long are you here for?'

'I'm flying back a week from Sunday. Chris is supposed to be out of the apartment by then. I assume you heard about the divorce.' I chew on my lip, wishing I hadn't brought it up. I'm supposed to be having fun tonight, not talking about my ex.

'Yeah, Matt mentioned it. I'm sorry to hear it didn't work out. That's gotta be tough.'

'It is, but I'm glad it's over. Now I just need him to move out. I don't want to go back to LA and find him still at the apartment.'

'You guys lived together while going through the divorce?'

'No,' I say, shaking my head. 'He just left his stuff there. He's been living with friends the past six months. He'd come back sometimes and sleep on the couch, but he'd be gone in the morning.'

'What's he doing for work?'

'Nothing,' I huff. 'At least not right now. He says he's considering his options.' I roll my eyes.

'What did he do before that?'

'Invested in businesses that turned out to be scams.' I sigh. 'I'd rather not talk about him.'

'I'm sorry. I shouldn't have asked.' Nick motions to the patio chairs. 'Why don't we go sit down?' He places his hand on my lower back as he leads us over to the chairs. His touch sends a tingle down me, the kind I haven't felt in years. Or maybe it's the wine making me feel this way, although I've only had half a glass.

'So tell me about you.' I turn more so I'm facing him, crossing my legs as I take a sip of wine.

'There's not much to say. I work a lot.'

'What's it like living in New York?'

'It's good. There's a lot to do. When I first moved there, it took me awhile to get used to a city that big after growing up in a small town.'

'I know what you mean. It took me a long time to get used to LA.'

'You ever miss it? Small-town living?'

'Sometimes I do. I miss being here in the fall, seeing the leaves, going to the orchard.'

He smiles. 'You miss the orchard?'

'I love that place. I grew up going there. Everyone did. I still like going. I told Diane I might even come back here for the fall festival.' I take another sip of wine. 'You think you'll be back for it?'

'Probably not. It's hard to get back here with my job. I was just in the office this morning so I've really only been gone a few hours and already have hundreds of messages waiting to be answered.'

'But you must love it, right? I mean, to work that much you kind of have to.'

'I like the job, but I don't like the long hours. Makes it hard to have a life.'

I tilt my head, eyeing him. 'So you never got married?'

'No. It's not that I'm against the idea. I just haven't met the right person. It's hard to meet people in a city that size, and I work a lot, so it's hard to find time to date.'

'I'm not looking forward to that.' I sip my wine. 'The whole dating thing. I'm not sure I even know how anymore.'

'It's not that hard. Just show up and be yourself. If the guy doesn't like you, that's his problem, not yours.' Nick takes a swig of his beer. 'You could practice on me if you want.'

'What do you mean?'

'We could go out. You could pretend you're on a date. Brush up on your skills.'

I can't tell if he's joking or serious. He's giving me this really sexy half smile and gazing at me with his deep blue eyes.

'Thanks, but it doesn't sound like you'll have time for that,' I say, looking down at my now empty wine glass.

'Want another?' he asks, pointing to my glass.

'Sure.' I hand him the glass as he gets up. I watch as he walks back to the bar cart. He even looks good from the back.

'White again?' he asks, holding the bottle.

'Yes, please.'

He pours the wine and brings me back the glass. I was going to stop at one, but I need another after that comment he made about us dating. He had to have been joking.

'We could do it on Sunday,' he says, sitting down. 'Your practice date.' He smiles. 'I can't say I'll be able to give you many tips given that I haven't been on a date myself in almost a year.'

'Really?'

'I just haven't had time.' He finishes his beer and gets up to get another. 'I'm sure I'm going to hear about that from my mom.' He laughs as he returns with his beer.

'She wants you to get married?'

'She's wanted that for ten years. If it were up to her, I'd be married with three kids by now.'

'What about your brothers? Did any of them get married?'

'No. Sawyer came close, but it didn't work out. My mom thinks my brothers are waiting for me to go first.' He shakes his head, smiling. 'If that's true, we'll all end up single.'

'You don't think you'll ever get married?'

'I think I will eventually, just not anytime soon. What about you? You think you'll get married again?'

'It's hard to say. Right now it sounds like a horrible idea, but maybe in a few years I'll feel differently.'

'Years? That's a long time.'

I laugh. 'It'll take me that long just to figure out how to date again.'

'What do you think of my offer? You want to use me for practice? I could use some practice too since it's been awhile.'

'Actually, yeah, that'd be great,' I say, wondering if he's just doing me a favor or if he's doing it because he wants to go out with me. But he's leaving on Monday, so he can't think the date would turn into anything. 'Where do you want to go?'

'We can figure it out on Sunday. We'll meet up at the brewery and leave from there.'

'Or the brewery could be our date,' I offer up, although I'd like to do more than that, like maybe have dinner somewhere.

'The brewery's not a date, especially with Matt there. He's going to join us.'

'Are you talking about me?' Matt asks as he comes out to the patio, a beer in his hand.

'I was telling her you'll be joining us for the beer tasting on Sunday,' Nick says.

'And then Nick and I are going on a pretend date,' I say, laughing. 'So I can practice my skills after being off the market for so long.'

'A pretend date, huh?' Matt smiles at Nick as he sits in the chair across from us. 'Who came up with that idea?'

'I did,' Nick says. 'I thought it'd be good for both of us since I haven't been out there either for a while.'

'What exactly do you do on a pretend date?' Matt asks before taking a drink of his beer.

Nick looks at me. 'I'm not really sure, but we'll figure it out.'

'You should go to that new restaurant,' Matt says. 'It's kind of fancy, but the food is really good. I took Tess there a couple weeks ago.'

'I think Sawyer told me about that,' Nick says. 'It's downtown, right? Across from the bakery?'

'Yeah, that's the one.'

'What do you think?' Nick asks me.

'Sounds perfect.' I take another sip of wine, nervous and excited about this date we just planned. Even if it's only pretend, I'm still looking forward to it.

'You sticking around for the reunion?' Matt asks me.

'I'll be here, but I don't think I'll go.'

'Why not?'

'I don't want people asking me about Chris and the divorce.'

'You could go with a date. People are less likely to ask you about Chris if you're with someone else.'

'I think it's a little late to find a date.' I take another sip of wine. 'And who would want to go to the reunion with me?'

'Maybe you could talk your fake boyfriend into going.' He looks at Nick.

'Now I'm a fake boyfriend?' Nick says to Matt, smiling.

'Why not? If you can be her fake date, you could be her fake boyfriend.'

'For the millionth time, I'm not going to the reunion,' Nick says. 'I have no desire to go back and relive high school.'

Matt leans toward me, hooking his thumb toward Nick. 'Would you please explain to him that reunions are about seeing old friends, not reliving high school? He doesn't seem to get how these work.'

'I think his mind is made up,' I say, looking at Nick. 'But it would be fun to go with him.'

'Are you serious?' Nick says.

I shrug. 'It doesn't matter. You're not going.'

'I could find you someone to go with,' Matt says, leaning back in his chair. 'There's a guy in my office who's single. He'd take you.'

'She said she doesn't want to go,' Nick says, staring at Matt.

'She doesn't want to go *alone*,' Matt clarifies. 'And since you're not an option, I'm offering up someone else.'

Nick's jaw tightens and he sits up straighter.

'Daddy!' A little girl with long blonde hair and a blue sundress comes running out of the house and up to Matt.

He pulls her onto his lap. 'What do you need?'

'Mommy said I should come outside and meet that lady.' She points to me.

'Hi!' I smile and lean toward her. 'I'm Lyndsay. What's your name?'

'Bella.' She lays her head on Matt's shoulder.

'She's six,' Matt says. 'And Mia's three.' He looks down at Bella. 'Lyndsay used to be a dancer like you. She taught ballet.'

I laugh. 'That's kind of a stretch. I just helped out at the dance school. It was a great job at the time. Better than working fast food.'

'You still dance?' Nick asks.

'Only for myself. I teach yoga, and after class, when the studio's empty, sometimes I'll stick around and do some ballet moves.'

'I can do ballet!' Bella jumps off Matt's lap and does some kind of squatting move that I think is supposed to be a plié.

'That's good!' I tell her. 'Now try it like this.' I get up and show her. She watches me, trying to move her feet like mine, her tongue at the side of her lip as she focuses. 'That's it! You got it!'

She smiles really wide and runs back to the house.

'You should get a job at the dance studio,' Matt says as I sit down. 'She's been taking lessons for three months and wasn't able to do that right until you showed her.'

'She's adorable,' I tell him.

'She's a good kid. Her sister's a little terror. Takes after her dad.'

Nick laughs.

'I should go check on dinner.' Matt gets up, leaving me alone with Nick.

'It's probably going to be an early night,' Nick says. 'Matt has to show a house in the morning and Tessa is taking the kids somewhere with Matt's mom.'

'That's fine. I wasn't planning to be out late.'

'Yeah, I suppose you're tired from the flight.'

'I'm really not. I slept on the plane. I just meant I didn't have any plans other than dinner.' I pause, wanting to suggest we go out, but feeling like I shouldn't. But if he's just a friend, then why not? 'If you wanted to do something later, I'd be open to that.'

'Yeah. Let's do it.'

'Great! I could start practicing my dating skills tonight!' I sound way too excited. I blame the wine. I've had two glasses and no food. I need to slow down before I say something I shouldn't.

'I just need to drop my stuff off at Sawyer's. Matt said I could borrow his car until the party tomorrow. After that, I'll use my dad's truck to get around. My dad didn't want me showing up there tonight and risking my mom seeing me. It'd ruin the surprise.'

'It's so sweet of him to throw her a party.'

'I can't believe he was able to pull it off. It's hard to hide stuff from my mom.' Nick nods at my empty wine glass. 'Can I get you another?'

'Not now, but thanks.' I set my glass down and turn more toward Nick.

His gaze drops down to my legs, then up my body. It turns me on seeing him look at me like that and having him not care that I noticed. He's much bolder and more confident than he was in high school.

I left home this morning feeling jaded about love and thinking I'd never have feelings for a man again. But here I am, having feelings for Nick that I haven't felt for a really long time. It gives me hope that maybe I could get married again, or at least be in a relationship. It's been so long since I felt this good around a man that I forgot what it's like. If only the man that makes me feel this way wasn't leaving on Monday.

Chapter 6

Nick

'Sawyer did a great job with the place,' Lyndsay says as she looks around the brewery.

'Yeah, it looks a lot better than it did,' I say, walking up to her. 'You should've seen it a few months ago. The fire nearly destroyed the place. I'm surprised the city didn't try to condemn it.'

'Why isn't anyone here?'

'It's closed tonight. It was open last night but only until ten. Sawyer's doing limited hours this week. He wants time to work out any issues before the official opening.'

Lyndsay walks over to the bar, running her hand over the reclaimed wood taken from an old shed that was original to the orchard. My dad tore the shed down last year, but some of the wood made it into Sawyer's brewery.

'Even though it's changed, I'll always think of this place as Meyer's Hardware,' Lyndsay says, sitting on one of the barstools. The seats were made using more of the reclaimed wood from the shed and then Sawyer added metal legs. It was my idea to make the barstools instead of buying them and Sawyer agreed. They turned out better than either of us imagined. 'I was really sad to hear it burned down.'

'I was too. I think everyone in town had a hard time accepting it was gone.' I take a seat beside her. 'Meyer's Hardware had been here forever. My dad loved the place. He likes Hal's Hardware too, but Meyer's was his favorite because it had been here longer. Dad's one of those guys who just can't bring himself to go into one of those big box hardware stores. He likes the small town store where he knows the owner.' I pause as I think back to all the times I came here with my dad when it was a hardware store. I miss those times. I like my life in New York, but I miss my family, and if I'm being honest, I miss this town. There just isn't anything here for me. The town's not big enough to need another lawyer, and after growing up here, I felt it was time to move on.

'How's he doing?' Lyndsay asks, turning to me. 'My mom said Mr. Meyer had a fall and might end up in a nursing home.'

I nod. 'He's already there. He's been there a few weeks. My dad went to see him yesterday. He said he's doing okay, but he misses being at home.'

'Did he sell his house?'

'Not yet. Matt's got the listing, but he said the place needs a lot of work before he puts it on the market. My cousin, Nash, is thinking of coming up here for a few weeks to fix the place up. He does construction, lots of old home renovations.'

'Doesn't he live in Chicago?'

I smile. 'You remembered that?'

'I remember a lot of stuff you told me,' she says, picking up a beer menu.

During her tutoring sessions, Lyndsay and I talked about more than just math. She was easy to talk to and asked a lot of questions, so what should've been an hour session would often end up being two, or sometimes three. We'd talk about most anything; movies, music, our families. The only topic we avoided was Chris and her relationship with him. It's like she sensed I didn't want to hear about him, or maybe she just didn't want to talk about him with me, knowing I didn't like him.

'Why would your cousin come all the way here to work?' she asks, looking over the menu.

'He likes being away from the city. He met Callie, his fiancé, in a small town south of Chicago, and kind of misses it. Sounds like they both do. Coming here for a few weeks would get him out of Chicago and he'd get paid for fixing up the house. It's a win-win.'

'Won't he miss his fiancé?'

'She might come with him. Nothing's definite yet. Mr. Meyer doesn't want to start the work until he's sure he's not going home.'

Lyndsay looks back at the area that used to be filled with shelves of tools and is now high-top tables and barstools. 'I always loved coming here as a kid. Remember the bubble gum machine? Mr. Meyer would always give us coins to put in it so we wouldn't have to pay.'

'That's right,' I say, smiling. 'He was a good man, or *is* a good man. I shouldn't be talking like he's gone, although at 85 he may not . . .' I decide not to finish that thought, not wanting to bring the mood down. 'He was thrilled when he found out Sawyer was buying the place. After the fire, everyone just assumed the building would be torn down.'

'Who restored it? Did Sawyer have to hire someone? There's no way he did all this himself.'

'He hired our cousin, Jake. Bryce helped too, but he was only here for part of it. Same with Nash.' I smile. 'We like to keep things in the family. They did it to help us out, but also to showcase what they can do. They'd never restored a place with that much damage. They took a lot of before and after photos and put them up on their website.'

'Jake and Bryce are Nash's brothers, right?'

'Yeah. You've got a good memory.'

'And there's another one.' She pauses to think. 'Austin?'

'Yeah. He's the youngest. I'm surprised you remembered their names after all this time.'

'It's because they reminded me of you and your brothers. Four boys close in age. Do they all do construction?'

'Yeah, Wheeler Construction. Their dad started the business and Nash and his brothers took it over, or they will when my uncle retires.' I pause, thinking how similar their situation is to my brothers and me. The four of us could've taken over the orchard, but none of us wanted it, and Dad never pressured us into taking it. He didn't want us doing something we didn't want to do out of obligation.

'You okay?' Lyndsay asks, putting her hand on my arm. 'You got quiet.'

'I was just thinking about something.' I smile at her. 'Ready to get out of here?'

'Sure.' She hops off the barstool and looks down at her clothes. 'I should've changed. I wore this on the plane because it's comfortable for the long flight.' She laughs. 'I look terrible for our pretend date.'

'You look beautiful,' I blurt out, then quickly say, 'I mean, what you're wearing is fine. But if you don't mind, I'd like to change into jeans.'

'Go ahead.'

'I'll just be a minute. You want anything to drink? I know the owner. I can get you whatever you want.'

She smiles. 'No, but thank you.'

I take off and go up the stairs to Sawyer's apartment. Tossing my suitcase on the couch, I quickly open it and take out a pair of jeans. I'd like to change out of my t-shirt but the button-up shirt I brought is wrinkled from being in the suitcase. I didn't bring many clothes, knowing I wouldn't be here long and figuring I'd end up helping out at the orchard. I brought work clothes and a nice shirt for the party. I definitely didn't pack for a date.

I'm going on a date with Lyndsay Davis, the girl I pined over all through high school. My teenage self can't believe this is happening. My adult self is struggling to believe it too. She seemed way out of my league back then, and still does. She's so incredibly beautiful, but still so easy to talk to. I feel like I can open up to her, which is not something I usually do, especially with women.

Grabbing my leather shaving bag, I go into the bathroom and set it on the counter. I open it up and take out my cologne. I spray some on and check myself in the mirror. This isn't a real date, but I still want to look good for her. I brush my teeth and rinse with mouthwash, then wonder why I'm doing it. It's not like I plan to kiss her. Then again, a date usually ends in a kiss, and if she really wants to know what it's like to get out there again, I shouldn't hold back. I should treat her like I would if we were really on a date.

I can't believe I suggested this. I threw it out there, half joking, never thinking she'd actually agree to it. I have no idea how tonight's going to turn out. Will we just forget the date and hang out as friends? I could see that happening, although I definitely feel some chemistry between us, the kind I didn't feel back in high school. Back then, she was so committed to Chris, she wouldn't even look at another guy.

'Hey,' I hear someone say as I go down the stairs. 'What are you doing here?'

As I walk into the brewery, I see Sawyer giving Lyndsay a hug.

'I'm home for a few days,' she says. 'It's good seeing you again.'

'You too,' he says, looking her up and down. He better not be checking her out. She's newly divorced. She's not ready to date, other than fake date, and that's only with me.

'I thought you had a date,' I say, coming up next to Sawyer.

'Didn't go well,' he says. 'So she came here with you?' he asks, pointing to Lyndsay.

'No,' I say, pretending to be surprised to see her. 'She must've broken in when I was upstairs. You should call the cops.'

'Wait—what?' Lyndsay grabs Sawyer's arm. 'He's lying. I didn't break in. I—'

'Relax,' Sawyer says with a laugh. 'He's just messing with you. He does that whenever he's—'

'With old friends,' I say, stopping him before he tells her the truth, which is that I tend to joke around with women I really like. I don't know why I do it. Maybe it's to calm my nerves, although I don't feel nervous around Lyndsay, so maybe it's something else.

'Right.' Sawyer smiles at me. 'Old friends.'

He better not say any more. He knows how much I wanted to date Lyndsay back in high school, and he knows I'll kick the shit out of him if he tells her that. I may play the role of sophisticated lawyer when I'm in New York, but when I come home, the rough-around-the-edges country boy comes out and I can throw a punch when needed, like if my stupid brother rats me out about my secret crush.

'So what are you guys doing here?' Sawyer asks.

'We just stopped by to drop off my suitcase,' I tell him. 'We're going to go find a place to get a drink.'

He motions to the bar. 'And what? This isn't good enough?'

'It's great!' Lyndsay says. 'I love how it turned out.'

'Thanks,' Sawyer says with pride in his voice. 'I put my heart and soul into it. Now I just need to make it a success, or at least make enough to keep the doors open.'

'Are you kidding?' Lyndsay laughs a little. 'You're the only brewery in town, and you know how much this town loves to drink. Add in the tourists in the fall and you'll be raking in the cash.'

'That *might've* been true,' he says, rolling his eyes, 'if another brewery wasn't about to open.'

'There's another one? Where?'

'Don't get him started,' I say to Lyndsay. 'We'll be here all night listening to him complain about the guy who will soon be his competitor.'

'Who is it?' Lyndsay asks Sawyer. 'Anyone I know?'

'The buyer wants to remain anonymous,' Sawyer says, rolling his eyes again. 'Why the hell is the guy trying to hide who he is? I'm gonna find out in a month or so when he opens. Why the big secret?'

'Maybe it's someone from high school,' Lyndsay says. 'Someone you didn't get along with.'

'Who? I got along with everyone, except Chris. I fucking hated that guy.' Sawyer realizes what he said and quickly backpedals. 'I meant back in high school. I'm sure we'd get along great now.' He folds his arms over his chest. 'So how's he doing?'

'I'm not sure,' Lyndsay says, her voice getting quieter. 'We're divorced.'

'It just happened,' I say to Sawyer. 'Probably not the best time to bring it up.'

'Sorry,' he says to Lyndsay. 'I didn't know.'

'It's fine.' She forces out a smile. 'I'm sure a lot of people will ask now that I'm back. Everyone knows us as Chris and Lyndsay. When they just see me, they're going to want to know what happened.'

'You don't have to answer them,' Sawyer says. 'Just tell them it's none of their business.'

'Sawyer, you know that doesn't work around here. It's a small town. If you don't tell them, someone else will, and whatever they say will be more rumor than the truth.'

'Yeah, you're right,' he says with a shrug. 'I'm sure after my date tonight everyone will be asking me who she was and if I'll be seeing her again.' He glances at me. 'I ran into Gertie outside the restaurant.'

I laugh. 'Yeah, you'll have the whole town talking about you, especially since the girl isn't from here.'

'Gertie.' Lyndsay laughs. 'Is she still trying to play matchmaker?'

'Hell yeah,' Sawyer says. 'The old lady isn't stopping until everyone in town is paired up.' He nudges me. 'You better lie low and not let her see that you're back. She told me she wants to set you up with Marilyn next time you're in town.'

'Her niece?' I say. 'The woman's as old as Mom.'

'Yeah, I know. I reminded her of that and she said your options are limited given your age.' He laughs. 'You can't afford to be picky.'

'*Me?* What about her? She's 85 and single.'

'Widowed,' Lyndsay says. 'That's different, especially for her generation. They commit to one man and don't think it's right to find someone else after he's gone.'

'Her husband's been dead for 25 years,' I say. 'I think he'd be okay with her dating.'

'Gertie might be right,' Sawyer says, going around to the other side of the bar. 'You're not getting any younger, Nick. You need to start dating again.' He leans back against the counter. 'What's it been . . . like over a year since you've been on a date?'

'It hasn't been that long. And I have a date tonight, not that it's any of your business.'

'Who's your date?'

'Me,' Lyndsay says, smiling as she wraps her arm around mine.

Sawyer looks at me to confirm it, thinking she's kidding.

'It's a practice date,' I explain. 'It's not real. I'm just doing her a favor.'

Sawyer looks confused.

Lyndsay lets go of me and steps up to the bar to talk to Sawyer. 'I've been with Chris for so long that I'm not sure I know how to date. Obviously I know the basics, but it's been so long since I've actually done it that I'm not sure I can anymore without feeling awkward and unsure of myself. So Nick offered to let me practice on him.'

'How generous of him,' Sawyer says, glancing at me.

'I know, right? He was always such a nice guy. Still is.'

The nice guy who never gets the girl, at least not in high school. If Lyndsay likes nice guys, why didn't she pick me instead of an asshole like Chris?

'So where are you going?' Sawyer asks.

'I'm not sure.' Lyndsay looks back at me. 'Where are you taking me?'

'Harley's on Main,' I say, deciding to take charge and just pick a place. I'm not the kid I was in high school, afraid to speak up. I'm bolder now, and a hell of a lot more confident.

'Is that new?' Lyndsay asks. 'I don't think I've been there.'

'It used to be Don's,' Sawyer says. 'His son took it over a few months ago.'

'It's a country bar,' I tell her. 'Nothing fancy, but it's a good time. Sawyer and I went there last time I was in town.'

'Since when are you a country boy?' Lyndsay asks in a tone that sounds kind of flirty. She's sounded that way more than once tonight, but it could be because she was drinking.

'I've always been a country boy,' I tell her. 'I grew up on an orchard.'

'But you live in New York now. I thought the city would've made you all fancy and sophisticated. I was thinking you'd suggest we go to a wine bar.'

'There aren't any wine bars here, and even if there were, I get enough of those in New York. When I come home, I like to kick back and hang out at places like Harley's. But if you want to go someplace nicer—'

'I don't. The country place sounds fun!' She walks up to me. 'I'm up for anything.'

Sawyer clears his throat. I look over at him and see him trying to hide a smile. By 'anything' she didn't mean what he's thinking. His mind always goes straight to sex.

'You two have fun,' he says.

'See ya later,' I tell him. I motion Lyndsay to go ahead of me. 'Ladies first.'

'Such a gentleman,' she says, giving me a smile before heading to the door.

'Nick,' Sawyer says under his breath.

I look back at him. 'What?'

He mouths the words, *What the fuck?* He points to Lyndsay.

'I'll try to be quiet when I get back,' I say, ignoring his question.

He's acting like I'm going on a real date, but I'm not. I'm just helping out an old friend. Helping her get ready to date again. It's fake. We're pretending.

I'm just not sure what exactly that means and how far to take it.

Chapter 7

Lyndsay

'What do you think?' Nick asks, bringing me another beer. I'm on my third one and it needs to be my last. I'm way past tipsy and might be drunk. I don't feel drunk, but after having wine at Matt's house followed by three beers, I have to be at least a little drunk. 'You okay staying a little longer?'

'Yeah, I love it!' I yell above the music.

Harley's is loud, mostly because of the music that's playing, but also from all the people. It's not a big place, and it's filled to capacity. I recognize at least half the people here and talked to a few of them, but was able to keep it short since it's so hard to hear. Brenda, a woman who lives a few houses down from my mom, asked me where Chris was, but I pretended not to hear her and talked about something else.

Tonight, I don't even want to think about Chris. I just want to have fun and hang out with Nick on our pretend date. I know that's what we're calling it, but it feels more real than fake. Nick's arm keeps going around my waist and pulling me closer. I think he's just protecting me from being bumped around by people going by, but it feels like more than that. And he keeps leaning down to talk to me, which I'm sure he's only doing because it's loud and hard to hear, but a few times he got close enough that his lips brushed over my ear. My body got all warm and tingly, like it did earlier, which I'm realizing is something I've missed. I've felt nothing for Chris for years, not even when we were intimate. It just shows how disconnected we were, and how the marriage should've ended a lot sooner than it did.

These feelings I'm having with Nick are showing me how alive I could feel with another man. It's giving me hope, making me believe I could someday find a man that I love and connect with, who makes me feel the sparks and tingles that I should've felt with Chris. I felt that way in the beginning with him, but those feelings faded away the longer we were together. I thought it was normal, just a side effect of being married. But then I'd see Diane and Tom and how they still flirted with each other and still had that spark, and realized my marriage was missing that. It took me a long time to admit that to myself, and even longer to admit it to Diane. She's the only one I told. I didn't want to tell anyone else, especially people here in town, who still, to this day, think Chris and I are the perfect couple.

I'm dreading people finding out about the divorce. I think my mom is too, which is why she hasn't told anyone. She hasn't said it, but I think she's disappointed in me for getting divorced. She's from a time when you just stuck it out and stayed in a marriage that made you miserable.

I stayed as long as I could with Chris, but I just couldn't do it anymore. Not only were Chris and I living together like strangers, but he was always draining our bank account with all his shady businesses.

'How about a dance?' Nick asks as a slow song comes through the speakers.

'Are you serious?' I ask, thinking he must be joking. Nick isn't the kind of guy who would dance. He's too shy and serious and doesn't like people watching him, or at least that's how he used to be.

'Come on.' He takes my hand. 'Just one. If you want to quit after that, we can.'

He's not kidding. He actually wants to dance. He's holding my hand and leading me to the middle of the bar, where three other couples are dancing. I can feel people staring at us, and if the music wasn't so loud, I'm sure I'd hear them talking about us, too.

Nick's arms go around me and I feel a warmth spread through me. It must be the alcohol, or maybe it's Nick. Maybe my feelings for him from the past are coming back, although it never felt like this. In high school, it was more of a teenage crush on the cute boy who helped me pass algebra. I liked talking to him and would've spent more time with him if Chris wasn't so jealous. He didn't want me even looking at another guy.

'This isn't so bad, is it?' Nick asks, leaning down to my ear as we sway to the music.

Why is he doing this? He knows this will be all over town tomorrow. People are going to talk about me being with Nick and wonder why I was with him and not Chris.

Why do I care? I don't live here, and it's not like my divorce is a secret. I'm sure by now someone's found out, which means everyone will know by the end of the week, maybe sooner.

I look up at Nick and smile. 'You're a good dancer.'

He chuckles. 'You're a good liar.'

'No, really, you are.'

Our eyes meet and I see a glimpse of the Nick I used to know, the smart, sweet guy I used to sit next to at the kitchen table as he explained my homework in a way I actually understood. I remember thinking he'd make a great dad someday. He was so patient, never getting frustrated or upset with me.

'You look beautiful tonight,' he says.

'You look good too.'

He looks better than good. He looks hot. His shirt clings to his chest muscles and has to stretch to fit over his ripped arms and shoulders. He was in good shape in high school from all the work he did on the orchard, but he has a lot more muscle now, and I swear he seems taller, way over six feet. I'm five seven and feel tiny in his arms.

The song ends and Nick asks, 'Could I talk you into another one?'

I nod, then rest my head on his chest as another song starts. His arms close around me as we move to the music. He smells amazing. I don't know what cologne he's wearing but it's my new favorite. And I love the way he's holding me, close but not too tight, and the way he moves us slowly around the dance floor.

It all feels so good, the way I wish things had felt with Chris but never did. I never felt safe or cared for when I was with Chris. I felt like a possession, like Chris had claimed me as his. When I was younger, I took that as a sign of how much he loved me and wanted me. But as I got older, I realized he just saw me as something pretty to keep at his side when we'd go out. Then when we'd get home, he'd ignore me and watch TV or talk on the phone or get on the computer. There was no closeness like I'm feeling now, no intimacy. Even sex with him didn't feel intimate.

As the song ends, I feel Nick pulling away. I want to hold on to him. I'm not ready to give up how I'm feeling right now. I've spent the past few months feeling sad and hopeless about my future as a divorced woman, thinking I'd never fall in love again. But now, being in a man's arms, a man who's kind and caring and makes me feel safe, I realize I want that. I want to find love again.

'Want to go sit down?' he asks.

I nod and step back. Nick takes my hand and walks us to our table. I glance at the table next to ours and see two women staring at us. I don't know them, but they seem to know me, or maybe they know Nick and they're trying to figure out who I am. Looking behind them, I see an older man with a young guy. They're also staring at us, and the young guy is saying something to the old man.

'Gary Stanton,' Nick says, noticing me looking at the table with the two men. 'He owns the gas station on Main. Bought it a few years ago from Whitfield.'

I look back at Nick. 'My mom mentioned someone bought it, but she didn't say who.'

'Gary grew up here, then moved away and came back after his kids were grown. That's his son, Jared. He helps him run the place.'

'I think they were talking about us.'

'Everyone is.' Nick laughs a little. 'You know how it is here, how people talk.'

'But I don't even know them.'

'They know me, and know my family. Brody goes to their gas station to fill up his equipment. They give him a discount because he spends so much.'

I turn to Nick. 'What equipment?'

He answers me, but it's so loud I can't hear him. Something about snow?

'I'm sorry, but I didn't hear you.'

'Brody has a lawn care and snow removal company,' Nick says, having to yell for me to hear him. 'You want to get out of here and go somewhere quieter?'

'Yes,' I say, happy he suggested it. I don't mind the music, but it's so loud we can't talk, and I really want to talk to him.

He pays for our drinks, then takes my hand and leads me through the packed bar to the outside.

This really does feel like a date, the way Nick keeps holding my hand and talking close. And that slow dance was definitely not something you'd do with a friend. The way Nick was holding me, the way we moved together, I almost felt like we were an actual couple. He's doing a great job playing along with this fake date idea. If he hadn't called it fake, I'd swear it was real. But I know Nick doesn't think of me that way, or he didn't when we were younger. If he had, maybe things would've turned out differently. Maybe we would've dated and I would've chosen him over Chris.

'Everything's closing soon,' Nick says, checking the time on his phone. 'We could head back to Sawyer's place. He should be up in his apartment by now. We'd have the brewery to ourselves.'

'Thanks, but I should probably get home,' I say, not wanting to go but thinking Nick must be tired after working all morning and traveling here.

'Oh,' he says, sounding surprised. 'I guess it is getting late. I'll take you home.'

We walk to the car and as he opens my door, I turn to him. 'I don't really want to go.'

'You don't want to go home?'

'No. Not yet. I just said that because I thought it's what *you* wanted. You had to work this morning and then make the trip here. I thought you might be tired and want to get some sleep.'

'Do I look tired?'

'No.' I gaze at his incredibly handsome face. The rounded jaw he had as a boy is now sharper, more pronounced, and his face seems longer and leaner. It's a man's face, a very good-looking man. 'It's just that you said how you had all that work to catch up on and I'm sure you'll be busy tomorrow with your family and the party.'

He leans closer, resting his hand on the roof of the car. 'We're on a date, right?'

'Yes, well, kind of,' I say, sounding breathless. My pulse sped up when he moved closer.

'And how's it going?' he asks, calmly and assuredly. This new confident Nick really turns me on.

'It's going great,' I say, glancing away.

'You're having a good time?'

'More than good.' My eyes return to his. 'Tonight's been really fun.'

'Then why would you want to end it?'

'I just thought you might want to, since you—'

His lips go to mine, taking my breath away and making my heart slam against my chest. I wasn't prepared for this—the kiss, or how amazing it'd be. His lips are soft and warm and he's giving me these slow, gentle kisses that are working me up in the most unexpected and wonderful way. I'm used to hard, fast kisses and Chris' tongue being shoved in my mouth. I've never been kissed like this. I had no idea what I was missing out on until now.

Nick's arm goes around my waist, pulling me closer. My lips part and he takes the kiss deeper, but not in a forced or rushed way. His pace is slow, his movements deliberate, like he knows exactly what to do to turn a woman on. Where did he learn this? In college? He didn't have a girlfriend in high school. He went out with some girls, but only a few times.

As his tongue moves over mine, I feel like my legs are about to give out. God, he's good at this. Who knew? I never would've guessed he was such a good kisser.

Before I'm ready for it to end, he pulls away. 'What do you think now? You think I'm in a hurry to take you home?'

I smile. 'I'm thinking no.'

Nick backs away, letting me in the car, then shuts the door and goes around to the other side.

We don't talk on the short drive back to the brewery. I'm too shocked to speak, still not believing how great that kiss was and how it made me feel. As for Nick, I'm not sure what's keeping him quiet. Is he feeling the same way I did about that kiss? He had to have felt something. That wasn't just any kiss.

Why did he do it? Why did he kiss me if we're just friends? Was he was just playing along with the fake date thing, preparing me for when a guy kisses me at the end of the night? I don't think I'm ready for that, at least not with someone else. But with Nick? I'm more than ready. I wish he'd do it again.

Chapter 8

Lyndsay

When we get to the brewery, Nick unlocks the door and we go inside. The lights are off except for the ones behind the bar, giving the place a dimly lit, almost romantic feel.

'Can I get you something to drink?' Nick asks.

'Maybe just some water. I've had enough drinks for tonight.'

He goes behind the bar to a cooler and takes out two bottles of water. He walks back to me and hands me the water.

'Let's sit over here.' He goes to a table, then nods toward the hall that leads to the stairs. 'I'll be able to see if Sawyer comes downstairs. I doubt he will, but you never know.'

'Why do you care?' I ask, sitting down.

'I don't want him interrupting us.' He opens his bottle of water and takes a sip.

What does he think Sawyer might interrupt? Is Nick planning to kiss me again? I wish that would happen, but I don't think it will. That kiss he gave me earlier was the kind that could lead to something more, something that would make us cross the friend line, which isn't a good idea. It'd make me want to date him for real, and I can't. We live on separate coasts.

'So tell me about LA,' Nick says, leaning back in his chair. 'How do you like it?'

'It's okay. I like the weather.'

'You think you'll stay there?'

'I don't know. The past few months I've been so focused on getting through the divorce that I never really considered what I'd do when it's finally over.'

'How are you feeling? Now that it's over.'

That's another thing I always loved about Nick. He'd always ask how I'm doing and seemed to actually care. I didn't always open up to him, thinking he didn't want to hear about whatever teenage drama I was going through, but in the few times I did tell him, he actually listened. Aside from Diane, Nick is the only person in my life that's ever made me feel heard. My parents never did. They're good people and I love them, but I never felt like they listened to me. They chose to hear what they wanted instead of what I actually said.

'Be honest,' Nick says. 'I don't want some bullshit story about how you're doing great and just happy to get rid of him. Or about how it's been over for years and the divorce was just a formality.'

'Have you been listening to my conversations?' I joke, but I'm serious. What he just said is what I've been telling people when they ask how I'm doing.

'I've heard that shit from my clients. I don't do a lot of divorces, but I've done a few, and when I ask them how they're doing, those are the responses I get.'

'Maybe they're telling the truth.'

'Or maybe they don't want to admit how much it hurts to see the life you thought you'd have crumble into pieces. Even if you hated the person, you're still having to say goodbye to something you thought would last forever. You can't tell me that doesn't hurt.'

'It does.' I look down at the table. 'And it doesn't make sense. The thing you said about it being over years ago is true. So why does it hurt so much? I should be happy about this. It's what I wanted.'

Nick leans toward me and puts his hand over mine. 'What you wanted was a guy who loved you and supported you and paid attention to you and did everything he could to make you happy.'

'Maybe that's too much to ask for,' I say with a humorless laugh.

'It's not. Just look at my parents. They've been married forever and they're more in love now than on their wedding day. They still hold hands. My dad still brings her flowers. My mom still makes his favorite meals. And now my dad's throwing her this surprise party, which is totally out of his comfort zone. He's never thrown a party, but he wanted to do something special for her birthday.'

I look up at Nick. 'I don't think that kind of love exists anymore, or if it does, it's rare.'

'That doesn't mean you give up on finding it. You're a beautiful woman with a beautiful heart. You deserve better than you had with him. I don't know what went on with you two, but I have an idea based on how much you've changed.'

'What do you mean?'

'You used to be the girl who smiled all the time and laughed so hard you'd have tears in your eyes and got all crazy when you saw a puppy. And your voice, you always sounded excited, even when you weren't. You had so much life to you, Lyndsay. You had this light about you, and now . . . it's like it burned out.'

I get up from my chair and walk away, keeping my back to him so he doesn't see the tears in my eyes. Why does he have to be so damn observant? And why is he pointing this out? I know I've lost a part of myself being with Chris, but I don't want to be reminded of it.

'Lyndsay?' Nick's behind me now, his hand on my shoulder.

'I should go,' I say, sniffling and wiping my eyes. 'Could you take me home?'

'Lyndsay, I'm sorry,' he says, turning me around. 'I didn't mean to upset you. I only said that because I wanted you to be honest with me. I know what you're going through has gotta hurt like hell and I just . . . I'm just trying to be a friend.'

'I know,' I say, nodding as I wipe the tears from my face. 'It's just what you said, I didn't want to hear it.'

'Why? Because you—'

'Because I don't know how to get her back!' I yell. I hear a noise upstairs and remember Sawyer is up there, trying to sleep. 'Shit,' I whisper. 'I forgot about Sawyer.'

'He'll be fine. He'll go back to sleep.' Nick pulls me into his arms. 'You'll get her back. It'll just take time.'

'I don't even know that girl anymore. I'm not sure she's even there.'

'She is. I saw a glimpse of her tonight when I asked you to pretend date me.'

'You did?' I look up at him.

'Your eyes lit up. You got some excitement back in your voice.'

'That might've been the wine.'

'It wasn't. I remember that girl pretty damn well, and I know I saw a glimpse of her tonight.'

I'm not sure how that's possible given how I've been feeling, but I did feel better being with Nick tonight. There were some moments where my mind didn't even think of Chris or the divorce or the empty apartment I'll be going home to.

'You've been a good distraction,' I say, pulling away from him.

'How about I distract you again tomorrow?'

'You can't. You have the party.'

'I don't have to be there until the afternoon. My morning's free.'

'Don't you want to do stuff with your brothers?'

'I see them all the time. I haven't seen you in 15 years. I'll take you to breakfast. Maury's Chicken Roost. Best pancakes in town. What do you say?'

I smile. 'I do love Maury's pancakes. But my mom will want me to have breakfast with her.'

'We'll bring her with.'

'On a date?'

'This is a date?'

'Isn't it?'

'I thought it was just breakfast, but okay, sure. It's a date.'

'You said you'd pretend to date me. Tonight wasn't enough.' I throw my hands in the air. 'I haven't dated in years! I need some serious help here!'

He laughs. 'There's that excitement again. See? The old Lyndsay is coming back.'

'That wasn't excitement. That was panic. Just the idea of dating is making me feel sick.' I sigh. 'Nick, I don't know if I can do this. I'm so out of practice. Everything's changed.'

'Okay, how about this? We go on a few more fake dates until I leave on Monday, and after that, we work together over the phone and online.'

'What do you mean by work together?'

'I'll be your tutor again, but this time I'll tutor you on dating instead of algebra.'

'Really? Or is this a joke?'

'I'm serious. I'm not an expert on dating, but I definitely got a lot of experience the past 15 years. You can ask me questions. We can do practice dates over the computer. Whatever you want.'

'Oh, Nick, you're amazing!' I say, hugging him. 'I can't thank you enough for doing this.' I pull back. 'But are you sure you'll have time? You must work like 100 hours a week.'

'I'll make time.' He takes my hand. 'Let's go sit down. We have a lot to catch up on.'

We talk until three in the morning. I would've talked longer if I wasn't staying with my mom. I texted her and told her Diane and I were having a girls' night and that I wouldn't be home until late and not to wait up for me.

'You're way past curfew,' Nick kids as he walks me to the door.

My mom left the porch light on. I wouldn't be surprised if she slept in the chair in the living room, just so she'd know when I got home. I wish she'd treat me like an adult instead of like I'm 16.

'I'll probably get grounded,' I say.

'Not if you tell her you were with me. Your mom loves me for helping you pass math.'

'You're right, she does,' I say, smiling. 'Well, goodnight. I'll see you tomorrow, or I guess in a few hours for breakfast.' I turn to the door.

'Lyndsay.'

'Yeah?' I turn back.

Nick steps up to me and wraps his hands around my face. He kisses me, like he did earlier, a soft, gentle kiss that makes me feel like I'm melting inside. He doesn't use tongue this time, just his lips, but it's still making sparks go off inside me.

He slowly back away. 'I'll see you at breakfast.'

Then he walks off, back to his car.

I remain on the porch. I feel like I can't move, my legs weak from that incredible kiss. How does he do it? How does he get me so worked up from just a kiss?

He's in the car now but hasn't left. He's waiting for me to go inside. That's Nick, caring about my safety. He's such a nice guy, but also a really hot, bold, confident guy that I can't believe is the same guy who tutored me in high school.

When I go in the house, the lamp is on but my mom's not in her chair. I sneak upstairs to my room and realize I don't have my suitcase. I left it at Diane's house. Oh well, I'll get it tomorrow.

Diane's not going to believe what happened tonight. I can hardly believe it myself.

Nick kissed me. Maybe it was real or maybe it was fake. Either way, it was the best kiss of my life.

Chapter 9

Lyndsay

'What time did you get in last night?' my mom asks, pouring coffee in her mug.

'Around three. Diane and I were talking and didn't realize it was so late. You know how it is when we get together.'

It's just after eight and I'm sitting at the kitchen table, dressed and ready to go meet Nick, but first I have to break the news to my mom that I won't be having breakfast with her.

She sets her coffee mug on the table. 'Give me a hug. I've missed you.'

I get up and give her a hug.

'You're too skinny,' she says, squeezing me tight before letting me go.

'I'm the same as always,' I tell her, but the truth is I've lost ten pounds while going through the divorce. I have trouble eating when I'm stressed.

My mom holds my face in her hands and looks into my eyes. 'How are you doing?'

'Mom, I'm fine,' I say, knowing it's better if I don't tell her the truth. I don't want her worrying about me, and it's not like there's anything she can do. I just need time to get past this and move on with my life.

Last night with Nick really gave me hope. I hadn't enjoyed a man's company that much in years. When Chris and I would go out, he'd always be checking his phone or checking out other women. We were one of those couples who'd go out for dinner and wouldn't talk.

'Is it really final?' my mom asks. 'There's no chance of reconciling with him?'

'It's final.' I look down, feeling like I disappointed her. She was hoping by now I would've given her a few grandkids, but instead I'm divorced and have no idea what to do next. Even if I start dating again, it'll be a long time before I'm married, and even longer before I have kids. What if I'm too old by then? I always wanted three kids, but now I may not even have one.

I sit back down at the table while Mom goes to the fridge to get the creamer. 'What would you like to do today?'

I'm relieved she didn't ask me more about the divorce. We've talked about it enough on the phone that there's nothing else to say, but I assumed she'd still ask me about it or try to get me to give Chris another chance.

'Maybe we could go to that place you like for lunch, the bed-and-breakfast.'

'We could, but I was thinking I'd take you out now. I know how much you love Maury's and we didn't get to go last time you were here.'

'Um, yeah, I kind of already made plans to go there.'

'With who?' Her brows rise. 'Diane?'

I could tell her I'm going with Diane, but my mom could easily find out I lied. A lot of her friends go to Maury's for breakfast on Saturday and if they saw me with Nick, they'd tell her.

'I'm going with Nick,' I say, sipping my coffee.

She sits across from me at the small kitchen table with the red-checkered tablecloth we've had for as long as I can remember. 'Nick who?'

'Nick Kanfield. The guy who tutored me back in high school.'

'Yes, I know Nick, but I thought he lived in New York now.'

'He does, but he's back to see his family. I ran into him at the airport and we thought it'd be fun to catch up so we're meeting for breakfast. Is it okay if I take the car?'

'I suppose it is, as long as you won't be gone long. I have a hair appointment at ten.'

That won't give Nick and me much time. I was hoping to spend the morning with him. We had such a good time last night. It's the first time in over a year that my mind didn't keep wandering to Chris and the divorce.

'Is Nick seeing anyone?' my mom asks.

'I don't think so.'

'I'm surprised. He's quite a catch, being a lawyer and all. And last time I saw him, he was quite handsome. He's certainly changed a lot since he was a boy, although I always thought the Kanfield boys were handsome. It's just that Nick was so skinny back in high school. Tall and skinny like a bean pole,' she says with a laugh.

My phone dings with a text from Diane. *You left your suitcase here. Should I bring it over?*

I'll come get it, I text back. *Be there in a few.*

'Was that Nick?' my mom asks.

'No, Diane. I was in such a hurry to leave last night that I forgot my suitcase. I'm going to go over there and pick it up.' I get up from the table and take my coffee mug to the sink.

'You're not going to keep running off like this, are you?' my mom asks. 'I want some time with you while you're here.'

'I'm just going to breakfast and then I'm all yours. See you later!' I grab the spare car keys from the drawer and my purse from the counter and head to the garage.

My mom's car is a really old blue sedan with matching blue vinyl seats. I'm surprised it still runs. I keep telling her to get a new car, but she's set in her ways and finds comfort in the familiar. In some ways, I'm the same. I married Chris because he was familiar, and stayed with him because I'd grown comfortable in our routine. Even if I wasn't happy, it was safer to stay than leave for the unknown.

'Come on in,' Diane says when I get to her house.

'I can't stay long. I'm meeting someone for breakfast at nine.'

'Who are you meeting?' she asks, stepping aside to let me in.

I stop just inside the door and whisper, 'Nick.'

'Nick Kanfield?'

'Yes.'

'Why are you whispering?'

'I don't know,' I say, raising my voice to its normal level. 'I guess because it seems kind of wrong.'

'Why is having breakfast with Nick wrong?'

'Because I just got divorced.'

'Oh, please,' she says, waving me off. 'Your marriage was over years ago.'

'Okay, but still, it's Nick.'

'Yeah? So?' She motions me to follow her to the kitchen. 'Hold that thought. We'll grab some coffee and go out back.'

'Hey, Tom,' I say, seeing him at the kitchen counter, pouring a bowl of cereal.

'Hey, Lyndsay.' He gives me his big goofy grin and comes over to give me a hug. 'How've you been?'

'I've been better.'

He frowns. 'Sorry. That was a really dumb thing to say. I'm still waking up.'

'Don't worry about it,' I say as I watch Diane pour coffee in two bright yellow mugs.

'Honey, could you make the kids breakfast?' Diane says, going past Tom to me. She hands me a mug. 'We're going to go out back and have some girl talk.'

'Sure.' He laughs. 'As long as this girl talk doesn't involve me.'

'Oh, and could you help Leah find her ballet shoes?' Diane says to Tom as we leave. 'Her lesson's at ten.'

'Ballet shoes,' he says. 'Got it.'

We go out to the patio and sit on the white Adirondack chairs.

'You got really lucky with Tom,' I say.

'He gets on my nerves sometimes, but yeah, he's one of the good ones. And a great father.'

'Is it wrong to say I'm jealous?'

'No.' She reaches over and puts her hand on mine. 'You're going to find someone just as great. It'll just take some time.'

'But I don't have time. I want to have kids. What if by the time I find someone I'm too old to be a mom?'

'Then you can adopt, or be a foster mom, or marry someone who has kids. There are all sorts of ways to have children in your life without actually having them.'

'You're right,' I say, giving her a half smile. 'And I could always borrow Leah and Adam.'

'I would love that. I could use a break.' She sips her coffee. 'So . . . what happened last night? It must've gone well if you're meeting him for breakfast.'

'Diane, it was perfect.' I set my coffee down and move to the end of my chair, turning toward her. 'I haven't had that great of a time in . . . I don't even know how long. Years.' I hear how excited I sound and am reminded of what Nick said last night about how much I've changed. He's right. I used to smile and laugh and get excited about silly things, but with Chris, that part of me faded away. He was always losing money in his business deals, which made him moody and cranky. He'd get annoyed at me for being happy because he wasn't, so I learned to hide any signs of joy and eventually joined him in his misery.

'What'd you guys do?'

'Not much. That's what's so amazing. We didn't do much and still had a great time. We went to a bar and danced and had some drinks, then went back to Sawyer's brewery and talked for hours. I didn't get home until after three. I told my mom I was with you, so if she says anything, just play along.'

'Why didn't you tell her the truth? You're a grown woman. You don't have to lie to your mom about being with Nick.'

'I do when I stay out all night with him. My mom still thinks there's a chance I could get back with Chris.'

'That's crazy! She knows the divorce is final, right?'

'Yes, but to her, that doesn't mean it's over. Her cousin, Bonnie, married the same man twice and they're still married. She's told me that story a million times the past year, hoping it'll make me change my mind about Chris.'

'But she knows you weren't happy with him.'

'She also knows I'm not getting any younger, and the older I get, the less of a chance she has to get grandkids.'

'Well, it's not her life. It's yours. Chris wasn't the right guy for you, and if you'd stayed with him, you'd never meet the guy who *is* right for you.'

'Assuming I can find him.'

'You will if you start dating. You can't wait. You need to get out there again.'

'I did, last night.'

'That wasn't a date.'

'That's what Nick called it.' I lean back in my chair and pick up my coffee.

'Nick said you guys were on a date?'

'A fake date.' I smile. 'He offered to be my dating tutor.'

'Dating tutor?' She laughs. 'Is this a joke?'

'No, I'm serious. I was telling him how I need practice dating and he offered to help. He's been on a lot more dates than I have and I think it'll be good to get a man's perspective.'

'But you live on separate coasts.'

'He's going to tutor me by phone or online. And tomorrow we're going out on another date.'

She sets her coffee down. 'There's something not right about this.'

'What do you mean?'

'I like Nick and don't think he'd do anything deceitful, but being your dating tutor? It sounds like he just made that up so he could try to get you for himself.'

'That's not it at all. He's just being a friend.'

'Maybe, but it doesn't make sense for a guy who works like 100 hours a week to give up his time to help you date. Why wouldn't he use that time to find a date for himself?'

'Maybe he doesn't want to date right now. Why are you acting like you don't want me seeing him? Just last night you were telling me to sleep with him.'

'But then I thought about it after you left and decided it wasn't a good idea. You don't even know Nick anymore. The small-town boy we grew up with is now a big city lawyer. Are you sure you can trust him?'

'Diane, why are you saying this stuff about Nick? He was the nicest guy in our high school. He never got into fights. He always volunteered for stuff. He helped his dad with the orchard.'

'That was 15 years ago. A person can change a lot in 15 years. Just look at Chris. You thought he was perfect back in high school and look how he turned out.'

'I didn't think he was perfect. I just couldn't see his flaws because I wanted so badly for things to work out with us. He promised me this great life in the big city, someplace completely different than Haydon Falls, and I believed him.'

'This town isn't that bad. I actually like it.'

'I like it too, but back then, Chris convinced me this place was boring and we'd be happier in a big city where there's more to do. But then we got there and spent all our time at home.'

'Chris should've taken you out,' Diane says, sounding disgusted with him. 'I can't believe how much he changed after high school. He was always the life of the party and then he got married and didn't want to leave the couch.'

'Except when he went on his *business trips*,' I say, rolling my eyes. 'Did he really think I wouldn't notice all the debt he was racking up with his scams?'

'Enough about him. We aren't supposed to be talking about Chris.' Diane turns to face me. 'Going back to Nick, what exactly happened last night?'

'I'm not sure I should tell you now that you think he's doing this for the wrong reasons.'

'He kissed you.'

I look away, trying to hold back the smile that desperately wants to appear.

'He did, didn't he? He kissed you.'

'It was a date,' I say, looking back at her. 'It's normal to kiss a girl on a date.'

'Not a fake one,' she scoffs. 'I can't believe he'd do this.'

'Do what? Kiss me? Why is that wrong?'

'Because he's pretending it's fake when it's not. He needs to be honest and stop making up excuses to go out with you.'

'It's not an excuse. Diane, I'm telling you, Nick is just being nice. He really wants to help me.'

She stares at me. 'The guy who had a huge crush on you in high school is just helping you learn to date? Do you really believe that?'

'He did not have a crush on me. He never even made a move on me.'

'Because he didn't think he had a chance with you. But now he's rich, successful, and a lot better looking. Maybe he thinks now is his chance to get the girl he's always wanted.'

I laugh. 'That's ridiculous.' I swirl what's left of my coffee around the bottom of the mug. 'And what if it's me that wants him?'

'Do you?'

I smile. 'Maybe.' I let out a dreamy sigh. 'Last night was so great. I was so into Nick that I barely even thought about Chris and the divorce. And when Nick and I talked, the hours just flew by. That never happened with Chris. We couldn't even talk for ten minutes. He had nothing to say and he got bored when I talked.'

She slowly smiles. 'Okay.'

'Okay what?'

'Okay, I'm going to support whatever this is between you and Nick, but I want you to be careful.'

'I don't need to be. Nick's a great guy. He's not going to hurt me.'

'He better not. If he does, I'll send Tom over there to beat him up.'

I roll my eyes. 'Tom wouldn't hurt a fly.'

'Yeah, you're right.'

'Mommy, I found them!' Leah yells, running outside with her ballet shoes.

'Did you have breakfast?'

She shakes her head, her long blonde hair flying everywhere. 'Go inside and have breakfast with Daddy.'

'Leah, can I have a hug?' I say to her. 'I didn't get to see you yesterday.'

She runs over and hugs me, then holds up her shoes. 'I have to go to ballet.'

'Okay, go ahead.'

She runs back into the house.

'I should get going.' I stand up. 'You mind if I change clothes while I'm here? I don't want to run back home.'

'Go ahead.' Diane gets up. 'You can use the guest room. Your suitcase is by the door.'

As we walk back to the house, Diane holds onto my arm, stopping me. 'I didn't mean to be a downer about

Nick. I just saw how excited you were about him and got concerned. I don't want you getting your hopes up with someone you're not actually dating.'

'I'm not. I know this isn't real. It's just nice to be with a guy who actually wants to hang out with me. Last night when I was with Nick, I felt better than I have in years. He made me feel hopeful about finding someone.'

She smiles. 'Tell him I said hi.'

'I will.'

We go in the house and I change into a sundress and sandals. If I were going to breakfast with my mom or Diane, I'd throw on shorts and a t-shirt, but this is a date so I want to look nice.

I'm not going to worry about what Diane said about Nick's motives. Right now I need to feel good about myself so I have the confidence to date again, and Nick gives me that confidence. The way he looked at me last night, and paid attention to me, held my hand, kissed me—it made me feel beautiful and desired, things I haven't felt with Chris in years. Last night, I even started to get excited about dating again, which is a huge deal since just a couple days ago I was dreading it.

When I get to Maury's Chicken Roost, I see Nick waiting outside. His head is down as he texts someone on his phone. He's wearing jeans and a white polo that fits tight against his chest. My pulse quickens just seeing him there and goes even faster as I approach him.

'Hey, Nick.' I stop just in front of him, a big smile on my face.

He glances up from his phone, blinking a few times as he takes a step back. 'Wow. You look gorgeous.' He smiles and pulls me in for a hug. I melt into his arms, inhaling his cologne, and wishing that this was real. A real date that might lead to more.

Chapter 10

Nick

Lyndsay looks absolutely gorgeous. Her hair is pulled back in a loose ponytail and she has just a touch of makeup on her face. She's wearing a sundress in a yellow floral print with thin straps at the top and white sandals. She's got that small-town, girl-next-door look that I love. It's not a look I see in New York. I didn't realize how much I missed it until now.

Damn, she's beautiful. How could Chris give her up? According to what Lyndsay told me last night, Chris didn't even try to save their marriage. She asked him to go to counseling and he refused. I can't believe she stayed with him as long as she did.

'I got us a table,' I tell her. 'It's really busy in there and I didn't want us having to wait.'

'Yeah, I don't have much time. My mom needs the car.'

'Oh. I was hoping we could go do something after this, but if you need to get home, I'll go hang out with my brothers. They're all going over to Sawyer's place before the party.'

'I could do something. I just need to drop off the car. I don't need to stay there.'

'You're trying to get all the dating practice you can before I leave, aren't you?' I smile and take her hand.

'Believe me, I need it,' she says as we walk to the door.

When I took her home this morning, I started feeling guilty for suggesting I tutor her in dating, knowing part of my offer was self-serving. I don't want to lose contact with her after this weekend. Last night was too great to just end it when we leave here. I could've just told her I want to stay in touch, but when I've said that to friends before, we get busy, time passes, and we never connect again. I didn't want that to happen with Lyndsay. With the tutoring sessions, we'll have a reason to talk, upping the chances of it actually happening.

As we sit down at the table, I feel like the whole restaurant's staring at us, wondering why the oldest Kanfield boy is back in town and why he's with Lyndsay Davis. I knew this would happen, but I really don't care if people gossip about us. I don't live here anymore. And when the rumors start, my mom will set everyone straight. She doesn't put up with people saying things about her family that aren't true.

'Everyone's staring,' Lyndsay whispers as she looks over her menu.

'Should we give them a show?' I smile at her.

'What do you mean?'

I reach over and hold her hand, keeping our hands on the table where everyone can see.

'Nick!' she whispers, glancing at our hands.

'What? I can't hold your hand?'

'Everyone's watching. They're going to think we're together.'

'We are. We're having breakfast together.'

'You know what I mean.'

'Yeah? So let them talk. This town could use some new gossip.'

She smiles a little, then glances at the table next to us. An older couple is there, watching us like they're watching a TV show.

'Can I get you something to drink?' the waitress asks, appearing at our table.

'I'll just have water,' Lyndsay says.

'I'll have orange juice,' I say.

'Nick?' The waitress smiles at me. 'Nick Kanfield?'

'Yeah,' I say, trying to figure out how she knows me.

'It's Lori.' She points to her name tag. 'We were partners in chem lab.'

Lori from high school? She looks totally different. Her long blonde hair is now short and dyed red, she's put on about 50 pounds, and she has tats running down both sides of her neck.

'Lori. Sorry, I didn't recognize you.' I get up and hug her, then sit back down. 'How have you been?'

'Okay. How about you?'

'I'm good.' I look over at Lyndsay. 'You remember Lyndsay?'

Lori's face lights up. 'Lyndsay Davis? I haven't seen you in forever!'

Lyndsay smiles. 'It's been awhile. I don't get home much.'

'I didn't know it was you with the darker hair.'

'I've been coloring it for a few years now.'

I don't know why she colors her hair. Her natural blonde color was beautiful and looked great with her light skin and blue eyes.

'I thought you moved to Texas,' Lyndsay says to Lori.

'I did, but it was too hot for me so I moved back. So how's Chris?'

'Um, he's fine. He's not here. He was busy with work.'

She doesn't want to tell Lori about the divorce. I don't know why she's hiding it. I'm guessing half the town knows by now. Chris still has friends here, who I'm sure have told people about the divorce. And anyone who saw Lyndsay at the bar last night could've figured it out. Lyndsay wasn't wearing her ring and we were acting like a couple, talking close, touching, slow dancing.

Thinking about it now, I probably took the fake date thing too far, but I had a few beers in me and was with the girl who appeared in most every one of my teen fantasies. I couldn't help but kiss her.

It was a damn good kiss. Too good. I was feeling things I shouldn't be feeling for someone I'm fake dating. I thought it might feel awkward, kissing a girl who's only ever been a friend, but it wasn't awkward at all. The moment our lips touched, I instantly felt something between us, something I'd been feeling all night but was trying to ignore. We definitely have a strong attraction to each other, but we also have something else that I can't put into words. It's whatever's been missing from all my other relationships, the reason they haven't gone anywhere.

'You and Chris were such a cute couple in high school,' Lori says to Lyndsay. 'Everyone was so jealous of you guys.'

I glance at Lyndsay, noticing how uncomfortable she looks.

'I'd love to talk more,' Lyndsay says, 'but I'm kind of in a hurry.'

'Yeah, of course, go ahead.' Lori gets her order pad out.

After she takes our order, she leaves, then comes back with our drinks. 'You guys will be at the reunion next weekend, right?'

'I won't be here,' I say. 'I'm leaving on Monday.'

'And I made plans to do something else,' Lyndsay says.

'Come on. You have to come. It's 15 years.'

'Maybe some other year,' I tell her.

'I really think you should come. People would love seeing you guys, especially you and Chris,' Lori says to Lyndsay. 'Maybe you could talk him into coming back for it.'

Lyndsay clears her throat. 'Um, Chris and I aren't together anymore.'

Lori gasps. 'You're separated?'

'Divorced,' Lyndsay says. 'Just this week, actually.'

'Did something happen or you just didn't get along?'

Lyndsay looks at me to help her out.

'Maybe you could give us a minute,' I say to Lori.

'Sure! I'll go check on your order,' she says, taking off.

'Thank you,' Lyndsay says quietly to me.

'Of course. You okay staying here?'

'Yeah,' she says with a sigh. 'I just wish people would stop assuming Chris and I are still a couple. A lot can happen in 15 years, and everyone knows high school relationships don't have the greatest success rate.'

'Lori didn't mean to upset you. She's just someone who asks a lot of questions.'

'I know, and I'm not mad at her. I just didn't know what to say.' She pauses. 'I actually do want to go to the reunion, but I can't, not now. All night people will be asking me about Chris. I won't be able to just go and have fun.'

'Kanfield,' a guy says, coming toward me, a big grin on his face.

'Kurt,' I say, getting up from the table to shake his hand. 'Good to see you.'

We went to high school together and were both on the debate team. He was a lawyer for a few years, but didn't like it and decided to open a gym with his wife. They live in Chicago now.

'You back for the reunion?' he asks.

'No, I'm just here to see my family. I'm heading out on Monday.'

'I'm trying to talk him into staying,' Lyndsay says, giving me a flirty smile. I can't tell what's going on with her. She's almost acting like she doesn't want our fake dating to be fake, like she's interested in me for real.

'Lyndsay Davis?' Kurt smiles at her. 'I didn't recognize you. Your hair's different.'

She laughs. 'I didn't realize I looked that different with brown hair. Lori just said the same thing.'

'Lori's here?' he asks.

'She's our waitress,' I tell him.

Just then, she returns to our table. She sees Kurt and her face lights up. 'Kurt!' She lunges at him, barely getting her arms around him because he's so big. He's really bulked up since high school. He's probably added 30 pounds of muscle.

'I didn't know you moved back,' Kurt says to her.

'A few months ago,' she says, letting him go. She looks him up and down, checking him out. 'You look good.'

'Thanks. I own a gym so I work out every day.'

'You own a gym?' Lori asks, sounding impressed.

'It's nothing fancy. It's one of those 24 hour places in a strip mall.'

'How's that going?' I ask. 'You like owning a gym?'

'It's better than being a lawyer,' he says, then quickly backtracks. 'I mean, nothing against being a lawyer. It just wasn't for me.'

'I get that. Some days I don't like it either. It's a lot of hours, a lot of stress.'

'You still working in New York?'

'Yeah. Hoping to make partner soon.'

'I need to check on my tables,' Lori says, taking off.

'Why don't you join us?' Lyndsay says to Kurt.

'I would, but I already ate. I was just heading out. The wife's waiting for me at her mom's house.'

'You didn't bring her with?' I ask, thinking it's odd he'd eat here by himself.

'She wanted to sleep in,' he says, glancing around the restaurant. He seems uncomfortable, like he doesn't want to talk about her. Maybe they're having problems. 'Anyway, I should get going.' He looks at Lyndsay. 'Hey, I heard about you and Chris. I'm sorry it didn't work out.'

She smiles a little. 'Thanks.'

'Who told you about it?' I ask him.

'The guys over at Loon's. I went there last night for a drink. Ted and Fink were there.' He laughs. 'Those idiots haven't changed. Fink even had on that shirt he always wore in high school, the black one with the skull on it that he thought got him girls.'

'It didn't,' Lyndsay says. 'He got girls because he was friends with Chris. So is he the one who told you about the divorce?'

'Ted did. He was working the bar when I got there. Fink didn't show up until later.'

Ted was one of Chris' best friends. They were on the football team together. Ted wasn't as obnoxious as Chris, but he was close. They were both jerks who thought way too highly of themselves. Fink was friends with them, but he wasn't on the football team. He messed up his knee freshman year and wasn't able to play. Fink is short for Finkenhauser, his last name, which people thought was too long, so everyone just called him Fink. They never used his first name because it's Chris and the other Chris wouldn't allow it. He wanted to be the only Chris, so the other one became Fink.

I wasn't friends with any of them. They ignored me, which was fine. Unlike the rest of the school, I didn't long for their attention. I had my own friends, and being a Kanfield meant Chris and his friends never tried to bully me. They knew if they did, they wouldn't just have to deal with me, but also my brothers and half the town. My family's orchard keeps this town in business, and back then, my dad was on city council. Even Chris, as dumb as he was, knew better than to mess with a Kanfield.

'I guess the secret is out,' Lyndsay says with a sigh.

'You didn't want people knowing?' Kurt asks.

'I don't care if they know. I just didn't want them finding out while I'm in town. I didn't want to have to answer all their questions.'

'So don't,' I say. 'You don't owe people answers. Just tell them you don't want to talk about it.'

'Is Chris coming to the reunion?' Kurt asks.

Lyndsay shakes her head. 'He's staying in LA. He's supposed to be moving out of the apartment this week. That's why I'm here.'

'You're not going to the reunion either?' he asks.

'No. I want to, but I don't want to show up alone.'

'Bring Nick.' Kurt looks at me. 'You could come back next weekend, right?'

'I can't. I need to work. I've only been gone a day and I'm already behind.'

'You see why I gave up law?' Kurt says to Lyndsay. 'You don't have time for a life.' His phone dings and he checks it. 'Shit, I gotta go. I'll see you guys later.'

He leaves just as Lori returns with our food. She almost drops one of the plates as she watches Kurt walk out the door. 'He sure looks different.' She smiles, almost like she has a thing for him.

'He had to get home to his wife,' I say.

'He's married?' she asks, her eyes going back to me.

'They've been married for like ten years.'

'Figures,' she says with a sigh. 'The good ones are always taken. Enjoy your food.'

When she's gone, I say to Lyndsay, 'This wasn't a good week to come here. Everyone thinks I'm home for the reunion.'

'Is there any way you'd considering coming back for it?' She pours syrup on her pancakes. 'I know you'd have to buy another plane ticket, but you'd get to see everyone, all your old friends.'

'I see most of them when I come home, and I doubt the ones who don't live here will be at the reunion.'

'Have you stayed in touched with any of them? Any of your friends that moved away?'

'Not really. I went to John's wedding a few years ago. He lives in Detroit now. I haven't talked to him since the wedding, but my dad saw his uncle at the hardware store and found out John's already divorced.'

'That's too bad.'

'It is, but it's not uncommon, which is why you shouldn't worry about people finding out about you and

Chris. Marriages end. People know that. It's nothing to be ashamed of.'

'But with Chris and me it's different. Everyone had all these expectations for us. I feel like I let them down.'

'Forget about them. It isn't their life. It's yours, and you're the only one who knows what happened. It's not fair for them to say what you should or shouldn't have done.'

She smiles. 'I really like talking to you. You always make me feel better. It was like that in high school, too. If I was having a bad day, you always made it better.'

'Didn't Chris do that?'

'No. He was too wrapped up in himself and football to notice if I was having a bad day. And he's not much of a talker. He'd rather watch TV or be looking at his phone than talk.'

Seriously, why did she stay with him for so long? She's funny, sweet, and fucking gorgeous. She could have any guy she wants, so why'd she stay with a jerk like Chris?

After breakfast, I follow her back to her mom's house.

'You can wait here,' Lyndsay says, coming up to the car as I get out. 'I just need to run in and tell my mom I'm leaving.'

As she says it, her mom comes out of the house, smiling when she sees me.

'I was hoping she wouldn't come out here,' Lyndsay mutters.

'It's fine.' I walk up to her mom, smiling. 'Hey, Mrs. Davis. It's good to see you again.'

'Nick, call me Patty.' She laughs. 'You're not a kid anymore.' She does a quick glance of my body, then says to Lyndsay, 'He's sure changed a lot, hasn't he?' She winks at her.

Lyndsay clears her throat. 'Mom, we were just leaving. I just came home to drop off the car.'

'Where are you going?'

'We're not sure yet, but Nick doesn't have much time. His mom's party is this afternoon.'

'Your father is such a sweetheart to do that for your mother,' Patty says to me. 'He's setting such a good example for you boys, that is, if you ever get married.' She smiles. 'Are you seeing anyone, Nick?'

'No, not right now. I'm trying to make partner at my law firm so I don't have much time to date.'

'Mom, we really need to go,' Lyndsay says.

'Nonsense.' Patty waves her hand in the air. 'I'm sure Nick has time to come in for a cup of coffee.'

'But don't you have to leave?' Lyndsay asks. 'You have to get to your hair appointment.'

'She just called. She's running behind and moved my appointment to 11. C'mon. I never see either of you. Can't you just come inside for a minute?'

Lyndsay glances at me, then back at her mom. I can tell she doesn't want to disappoint her mom, but doesn't want me feeling like I have to go inside.

'I'd love some coffee,' I tell Patty.

'Wonderful! I'll go start a fresh pot!'

As she goes back inside, Lyndsay walks up to me. 'You don't have to do this.'

'She's your mom, and she never sees you, and she really seems excited about that coffee.'

'But what about our . . .' Lyndsay pauses, like she's searching for the word. 'Pretend date?'

'Part of dating someone is meeting the parents, getting to know their family. This will be good practice for when you have to bring a guy home to meet your mom.'

She smiles and rolls her eyes. 'My mom already knows you. She's known you forever.'

'As a kid. She doesn't know me as a grown man. I'm totally different now.'

'You kind of are,' she says, that flirty smile appearing again. 'Just don't tell my mom this is a date. I don't want her getting her hopes up.' She walks off, giving me a view of the back of her in that dress. Damn, she's hot. Her body looks even better now than it did in high school.

'You coming?' she asks, turning back.

'Yeah.' I force my mind off the dirty thoughts it's having and follow her inside the house.

I need to stop looking at Lyndsay that way, and stop thinking this dating thing we're doing is real. It feels real, but it's not. I'm going back to New York on Monday, and in a week she'll be going back to LA. We might continue to talk, but I doubt I'll ever see her again, and if I do, she'll probably be with someone else. I just hope it's not another guy like Chris.

Chapter 11

Nick

It's like stepping back in time. Lyndsay's house hasn't changed in 15 years, not even a little. The stuffed bear Lyndsay had as a kid is still sitting on a tiny chair next to the fireplace. The green and white Packers quilt her mom made is still draped over the couch, next to the brown leather chair Lyndsay's dad always sat in. He died when she was 14. We weren't really friends back then, but I knew her from school. Her family had been to the orchard that day. It was a Saturday and the place was packed. I was driving the tractor, taking people to the fields to pick apples. I remember seeing Lyndsay, wondering how it was possible she got prettier every time I saw her. I knew I didn't have a chance with her, but that didn't stop me from imagining what it'd be like to be with her, take her out, kiss her.

She was so happy that day at the orchard, laughing at her dad's lame jokes. He was one of those guys who told really bad dad jokes, but Lyndsay laughed at them even if nobody else did. She loved her dad. She was devastated when he passed. It happened that night. He was in the bathroom and collapsed from a heart attack.

'Coffee's almost ready,' Patty says, coming into the living room. 'Lyndsay, when's the last time Nick was over? Do you remember?'

'May of our senior year,' I say. 'Right before we graduated.'

I remember because it's the day Chris proposed to Lyndsay, and the day I gave up any dreams that she'd ever be mine. I always knew it was a long shot, but I held out hope, my naïve teenage self thinking anything was possible. But that day, when he gave her the ring, my hope fizzled out. She was Chris' girl and always would be. He didn't really propose to her that day. He gave her a promise ring and told her he'd marry her someday, but to Lyndsay, it was as good as a proposal. She and her friends even went out and bought bridal magazines.

'You have a good memory,' Lyndsay says, walking over to me. 'But I bet you don't know the day.'

'The tenth. I only remember that because it was Jason's birthday and I couldn't stay long because I had to be home for his party.'

'That's right,' Lyndsay says, nodding like she's remembering it. 'You saved up your money and got him that baseball card he wanted.'

'You remember that?' My brows rise. 'I didn't think you were listening when I was telling you.'

'Of course I was listening. Why did you think I wasn't?'

'You were staring at your hand, at the ring.'

She looks down. 'Oh. Yeah.'

'Sorry. I shouldn't have brought it up.'

'No, it's true.' She looks up. 'I was staring at the ring, but I still heard what you said. I remember you telling me how you gave up buying that part for your car so you could afford to get Jason that baseball card.'

'It all worked out. My dad ended up loaning me money for the part.'

'Your father's a good man,' Patty says.

'So is his son,' Lyndsay says, gazing up at me.

Something beeps from the kitchen. 'That's the coffee,' Patty says. 'Come into the kitchen. I put out some zucchini bread.'

'Mom, we just ate,' Lyndsay says as we follow her mom to the kitchen table.

'I know, but I have to at least offer Nick some. He's our guest.'

'I'd love some,' I say, sitting down next to Lyndsay. I'm still full from breakfast, but I could find room for a piece of zucchini bread. It's not often I get homemade baked goods. My mom stuffs me full of them when I'm here in town, but back in New York, breakfast is usually dark coffee and a protein bar on my way into the office.

'So how long are you here for?' Patty asks as she serves me a piece of zucchini bread on a small white plate with a scalloped edge. I smile, feeling like I'm back in high school, sitting here at the kitchen table tutoring Lyndsay, her mom serving me cookies on these same tiny plates.

'I'm leaving on Monday,' I tell her.

'Oh, that's a shame.' Patty goes to get the coffee. 'It's too bad you can't stick around for the reunion.'

'Reunions aren't really my thing,' I say with a laugh. 'I'm trying to forget high school, not return to it.'

'C'mon, it wasn't that bad,' Lyndsay says, putting her hand on my arm.

'Perhaps you could take Lyndsay,' Patty says, setting my coffee down and noticing Lyndsay's hand on my arm.

'As a friend,' Lyndsay says, taking her hand off me.

'Or otherwise,' Patty mutters, going to get the other two coffee mugs.

'So Mom, what do you want to do today?' Lyndsay asks, trying to change the subject.

'I need to run some errands,' she says, setting the mugs down on the table and sitting across from us. 'If you wouldn't mind going to the hardware store, I'd like to go there and ask Hal what he thinks might be wrong with the dishwasher.'

'It's broken?' Lyndsay asks, sipping her coffee.

'It hasn't worked in months,' Patty says. 'I didn't want to spend the money to fix it so I've just been washing the dishes by hand. But maybe if I knew what was wrong I could fix it myself.'

'I could take a look at it,' I say, getting up and going over to the dishwasher.

'Nick, no,' Lyndsay says. 'You don't have to do that.'

'I don't mind.' I open the dishwasher door. 'What are you having problems with? Is it not running?'

'It runs, but leaks all over the floor,' Patty says, coming over to me. 'It got so bad I just stopped using it.'

'You got a screwdriver handy?' I ask.

She nods. 'In Harold's toolbox. It's in the garage.'

'I can show you,' Lyndsay says, getting up.

We go in the garage and I see the toolbox sitting on the workbench, the same place it was 15 years ago. I'm starting to wonder if Patty kept everything the same because it made her feel like Harold was still around. She took his death really hard, barely leaving the house after he was gone.

'Nick, you really don't have to do this,' Lyndsay says as I go over to the toolbox. 'You're on vacation. You shouldn't be doing chores.'

I open the toolbox and take out the screwdriver and a wrench. 'It's not a chore. I'm helping out your mom. She's a nice lady, and maybe if I fix her dishwasher she'll let me take her daughter out tonight.'

'Tonight?' Lyndsay says, sounding confused. 'You have the party tonight.'

'It's not going to go on all night. It'll wrap up around eight or nine. What do you say? You want another practice date?'

'I'd love that!' She leans against the workbench and looks up at me. 'You really are a great guy, Nick. How are you not married by now?'

'Just haven't found the right girl.' I nod toward the house. 'We should get back in there.'

'Yeah.' She nods and hurries back to the house.

Why the hell did I do that? Why did I ask her out again? First breakfast, then I asked her to spend the morning with me, and now I'm asking her out for tonight?

I know I'm supposed to be helping her learn to date, but spending all this time with her is making me have feelings for her again. I shouldn't be having feelings for a girl I can't be with, so why am I doing this?

Five minutes later, I've got the dishwasher door off and notice the rubber seal is damaged.

'It's the seal,' I say to Patty, showing her where it's coming apart. 'It's old and worn out so it's not keeping the water in anymore. I could stop at Hal's and pick you up a new one. If you'll be here tomorrow morning, I'll come back then and put it in. You'll be able to use it after that.'

'Oh, Nick, I couldn't ask you to do all that,' Patty says. 'You're not home for long. You need to spend time with your family.'

'It won't take long, and I'll see my family at the party. You go ahead to your hair appointment and Lyndsay and I will go to the hardware store.'

Patty looks like she's about to cry, but then smiles. 'Your father raised a very nice young man. Let me get you some money.' She hurries over to her purse which is on the counter.

'Mrs. Davis, I got this. Don't worry about it.'

'Nick, I have to pay you, at least for the part.' She comes over to me, holding a $20 bill. 'Is that enough?'

'How about you let me take some of that zucchini bread instead?'

'Of course! Take all you want. I'll wrap it up for you.' She goes to the pantry and takes out a box of foil.

'Mom, I got it,' Lyndsay tells her. 'You go ahead and get ready.'

Patty sets the foil down and walks up to me. 'I can't thank you enough. With my arthritis, it's been such a pain, literally, having to wash dishes by hand.'

'It'll be fixed by tomorrow,' I assure her.

'And you're sure I can't pay you?'

'You can try, but I won't take it.'

'You sound just like your father,' she says with a smile. Her phone dings and she picks it up. 'Oh, she's ready for me! I need to head out.'

'Bye, Mom,' Lyndsay says as Patty leaves.

When she's gone, I walk up to Lyndsay. 'If you want to skip the hardware store, I can go by myself.'

'I'll go.' She rips off some foil and starts wrapping up the bread. 'Just let me get your payment.' She seals the foil over the bread and hands it to me. 'I still can't believe you're doing this. Chris would never do this, and he was her son-in-law.'

'Maybe he didn't know how to fix stuff.'

'Yeah, I guess he didn't, but he could've helped her with the yard. She asked him to cut a tree branch one time and he wouldn't do it. He said his shoulder hurt and he didn't want to strain it. He was such a liar, but a good one. People always believed him, including me.' She forces out a smile. 'Okay, I'm ready if you are.'

We go out to the car and head to the hardware store.

'How do you know this stuff?' Lyndsay asks as we're driving. 'You're a lawyer. How do you know how to fix stuff?'

'My dad taught me. He taught all of us. He said we shouldn't be paying someone to fix stuff when we could just as easily do it ourselves. I remember being ten and one of the tillers broke down. The thing we use to till up the fields?'

She nods. 'Yeah, I know what they are.'

'My dad wasn't around so I took it apart and fixed it. The thing was fucking sharp. I'm surprised I didn't cut off a finger. My mom yelled at me later for doing it, but my dad just gave me a smile. I think he was proud I figured it out at that age.'

'That *is* impressive. You have many talents, Nick Kanfield.'

I glance at her. 'So do you.'

She laughs. 'Yeah, I can teach yoga. And do bookkeeping. That's about it.'

'You do bookkeeping?' I ask, thinking she must be kidding. She hated math, and bookkeeping involves math.

'I had to get another job since Chris kept spending all our money investing in businesses that never made anything.'

'You went to school for this?'

'Just community college. I got my associate degree in accounting.'

'Lyndsay, that's awesome!' I say, pulling into the hardware store parking lot. 'Why didn't you tell me?'

'It just didn't come up. We haven't seen each other in 15 years. There's a lot to catch up on.'

'I mean, why didn't you tell me when you got the degree? I would've sent a card, a gift. Hell, I might've even flown out for your graduation.'

She laughs. 'Nick, you're making too much of this. It wasn't a big deal.'

'Are you kidding?' I take off my seatbelt and turn to her. 'This is huge! I was your math tutor and you ended up getting a degree in accounting. I would've liked to have been informed of my student's achievements.'

She laughs again. 'You're right. I apologize. I should've sent you a note, letting you know. But you couldn't have gone to the graduation. I wasn't even there. Chris made us go to a convention that weekend in Vegas.'

'Instead of your graduation? What the hell?' I say, hearing the anger in my voice. I want to kill that asshole for doing that. Lyndsay always struggled in school, especially math, so for her to get a degree in accounting is a huge accomplishment, and then her loser husband doesn't let her attend the graduation? That's fucking wrong.

'It's fine,' she says. 'I didn't need to go. I mean, I kind of wanted to, but Chris really wanted to go to this convention and they were on the same weekend so it just wasn't possible to do both.' She takes off her seatbelt. 'Anyway, should we go in?'

She's out of the car before I can ask her how this even happened, why she picked bookkeeping over some other job. How does a person who hates math end up getting a degree in it?

We go inside the hardware store. I go straight to the section I need, knowing exactly where it is because of all the hours I spent here with my dad growing up. The store hasn't changed, and probably never will. There's comfort in that, which I like. I didn't use to feel that way. When I left here, I craved change. I was sick of living in this small town and nothing ever changing, but now I appreciate it.

'Helping out your mom while you're home?' Hal asks as he checks me out at the register.

'Not this time,' I say, handing him some cash. 'I'm helping Mrs. Davis with her dishwasher. Lyndsay and I went out for breakfast to catch up and when I took her home, her mom mentioned the dishwasher wasn't working.'

Hal looks over at Lyndsay as he hands me my change and receipt. 'Sorry to hear about you and Chris.' The old man leans toward her over the register, squinting his eyes and scowling. 'Between you and me, I never liked that kid. He was a troublemaker. Of course, nobody ever believed me since the boy was winning us games, but him and his friends didn't come in here buying all that spray paint to be fixing up old patio furniture. I can tell you that.'

'We should get going,' I say, knowing Lyndsay doesn't want to stand here and listen to Hal talk about her ex. But I like that Hal didn't stick up for Chris. He's one of the few people in town who didn't like him, or at least admitted to it. I think a lot of people didn't like him, but as Hal said, people were willing to overlook his flaws as long as he kept winning us football games.

'It was nice seeing you,' Lyndsay says, waving at Hal as we leave.

'You kids have fun!' he calls out as we walk to the door.

'It's true,' Lyndsay says as we head to the car. 'What he said about Chris? He'd get bored and vandalize stuff.' Lyndsay stops and points to the back of the brick building next to Hal's. 'You can still see the spray paint. It's faint, but it's there. He did it because Mr. Kramer gave him a C in English. His wife owned the bakery that used to be there.'

'The penis with the blue balls?' I say, remembering the spray-painted wall. 'That was Chris' work?'

'Yes. He told me about it later. He thought it was hilarious. I thought it was mean.'

'He put it on the front door too. Kramer's wife had to shut the place down for a day to clean it.'

'I can't believe he did that. Mr. Kramer was just doing his job. Chris got the grade he earned, but because he thought he deserved an A, he goes and vandalizes a building.' She sighs as we continue to the car. 'I shouldn't keep talking about him. I promised I wouldn't talk about him at all this week.'

'I think it's kind of inevitable.' I toss the sack in the trunk and walk over to Lyndsay. 'Just because the papers are signed and a judge made it official doesn't mean you stop thinking about it.'

'I know, but I shouldn't be talking about it, or about him, especially to you.'

'Why me?'

'Because I know how much you didn't like him.' She smiles. 'And because we're supposed to be on a date. I'm supposed to be learning how to do this, and I'm pretty sure talking about your ex is a bad idea on a date.'

'It is, but I'm just your fake date. I'm also your friend, and if you want to talk to me, I'm here, even if it's about . . . him.' I take a breath, trying to remain calm, but the more I hear about Chris, the more I want to strangle him. I'm still furious that he made Lyndsay miss her graduation.

'Did you even get dinner? A cake? Anything?'

She tilts her head. 'What are you talking about?'

'When you graduated. Did he get you anything? Take you anywhere to celebrate?'

'No, we didn't have time. We drove to the convention and were there for almost a week.'

'Then we're celebrating now. No, tomorrow night. I'm taking you someplace nice. And I'm getting you a cake. How could he not even get you a cake? What the fuck? It's not that hard. Just drive to a damn grocery store and pick one up.'

She laughs. 'Nick, why are you getting so upset about this?'

I hold her shoulders and lean down to her. 'Because you did something amazing and it wasn't even acknowledged. When did this happen? When did you graduate?'

'Five years ago. But Nick, really, we don't need to do anything. It was a long time ago.'

Letting her go, I lean back against the car, folding my arms over my chest. 'Why accounting? Why'd you choose that over something else?'

She shrugs. 'It seemed like something that could get me a job. And the hours would be during the day so I could still teach yoga at night and on the weekends.'

'That's it? That's the only reason you chose it?'

She looks down. 'It might've also been because of you.'

'Me? Why me?'

Her eyes go back to mine. 'You made me feel smart. You made me believe I could do more than I thought I could. I knew accounting would be hard, but I remembered what you used to say about taking things one step at a time. Like when we'd be working out a problem. You'd break it down into steps and tell me to just try to get to the next step, and then the next. Eventually, I'd get to the end of the problem and realize I'd done it. I'd solved the problem.'

'And then you'd jump up and down and scare your mom,' I say, laughing. 'She thought you'd seen a mouse the way you were jumping around like that.'

'I was just so happy that I'd done it. I'd done something I didn't think was possible. I thought about that when I was trying to decide what to go to school for. I thought about how good it felt to do something I didn't think I could do, how happy I felt when I actually did it. So I picked accounting. I decided to just take one class to start to see if I could do it. When I passed the class, I decided to take another. And two years later, I'd done it. I got my degree.'

I step up to her. 'I'm so damn proud of you, Lyndsay. I can't even tell you how fucking proud I am.'

'It just shows what a good teacher you were.'

'It wasn't me. I helped you get through high school algebra. College is a whole different level. That was all you. You did whatever it took to get through those classes and graduate. Do you get what a huge accomplishment that is?'

'What about you? You got through college, then law school, and now you work at some fancy law firm in New York. That's more of an accomplishment than me getting my associate degree.'

'Would you stop comparing us and focus on what you've done? How far you've come? When I started tutoring you, you were flunking math, and now you have an accounting degree and work as a bookkeeper. That's a huge accomplishment.'

'I guess it is,' she says, smiling a little. 'I never really thought of it that way. I was just trying to get through school so I could get a job and pay the rent. Chris never said much about me going back to school so I guess it just didn't seem like that big of a deal.'

'Well, it is, and we're going to celebrate tomorrow.'

'With cake?' She smiles. 'Or was that a joke?'

'I don't joke about cake. Is chocolate still your favorite?'

'You remembered.' She looks into my eyes. 'How do you remember so much?'

'I've got a good memory.'

I really don't, but I remember almost everything about Lyndsay. All those times we talked during her tutoring sessions, I listened to her every word, and whatever she told me stuck around, even all these years later.

For the past 15 years, I haven't been able to get Lyndsay out of my head. I tried to, especially after I found out she got married, but then I'd hear a song that reminded me of her or see something that made me think of her, and there'd she be again, consuming my thoughts.

Maybe that's why I'm still single. I was too hung up on this fantasy of being with Lyndsay that I couldn't see myself being with someone else. If that's true, I need to end this fake dating thing. Being with her is just going to make me think of her even more when I get back to New York.

But I don't want to stop seeing her. And I don't want to fake date her. I want to date her for real.

Chapter 12

Lyndsay

Why didn't I marry someone like Nick? Someone who's kind and supportive and smart and can fix stuff. He's like the perfect guy, but back in high school I never saw myself dating him. I was too focused on Chris.

But now? All I can think about is Nick. I want these fake dates to be real, but I know that'll just lead to me missing him more when he leaves. I'm trying to keep my heart out of this, but when he does things like help out my mom or insists on taking me out to celebrate my graduation, I feel myself falling for him in a way I didn't expect. I just got out of my marriage. I shouldn't be feeling this way for another guy so soon after getting divorced.

We're back at my mom's house now, dropping off the part for the dishwasher. As we're standing in the kitchen, about to leave, Nick's phone dings.

He checks it. 'It's Brody. Jason and him just got to Sawyer's. He's asking when I'll be over. I'll tell him I'll see them at the party.' He starts to text him.

'Wait.' I walk up to him. 'Why don't you just go?'

'Because I'm going out with you.'

'We can go out later. You should spend time with your brothers. You don't see them much.'

'I see them more than I see you. And we don't have much time left for you to practice dating. We need to go out.'

'Maybe I could come with you.'

'Where? To hang out with my brothers?'

'Yeah. It's the whole meet the family thing. Like you said, it's part of dating, right? Meeting the family?'

'But you already know my family.'

'And you already know my mom, but you still came inside to meet her.' I rest my hand on his arm and look up at him. 'We're pretending, remember? This is just practice for the real thing. And I haven't seen your brothers since high school. They're all grown up now. It'll be like I'm meeting them for the first time.'

Nick smiles. 'You really want to hang out with my brothers?'

I smile back. 'I'd love to, if you don't mind.'

'I'd rather have you all to myself, but if you really want to do this, then yeah, we can go over there.'

When he says things like that—that he wants me to himself—it makes me think he wants to date me for real. But he's made it clear that's not what he wants. He keeps saying he doesn't have time for a girlfriend and that he needs to focus on work.

'I told him we'll be over in a few minutes,' Nick says, sending the text. He slides his phone in his pocket. 'You sure about this? Because I'd be happy to take you out.'

'Nick, I want to do this. It'll be fun to see all the Kanfield boys again.'

'I used to get really annoyed when people called us that. It's like we were all the same, like we didn't have our own identity.'

'Sorry, I didn't mean anything by it.'

'No, it's fine. I actually like it now, although men would be better than boys.' He chuckles. 'I think we've all outgrown being called boys. Brody's six five now, taller than all of us.'

'How tall are you?' I ask, looking up at him.

'Six three, same as Jason and Sawyer.'

'Your parents made some tall boys, I mean men.' I remain in front of him, wishing he'd kiss me. I know he shouldn't since we're not actually dating, but I love how I feel when he kisses me and I'm starting to crave it whenever he's around, especially when we're close like this.

'Nick?' I say, sounding breathless, my heart thundering in my chest. I shouldn't do this. But I really want to.

'Yeah?'

I hold on to his shoulders and reach up on my toes and kiss him. I make it quick and wait to see what he'll do. Our eyes meet for just a second, but it's long enough for me to see his desire and feel that intense spark between us.

He grabs me around the waist and kisses me back, a scorching hot kiss that sends tingles down my core. He backs me up and lifts me up on the counter, his lips returning to mine as his hands rest on my legs, just below the hem of my dress.

'Tell me to stop,' he whispers over my mouth.

I shake my head and hear him groan. He pushes my dress up higher and spreads my legs, then yanks me to the edge of the counter. His large hands grip my thighs as he kisses me again, his soft lips moving gently over mine. The tingles I felt before have exploded throughout my body, making me feel alive in a way I never have, not even in all my years with Chris. Maybe I trust Nick more, or maybe it's because I'm older and more experienced. Or maybe he's just really good at this.

I had a friend in LA that used to tell me that smart, studious guys make the best lovers. Maybe she was right. I'd like to test that theory, but I can't, not with Nick. He's just a friend, and he's leaving.

He kisses the side of my neck as he slides off the straps of my dress. It has a built-in bra so when he lowers the dress to my waist, my top half is exposed. When his mouth moves to my breast, I'm filled with more of those pleasurable tingles. I lean back, pushing my chest out, wanting more. If he keeps this up, I'm going to come right here in the kitchen. If my mom knew I was doing this on her counter, she'd kill me, but there's no way I'm stopping this. It's too good. I never would've guessed Nick had these kind of skills, although the kisses he gave me earlier should've been a clue.

When his hand slides under my dress, under my panties, my head falls back against the cabinet. I'm panting, moaning, wishing I could touch him, but I'm too wrapped up in how I'm feeling to do anything right now. My head's spinning. The pleasure's building. My body's writhing under Nick's touch, trying to get closer but then pulling away, not ready for this to end.

His lips return to mine and his tongue slips in my mouth. It's a slow, sensual kiss and so damn good. His fingers are pumping in and out of me, his thumb circling my clit. I'm drowning in a type of pleasure I've never known, never experienced, breathing so hard I feel like I could pass out. His thumb presses down harder and his fingers plunge deeper.

'Nick!' I cry out, grabbing hold of his shirt as the most glorious feeling pulses through me. He rests his forehead against mine and slowly removes his hand from between my legs. I take a moment to catch my breath and feel Nick pulling away.

I open my eyes and see him looking at me. He almost looks regretful, like he shouldn't have done it. But I wanted him to. What he just did was incredible.

'We should go,' he says, heading to the door.

I put the straps of my dress back in place, then jump off the counter and race to catch up with him. 'What's wrong?'

'Nothing. We just need to get going. Your mom will be back soon.'

'Don't you want to talk about this?'

He stops and turns to me. 'I shouldn't have done it. I took it too far.'

'It wasn't too far. Why would you say that?'

'I don't want you thinking I'm only helping you out to . . .' He glances away. 'Be with you that way.'

'I don't.' I grip his arm. 'Nick, look at me.' I wait until he does. 'You're a great guy, and I know you'd never use me like that. What happened just now is what I wanted, and I think you might've wanted it too.'

He blows out a breath. 'I did, but that's the problem. We almost—' He shakes his head.

'Nick, we're both adults. We didn't do anything wrong. And doing more wouldn't be wrong either. I mean, if we both wanted that.'

His phone dings. 'That's probably Sawyer. We should get over there.'

He doesn't want to talk about it. Nick and I have always been able to talk about most anything, but maybe that's not true anymore. Or maybe he needs time to process this and accept that it's not wrong. I need to do that too. There's a part of me that still feels a loyalty to Chris, but I shouldn't. He's not my husband anymore. Even when he was, we hadn't been intimate for over a year. We didn't even live together for most of the last six months. So why would I feel even an ounce of guilt about being with Nick? I can be with whoever I want. It's not wrong.

'I don't regret it,' I say. 'Do you?'

'No.' He leans down and kisses me, a quick friend-like kiss, nothing like the hot passionate kiss he gave me just moments ago. I hope that doesn't mean he's changed his mind about the fake-dating thing. I want to keep seeing him before he has to leave.

He takes my hand and we go out to the driveway. Holding my hand is a good sign, so maybe the fake dating thing will keep going. Nick isn't someone who goes back on his word. If he commits to something, he follows through.

When we get to the brewery, I see a sign outside saying it's closed today. Sawyer mentioned last night that he'd be closing the place so he could go to his mom's party. He doesn't have enough staff yet to keep it open. Right now, it's just him and the bartender he hired. I'm impressed he's doing this. Opening a business is a lot of work, and keeping it open in a small town like this could be a challenge. Hopefully, the town's loyalty to the Kanfield name will be enough to draw in a crowd every night.

'About time you got here,' Brody says as Nick and I walk in. Brody looks completely different than when I saw him last. He was only 11 then, which means he's around 26 now. He shot up in height and filled out with muscle, and his brown hair is darker than I remember.

'What are you drinking?' Sawyer asks from the bar.

'I'll take the lager,' Nick yells back.

'I was asking Lyndsay. Ladies first. Where's your manners?' Sawyer smiles at me. 'What can I get you?'

'I'll do the pale ale.'

'Good choice,' he says, going to fill the glass.

'Lyndsay?' Brody says, eyeing me. 'You're not the Lyndsay who—'

'The one I used to tutor,' Nick says, interrupting him.

'No shit?' Jason walks up to us. 'I thought you moved to California.'

'I did, but I'm back visiting my mom.'

Jason's as tall as Nick with thick dark hair and the start of a beard. Looking at Nick, Brody, and Jason standing next to each other, I can't believe how good they look. They're all really hot, although Nick's the hottest, at least to me. I'm still burning up from what he did to me. How in the world is he still single? How are any of these guys single? Girls would be crazy not to date them, or maybe they do, but the guys just don't want to commit.

Jason looks between Nick and me. 'How did this happen? How'd you two connect?'

'I ran into her at the airport,' Nick says. He looks over at Sawyer. 'You were supposed to tell them all this before we got here.'

He shrugs. 'I've been busy. I got a lot going on.' He sets the beers on the bar. 'You hungry? We got sandwiches in the back.'

'I'm good,' Nick says as we walk to the bar. 'We had a big breakfast.'

Sawyer stands across from us at the bar, smiling. 'You had breakfast? Must've been a late night.'

'You know what time I got in,' Nick says, sounding annoyed at what Sawyer's insinuating. 'You woke up and yelled at me to be quiet.'

'Did I?' Sawyer says. 'I don't remember doing that. I don't even remember you getting home.'

'It was pretty late,' I say, taking a sip of my beer. 'Nick and I sat down here and talked after we left the bar.'

'You coming to the party?' Jason asks, sitting next to me.

'No, I'll be going home after this. I'll probably do something with my mom this afternoon.'

But I'd rather be with Nick. Knowing he's leaving Monday makes me want more time with him. I'm getting too close to him, having feelings I shouldn't be having. But being with him feels so good, I don't want to stop.

Chapter 13

Lyndsay

'She could come to the party, right?' Jason asks Nick. 'Did Dad say we could bring guests?'

'He didn't say, but I'm sure he wouldn't care if we did,' Sawyer says, answering for Nick. 'And it's Lyndsay. She's like family.'

I laugh. 'Nick tutored me in high school. I'd hardly call that family.'

'Yeah, but you're from here. A local. That makes you family.'

'You should come to the party,' Brody says, going behind the bar to refill his beer.

'Slow down there,' Sawyer says to him. 'Dad doesn't want you showing up drunk.'

'I'm not even close to being drunk.' Brody stands next to Sawyer behind the bar. 'And the party isn't for a few more hours. Whatever I drink will be out of me by then.'

Looking at Brody, I'm amazed at how much he's changed. I can't believe how tall he is now, even taller than his brothers. Nick was probably six feet back in high school, but now he's taller and a lot bigger, like he spends hours at the gym. Maybe he works out to burn off stress from his job. That's why I started doing yoga, except my stress was from Chris and all the scams he got involved in that drained our bank account.

'Who's running your business today?' Nick asks Brody.

'This guy, Kevin. He's Dale's stepson. He dropped out of college so I hired him before someone else got him. He's still got a lot to learn, but he knows enough to handle the afternoon for me.'

'I can't believe this idiot's running a business,' Sawyer says, hooking a thumb toward Brody. 'He couldn't even run a lemonade stand.'

Jason laughs. 'That's because he gave it all away to cute girls that walked by.'

'You gave girls free lemonade?' I say. 'That's so sweet.'

'His motives aren't what you're thinking,' Nick says before taking a drink of his beer.

'He was trying to get them to kiss him,' Jason says, laughing. 'He tried with this one girl and she threw the lemonade in his face.'

'Bet she's regretting that now,' Brody says.

'Yeah, you're a real catch,' Sawyer says, rolling his eyes.

'Is this where the party's at?' a deep voice says.

We all look back and see a guy coming into the brewery.

'What the hell you doing here?' Sawyer asks, smiling at the guy.

'I was invited. Your dad didn't tell you?'

Nick and his brothers walk over to the guy.

'He said you couldn't make it,' Nick says. 'Something about being behind on one of your renovations.'

The guy nods. 'We brought in a crew to finish it up so we could be here for Aunt Martha's party.'

Aunt Martha. So this guy is Nick's cousin, one of the Wheeler brothers. I've only heard about them. I've never met any of them until now.

Two more guys walk in.

'Nash, here's your keys,' one of the guys says, tossing the keys to Nick's cousin.

So that's Nash. I'm guessing the other guys are his brothers. I think Nash is the oldest. He's about as tall as Nick, with short dark hair and gorgeous blue eyes. He's really hot, like Nick and his brothers. This entire family was blessed with good genes.

'I'll take an amber ale,' one of the guys says to Sawyer. He looks similar to Nash—tall, dark hair, really hot.

'Help yourself,' Sawyer says. 'You know where to go. You put the taps in yourself.'

'When'd you get here?' the guy says to Nick.

'Yesterday. I've been hiding out here so Mom doesn't see me. Dad wanted to keep it a surprise.'

'With us too. She doesn't know we're here.' The guy glances back at me at the bar. 'Is that your girlfriend?'

'No. She's a friend from high school. Lyndsay, get over here.'

I walk over to him, feeling overwhelmed being surrounded by seven very tall, very hot guys.

'Hi.' I smile at Nash and the other two guys. 'You're Nick's cousins, right?'

'So you've heard about us,' Nash says with a laugh. He shakes my hand. 'Nash Wheeler. And these are my brothers, Jake and Bryce.'

'Nice to meet you.' I shake Jake's hand and then Bryce's. They both have huge hands and firm handshakes, like Nick and his brothers. I feel like I'm drowning in testosterone with all these guys.

'Where's Austin?' Brody asks.

'He's coming up later,' Nash says. 'He's bringing the band. They'll be playing tonight.'

'Did that just happen?' Sawyer asks. 'Dad didn't tell us Austin was doing the music.'

'It was a last-minute thing,' Nash says. 'Austin had another gig, but he cancelled so he could be here tonight. Keep that between us. Dad doesn't want Aunt Martha knowing Austin cancelled a gig to do this. You know how she is.'

'Never wants anyone being inconvenienced because of her,' Nick says to me. 'Drives us all crazy.'

'Just wait until she finds out about all the work Dad did for this party,' Brody says. 'I bet she yells at him for it.'

Nick shakes his head. 'She won't. She'll probably cry because he's never done anything like this before.'

'Want a beer?' Jake says to Bryce, who is also gorgeous—big and tall and covered in tats.

'Yeah,' Bryce says. 'Get me a lager.'

Jake takes off for the bar.

'Where are the girls?' Jason asks Nash.

'They're coming up later today. They didn't want to sit around here while we drink and talk sports. They're back at Dad's place, baking stuff for the party. Callie insisted on making all the desserts. Jen and Kira are helping and Ivy offered to clean up.'

'Those are your girlfriends?' I ask, looking at Nash.

'Yeah. Callie's my fiancé. Kira is Austin's girl.' Nash points to Bryce. 'He's dating Jen and Jake's with Ivy, although I still don't understand why. I think she could do better.'

'What the hell?' Jake yells from the bar. 'I was Chicago's most eligible bachelor! I'm a fucking catch!'

'Was he really Chicago's most eligible bachelor?' I ask.

'Yes.' Nash rolls his eyes. 'And he loves bringing it up.'

'When's your dad getting here?' Nick asks Nash.

'He's already here. He's helping your dad set up the barn.'

'Mom's gonna see his truck and know something's up,' Nick says.

Nash shakes his head. 'Your dad got one of her friends to take her out to lunch and then to the salon to get her hair done.'

'How do you know this shit and we don't?' Brody asks.

'He probably didn't even think to tell us,' Nick says. 'He's too busy trying to get this party put together. I haven't even talked to him since I got into town. I texted him and just got something back saying he'd see me at the party.'

'Same here,' Jason says. 'He hasn't talked to me in days. Bet he'll be glad when this party's over.'

'I think I'll go,' I say to Nick, 'so you can spend time with your family.'

'You don't have to go. Stay and hang out with us.'

'Aren't you going to the party?' Nash asks.

'Yeah, why don't you come?' Nick says to me.

'It's for family. I'd feel out of place.'

'It's not just family,' Jason says. 'It's friends too, and you're Nick's friend, so consider yourself invited.'

It's really nice of them to invite me, but I don't think I should go. It seems like something a girlfriend would do, and I'm not Nick's girlfriend. I'm just a girl from his past. And I should probably spend time with my mom. I've barely seen her since I got into town.

'Thanks, but I think my mom already has plans for us this afternoon.'

'You can at least stay and finish your beer,' Nick says.

'Okay.' I give him a smile, noticing how far away from me he's standing. And he hasn't held my hand since we got here. He's been really affectionate with me since we started fake dating, but now he's staying away from me. Is it because of what happened back at my mom's house? Or does he just not want to be that way with me in front of his family? I guess I can understand why. If we're not really dating, it'd seem odd for his family to see us holding hands or standing close.

'Let's go have a seat,' Nash says, heading to the bar.

We go over there and Nash starts telling Nick about one of the projects he's working on. Then Nick tells him about his job in New York and how he's been working extra hours, trying to make partner. I join in now and then but mostly keep quiet, just listening and drinking my beer. Brody and Bryce are talking on the other side of me and Jake and Sawyer are behind the bar talking. They're all really loud, talking and laughing, but I like it. It feels comfortable, like I'm surrounded by family.

'So Lyndsay,' Nash says. 'What do you do around here?'

'Oh, I'm just here to see my mom. I live in California now.'

'She's a bookkeeper,' Nick says, smiling at me. 'And she teaches yoga.'

'You married?' Nash asks. 'Got any kids?'

'I'm divorced,' I say, getting that sick feeling in my stomach that shows up whenever I talk about the divorce. 'And no kids.' I get off the barstool. 'I should get going. Nick, I hate to make you leave, but would you mind giving me a ride home? Or I could call my mom and see if she could get me.'

'I can take you.' He looks back at Nash. 'She doesn't live far from here. I'll be back in a few minutes.'

'Take your time. No rush.'

Nick and I go out to the car.

'What's wrong?' he asks, opening my door.

'Nothing. It's just getting late and you need to get to the party soon.'

'You sure you don't want to come? It'll be a good time. Live band. Good food.'

'Thanks, but I should really spend time with my mom.' I get in the car.

He's quiet as we drive back to my house. The closeness I felt between us earlier seems to have disappeared. It's like Nick shut down after we made out at my mom's house, but why? Does he think it's too soon after the divorce for me to be doing stuff with him? Or maybe this just isn't what he wants and he's starting to regret us getting together.

'We can skip tonight,' I say as he pulls into my mom's driveway.

He puts the car in park and turns to me. 'You don't want to go out?'

'Your cousins are here. You should spend time with them.'

'Lyndsay, what's going on? Why are you trying to get out of our date?'

'Because it's not a date. It's just pretend.'

'Isn't that what you wanted? Someone to practice on?'

'I did at first, but now . . .' I look down.

'Now *what*?'

I get out of the car. 'I'll talk to you tomorrow, Nick.'

'Lyndsay, wait!' He gets out of the car and comes up to me. 'What's going on? What happened?'

My eyes lift to his. 'I don't think I can do this. These fake dates are starting to feel real.'

'Yeah,' he says with a sigh. 'I know.'

'So maybe we should just end this.'

'Is that what you want?'

'No, but I don't know how we keep doing this without having our feelings get involved.'

He's looking at me but doesn't say anything. Does that mean he agrees with me, that we should stop seeing each other?

'Bye, Nick.' I race to the house and go inside, my heart pounding, tears stinging my eyes.

Just a few dates with Nick and I'm this upset about it ending? I take that to mean I did the right thing. Giving my heart to a guy I can't have is just setting me up to have it broken again, and that's the last thing I need right now.

Checking out the window, I see that Nick is gone. I go to the kitchen and my gaze immediately goes to where Nick lifted me up on the counter. Now every time I come in here I'll think about that, about what we did and how it felt.

Why did I have to run into him again? Why now? I just got out of my marriage. My heart's still healing from Chris. This is not the time to be falling for some other guy, especially some guy who lives thousands of miles away.

My phone rings. It's Diane calling, just the person I need to talk to.

'Hey, Diane,' I answer.

'Hey, are you with your mom?'

'No. I think she's still out.' I go to the garage to check. 'Yeah, her car's not here.'

'Do you guys have plans later? Because I was thinking of having a girls' night. Tom said he'd watch the kids. We could go out for drinks, get dinner somewhere.'

'Maybe. Let me talk to my mom and see if she has anything planned.'

'Oh, wait, aren't you going out with Nick tonight?'

'No. We decided not to, or *I* did.'

'What happened?' she asks in her protective best friend tone. 'What'd he do?'

'Nothing,' I say, going upstairs. 'I just decided this fake dating thing wasn't a good idea.' I go in my room and lay down on the twin bed that still has the pink comforter on it that I picked out in tenth grade.

'You had sex with him,' Diane says.

'What? No. I mean, we could've, but we didn't.'

'Lyndsay, just spill it. What happened?'

'I'm starting to have feelings for him. And I can't let that happen knowing he's leaving on Monday.'

'What are you saying? You're falling in love with him? After a day?'

'It's not love. It feels like . . . I don't know how to describe it. I just know if I keep letting myself fall for him I'll end up getting hurt.'

'Then it's good you're not going to see him anymore. I never liked the fake date thing anyway.'

'But I really like Nick. He's sweet and funny and easy to talk to. And damn, does that boy know how to kiss.'

'Maybe what you're feeling is less about Nick and more about being with someone new after all those years with Chris.'

'What do you mean?'

'Think about it. Chris ignored you. He never took you out. Never spent time with you. You guys weren't even having sex. And now you're going out with this really hot guy who's giving you attention, making you feel desirable again, listening to you. It's totally normal to feel like you're falling for him. I think you're worrying about nothing. You're not in love with Nick. You're just getting a taste of what it feels like to be with a guy who actually likes spending time with you. That guy doesn't have to be Nick. Once you start dating again, you'll get those same feelings with someone else.'

'Really? You really think that's true?'

'I know it is. Back in college, I went out with a bunch of guys I thought I was in love with, but it wasn't love. They were just guys I really liked who were hot and gave me a lot of attention and were good in bed. It was hormones making me feel that way, not actual love. And after not having sex for over a year, your hormones are probably going crazy just kissing Nick.'

'They are. I almost had sex with him today. If we didn't have to meet up with his brothers, it might have happened.'

'You met up with his brothers?'

'At Sawyer's brewery. Nick's cousins showed up, too. They're all in town for the party. They invited me to go, but I didn't think I should. It seemed like a family thing. And Nick was acting weird. I felt like he didn't really want me there. He said he did, but I think he was just being nice.'

'How was he acting weird?'

'He was acting like we're friends. He wasn't holding my hand, wasn't putting his arm around me.'

'Because you're not dating. Lyndsay, you can't tell the guy you want to fake date him and then expect him to act like you're actually dating when he's around his family. Sorry, but I'm gonna have to take Nick's side on this.'

'Yeah, I guess you're right. See, this is why it doesn't work. The fake dating thing is helping me feel more comfortable about dating again, but I'm getting confused about what's real and what's fake.'

'Did you talk to Nick about it?'

'I told him the fake dates were starting to feel real and he agreed. But he didn't offer a solution. He just left.'

'So what are you going to do?'

'I don't know. I really want to see him tonight, but I don't know if I should.'

'If you knew getting hurt wasn't possible, what would you do?'

'Go out with Nick. A hundred percent. I'd have no doubts.'

'Why? Why would you want to go out with him?'

'Because he makes me feel alive and happy and excited and . . . like me again. I didn't realize how much of myself I'd lost being with Chris, but being with Nick, I feel like the old me is starting to come back. I can't tell you how great that feels.'

'And you think Nick's the one making you feel like that?'

'He's part of the reason. In fact, he's the one that pointed out how much I've changed. How I don't smile like I used to, or laugh, or get excited. He was right. That part of me got lost when I was with Chris.' The phone is silent and I check that we're still connected. 'Diane? You still there?'

'Yeah.'

'So what do you think? Do I tell Nick I can't see him anymore?'

'That's up to you. I can't tell you what to do. But I can tell you that getting hurt can happen no matter who you're with. When you start dating again, you're going to get your heart broken, probably more than once. It's just what happens when you put yourself out there.'

'What are you saying? That I shouldn't date?'

'No, of course you should date. I'm just saying you can't expect not to get hurt. It's going to happen, but it's up to you to decide who you're willing to risk your heart with. Maybe that guy is Nick, maybe it's not.'

'It's not Nick. I mean, it could be, but we live on different coasts. It'd never work. I just need to find someone just like him who lives in LA.'

She's quiet, then says, 'Is Nick worth it?'

'What do you mean?'

'Is dating Nick worth it, knowing you'll probably end up getting hurt?'

'You're saying I should date him for real?'

'I'm just asking a question. Are you willing to risk your heart being broken if you start something with Nick and it doesn't work out?'

'I don't know. I haven't even thought about dating him for real because of where we live. Why would I date him, knowing it wouldn't work?'

'I'm not saying you should. But if he makes you feel as good as you say he does, maybe you give it a chance.'

'I don't think Nick wants to date me. He doesn't even want a girlfriend. And how would that work when we live on different coasts?'

'You talk on the phone. Do video dates. Being apart might make it easier to keep your heart from getting involved. Maybe you both agree to keep it casual and only keep it going until you find someone else.'

'I'm not sure I could keep my heart out of it. Nick's not a stranger I met on a dating app. He's a guy I grew up with. A friend. I know his family, his brothers. I had feelings for him even back in high school.'

'You did?'

'They weren't romantic feelings. It was the type of feelings you'd have for a friend. I cared about him. I looked forward to our tutoring sessions because I really liked spending time with him. Sometimes I'd call him to tell him something because I didn't want to wait until our next session. He was the guy I wish Chris had been, but that just wasn't him.'

'Okay, this is getting complicated. I know you think you only saw Nick as a friend back in high school, but it sounds like more than that, which would explain why you're having such strong feelings for him now. Maybe you shouldn't see him anymore.'

'Except I really want to, even if it's only for one more day. Would it be that bad to go on a real date with Nick, knowing it won't go anywhere?'

'That's up to you. Just make sure you let him know that's what you're doing. Don't pretend to fake date him and then tell yourself it's real.'

'I don't think he'll do it if I tell him that. He doesn't want this turning into anything.'

'Then don't do it. Lying about what you're doing isn't fair to either of you and will definitely end with one or both of you getting hurt.'

I sigh. 'I need to think about this.'

'Let's plan our girls' night for next week, once Nick is gone.'

'Sorry. I'm not being a very good friend.'

'You're a great friend. You're just going through a tough time. You need to do what you need to do. I get that. I'm here if you need me, okay?'

'Yeah. Thanks, Diane. I'll let you know what happens.'

There's a knock on my door. 'Honey, are you in there?'

'Yeah, Mom. Just a minute.' I get up and open the door. 'Your hair looks nice.'

She's had the same hairstyle for as long as I can remember, a short bob that she curls under at the ends.

'Thank you.' She smooths her hand over it. 'It always feels good to get it trimmed up. Did Nick leave?'

'Yeah, he's with his brothers and his cousins from Chicago. They'll all be going to the party soon.'

'He's such a nice young man.' She smiles. 'And he seems to think an awful lot of you. The way he was looking at you?' She winks at me.

'We're just friends, Mom.' I walk over to the mirror above my dresser to check that my mascara didn't smear when I was tearing up. I don't want my mom knowing I was crying and asking why. 'Besides, I thought you were still holding out hope that I'd get back with Chris.'

'Honey, I know it's over between you two,' she says, coming into my room. 'I was hoping you two might be able to reconcile, but now that the divorce is final, I think it's time for you to find someone else.'

'I'm not sure I'm ready for that.' I turn to face her. 'Dating. Getting into another relationship.'

'You're not getting any younger, and if you want children—'

'Yeah, Mom, I know.'

I don't need a reminder of how old I'm getting and how my time's running out to have kids. I already think about that all that time. It's the reason I need to force myself to start dating again. So maybe I shouldn't be pursuing anything with Nick. Maybe my time should be spent getting back out there, finding someone I could actually date and maybe marry. I wish that guy could be Nick, but it's not, and never will be.

Chapter 14

Nick

The party's been going on for a few hours now and my mom's had a smile on her face the entire time. I don't think I've ever seen her this happy, or this in love with my dad. When he walked her into the barn and she saw us all there, her jaw dropped. She was stunned and overwhelmed, and probably wondering how my dad pulled this off.

We all stayed quiet, waiting for her to say something. But she didn't, not right away. Instead, she slowly looked around the barn, at the long tables that were set up with white tablecloths and white wooden folding chairs. Dad put wildflowers—my mom's favorite—down the center of each table and hung white lights from the wood beams along the ceiling. He put lanterns around the perimeter of the room for extra light. The barn has electricity, but Dad was going for mood lighting. He wanted the space to feel romantic and special.

When Mom was done checking it out, she turned to Dad, took his face in her hands, and kissed him. My brothers hooted and hollered like idiots, ruining the moment, but Mom just laughed. Austin's band started playing Mom's favorite song—a slow country song—and Dad took her hand and led her to the dance floor.

We all watched as they danced. They didn't take their eyes off each other. It was then that I knew how completely and totally in love they were. I'd never really thought about it before. I knew they were in love, but it didn't seem like anything special. They held hands sometimes and gave each other the occasional peck on the cheek, but other than that, they reserved affection for when they were alone together. And I never saw them look at each other the way they did tonight. Or maybe they did and I just didn't notice.

'You seem lost in your thoughts,' Nash says, coming up beside me as I watch Dad serve Mom a piece of cake. 'You thinking about that girl?'

'No,' I say, but I actually was thinking about Lyndsay, and about what she said when I dropped her off. She's right. Our fake dates aren't feeling so fake anymore. I tried to keep my feelings out of it, but I couldn't. The crush I had on Lyndsay 15 years ago is still there, except now it's becoming more than a crush. I'm developing real feelings for her and it needs to stop.

'So there's nothing going on with you two?' Nash asks.

'She's just a friend.'

He laughs a little. 'So was Callie, and now I'm engaged to her.'

I turn to him. 'You set a date yet?'

'We've talked about it, but we haven't decided. You think you'll make it back for the wedding? I'd love to have you there.'

'I'm sure I could make it work. As soon as you set the date, let me know so I can get the time off.'

'You should bring that girl you were with today. I know you say she's just a friend, but I sensed some chemistry there.'

'We definitely have chemistry, but we live on different coasts. And she just got divorced. I don't think she's ready to get involved with someone again.'

'It's never the right time. You can't let that stop you from being with someone.' The music gets louder as Austin's band plays a new song. 'Let's get out of here where we can talk.'

We walk to the door that goes outside. There's a grassy area before the orchard starts where we have chairs and benches set up. Nash goes over to one of the benches and takes a seat at the end. I sit on the other end, turning to him.

'What'd you want to talk about?' I ask.

He shrugs. 'Just catching up. I haven't seen you much since you moved away.'

'Yeah, I don't get back that often.'

'You miss it?'

'I do, but small-town life just isn't for me. I liked growing up here, but I needed a change. There's so much to do in New York, so many places to go.'

'It can't be that great if you're doing it alone, or do you have someone there?'

'I'm not seeing anyone. I haven't had the best luck dating there. I've gone out on plenty of dates. They just don't go anywhere. I've decided to take some time off from dating and focus on work. Maybe in a few months I'll get back out there again.'

'You don't see yourself dating Lyndsay? That's her name, right?'

'Yes. And no, I wouldn't date her. It wouldn't work with us living so far apart. And like I said, she's not ready for a relationship.'

'Neither was Callie. She turned me away so many times I lost count. But I didn't give up on her. I just kept showing up at her door.'

'Why? If you knew she didn't want to date you, why'd you keep asking her?'

'Because I felt something between us, something I hadn't felt with other girls, not even the girl I was engaged to.'

I'd forgotten Nash was engaged to a girl before Callie. It wasn't a long engagement so maybe that's why I didn't remember it.

'I wasn't going to just let that go,' Nash continues. 'When you feel that kind of connection with someone, you don't just give up without at least putting some effort in.'

'So what'd you do?'

'I hired her. Had her help me clean up that house I inherited. It gave me an excuse to spend time with her. Our attraction to each other was insane, but we didn't act on it, at least not right away. I kissed her a few times, but she made it clear she didn't want that, so we were just friends for a while.'

'How'd you end up becoming more?'

'I kept being a friend to her until she was ready. It's different with Callie because she'd been through a huge loss and was still grieving. But I was willing to wait for her, even knowing I'd be going back to Chicago.'

'That's right. She didn't live there.'

'No, and she had no plans to move. I took a big risk with her, but it ended up working out. And now I couldn't be happier. She's the love of my life.'

'It's a great story, but why are you telling me this?'

'Because I'd hate to see you give up on this girl before giving it a chance. Sawyer said you stayed up all night talking to her. You don't do that with some girl you don't feel something for.'

'You were talking to Sawyer about this?' I shake my head. 'Ignore him. He doesn't know shit.'

'I remember you talking about her back in high school. It's no secret you liked her back then.'

'Every guy liked her. She was hot and a cheerleader.'

'But you were the guy she was friends with. Am I right? Weren't you guys friends?'

'Yeah, but only because I was tutoring her. If I wasn't her tutor, we would've just passed each other in the halls and never spoken.'

'Did she have a boyfriend?'

'Yeah, this jerk, Chris. Quarterback of the football team. He treated Lyndsay like shit. I hated him. She ended up marrying him.'

Nash leans back on the bench and looks out at the orchard. 'If I were you, I wouldn't give up on her. A girl with a boyfriend doesn't confide in some other guy unless she trusts him and feels something for him. I'm guessing her feelings for you back then were more than she was letting on.'

'I doubt it, but even if that were true, it doesn't change the fact that we live on opposite coasts. I can't date a girl from thousands of miles away.'

'Is she staying in California?'

'I don't know. I assume she will. She has friends there, a life, a job.'

'And you're determined to stay in New York?'

'I'm about to make partner at my firm, so yeah.'

'Nash?'

We turn back and see Callie, Nash's fiancé, coming up behind us.

'Hey, babe,' Nash says. 'You need something?'

'I just didn't know where you went. Sorry, I didn't mean to interrupt.' She smiles at me. 'Hey, Nick.'

'Hey, Callie. Congrats on the engagement. You sure you want to commit to this guy?' I nod at Nash.

She laughs. 'There's no one I'd rather be with.' She leans down to him and he kisses her.

'I'll be in there in a minute,' he says.

'No rush,' she says, going back inside.

Nash watches her with the same look on his face that my parents had as they gazed at each other on the dance floor.

'You guys seem made for each other,' I say.

'I'm lucky I found her. But like I said, nothing would've happened with us if I hadn't put in the effort.' He gets up. 'If you really want Lyndsay, you could make it work. I'll see you inside.' He goes back into the barn.

I get up and walk over to the line of trees at the edge of the orchard. It's dark out, but the area around the barn is lit, casting light on the rolling hills lined with apple trees. My dad built this place from nothing. He inherited the land from his father, along with the house. The land was covered in tall prairie grass back then, but my dad imagined it being an orchard. He had no experience in farming, but he read books and talked to tree experts and drove to other orchards asking for advice, then took out a loan and got to work planting trees.

The orchard took off soon after it opened. There weren't any others in the area so he had an advantage. He made a decent living off the apples, but Mom suggested they sell more than just apples to bring in more people. She started making pies and apple fritters and selling them on the weekends when we got the most visitors. They sold out within hours and soon people were showing up just to get her homemade pies and fritters. The following year, they added a store with apple-themed products and baked goods. Then Dad started growing pumpkins, which drew in even more people. And a few years ago, he planted strawberry fields to get income coming in during the summer.

Dad never went to college, but he didn't need to. He grew a successful business out of nothing and made it more profitable every year by adding the stuff people wanted, like tractor rides to the fields and pumpkin painting for kids. And he's helped the town. Not only does this place draw in tourists, but he also gives part of what he makes back to the community. And on his two busiest weekends of the fall, he hosts a vendor fair, where locals can sell their craft items.

'What are you doing out here?' I hear Matt say.

Turning around, I see him coming toward me.

'Just checking out the orchard. The trees are looking good this year.'

He stands beside me and gazes out at the fields. 'Remember that time we were cutting branches and you made me laugh so hard I fell out of the tree?'

'I don't even remember what I said.'

'I don't either, but I couldn't walk for a week thanks to you.' He laughs. 'Lot of memories out here.' He turns to me. 'The party turned out well.'

'Yeah, Dad did a good job. I've never seen Mom this happy.'

'Speaking of happy, you and Lyndsay seemed pretty happy at my house last night. You two couldn't stop talking.'

That was last night? God, it seemed like a week ago, probably because I've spent all my time with her since I got into town. How is it possible I'm feeling this much for her after only a day? Is it just old feelings from the past coming back?

'I saw her again this morning. I took her to breakfast, then she went to the brewery with me and we hung out with the family.'

'No shit?' His brows rise. 'What's going on with you two? Is it serious?'

'We just like spending time together. I was going to see her tonight, but she decided to stay home.'

I'm still bothered by that. I understand her reasoning, but I really want to see her. I miss her. It's only been a few hours since I dropped her off and I miss her. Why would I miss her? I'm not even dating her.

'But you're taking her out tomorrow, right? After the beer tasting?'

'I don't know. Probably not. I think she's done with the fake dating thing.'

'Why is that?'

'I don't want to get into it.'

'She's not getting back with Chris, is she?'

'Hell no. She just divorced him. Why would you even say that?'

He shrugs. 'No reason.' He glances back at the barn. 'I should get in there. Tessa's probably looking for me.'

'Matt, hold on,' I say, stopping him on his way back to the barn. 'What are you not telling me?'

'It's nothing. Just forget it.'

'I know you're lying. Now tell me what it is.'

'Why? You're not dating her.' He eyes me. 'Are you?'

'Lyndsay? No, but what does that have to do with anything?'

'Just forget it. I shouldn't have brought it up.'

'Brought what up? Chris?'

'Let it go. Just forget I said anything.' He continues to the barn.

'Matt, wait!' I get in front of him. 'Tell me what's going on.'

He sighs. 'There's a rumor going around that Chris is coming to the reunion.'

'Yeah? So?'

'Think about it. He's there with Lyndsay, reliving memories from high school, the place they fell in love. Shit like that gets people back together. I'm not saying it'll happen, but it's possible.'

'Lyndsay's not even going to the reunion.'

'She bought a ticket like an hour ago.'

'How do you know?'

'I'm on the planning committee. I get a notification every time someone buys a ticket online.'

Lyndsay said she wanted to go to the reunion, but only if she didn't have to go alone. There's no way she'd go with Chris. She doesn't want to get back together with him. She doesn't even want to see him. That's why she's here while he moves out of their apartment.

'There's no way she'd get back with him. She's the one who filed for divorce.'

'And we both know how much Chris hates to lose. If the divorce was his idea, he'd leave her alone. But if Lyndsay wanted it and he didn't? He might try to get her back, especially if he heard she was seeing someone else.'

'But she's not.'

'That's not what people around town are saying.'

'What do you mean?'

'You and her getting all close at the country bar? People saw you guys together and now that shit's all over town.'

'And made its way to Chris?'

'He still has friends here. You know one of those shitheads told him they saw her with you.'

Part of me is glad Chris knows I was out with Lyndsay. The asshole never acknowledged me in high school. He acted like I was invisible. Now he thinks I'm dating his ex, which will piss him off more than if she were dating someone he didn't know. But I don't want him going after Lyndsay because of it.

'Did he buy a ticket?' I ask.

'Not yet, but I'll let you know if he does. I don't think he'll actually show up, especially if he finds out you left town and went back to New York. But you never know. If he really wants Lyndsay back, returning to the good old days is the way to do it.'

'She'd never go back to him,' I say, shaking my head.

'Yeah, you're probably right. I'm gonna head back in.'

I follow him into the barn and go back to my seat. Nash is on the dance floor with Callie. Bryce is there too, dancing with Jen. Matt's with Tessa and Mom's with Dad. They all look ridiculously happy and in love, which I have to admit makes me kind of jealous. I'd like to settle down, get married, have the kind of love they have, but I just can't find the right girl.

Getting out my phone, I check for any messages from Lyndsay, thinking she might've changed her mind about tonight. But I don't see any texts and no missed calls. Damn, I really screwed this up. I shouldn't have suggested the fake dating thing. I shouldn't have kissed her. And I definitely shouldn't have done what I did to her in her mom's kitchen earlier today.

What the hell was I thinking? I wasn't. I was so wrapped up in how it felt to kiss her and touch her that I couldn't stop myself. If we hadn't gotten out of there, things might've gone even farther.

Now she doesn't trust me, or maybe she doesn't trust herself. We agreed this wouldn't turn into anything and it has, or it was starting to. Maybe I should just leave her alone. Go back to my life in New York and try to forget about her. It's not what I want, but I don't know what else to do.

What if we truly were just friends? Would it work? Could we be friends without it becoming more?

Before I can talk myself out of it, I text her, *Can we be friends?*

Several minutes pass before I get a text back. *Isn't that what we are?*

It's a loaded question and not one I can answer over text. It needs to be in person.

I need to talk to you. Can I see you tonight?

When?

Now.

I'd planned to stay at the party longer, but I don't need to. The dinner is done, the cake's been served, and Mom opened all her gifts. If I stay here, I'll just be sitting at this table alone, watching couples in love on the dance floor. I really don't need to see that.

My mom's here, Lyndsay texts.

I'll pick you up. We can go somewhere.

Okay.

I get up and go over to Matt and Tessa on the dance floor. 'Hey, sorry to interrupt, but I'm heading out. I'm gonna take my dad's truck so you guys can have your car back.' I hand Matt the key.

'Where are you going?' he asks.

'I need to go talk to someone.'

He nods, smiling, because he knows that someone is Lyndsay. 'Good luck.'

I might need it. I'm worried Lyndsay's going to tell me she doesn't even want us being friends, which I totally get, but I hate the idea of never talking to her again.

I walk up to my parents. 'I'm gonna head out, if that's okay.'

'Of course.' Mom lets go of Dad and gives me a hug. 'It's so good having you home. It's the only gift I needed.'

Dad smiles at me. 'Where are you off to? You got a date?'

'How could I have a date?' I say, laughing. 'I just got here.'

'Word around town is you've been spending time with the Davis girl.' He winks at me. 'You had quite a crush on her back in the day.'

'Dad, I'm not—'

'She's such a sweet girl,' Mom says. 'I'm glad she finally got rid of that husband of hers. The things I've heard . . .' She sighs. 'You go off and have a nice time. Tell her we said hello.'

Why are they assuming I'm going to see Lyndsay? I didn't tell them I've been hanging out with her. Maybe my brothers told them.

'Is it okay if I take the new truck?' I ask Dad, feeling like I'm 16 again, asking to borrow the car.

'Go ahead. Keys are by the door.'

'Thanks. See you tomorrow.'

I go back to the house, where I'll be staying tonight. I kind of wish I was staying with Sawyer again instead of my parents. If I'm out late, they'll question me about it and I don't want to answer their questions.

When I get to Lyndsay's house, she's sitting outside on the porch swing, wearing jeans and a t-shirt. My pulse rises the moment I see her. The girl takes my breath away, always has, always will.

She sees me and heads to the truck. I'm about to get out to open her door, but she's already there, opening the door for herself.

'Hi, Nick,' she says in a tone that's friendly but not at all flirtatious. She's made her decision. She just wants to be friends, nothing more, or maybe she doesn't even want to be friends.

'Are you hungry?' I ask. 'We could get something to eat.'

'I already had dinner. Maybe we could just go somewhere and talk.'

I drive to a coffee shop that also serves food, just in case she changes her mind and decides she wants to eat.

'Let's just stay here,' she says as I open my door.

'In the truck?'

'Yeah.' She turns to me. 'I'm guessing this won't take long, whatever it is you wanted to say.'

'Um, I guess not. Are you in a hurry?'

'No.' She looks down. She seems sad. I hope it's not because of me. The last thing I'd ever want to do is hurt her, which is why I'm not letting myself get more involved with her.

'Lyndsay, I know things were moving fast with us, but I promise you, that wasn't my intention.'

She looks up at me. 'I know.'

'It's just that seeing you again brought up old feelings. And spending time with you has made those feelings even stronger. Knowing that, I shouldn't have taken things as far as I did.'

'We both played a part in that. I liked what we were doing. I just wanted it to be real.'

'I get that, and I never should've suggested the fake dating thing.' I take her hand. 'Being with you has never felt fake. I tried to keep my feelings out of it, but I couldn't. There's just something about you . . . about us.'

'I agree.' She smiles. 'So what are you saying?'

'I'm saying you need to be with someone who can give you what you want. Someone you can have a future with. I don't want to get in the way of that. When I get back to New York, I want us to remain friends, but if you decide that won't work, I'll understand.'

Saying this to her is killing me. I want to tell her I want this, that I want her more than anything, but why would I tell her that if it can't happen? Nash's advice that I need to put in the effort if I really want to be with her is true if we lived in the same town, but we don't. I can't date a girl who lives thousands of miles away. It just won't work.

Chapter 15

Lyndsay

Nick wants me to find someone else. My heart broke when he said it because I thought he was going to tell me he wanted us to date for real. And I was going to agree with him. It's what I'd decided after spending all day thinking about it.

People date long distance all the time. Nick and I could at least try to make it work. We could talk on the phone, do video chats, and if things were going well, maybe I'd move to New York to be with him.

But that's not what he wants. He doesn't see a future with me. I guess I can understand that. Even though he admitted he has feelings for me, I'm not his type. I barely got through school and he was valedictorian. I teach yoga and he's a successful lawyer. The two of us don't make sense. And I don't fit in his world. He'd probably be embarrassed having me in New York with all his smart, successful friends.

'Lyndsay, say something,' he says, still waiting for my answer.

'Friends.' I force out a smile as I choke back tears. 'Yeah. We could be friends.'

'Are you sure? You seem like you're not.'

'I'm just not sure what you mean by that. Are you saying we'll just talk on the phone?'

'We could do that, or a video call so we could see each other.'

'We could try it.' I look out the window.

'Lyndsay, what's wrong? You're acting like you don't want to do this. If you don't want to stay in touch, just tell me.'

'I just don't think it'll work. You're busy with your job and I'll be busy trying to make a new life for myself. Meeting new people. Dating.'

'That doesn't mean we can't at least try. Unless you don't want to.'

It'd probably be easier if we made a clean break and I just forgot all about this weekend, but I'm not ready to do that. I'm not ready to let Nick go.

'We can try it,' I say, looking over at him.

'Good.' He smiles, and when our eyes meet, I feel the attraction between us and whatever it is that makes me feel like we belong together. I've always felt a connection with Nick, but I ignored it when I was younger. Now that I'm older, I can't. It's there and stronger than ever, but I guess Nick and I just weren't meant to be.

'How about a round of mini golf?' Nick says.

'You want to play mini golf?' I ask, thinking he's kidding.

'Over there.' He points to the mini golf course that I don't even think is open anymore. It's got weeds growing around it and the paint on the building where you pay is chipped off. 'I'm not ready to go home yet, and if you don't want to eat or go get a drink, this might be our only option.'

'I don't think it's open. I think my mom said it closed a few years ago.'

'Let's go check it out. If it's closed, we'll find something else to do.' He gets out of the truck.

I really thought he was kidding, but he seems to be serious. He's walking across the parking lot toward the mini golf course.

'Nick, wait!' I race to catch up to him, almost grabbing his hand, but then realizing I can't. He doesn't want that.

We get to the building and see it's all boarded up.

'I think the owner retired a few years ago,' I say. 'Nobody bought it, so now it just sits here.'

'Why wouldn't anyone buy it? People used to love this place. They'd still go if it was open.'

I smile as I look out at it. 'My dad used to take us here. I'd always hit the ball off the course and it'd land in that little pond that used to be there.' I point to it. 'My dad would get his shoes wet trying to get it. And one time he fell and got his pants wet.' I laugh, thinking about it.

'But didn't you end up getting a free game?'

'I did. The owner felt bad and gave us a free game. How'd you know that?'

'You told me during one of our study sessions.'

'I can't believe you remembered that.'

'Good memory.' Nick taps his head. 'Worked out great during law school. They make you memorize a lot.' He walks around the building.

'Where are you going?'

'Ha! I knew it!' He comes back holding two rusty golf clubs and two balls, one orange and one blue.

'Where'd you get that?'

'Side of the building. There's a sign saying anyone can play for free and to have fun.' He smiles. 'Ready to have fun?'

I glance back at the course. It looks terrible. The concrete paths are cracked and pushing up from the ground. The red windmill has a blade broken off. The clown at the end has an eye missing and a mustache that someone drew on with a marker.

'Come on.' Nick holds onto my arm and pulls on me to follow him.

'Are you sure it's okay to do this? We're not trespassing?'

'If we were, you really think anyone would care? Look at this place. The gnome over there doesn't even have a head.'

I laugh. 'I'm pretty sure that used to be a squirrel, not a gnome. See the tail?'

'Here.' He hands me a club and the orange ball. Orange is my favorite color. I wonder if he remembered that. 'You want to go first?'

'You go. I haven't golfed in a while. I need to warm up.'

He eyes me like he's not sure if I'm kidding, then gives me a slight smile before focusing back on the course. He's still wearing what he had on at the party; black dress pants and a light blue shirt with the sleeves rolled up. He looks really hot, and of course, he's wearing that great cologne I love. I'm getting that tingly feeling again and he's not even touching me. Why am I having all these feelings for him? I mean, yes, we've spent almost every moment together since he got here, but that shouldn't be enough time to get all crazy about him. Is Diane right and my feelings for him in high school were more than I thought? Maybe I just wouldn't admit to myself how much I liked him back then because I was with Chris.

'I gotta think of a strategy here,' Nick says, kicking the ball in place with his foot. He swings the club back a little, then does it again, like pro golfers on TV do before taking a shot.

'You're taking this very seriously,' I kid.

'Miniature golf is a serious sport. You've got obstacles to get past. Water traps. Volcanos. Psychotic clowns.'

I laugh. 'You're right. I didn't think about that. I'll be quiet so you can concentrate.'

'You can make noise. I don't mind. Play some music if you want.'

As he's lining up his shot, I get out my phone and find a song that was popular when we were in high school.

'Good song,' he says as he follows his ball to the other side of the hill that leads to the hole. 'Holy shit, I got it on the first try.'

'Really?' I race over to see and there it is, in the cup. 'Nick, that's great!' I hug him without even thinking. But friends can hug, right? It doesn't have to mean anything.

He hugs me back, but then quickly lets me go. 'Your turn.'

'Any tips to share before I do this?' I ask as I line up my ball.

'Try to get it in the hole.'

I glance at him. 'That's what she said.'

He laughs. 'Seriously?'

'What? It was right there. I had to.' I hit the ball, but with way too much force. It flies up in the air and hits Nick in the face.

'Okay, maybe this was a bad idea,' he says, rubbing his cheek where the ball hit.

I run up to him. 'Oh my God, I'm so sorry. Let me see.' I take his hand from his face and see the red mark the ball left behind. 'We should go get some ice.'

'Yeah, and maybe hit the emergency room.'

'It's that bad?' I grab his arm. 'Nick, I am so sorry. Let's go!'

He smiles. 'I'm joking. I'm fine.' He picks up the ball and hands it to me. 'Here. Try again.'

'Are you really okay?'

'Yes. It didn't even hurt. When you grow up with three brothers and on a farm with dangerous equipment, getting hit with a golf ball is nothing.'

I put the ball in place and hit it so softly it barely moves.

'Do it harder,' Nick says.

'That's what—never mind.'

Nick laughs. 'I didn't know you had such a dirty mind.'

'I don't. I swear.' I hit the ball again and this time it actually stays on the course and goes over the tiny hill. 'It's this music from high school. It's making me act like a teenager again.'

'These are some good songs,' he says as another one starts to play.

'Chris hated this one. He didn't like any of the ones I liked. We had opposite tastes in music.' I tap the ball into the hole. 'I did it! And it only took four tries.'

'I'm not keeping score. We're just here to have fun.' He moves to the next hole, which has a fish statue sticking out of some concrete painted blue to look like water.

'You think Chris will come to the reunion?' Nick asks as he hits his ball.

'No. He's going to San Diego next weekend. He has a meeting with some guy for another one of his business investments.' Nick moves out of the way as I step up to the tee-off area. 'Why do you ask?'

'I just wondered.'

I hit the ball, but it only moves a few feet. 'You still don't think you'll go?'

'Probably not.' He taps his ball in the hole. 'How about you?'

'I got a ticket, but I haven't decided if I'll go.' I pass in front of him as I hit my next shot and get a whiff of his cologne. God, he smells good. Good thing I'm not drinking or I'd lose all control and kiss him.

'If you decide to go, will you go with Diane?'

'She's going with Tom, but I'll see her there. Why? Do you know someone who would go with me?'

I wish he'd say him, but he won't.

'You mean as a date?'

'Or a friend.'

'Sawyer would go with you. As a friend,' Nick clarifies. 'You want me to ask him?'

'No, that's okay. He needs to be at the brewery. I'll just meet up with Diane when I get there, assuming I go. I might skip it and do something with my mom since I'm flying back to LA the next day.'

'You ever consider moving?' Nick asks as we continue to the next hole. It has a pyramid on it that you have to go through to get to the other side. I didn't realize until now that these obstacles don't fit any kind of theme. A clown, a pyramid, a fish. But I like that it doesn't make sense. It makes it more quirky and fun. I'm glad Nick suggested this. It lets us talk while also giving us something to do so we aren't tempted to do things we shouldn't.

'You mean out of my apartment?' I ask as Nick hits the ball directly through the pyramid.

'No, out of California.'

'Oh. I don't know. I haven't really thought about it.' I hit the ball and it bounces off the pyramid, not even close to the little tunnel it's supposed to go through. 'Where would I go if I moved?'

'You could move back here, be close to your mom.'

'I've thought about it, but how would I meet someone here? I know all the guys my age and I'm not interested in any of them.'

'You could go older. Hal's single.'

'Hal who?'

'Hal of Hal's Hardware. He winked at you when we were checking out today. He's definitely interested.'

'Yeah, I'll pass,' I say, laughing. 'I'd like someone a little younger.'

We continue the game, talking and laughing and listening to old songs. It's the most fun I've had in years. I wish it didn't have to end.

'Last hole,' Nick says, lining up his shot. 'The one-eyed clown.'

I laugh. 'It used to have two.'

Nick makes his shot, landing it in the clown's mouth. 'Guess that's it.'

'You're way too good at this.' I hit the ball harder than I intended. It bounces off the clown's nose, hits the green, and bounces into the mouth.

'Trick shot,' Nick says. 'Impressive.'

'It was pure luck. I didn't mean to do that.'

He takes my club and collects the balls and takes them back to where he found them.

'I can't believe this course hasn't been torn down,' I say as we walk back to the truck.

'Why would they tear it down? It's great.'

I stop at the truck. 'I don't get you, Nick.'

'What do you mean?'

'You live in a fancy apartment in New York. Go to all these fancy places and expensive restaurants, and yet you're still okay going to a place like this.'

'Why wouldn't I be?'

I shrug. 'I don't know. I thought you might've turned kind of snobby living in the big city and looked down on places like this.'

'Are you kidding? I love places like this. I also love dive bars and greasy diners. I live in a big city, but I'm still a small-town guy. Always will be.'

'But how does that work? How can you be happy there but still like being here? They're totally different.'

'I don't know. I never really thought about it that way.' He reaches past me and opens my door. I guess that means we're leaving. I was hoping we could talk more.

'Want to stop anywhere else?' Nick asks as we're driving, but he's already heading to my house.

'I should probably get home. So should you. You have a repair job in the morning.'

'That's right. I almost forgot about that. What time should I come by?'

'Maybe around ten? My mom will be at church, but I'll stay home so I can let you in.'

'Could it be earlier? Like nine?'

'Sure.' Nine is probably better because my mom will be home, keeping Nick and me from doing anything. 'Am I still invited to the beer tasting?'

'Of course. Why wouldn't you be?'

'I wasn't sure with our new arrangement.'

'We were friends before and we still are. That hasn't changed. And I'm still taking you to dinner afterward. We're going to celebrate your graduation.'

'Nick, you really don't have to do that. It was a long time ago.'

'And you never celebrated it, so we're doing it tomorrow.'

We're at my house and he pulls into the driveway.

'Thanks for tonight,' I say as I get out of the truck. 'It was fun.'

'It was.' He smiles. 'I'll see you tomorrow.'

When he's gone, I already miss him. I'm going to miss him even more when he leaves on Monday. We'll talk on the phone, but it won't be the same.

Why did this have to happen? I came here to grieve the loss of my marriage and ended up having the best time of my life with a guy I can't date. I'm more sad about that than about the divorce.

Chapter 16

Nick

'You're going *where*?' Mom asks as she pours me another cup of coffee.

We just finished a breakfast of pancakes, eggs, toast, and bacon. I'm not used to eating that much. I did when I lived here, but I was a growing boy who spent hours a day working outside in the fields. Now I just sit at a computer all day.

'To Lyndsay's house,' I say. 'I'm fixing her mom's dishwasher.'

'That's interesting,' Dad says, his bushy gray brows rising as he sips his coffee.

'I'm doing it to be nice, not for whatever you're thinking.'

Dad glances at Mom. 'Tell him what I did for your mother back in the day.'

'He fixed her car,' Mom says to me. 'Built her a whole new engine. It was when your grandfather had to be on the road for work. Your grandma's car completely died one day and she didn't have the money to take it in.'

'So I offered to fix it for free,' Dad says. 'Her mother liked me from that day on.'

'Are you saying Grandma didn't like you before that?' I ask.

'She called me a dreamer, thought I had my head in the clouds because I was always talking about having my own business. She didn't think I could do it, which meant I wouldn't be able to support her daughter.'

'You sure proved her wrong,' Mom says, going to get more coffee.

Dad leans back, cringing and rubbing his stomach.

'You okay?' I ask.

He shakes his head. 'I've been having some bad indigestion lately. Your mom says I'm working too hard, but I think I just need to eat less.'

'You've *been* eating less and you still have that pain,' Mom says, taking our plates to the sink.

'How long's this been going on?' I ask.

'A few weeks.' He gets up. 'It's just part of getting old. I'm going to take a short nap before going out in the fields.'

When he's upstairs, I walk over to Mom. 'Is Dad okay?'

'He's fine. He just overworks himself. I keep telling him to hire another helper, but he insists he can do it alone.'

'He's getting older. He needs to slow down.'

'Maybe you can talk him into it. He won't listen to me.'

'I'll talk to him when I get home. Thanks for breakfast.'

Mom winks at me. 'Tell Lyndsay I said hello.'

'For the last time, I'm not dating her.'

My mom would love it if I dated Lyndsay. She's always liked her. They worked together on some school fundraisers. Lyndsay always volunteered for that stuff; school fundraisers, bake sales to support local kid programs, charity events to raise money for people in town that needed it. She was always helping out, and because she was popular, she got other people to help out too.

When I get to her house, she answers the door.

'Hey, I'm Nick, your repair guy. I believe you have an issue with your dishwasher?'

Lyndsay smiles. 'Yes, it's leaking. I couldn't wait for you to get here.'

The way she says it makes me think she's not kidding, that she really couldn't wait to see me. I'm so damn confused about her. Last night had me even more confused. I told her what I thought she wanted, for us to stay friends, but she looked sad when I said it. I don't know what that means, and when I asked her about it, she acted like everything was fine.

Was she hoping for something else, like for us to date? Why would she want that, knowing I'm leaving? And if she wanted us to date, why didn't she tell me that? I don't think she does. I think she's just sad we won't see each other anymore. I'm sad about that too, but there's nothing I can do about it. I have to get back to New York.

'Nick, can I get you anything?' Patty asks as I bring the toolbox into the kitchen. 'Some coffee? A cinnamon roll?'

'No thanks. I just had breakfast. But I might take one of those cinnamon rolls to go.'

'You can have the whole pan,' she says, sounding excited that I asked for one. She's always been an excellent baker. She loved feeding me when I'd come over to tutor Lyndsay.

'How are your parents doing?' Patty asks as she wraps up the cinnamon rolls.

'I think they're worn out from the party last night. They were up pretty late.' I get to work taking the door off the dishwasher, noticing Lyndsay watching me.

I'm watching her too. She's got on ripped denim shorts and a pink-and-white plaid button-up shirt that's tied in front, just below her breasts, exposing her stomach. If she's trying to tempt me to cross the friend line, she's doing a damn good job.

'You want to help?' I ask, smiling at her.

'I'm good over here,' she says, smiling back as she picks up her coffee.

The job only takes ten minutes. When I'm done, Patty runs the dishwasher and not a single drop of water leaks out.

'It works!' Patty hugs me. 'Oh, Nick, I can't thank you enough.' She lets me go and races over to her purse. 'Let me pay you for the parts.'

'I'm not taking your money,' I tell her. 'You can pay me in cinnamon rolls, but that's it.'

'You're such a nice young man.' She walks over to me. 'I need to go get ready for church, but thank you again for all your help.'

'You're welcome. I'm glad I could fix it.'

She leaves and Lyndsay walks up to me. 'Want some coffee?'

Before I can answer, my phone rings. It's my mom calling.

'Just a minute,' I say to Lyndsay as I answer the phone. 'Hey, Mom, I'm just finishing up. You need me to stop somewhere?'

'No. I was calling because I wanted to know if you'd be willing to fill in for your father today out in the orchard.'

'Sure, but why? Is he okay?'

'He isn't feeling well and I want him to rest, but I know he won't if his chores don't get done.'

'What's wrong? Is it his stomach?'

'I believe so, but he's not saying much. You know how he is. He doesn't like me to worry. I know you had plans today, but if you could just help out for a few hours.'

'Of course. I'll be right over.' I end the call and gather up my tools. 'Sorry to rush out, but I need to get home.'

'Is everything okay?' Lyndsay asks.

'My dad's not feeling well. He needs me to cover for him in the orchard today.'

'Can I help?'

I smile at her. 'I'm not sure you'd want to do this kind of work. It gets hot in the fields and there's a good chance you'll run into a snake or some mice.'

'I could help clean up from last night. I'm sure your mom hasn't had time to do it and she really shouldn't since it was her party.'

'I'll see if one of my brothers can do it.'

'Nick, really, I don't mind.'

I pause a moment, wondering if this is a good idea. I should be keeping my distance from her, trying to stop these feelings I'm having, but I can tell she really wants to help. It's just how she is, how she was raised. We were both raised to help people out.

'That'd be great,' I tell her. 'I'm sure my mom would appreciate it.'

'Let me just run up and grab my shoes. Can I ride with you? My mom will want the car.'

'Sure.'

While Lyndsay's upstairs, I call Sawyer.

'Hey, what's up?' he answers.

'You hear about Dad?'

'No. Why? What happened?'

'Mom said he's not feeling well. I'm going to fill in for him at the orchard today. I may not make it to your beer tasting.'

'Why don't I just close for a few hours and help you out in the fields?'

'I don't think I'll need it. I'll probably just be cleaning up the rows. And I don't want you closing the place and losing business.'

'Okay, but let me know if you change your mind. Do you know if Lyndsay's still coming to the tasting?'

'Probably not. I'm with her right now. She's coming over to the house with me to help Mom clean up from the party.'

'Sounds like something a girlfriend would do,' he says, a smile in his voice.

'Don't start with that shit. She's just being a friend. Hey, I need to go. Call Brody and Jason and tell them about Dad.'

'What do you think is wrong with him? Is it the flu or something he ate?'

'He said his stomach was bothering him. He didn't look too good at breakfast.' I hear Lyndsay running down the stairs. 'I gotta go. Talk to you later.'

'I'm ready,' Lyndsay says, her sneakers on, her hair in a ponytail, and wearing a white baseball cap. She looks adorable, and fucking hot in that plaid shirt and those tiny shorts. I want to take her in my arms and kiss her, but I can't. We're not dating, not even fake dating.

Last night sure felt like a date. It took everything in me to stay away from her. More than once, I reached out to touch her, but then realized I couldn't. I couldn't kiss her either, even though I was dying to. We had such a great time at that run-down mini golf course. It was in such bad shape, it was comical. We couldn't stop laughing, especially at the one-eyed clown, which was both frightening and funny. I haven't laughed that much in years. Back in New York, I'm always so serious. I have to be for my job. It was nice to just kick back and relax and let myself laugh and have a good time.

When we get to the house, my mom looks surprised when she sees Lyndsay.

'Well, hello,' Mom says, smiling as she goes up to her. 'Nick didn't say he was bringing a friend.'

'I thought you might need some help cleaning up from the party last night,' Lyndsay says. 'I probably should've asked you first, but Nick was in such a hurry to get over here.'

'Do you mind if she helps?' I ask, realizing Mom may want to tend to Dad rather than deal with the party cleanup.

'I'd love some help,' she says, looking at Lyndsay, 'and the company. I haven't seen you since Nick's graduation party. That's been what . . . ten years?'

'Fifteen,' I say, laughing. 'I'm 33, Mom.'

She pauses to think. 'That's right. I guess it was 15 years. Time sure does fly.'

'What's Dad got on the chore list?'

'Cleaning up the fields. We had a storm last week and your father wasn't able to get out there and clean up all the debris it left behind.'

'Because he didn't have time or because he wasn't feeling well?' I ask, hoping it was time and not his health.

'He didn't have the energy. He'd go out there and end up coming in an hour later and taking a nap.'

'That doesn't sound like Dad.' I glance at Lyndsay, who looks as worried as I am. My dad doesn't take naps. He works nonstop from sunrise to sunset. He's always been that way.

'I'm sure planning the party took a lot out of him,' Mom says with a strained smile. 'He'll be fine after he rests.'

She's worried too, but trying to hide it. She and Dad never wanted us kids to worry so they'd never tell us when something was wrong.

'I'll go out to the fields and see what needs to be done,' I say. 'Maybe I'll call Brody, see if he can help.'

'Nick, don't,' Mom says, racing up to me. 'I don't want your brothers knowing your father's not feeling well. Just do what you can and if your father still isn't feeling well tomorrow, we'll bring in some help.'

'I already told Sawyer, and he's telling Jason and Brody. Mom, this could be serious, and we're all adults. You don't need to hide this stuff from us anymore.'

She nods. 'Maybe you're right, but I still don't want you asking Brody. Sunday is one of his busiest days and I don't want him cancelling on his customers. And Jason's summer classes start tomorrow. He needs today to prepare.'

Jason teaches summer school to kids who are falling behind. He loves teaching and didn't want to take the summer off. He also coaches baseball, so he's always busy. It's hard to find time to see him when I'm home. It's the same with Brody. With his lawn business taking off, he's working all the time. And Sawyer just opened the brewery, so he's working a lot too.

All of us are like are our dad, working hard to achieve our goals. Growing up, we watched Dad work long days, seven days a week, to make the orchard a success. But he always told us it didn't feel like work because he loved it. He told us to do the same; to find something we loved to do and find a way to make money doing it. That way, we'd never dread going to work.

My brothers managed to do that, but I'm not sure I did. I like practicing law, but I don't love it. Honestly, some days I hate it. Writing contracts, doing research, dealing with angry clients who demand I get them what they want. And no matter how hard I work, the partners at my law firm always want more. It's never enough. It's exhausting, and the only reward I get from it is money, which isn't nearly as meaningful as the reward Dad gets from this orchard. Seeing all the families here, making memories. Tourists stopping by, bringing income to the town. He's even had a few couples get married here. He's created something that brings people joy, and made a good living doing it.

'I'll get out there and see how much I can get done,' I say to Mom. I walk over to Lyndsay. 'Let me know when you need to go. I'll give you a ride.'

She nods, a determined look on her face, like she's not leaving until her work here is done. I love her for helping us like this. She didn't have to do it, but the fact that she is makes those feelings I'm having for her even stronger.

'Where should I start?' I hear Lyndsay ask my mom as I leave.

Going out to the orchard, I see the damage left behind from the storm. I didn't notice it last night because Dad cleaned up the rows closest to the barn where the party was being held. But farther into the fields, there's storm debris everywhere I look. In addition to all the cleanup that has to be done, some branches on the younger trees were damaged and need to be cut. Doing this myself, it's going to take all day. I won't have time to take Lyndsay out for her graduation dinner. I told her I would and she was so excited about it. I really don't want to have to cancel on her, although I know she'd understand if I did.

I call up Matt.

'Hey, what's up?' he answers.

'What have you got going on today?'

'Besides the beer tasting? I have some people who might want to look at the house that's for sale over on Maple Street, but they're not sure yet. I'm waiting for them to call me back. Why?'

'How would you feel about helping me in the orchard for a couple hours? I'd pay you for it.'

'You're not paying me. What do you need help with?'

'Cutting some branches. Cleaning up the storm debris. It's kind of a mess out here and I don't think I can do it all myself. Dad's not feeling well and hasn't been able to get to it.'

'What's wrong with your dad?'

'I'm not sure, but Mom wants him to rest, so I'm filling in. But I know Sunday is your busiest day so—'

'Today is slow. I got nothing going on other than those people wanting to see that house. I'll call and tell them we can do it tomorrow.'

'Are you sure? I don't want you losing business over this.'

'Don't worry about it. They can wait a day. That house isn't going anywhere. Did you tell Sawyer we won't be at the tasting?'

'I told him I wouldn't, but I'll call him back and let him know you won't be there either.'

'You want me to come over right now?'

'If you could, yeah.'

'Be there soon.'

I knew I could count on him to help. I could call most anyone in town to help out. But my dad wouldn't want that. He wouldn't want people knowing he needs help, but they'd be here if he asked. That's small-town living. People help each other out.

As I go in the barn to get the equipment I need, I call up Sawyer.

'Hey, are you at home?' he answers.

'Yeah, I was just out in the fields. It's a mess out there. That storm did some damage.'

'You want some help?'

'I already called Matt. He's coming over, so he won't be at your tasting.'

'That's fine. Is Matt going to be enough? Because I can still close the place and help you out.'

'I'd tell you yes, but if Dad found out, he'd be pissed. You just opened. He'd want you there, running your business, not here.'

'So don't tell him.'

'Let me see what I can get done with Matt. If I need help later, I'll give you a call.'

'How's Dad doing?'

'I don't know. He's resting. I haven't seen him.'

'Hey, Nick, thanks for doing this.'

'What do you mean? Of course I'm doing it. Why wouldn't I?'

'You're a big city guy now. You haven't worked in those fields in years. I didn't think you'd want to do it anymore.'

'Actually, I kind of miss it.' I walk out of the barn and look out at the fields. 'It's nice being out here, getting some fresh air. And Dad needs the help.'

'Well, let me know if you need some extra hands.'

'I will. Bye.'

I'm surprised Sawyer thinks I wouldn't step in and help. It's true it's been awhile since I've worked in the fields, but that doesn't mean I wouldn't do it. It's not like I forgot how. I grew up helping my dad. I spent more time out here than any of my brothers. I was one of those kids who liked learning stuff, so I'd come out here and ask my dad to teach me everything he knew. I had no intention of ever running an orchard, but I still wanted to learn about it.

'Where should I start?' I hear Matt yell as he makes his way over to me. He's got on an old pair of jeans, a baseball cap, and a t-shirt with the name of our high school on it.

'That was fast.'

'I just had to change clothes, then I headed over. What do you want me to do?'

'You get to pick. Rake or cut branches?'

'Cut branches.' He smirks. 'I'm faster at it than you.'

'What the hell? You're not faster than me.'

We go in the barn to get what we need.

'Don't you remember?' he says. 'I'd be done with an entire row and you'd be only halfway done with yours.'

'Yeah, well, I was more precise. I didn't just hack at the trees.'

'I think it was more about you having your mind on something else.'

'Like what?'

We take our tools and head out to the orchard.

'Not *what*. Who,' he says. 'You couldn't stop thinking about Lyndsay. That summer we worked together was her last summer here before she moved away with Chris.'

'Yeah? So?'

'You were pissed she was leaving with him and trying to find a way to get her to stay. That's why you were so slow with those trees.'

'I was not thinking about Lyndsay. And why would I try to get her to stay? She chose Chris. She chose to move away with him and marry him. That was her decision. I wasn't getting in the way of that.'

He shrugs. 'It was just a theory. I don't know how else to explain why you were so freaking slow.' He holds back a laugh.

'I wasn't slow,' I insist.

We get down to the trees and Matt stops. 'Holy shit, this is a mess. That storm was over a week ago. I can't believe it still looks like this.'

'Dad wasn't able to do the work. Matt, I'm getting worried. You know my dad. He never takes a day off. Something like a storm happens and he's out here until sunset every day cleaning it up.'

'But he had the party to plan. Maybe that's why he didn't do it. He didn't have time.'

'Yeah, I thought about that, but still, it's not like him to take a nap after breakfast. I know he's tired from being up late last night, but he'd normally fight through it and be out here.'

'I'm sure he's fine. Getting that party ready probably just wore him out.'

I hope that's it and not anything more serious than that.

Chapter 17

Nick

'So what's the latest on you and Lyndsay?' Matt asks as he sets the ladder up by one of the damaged trees.

'Nothing. We're just friends.'

'You wouldn't leave your mom's party to go see a friend.'

'The party was almost over. I didn't want to sit there for another hour watching couples make out on the dance floor.'

Matt smiles. 'What can I say? I got a beautiful wife. I can't help myself. And it was romantic with all those little white lights and the lanterns. Add in a few glasses of wine and Tessa couldn't wait to get me home. We might've made another kid last night.'

'Are you serious?'

'No.' He laughs as he climbs up the ladder. 'I'm just saying, it was a good night. Great party. So what'd you end up doing after you left?'

'I took Lyndsay to play mini golf.'

He was cutting a branch, but stops and looks down at me. 'You took her to do *what*?'

'Play mini golf.'

'Aren't you a little old for that? And where the hell is a mini golf course around here?'

'It's that one behind the coffee shop. Behind the parking lot.'

'That thing hasn't been open for like two years.'

'Yeah, well, they left the equipment out for anyone who wants to play.'

'That was your romantic date?' he asks, going back to cutting branches. 'Taking her to a mini golf course that looks like shit and isn't even open?'

'It wasn't a date,' I say, raking up the leaves and branches that collected in the grass. The grass needs to be mowed. That's Brody's job, but Dad probably told him to hold off mowing until he cleaned up the mess from the storm.

'Then what was it?'

'Just two friends going out.'

'Let me get this straight. You left your mom's party to go out with Lyndsay, on a Saturday night, but it wasn't a date.'

'Okay, for the last time, the party was almost over, and no, it wasn't a date. I went to see her because when I dropped her off yesterday she seemed . . . I don't know . . . upset.'

'About what?'

'The fake dating thing. I told you this yesterday.'

'Actually, you didn't. You said you didn't want to talk about it.'

'And I still don't.'

'Just tell me what she said. Does she want to date you for real?'

'No. She knows it wouldn't work. We both do. That's what we talked about last night. I went to see her to make sure there wasn't any confusion about what this is between us. And we agreed we should just be friends and forget the fake dating thing.'

'What does that mean? Be friends?'

'It means we stay in touch, talk on the phone.'

'Until she finds someone else.'

'Yeah,' I mutter, not wanting to think about that. 'Oh, and I asked her about Chris coming back for the reunion. She said he won't. He has a meeting that weekend with some guy in San Diego.'

'See, this is why I shouldn't listen to rumors. Half the time they're not true.'

'I'm going to finish this row, then go down a few. You need anything?'

'No, I'm good.'

We continue to work, and an hour later we're farther along than I thought we'd be. Matt really is a fast worker. With his help, we'll get a lot more done than I could've done on my own. But we won't be able to finish today, not even close. The orchard is huge. Dad needs to hire a crew to maintain it, but he won't. He just hires temp help when he needs it.

'You guys want something to drink?' I hear Lyndsay yell from up the hill.

'Yeah!' Matt yells back. He's on the ladder and can see her. I can't from the ground.

'Tell her we'll go up and get it,' I say.

'We'll be there in a minute!' Matt yells.

'I'll just bring it down!' she yells.

Moments later, she appears with two big jugs of water, setting them on the ground. She looks so damn hot in those denim shorts and wearing that baseball hat. She changed out of the plaid shirt and has on a t-shirt, a fitted white one with 'Kanfield Orchard' printed on it. The shirt clings to her breasts and tiny waist. She should do ads for us. We'd sell a hell of a lot more shirts if she did.

'Nice shirt,' I say, smiling at her.

'Your mom let me have it in exchange for my help. I was getting too warm in the shirt I had on. I needed something cooler.'

'It looks good on you,' I say, loving seeing my family name spread across her chest. If things had been different, if she'd seen me as more than a friend back in school, maybe she and I would've ended up together. Maybe she'd have *my* last name instead of Chris'.

'How's it going, Lyndsay?' Matt asks as he picks up the jug of water. 'Nick says you're helping in the barn?'

'Yeah. We got all the tables cleaned up and the chairs put away.' She looks over at me. 'I love the new barn. It looks great.'

'Yeah, it's a lot better than the old one.'

'It'd be good to rent out for parties or weddings.'

'They've thought about that, but it's a lot of work. It's basically starting another business. I'm not sure my parents are up for that.'

'So they only use it in the fall?'

'Yeah, as a store and as a place for people to wait before taking the tractor to the fields. And they have the fall festival in there. The festival is so big now that the outdoor space just wasn't enough.'

'It's so awesome what they've built here. It's really amazing.'

'Yeah, it really is,' I say, thinking about how much the place has grown over the years. I remember when it was just a roadside stand that sold apples, and now it's a huge business.

'Are you guys hungry? Martha and I were going to start lunch soon.'

'Martha?' I say, kidding her. I've never heard Lyndsay use my mom's name.

'She told me to call her that but it feels weird. I keep wanting to call her Mrs. Kanfield.'

'I'm the same way with your mom. Calling her Patty feels wrong.'

'I still call her Mrs. Kanfield,' Matt says, leaning against a tree as he gulps down his water.

'We should get back to work,' I say to Matt, then I look back at Lyndsay. 'We can eat whenever you guys are ready.'

'Okay!' She smiles and goes back up the hill to the house.

My gaze remains on her the entire time. That cute little ass. Those tan, lean legs.

'You gonna stare at her all day or get back to work?'

'What?' I look over at Matt and see him smiling at me.

'She *is* pretty fucking hot,' he says. 'She's even hotter than she was in high school.'

'Yeah, she is,' I mutter, picking up the rake.

'I don't know how you keep going out with her without something happening.'

Things *did* happen, but I'm not going to tell him that.

'I told you, we're just friends.'

'You sure about that? Because the way Lyndsay was looking at you, I'd say she wants you.'

'She wasn't looking at me.' I start raking. 'You're just giving me shit.'

'You didn't notice?'

'Notice what?'

He laughs. 'She couldn't stop staring at your chest. How the hell did you get like that, anyway? You got a trainer or something?'

'I did, but now I just work out on my own. I lift to relieve stress.' I look down at myself, shirtless and covered in sweat and dirt. 'I look like shit. If she was looking at me, it's because she thinks I need a shower.'

'Yeah. With her.'

I laugh. 'You're full of shit. Get back to work.'

A half hour later, Lyndsay returns to tell us lunch is ready. This time I notice her looking at me, at my chest and arms, but I'm not going to read anything into it. She made it clear she only wanted to be friends when we talked last night.

'This salad is great,' Matt says to my mom as we're having lunch. We're eating outside on one of the picnic tables since Matt and I are too much of a mess to go inside. We're both sweaty and covered in grass, dirt, and leaves.

'Lyndsay made it,' Mom says, smiling at her.

'One of my yoga students gave me the recipe,' she says.

'The steaks are good too,' Matt says.

'Mrs. Kanfield made those,' Lyndsay says. 'I mean Martha.'

Mom laughs. 'Old habits die hard. Earlier I called her little Lyndsay, like I used to do when she was younger.'

'How's the barn coming?' I ask. 'You guys almost done?'

'We still have to put the tables away,' Lyndsay says.

'I can do that. Those tables are heavy.'

'I don't mind doing it,' Lyndsay says. 'It's a good workout. And I'm not in a hurry to leave. My mom went to lunch with a friend. If I go home, I'll just be alone.'

'You're welcome to stay,' Mom tells her. 'But you don't have to keep working. You've done enough.' She looks at Matt and me. 'The same goes for you two. You boys have done enough for today. I don't want you spending what's left of your weekend out working in the fields.'

'Mom, I want to. Dad needs the help.'

'And I don't mind staying,' Matt says. 'Tessa's out with the kids and I don't have any appointments this afternoon.'

She sighs. 'Okay, but no later than three. After that, you quit for the day. And Nick, I'm making you a nice dinner tonight before you have to head home tomorrow.'

I glance at Lyndsay. 'Mom, I'd love to, but I kind of already have plans.'

'Nick, it's okay,' Lyndsay rushes to say. 'We can skip it.'

'Skip what?' Mom asks. 'Were you two going to dinner?'

'We don't need to,' Lyndsay says. 'You go ahead with your plans.'

'I'm taking Lyndsay to dinner to celebrate her graduation from college,' I tell my mom. 'She never celebrated it and I wanted to do something special for her.'

'I didn't know you went to college,' Matt says, munching on his salad.

'Community college,' she says. 'I got an associate degree in accounting.'

'Accounting? I thought you hated math.'

'Nick convinced me it's not as bad as I thought.' She smiles at me. 'He was an excellent tutor.'

'What if we celebrate here?' Mom says to Lyndsay. 'The boys could come over. You could invite some friends and your mother. It'd be like a little party.'

'Oh, no, I couldn't have you go to all that work,' Lyndsay says. 'And you need to take care of your husband. You don't need to throw me a party.'

'Did I hear something about a party?'

Dad appears, looking much better than he did this morning, and he's walking like he has more energy.

'Where'd you come from?' Mom asks, getting up. 'I didn't hear you come out.'

'I'm sneaky that way.' He smiles and gives her a kiss.

'You feeling better?' I ask.

'I'm not a hundred percent, but I'm better than I was this morning. I think all that party planning wore me out.' He stands at the end of the table, looking at Matt and Lyndsay. 'What are you two doing here?'

'They're helping us out,' Mom says. 'Matt's helping Nick in the fields and Lyndsay's helping me clean up the barn from last night.'

'Why are you putting these kids to work?' Dad says to Mom. 'I told you I'd take care of all that.'

'And I told you I wanted you to rest,' she says, patting his chest. 'You haven't been feeling well all week and working in those fields isn't going to make you better.'

'I needed the workout,' I say, knowing Dad has a hard time admitting he needs help. If I make it about me, he's more likely to be okay with it. 'I haven't been to the gym for days.'

'And I haven't been in years,' Matt says, which makes everyone laugh.

'We made it about halfway down the hill,' I tell Dad. 'After lunch, Matt and I will keep going and hopefully make it down to the property line.'

'That's almost a third of the orchard,' Mom says. 'You boys are fast.'

Dad nods. 'Thanks for helping out.'

'Anytime, Mr. Kanfield,' Matt says.

Dad chuckles at Matt calling him that. 'So what's this talk about a party?'

'We're thinking of having a graduation party for Lyndsay,' Mom says. 'She got her associate degree.'

'Congratulations.' Dad smiles at her.

'Thanks, but it was five years ago.' She laughs. 'I really don't need to celebrate.'

'Chris didn't throw you a party?' Matt asks.

'No, we went to a convention out of town that weekend.'

Matt glances at me.

I keep my focus on Lyndsay. 'If you don't want to do this, it's fine. We can still go out like we planned.'

Lyndsay's gaze goes to my parents. I can tell she's struggling with what to do. She thinks it's silly to have a party, but she doesn't want to disappoint my mom, who seems to really want to do this.

'If it's not too much trouble,' Lyndsay says, 'then yes, I'd love a party. But I insist on helping with it and I'm sure my mom will want to bring dessert. You know how she loves to bake.'

'Wonderful!' Mom claps her hands. 'I'm going to go call her. It'll be nice to see her again. It's been forever since we've had a chance to sit down and chat.'

'Lyndsay, can I talk to you a minute?' I say.

'Sure.'

We get up and walk around the side of the barn where my parents can't see us.

'Are you really okay with this?'

'Of course. It's so sweet of them to offer. I just feel bad making your mom have to go to all that work.'

'She was going to make dinner anyway and this gives her a chance to have my brothers over and your mom. She wants to do this. You saw how excited she was. And if you want to go out after dinner, just the two of us, the offer's still open.'

'Don't you have to leave early tomorrow?'

'It doesn't matter. I can be up late.'

'Then yeah, maybe, if you're not too exhausted from working in the fields.' Her eyes dart down to my arms, then my chest, before returning to my face. Okay, that time she was definitely checking me out, and I even put a shirt on.

'I should get back out there,' I say.

'Yeah.' She smiles and walks back to the table.

'Matt!' I yell at him as I head to the fields. 'Let's go!'

'What was that about?' he asks as we walk through the orchard. 'Your little private chat with Lyndsay?'

'I was just making sure she's okay with the party. She didn't even want me taking her to dinner to celebrate. She thought it'd been too long since she graduated, but I told her it didn't matter. She had to have worked her ass off for that degree given how much she struggled in school, and Chris didn't even let her go to her graduation.'

'He's always been a selfish bastard. You know that.'

'Yeah, but she was his wife. He can't miss some stupid convention to go to his wife's graduation? That's bullshit.'

'Yeah, well, that's Chris. He hasn't changed.'

We're back at the place where we left off. I pick up the rake and get back to work while Matt moves the ladder to another section of trees.

'You taking her out later?' Matt asks.

'Maybe. If she wants to.'

'I'd say that's a yes.'

'Why?' I look up at him on the ladder.

He chuckles. 'She fucking wants you, dude. Didn't you see how she was looking at you? I only got that look from Tessa when we were dating, and when I did . . .' He shakes his head. 'Those were some damn good nights. Not that the sex isn't good now, but you know how it is when the relationship's new and hot and you haven't had to clean up kid puke together in the middle of the night.'

'I'm glad to say I've never had to do that.'

'You will, and let me tell you, it sucks, but it's part of having kids. Anyway, going back to Lyndsay, she totally wants you. Too bad you're leaving tomorrow. But hey, you still have tonight.'

'We're just friends. How many times do I need to say it?'

'You can say it all you want, but you two are not just friends. You both want each other. You just refuse to act on it.'

'Because I'm leaving, and so is she. Now can we stop talking about this and get to work? We don't have much time left.'

We work until three, getting as much done as we could. I would've liked to do more, but I wanted to have time to clean up and get ready for Lyndsay's party. I have some errands to run before it starts, like getting the cake I promised her.

I'm not ready to say goodbye to her, especially knowing it might be the last time I see her. Reconnecting with Lyndsay this weekend has really messed with my head. This trip was supposed to just be a quick trip home for my mom's birthday but ended up making me reevaluate my life. Seeing Matt with his family and my parents so in love . . . it really got to me, which is odd because it usually doesn't affect me. I've been here plenty of times and never felt this way. But this time was different. Seeing Lyndsay again and having these feelings for her has made me think about how much I need that in my life . . . someone to love the way Matt loves his wife, or the kind of enduring love my parents have. I'm starting to wonder if I'll ever find that, or if I already have, with Lyndsay.

Chapter 18

Lyndsay

'The dinner was wonderful,' I say to Martha.

'I'm glad you enjoyed it.' She looks around the table, smiling. 'It's nice having everyone here. It's rare I get all my boys in one place. They're all so busy now, and of course with Nick in New York it's even harder.'

'But it sounds like he's very successful,' my mom says.

'About to make partner,' Mr. Kanfield proudly says.

'Not yet,' Nick says, 'but I'm working on it.'

I've been trying not to stare at Nick all night, but I keep doing it. He wore a shirt and tie to the party and paired it with jeans, the perfect look for dinner in the barn. We had the party out here since the tables were already set up and we still had all the decorations from the night before.

I'm doing it again. I'm staring at Nick. He's just so damn handsome. And today in the fields . . . I'm getting hot just thinking about it. He wasn't wearing a shirt and I couldn't take my eyes off his muscular chest and arms and his washboard abs. Even Chris never looked that good back when he was playing football and worked out all the time. If you saw him now, you'd never guess he used to be an athlete. He's put on at least 40 pounds and none of it is muscle. Most of it went to his stomach. I used to ask him to work out with me, but he wouldn't do it. He's not even close to looking like the guy I dated in high school. I think that's why he won't go to the reunion. He doesn't want anyone seeing him like that.

'I'll be right back,' Nick says, getting up.

'Where's he going?' Brody asks, looking to see where Nick went.

'Shut up,' Sawyer whispers to him. 'It's a surprise.'

Nick returns holding a huge chocolate cake. He sets it on the table and I see 'Congratulations, Lyndsay!' written on top in pink frosting. Around it are math symbols and a math book.

'Nick, I love it!' I jump up and run to the end of the table to give him a hug. 'Thank you!'

'He had to get Agnes to open the bakery for that,' my mom says. 'She's usually closed on Sundays.'

'How'd you get her to come in?' I ask Nick.

'I promised her Broadway tickets for a show she wants to see. She's going to New York in August to see her granddaughter.'

'Nick, you have to let me pay you for those.'

'Yeah, that's not happening. Go try your cake.'

Martha gets the knife to cut it.

'Wait!' I run to the table to get my phone. 'I need a picture!'

'I'll take it,' Nick says, coming over to me.

'You should be in it too since you're the reason I did it.' I look up at him, wishing he knew how much he meant to me. How much he inspired me to go back to school. How he made me believe in myself more than anyone else.

He catches my eye and I get that feeling again, the one that tells me there's so much more to this relationship than just a friendship. I wish it could be more. I wish he wanted that and that we could find a way to make it work.

'I'll take it,' Jason says, getting up.

I give Jason my camera as Nick picks up the cake.

'Where do you want to stand?' he asks.

'Under the banner.'

Nick got me a graduation banner and balloons. I don't know when he had time to do all this but it melts my heart knowing he did. I'm trying to stop having feelings for him, but he keeps doing things that make it impossible not to.

'Stand closer,' Jason instructs as he aims the camera at us.

I move closer to Nick, close enough that our sides are touching. He's wearing that great cologne and it's driving me wild. These past few days have revealed to me a side of myself I didn't know I had. A wild, passionate side that makes me want to do things with Nick, things I was never that interested in doing with Chris. Our sex life was never good, but it's all I knew so I never questioned it. I thought my lack of desire was normal and that women just don't get aroused the way men do.

It wasn't until this weekend that I realized that isn't true. Just being around Nick arouses me. The sexual tension between us is almost unbearable and yet we're acting like it doesn't exist. The only time we even hinted at it was yesterday in the kitchen, but then Nick acted like he regretted it. I understand why he doesn't want to act on our attraction to each other. He's going away, and there's a good chance I won't see him again, but if he were willing to take things all the way tonight, I'd do it. And I wouldn't regret it.

'I think I got some good ones,' Jason says, coming up to me to give me the camera.

'You want any others?' Nick asks. 'Like maybe you and your mom?'

'Yeah, that's a good idea.' I wave at her. 'Mom, come over here!'

'Oh, honey, you know I hate having my picture taken,' she says as she makes her way over to me.

'You look great, Mom.' I put my arm around her and Jason takes the picture.

When he's done, my mom turns to me and whispers, 'I'm so proud of you.'

I tear up when she says it. She wanted to come to my graduation, but I didn't want her spending the money. She doesn't have much, and what little she has, I'd like her to spend on herself. I almost bought her a plane ticket, but then Chris insisted we go to Vegas so she didn't need to make the trip.

We have the cake, which is delicious and big enough that it'll take us all week to finish. As I sip my coffee and look around the table at my mom talking to Martha, and Nick talking to his dad, and Jason and Sawyer laughing about something Brody said, I realize how much I miss being here and being around family and friends. I have friends in LA, but they're not like the ones I have here, who would do most anything for me. Even Nick's brothers, who I really don't know that well, would help me without question if I needed it. Like in high school when my car broke down and Sawyer gave me a ride home. I knew him from school, but we weren't friends and had hardly even talked before that day. But he saw I needed help, called for a tow truck, and gave me a ride home.

'I think it's time I call it a night,' Mr. Kanfield says, getting up. 'I've got to be up early tomorrow.' He walks over to me as I stand up. 'I'm glad we could do this for you. Next time you're in town, come back again. I can't promise you a party, but we'll give you a damn fine dinner.'

'Thank you, Mr. Kanfield.'

He gives me a hug. 'Have a safe trip back.'

'I will.' I smile at him as I sit back down beside Nick.

'Goodnight everyone,' Mr. Kanfield says as he leaves.

We all tell him goodnight.

'I should get started on the dishes,' Martha says, getting up.

'We got it, Mom,' Sawyer says, motioning his brothers to help out.

'You boys need to get home,' she says. 'Go ahead and go.'

'Too late,' Sawyer says. 'Once we start, we gotta finish.' He nods toward Nick and me. 'You two can get out of here. We got this.'

'Thanks,' Nick says, pushing away from the table. 'Sorry about the beer tasting. Next time I'm home, okay?'

'By then I'll be doing my winter brews,' he says as he stacks the plates.

'I'll be home before then.' Nick helps me with my chair. 'Ready to go?'

'I think so.' I stand up, holding my stomach. 'I'm so full I can barely walk.'

'You two have fun!' Martha says as we leave.

I wonder what she thinks we're going to do. Nick's whole family kept looking at us like we're a couple, which makes me think he told them something about us. But he couldn't have told them we're dating after telling me we're not.

'Where should we go?' I ask as Nick helps me into the truck. I wore a dress, which makes it difficult to climb in.

'Well, our options on a Sunday night in a small town are limited. Give me a minute.' He goes around the truck and gets in on the driver's side. 'There's the grocery store, the drugstore. Any of those sound fun?'

I laugh. 'Not really.'

'How about a drink? A congratulatory cocktail?'

'That sounds good, but I'm overdressed for the bars around here.'

'We could go to Clancie's. It's that new restaurant that opened. It's nice, or nice for around here. It's where I was going to take you to dinner tonight.'

'Yeah, let's go there. My mom mentioned that it'd opened, but she didn't say much about it other than that it's expensive.'

'It's not expensive. Well, not compared to New York.'

'Are you looking forward to going back?'

'Not at all. I'll have about a million things to do when I get back to work and I'm sure the landlord didn't fix the sink in my apartment, so I'll have to deal with that. It takes like three or four requests before anything gets fixed.'

He didn't list us as a reason he doesn't want to go back, but that shouldn't surprise me. There is no us. I'm worried we won't even be friends once we're back to our regular lives. People always say they'll stay in touch, but it never happens.

'What can I get you to drink?' the waitress asks when we're seated at the restaurant. She hands us some menus.

'I'll have a glass of merlot,' I tell her.

'Jack and Coke,' Nick says. 'And we don't need menus.' He hands them to her. 'We're just having drinks.'

She takes the menus, smiling at him. 'I'll be right back.

'What do you think?' Nick asks, looking around. 'It's not great, but it's fancy compared to what was here before.'

It used to be a barbecue restaurant, but the owner retired last year. The whole place has been renovated with black-and-white tile floors, black booths and tables, and white pendant lights hanging from the ceiling.

'The design is nice. Modern. Kind of a big city look.'

'That's what I was thinking. I'm not sure how popular it'll be around here. I'm thinking Sawyer's place has a better chance of staying in business.'

'Is he going to serve food?'

'Not right away. He'd like to eventually, but for now he's focusing on the beer.'

The waitress returns with our drinks. The hostess must've thought Nick and I were on a date because she put us at a table near the window that looks out at the downtown. It's a small but nice downtown with little shops and a few restaurants.

'I had a great weekend.' I take a sip of my wine.

'I did too. It went too fast.'

'When do you think you'll be back?'

'Probably Thanksgiving. I'd like to come back for the fall festival if I can get the time off, but I doubt it'll happen.'

I take another sip of wine, hoping it'll lessen the sadness I'm feeling about not seeing Nick again.

'I got you something.' He pulls an envelope out of his pocket and sets it on the table. 'I didn't want to give it to you in front of everyone.'

'Nick, you didn't have to get me anything.'

'I wanted to. It's a graduation gift.'

'You've already done enough with the party and the cake.'

'The party was my mom's idea.' He nods toward the envelope. 'Go ahead and open it.'

I pick up the envelope and open it to find a card inside. It's a graduation card, the only one I got other than the one my mom sent me.

'Open it up,' he says.

I open the card and another envelope falls out. I hold it up. 'What's this?'

He smiles. 'Open it and find out.'

When I do, I find a gift card inside. It's an airline gift card and has $500 on it.

'It's so you can fly home,' Nick says. 'See your mom. Spend time with Diane. Or when you need to get a break from LA and go back to small-town life.'

'Nick, I can't take this. It's too much.'

'It's not too much. You know what I make an hour?' He reaches across the table and holds my hand, something I've missed and will miss even more when he's gone. 'I know it's tough being away from family and the friends you grew up with. And now that you're divorced I'm sure it's even tougher, adjusting to a new life on your own. This way you can make a trip home and not have to worry about paying for it.'

'Nick.' I squeeze my eyes shut, trying to hold back the tears, but one manages to slide down my cheek.

'Hey.' Nick rubs my hand. 'This was supposed to be a good thing. Why are you crying?'

'Because it's perfect.' I wipe my eyes. 'It's exactly what I needed. Chris cleaned out our savings and I didn't know when I'd be able to come back here.' I smile. 'These are happy tears. I can't thank you enough.'

'You're welcome. I'm glad I could do it.'

'You're a great guy, Nick. I'm going to miss you.'

'I'll miss you too.' He takes his hand from mine and picks up his drink, swigging down half of it.

'You think your dad will be okay?'

'I think so. He was probably just exhausted from getting the party ready. He was looking better tonight.'

'It was nice of you to do all that work in the orchard for him.'

'I liked doing it. It was hard work, but it was also kind of relaxing, being out there in the fresh air, the beautiful scenery. You don't appreciate that shit when you're younger. Back in high school, I couldn't wait to get away from it and away from this town.'

'And now?'

'Now I kind of miss it, but I wouldn't want to be here all the time. A few times a year is enough.'

He seems determined to stay in New York, and my life is in LA. So why do I keep holding out hope that Nick and I could be together someday?

'You think you'll start dating again?' I blurt out.

He smiles. 'That came out of nowhere.'

I feel my face burning up. 'Yeah, sorry, I don't know why I asked that. It's none of my business.'

'You can ask. We're friends. You can ask me anything. And the answer is no. I don't think I'll be dating anytime soon.'

'Why?'

'I'm too busy with work to give a relationship the time it needs.'

I nod, my gaze going to my wine as I swirl it around the glass.

'How about you? You going to sign up for some dating apps when you get back?'

I shrug. 'I don't know. I probably should, but I'm dreading it. I don't even know how those things work.'

'They're easy. I can help if you have questions. But if you're dreading getting back out there, you might want to wait. Attitude is a big part of having success on those things. If you're only on there because you think you have to be, it'll come across on the date. I went out with some women who were clearly sick of dating and fed up with men and it made for a really uncomfortable date.'

'I just don't think I can wait. I'm not getting any younger.'

'Maybe just wait a month or two. Focus on yourself and doing all the things you didn't get to do when you were with Chris. That might help you get in a better frame of mind before getting out there again.'

'That's a good idea.' I take another drink of my wine, then set the glass down. 'Or maybe I'll just be single.'

'You don't want that, do you? To be single the rest of your life?'

'No, but it's better than settling down with the wrong person just so I'm not alone.'

'The right person is out there. You just need to find him.'

I have. He's sitting across the table from me.

The waitress returns. 'Can I get you anything else?'

Nick looks at me to answer.

'I'm good,' I tell her.

'You don't want another glass?' Nick asks, noticing my wine is almost gone.

'No. I should probably get home.'

His gaze pauses on me a moment before he looks back at the waitress. 'We'll take the check.'

She leaves and comes right back with the check, setting it on the table before taking off again.

'Is everything okay?' Nick asks.

'Yeah.' I force out a smile. 'I'm just tired. It was a long day.'

'You want to get out of here?'

I nod and get up as he puts money down for the check.

I'm quiet on the drive back to the house, my heart already breaking from the loss of a guy I never even dated.

'You don't have to walk me to the door,' I say as Nick takes off his seatbelt.

He pretends not to hear me and follows me to the door. The porch light is on and I can hear the TV on inside, which means my mom's still up. Hopefully, she's not looking out the window, spying on me like she did when I was a teenager.

'Have a safe trip back,' Nick says, awkwardly stuffing his hands in his pockets.

'Yeah. You too.'

'Maybe we can talk sometime this week.'

'Sure. If you have time.' I look down, my heart pounding and tears stinging my eyes. Why does this hurt so much? I only spent a few days with him. How did I get so attached to him in such a short amount of time?

'It was really good seeing you again.'

I nod, avoiding his gaze. 'I should get inside.'

When I turn to open the door, I feel Nick's hand on my arm. 'Wait.'

I turn back to him and he pulls me into his arms. I breathe in his scent one last time and tuck away the memory of how this feels, to be wrapped in his arms, listening to his heart beat as my head rests on his chest.

'I wish things could be different,' I hear him whisper.

They could be, if he'd just tell me he wants this. But he doesn't, and he won't. He has a life in New York and a career that takes up all his time. He's not looking for a girlfriend. He's not even looking for someone to date.

We're at different places in our lives. We want different things. So as much as it hurts, I have to accept that this is goodbye.

Chapter 19

Nick

I've been back in New York for four days and have never been more miserable in my entire life. I used to love this city. I loved the excitement of it, the opportunities it offered, the great museums, the great restaurants. I loved my apartment.

But when I got back here Monday, everything felt different. The city seemed crowded and loud, my apartment felt cold and dark, and when I went to bed that night, I'd never felt more lonely. I tried to ignore how I was feeling and focus on work, but that, too, felt different. I didn't even want to be there. I had hundreds of messages to follow up on after being gone for a day, and my boss yelled at me for being late to a meeting. Then he piled more work on me, so much that I stayed in the office until midnight on Monday. I was hoping to call Lyndsay that night, but I couldn't because of work. I tried to call her Tuesday, but she didn't pick up. Later, she sent me a text saying she was out having drinks with Diane. Then on Wednesday I had to go to a dinner for work that went until late that night, so again, I couldn't call Lyndsay.

If things continue like this, I can't see Lyndsay and me staying in touch. I told myself that wouldn't happen, but I know it will. It's inevitable. Life gets busy, days go by, and soon it's been weeks since you've talked to the person. Even if we made a real effort to talk, our calls would end once Lyndsay finds someone else. Her new boyfriend won't want her talking to some other guy.

Why did I start something with her, knowing it could never turn into anything? I never intended for that to happen. But from the moment I saw her, that brief encounter in the airport, all the feelings I had for her back in high school came rushing back. And they just got stronger the more time I spent with her.

Now she's all I can think about. I can't concentrate at work. I go home to my empty apartment and wish she was there. I go to bed at night and imagine her beside me. I even have dreams about her, about us, and our future together. But there isn't a future for us, so why can't I let her go?

'You going to open the door?' Tim asks, sounding annoyed.

I wake from my thoughts and notice I'm standing in front of our office building, not moving, a Starbucks cup in my hand. I barely remember going there. Since getting back here, I feel like I'm just going through the motions, without any joy or meaning behind my actions.

'Sorry,' I say, opening the door.

We go into the building with its shiny white tile floors, people racing around with phones plastered to their ears. I think back to being at the orchard last weekend, being out in the fields, the open space, the stillness, the only sounds being birds chirping overhead or the leaves rustling in the breeze. It was calm. Peaceful. I didn't have a boss yelling at me or a client demanding my attention or a slew of emails to return.

This is the life I chose, and I accept that, but it was nice to get away. I'm realizing now that I need to do that more. Like maybe this weekend. I know it's crazy. I was just there. But the reunion's this weekend and Matt ran into Diane at the store and found out Lyndsay's planning to go. What if I showed up there and surprised her? Would she be happy to see me or angry that I didn't tell her?

What the hell am I thinking? I can't do that. I'd be leading her on, making her think I want something we both know we can't have. But I'm desperate to see her. I can't take another moment of thinking about her without being able to see her or talk to her. Maybe I need closure. Maybe our goodbye on Sunday just wasn't enough. It was too fast, too abrupt. Maybe if we'd talked more, stayed at the restaurant longer, or played another round of mini golf, our goodbye wouldn't have seemed so unfinished and I'd be able to move on.

'Nick?'

I look up and see Tim outside the elevator, staring at me because I'm still standing in it, not moving. I don't even remember getting on it or going up to our floor.

'What the hell's wrong with you?' he asks as we're walking down the hall. 'You've been like this all week.'

'I don't know. I'm just tired, I guess.'

I'm more than tired. I'm exhausted. It's after five and I have six or seven more hours of work to do before I can leave. That's why I went with Tim to get a coffee, but I don't think even a double espresso will be able to keep me alert enough to get my work done.

'What are you doing?' I ask as Tim races in front of me, stopping me.

'I need to show you something.' He grins and nods toward the conference room. 'It's in there.'

'What is it?'

'Come on. I'll show you.' He starts heading to the conference room.

'Tim, I don't have time for this. I need to get back to work.'

'Trust me, you have time for this.'

Sighing, I follow him to the conference room. He opens the door and I see all the partners standing there, big smiles on their faces.

'Nick.' Sal, one of the partners, walks up to me. 'Let me be the first to congratulate you on making partner.'

I'm shocked, thinking this is some kind of joke. I didn't expect to make partner until the end of the year at the earliest.

'Say something,' Tim mutters, nudging me.

'Thank you,' I blurt out. 'This is great. And a surprise. I wasn't expecting this today.'

Sal smiles and pats my shoulder. 'It's well deserved. You've done a fine job since joining the firm. You're a hard worker. Dedicated to your clients. We look forward to having you here for a very long time.'

A very long time. This is my future. Here at this firm. It's all planned out, and it's exactly what I wanted. I should be happy, jumping for fucking joy. I worked my ass off for this. I sacrificed a personal life, a social life, and trips back home, all for this moment. I achieved my goal. So why don't I feel happy? Why am I not excited?

'Congratulations,' the other partners say as they politely smile and shake my hand on their way out of the conference room.

'We'll get all the paperwork settled up tomorrow,' Sal says, smiling at me. 'Why don't you get out of here and celebrate?'

'I've got too much work to do, but maybe this weekend.'

He nods. 'Good to have you on board, Nick.' He pats my shoulder before leaving.

'You don't want to go out?' Tim asks. 'What the fuck, man? You just made partner.'

'I can't leave. I have shit that needs to be done by the morning.'

'So we'll go get a drink and you can come back here later.'

'Sorry, but I'm going to have to pass. Maybe we could go out tomorrow.'

'Can't. Rach and I are going to a play, but maybe next week sometime.' Rachel is his girlfriend. They've been living together for two years. 'I need to get back to work, but let me know if you change your mind about that drink.'

We go back to our offices. I shut my door and sit at my desk, staring at my phone, wanting to call Lyndsay but not sure if I should. It's Thursday and I haven't talked to her all week. We keep missing each other and end up sending texts saying we'll try to connect later, which never happens.

I want to call and tell her my news. She's the first person I thought of calling when Sal said I made partner. I thought of Lyndsay even before my parents, or my brothers, or Matt. What does that say? That I miss her, or is it more than that?

Before I change my mind, I call her. The phone rings and rings and I almost hang up, not wanting to leave yet another message.

'Hello?'

She actually answered. Shit. I'm not prepared.

I take a breath. 'Hey, it's me.'

'Nick. Um, hey.' She sounds as nervous as I do. Why are we nervous? We weren't like this when we were together last weekend.

'How are you doing?'

'Fine. I'm over at Diane's place. She had to run an errand so I'm watching the kids.'

'Oh. Do you need to go?'

'No, they're fine. They're in the other room watching a movie. I'm in the kitchen, but I can see them from here, so we're good. So how are you?'

'Busy. Work's been crazy.'

'Sounds like it's always that way.'

'Yeah. Unfortunately.'

'You sound tired.'

'I am. I haven't slept much this week.'

'Because of work?'

'Yeah,' I lie, not wanting to tell her my lack of sleep is because I can't stop thinking about her. 'I've been staying late at the office.'

We're both silent a moment.

'So I have some news,' I say, trying to sound excited.

Seriously, why am I not more excited about this? Am I in shock? Do I just need some time to let it sink in?

'What is it?' she asks.

'I made partner. I just found out.'

'Nick, that's great! Congratulations!'

'Thanks. It's sooner than I thought. I was thinking it wouldn't happen for a few months or maybe not until next year.'

'Your parents must be thrilled! They're so proud of you.'

'My parents don't know yet. You're the first person I told.'

'Really?'

'Yeah. So anyway, I just wanted you to know.'

'It's really great, Nick. I'm proud of you.'

Just hearing her voice again makes my heart ache to be with her, to hold her in my arms, kiss her. God, I miss her. I miss her so fucking bad.

'I should probably let you go,' I say.

'Oh. Yeah, okay. It was nice talking to you, Nick.'

'You too.' I pause. 'Lyndsay, wait. Before you go . . .'

'Yeah?'

'Are you still planning on going to the reunion?'

'I am. How'd you know I was going?'

'Matt mentioned it. He said Diane told him when he ran into her at the store.'

'Yeah, I'm going with her and Tom. I'll feel like a third wheel, but I guess it's better than going alone.'

'What if I went with you?' I ask, my heart pounding as my thoughts race back and forth about whether this is a good idea. But now that I've thrown it out there, I can't take it back.

'Are you serious?'

'I was thinking of flying back for it, but I don't want to go alone. Maybe you could with me?'

'Yes! Nick, I'd love to,' she says, sounding out of breath. 'When could you be here?'

'I'll try to get a flight out tomorrow night. Maybe we could get together before the reunion.'

'Yes, definitely. When are you thinking?'

'Saturday morning? I could take you to breakfast and we could go from there.'

'That sounds great!'

'I'll check on flights and let you know when I'll be there. I have to get back to work. I just wanted to let you know my news and that I'd coming out there. I'll see you on Saturday.'

'Wait. Nick?'

'Yeah?'

'What made you change your mind? About the reunion?'

'Matt talked me into it. I couldn't take him nagging me, so I finally gave in.'

'Oh. Okay, well, I'm glad you're coming. See you soon.'

Why the hell did I lie to her? Why couldn't I just tell her the truth, that she's the reason I'm flying back? Because it'd be leading her on, that's why. I don't want her thinking Saturday is a date, or that I'm coming back to continue where we left off.

Shit. Why did I do this? It's going to be nearly impossible to be around her without holding her hand, touching her, kissing her. It's all I've thought about all week. Being with her is only going to make me want to act on those thoughts, and I can't.

As I look for flights on my laptop, I call up Matt.

'Hey, buddy, what's up?'

'I made partner,' I say, like it's not a big deal.

'No shit? That's awesome! Congratulations!'

'Yeah, it's good, but I don't think my workload will get any better. I'm stuck at the office tonight. I've been here every night since I got back.'

I find a flight that gets me to Wisconsin at eight tomorrow night. I get out my credit card to book it.

'I'm glad I don't have a job like that,' Matt says. 'At least you make a lot of money.'

'Yeah. Hey, can you get me a ticket for the reunion?'

'Wait—what? You're going to the reunion?'

'I'm flying there tomorrow night.'

'What changed your mind? The hot girl you used to tutor in math?' He laughs.

'She might've factored into my decision.' I sigh. 'Matt, what the fuck am I doing? I can't be with her, so why am I going to see her?'

'Because you love her. And you *can* be with her. You just need to figure out how.'

'She's not moving to New York. She has a life in LA, and I just made partner. I can't quit.'

'How do you know she wouldn't move? Did you ask her?'

'No, and I wouldn't. I don't want her relocating her entire life, leaving her friends and her job, to be with me. What if it didn't work out?'

'What if it did?'

'I can't predict that, and since I can't, I don't think it's fair for me to ask her to move. I'd feel like shit if she did all that and then we broke up.'

'Why don't you just ask and let her make the decision?'

'You know Lyndsay. She'd do it just to make me happy. She's not good at putting herself first. That's why she ended up with an asshole like Chris. She did everything for that jerk at her own expense.'

'I don't think that's the case here. I think she'd be doing this for her. She wants to be with you, Nick, just as much as you want to be with her.'

'You don't know that.'

He blows out a breath. 'I'm not supposed to say anything, but I think you need to hear this.'

'Hear what?'

'When I ran into Diane at the store the other day, she said Lyndsay's been miserable since you left. She doesn't want to go out. She hasn't been sleeping. Diane keeps trying to cheer her up but nothing's working.'

'She just got divorced. That's why she's feeling that way.'

'It's not the divorce. Last weekend, she wasn't even thinking about the divorce. She was happier than I've ever seen her. Diane agreed. Then on Monday everything changed. I'm telling you, man, she misses you. And she doesn't want to just be your friend. She wants more than that.'

'I can't give her more. Even if she moved here, I wouldn't be able to give her the life she wanted. A big house. Kids. A guy who can spend time with her and isn't at work all the time. My whole life is this job. I barely have time to even get to the gym these days and every meal's been takeout that I eat at my desk.'

'And you're okay with that?'

'No, but I don't know how to change it. It's not like the work's going away. Every day I seem to get more piled on me.'

'How long are you going to keep doing this?'

'What do you mean?'

'What's your goal here? To make a certain amount of money? Be able to buy a fancy car? Get a better apartment?'

'Honestly, I don't know anymore. My goal was to make partner, but now that I have, I don't know what's next.'

'Marriage? Kids? You're just giving that up?'

'I wasn't going to, but I don't see myself having that life here. Like I told you last weekend, I wouldn't want my kids growing up in the city. I'd want them to grow up in a place like we did, a smaller town that's safe and has a sense of community where people know each other.'

'So it's your job or a family? Is that what you're saying?'

'Maybe. Maybe I just need to accept that I can't have both.'

'If that's true, then I feel sorry for you. There's more to life than a job. I love my job, but if keeping it meant I'd lose Tessa and the kids, I'd give it up in a heartbeat.' I hear voices in the background. 'Speaking of kids, I just got to Mia's daycare. Can we talk later?'

'I'll just call you when I get in tomorrow. I'll be there around eight.'

'You want me to pick you up?'

'I'll see if Sawyer can do it. What about the reunion? You'll get me a ticket?'

'Yeah, you can just pick it up that night. I'll put your name on it. You going to ask Lyndsay to go with you?'

'Already did. I called her before I called you.'

'I'm guessing she said yes?'

'Yeah. She sounded excited. I'm excited too. I'm just not sure I'm doing the right thing here.'

'Just talk to her and see how committed she is to staying in LA. If I were her, I'd want to get out of there. She's not from there and doesn't have family there. And why would she want to be in the same town as Chris? Hey, I gotta go. I gotta get Mia. We'll talk later.'

'Yeah, bye.'

Sometimes I can't believe Matt and I are the same age and he's married with two kids. That could've been me picking up my kid at daycare, but instead I'm spending my night at a desk and going home to an empty apartment.

What Matt said really got to me. Why am I doing this? Is it for the money? The prestige of working for a big law firm in the heart of New York City? Am I trying to prove something to myself? Or to my parents? My parents don't care what I do for a job. They just want me to be happy. But I'm not. Even after finding out I made partner, I'm still not happy. There's something not right about that.

Chapter 20

Lyndsay

'What if he doesn't show up?' I ask Diane as I paint sparkly purple nail polish on Leah's tiny fingers. She insists I'm better at painting her nails than her mom.

'This is Nick you're talking about,' Diane says. 'He's very reliable. Always has been. He's nothing like Chris.'

'Is Nick your boyfriend?' Leah asks, smiling at me, her head tilted.

'No. He's just a friend who's a boy.'

'Did he kiss you? Because if he kissed you, he's for sure your boyfriend.'

'Who told you that?' Diane asks in her concerned mom tone.

'Shana.' Leah rocks side to side on her chair, causing me to almost paint her finger instead of her nail. 'Tommy Mayfield kissed her and now he's her boyfriend.'

'Leah, can you hold still a minute so I can finish?' I ask.

She nods really fast, then watches as I finish the last two nails. 'Do you *have* to go back to California?'

'Yes, but I'll come back to visit.'

'When?'

'I'm not sure yet. Maybe Thanksgiving.'

'That long?' Diane says. 'I thought you were coming back for the fall festival.'

'I was, but . . .' I finish painting Leah's nails and sit back, looking at Diane across the kitchen table. 'It'll just remind me of Nick.'

'Maybe he's coming here to tell you he wants to try to make this work.'

'I doubt it. He said it's because Matt talked him into going to the reunion. He's not here to see me.'

'Then why is he taking you to breakfast?'

'Because we're friends.'

'Mommy, look!' Leah jumps off her chair and runs over to her mom. 'Isn't it pretty?'

'Super pretty. And I like the sparkles. You should thank Lyndsay for buying you that.'

Leah runs over to me and gives me a hug. 'Thank you!'

'You're welcome, sweetie.'

'I'm gonna go show Daddy!' Leah runs off.

'She's going to miss you,' Diane says. 'We all are.'

'I'm going to miss you guys too.'

'There isn't any chance you'd consider moving back?'

'I don't know. Maybe. But what would I do here? And how would I find someone to date? The only single guys around here are either too old, too young, or friends with Chris.'

'What about going somewhere else?'

'I might've considered moving to New York if I thought Nick and I might have a chance.'

'Did you tell him that?'

'No. If he wanted me to move there, he would've asked. The fact that he didn't tells me he doesn't want to even try having a relationship. He's consumed with his job and maybe that's all he wants out of life.'

'I don't think that's true. I could easily see Nick married with kids.'

'I could too, but I don't think that's what he wants. Maybe this weekend is his way of telling me goodbye, for good this time. Maybe he'll tell me he doesn't even want to be friends.' I fight back tears, telling myself for the millionth time that I'm not going to cry over Nick. He's a great guy and I wish things had turned out differently between us, but I need to end this fantasy of us being together and just accept that it wasn't meant to be.

'I don't think he'd come here just to tell you goodbye,' Diane says, getting up to get some wine. 'Want some?'

'No, thanks.' I watch as she pours wine in a glass. 'Maybe when he's here, he won't even talk about us. Maybe last weekend didn't mean anything to him and I'm making it into more than it was. I mean, he said he's coming back for the reunion, not to see me.'

Diane comes back to the table, holding her wine glass. 'We both know he's coming to see you. The reunion is just an excuse. He didn't even want to go.'

'I can't tell you how much I want to see him. He's not even here yet and my heart's already racing, I'm so excited.'

'That's why I'm worried.' Diane takes a sip of her wine. 'Part of me wishes he wasn't coming.'

'You don't have to worry. I'm not getting my hopes up. I know Nick and I don't have a future together, but I'm still excited to see him. I feel like it's been months, but it hasn't even been a week.' I check my phone for the time. 'He should be here by now. I wonder who's picking him up.'

'Probably Sawyer. Hey, Tom went to the brewery last night with some friends and said the place was packed.'

'I'm not surprised. I think it'll do well. It's a fun atmosphere and the beer's really good.' My phone rings. I check the screen. 'It's him! It's Nick!'

'Are you going to answer it?'

'Hey, Nick,' I say, trying to sound cool and not crazy excited.

'Hey, I just got into town and was wondering if you want to go to Sawyer's for a drink. He picked me up from the airport and we're heading back to the brewery. We can stop and get you if you want.'

'Um, yeah, that sounds fun!' I look at Diane. 'But I'm not at home. I'm at Diane's house.'

'Perfect! We're like a mile from there. We'll be there in a minute.'

I end the call and jump up from my chair. 'He's coming to pick me up. How do I look?'

'Great, but why is he picking you up? Where are you going?'

'To the brewery. Sawyer got Nick at the airport and they're heading over there. He's going to be here in a minute.' I look down at my baggy t-shirt and faded jeans. 'I'm a mess. I can't go out like this. Do you have anything I could borrow?'

She laughs. 'You're like three sizes smaller than me. You'd be swimming in anything of mine.' She comes over to me, putting her arm around me as she walks me out of the kitchen. 'You look fine.'

'I'm not ready,' I say, turning to her. 'I'm not supposed to see him until tomorrow.'

'Well, apparently he couldn't wait that long.'

'I'm so confused. Does he like me or are we just friends?'

'I think you two need to have a talk this weekend and figure that out.'

The doorbell rings.

'I'll get it!' Leah yells.

As Diane and I walk to the door, my heart nearly stops when I see him. He has on dark jeans and a white dress shirt with the sleeves rolled up. There's a thick layer of stubble on his face and his hair looks kind of messy, like he ran his hand through it. He looks so damn hot. I've missed him so much.

He hasn't noticed me yet. He's leaned down to Leah, listening to her talk and smiling at whatever she said.

'Hey, Nick,' I say, feeling breathless.

'Lyndsay.' He slowly rises to standing, his eyes not leaving mine. 'It's good to see you again.'

'You too.'

Leah turns to me. 'I told him if he kisses you, he's your boyfriend.'

'Apparently it's a rule,' Nick says, smiling. 'I'd never heard that one before.'

'Me either.'

'I'm not sure I'd trust a seven-year-old on that,' Diane says.

'Hey, Diane,' Nick says.

'Hi, Nick,' she says in the same protective tone she uses with her kids. She likes Nick, but she's worried he'll break my heart. But he's already done that, and it wasn't his fault. It was mine, for imagining something that wasn't there.

'You ready to go?' Nick asks me. 'Sawyer's waiting in the car.'

'Yeah.' I hug Diane. 'I'll call you tomorrow.'

'Me too!' Leah says, holding her arms out to me.

I hug her. 'Goodnight, sweetie.'

Nick and I go outside to Sawyer's car. Nick opens the door for me and I get in the back seat. Nick slides in beside me.

'What am I . . . your chauffeur?' Sawyer asks, glancing at Nick in the rearview mirror. 'Why are you sitting back there?'

'So I can talk to Lyndsay without straining my neck. Just shut up and drive.'

'Hi, Sawyer,' I say. 'Thanks for the ride.'

'Anytime.' Sawyer pulls out of the driveway and heads down the street.

'How was your flight?' I ask Nick.

'Uneventful. I slept for most of it.'

'Sounds like you needed the rest after all the hours you worked this week.'

'Yeah, it wasn't a good week,' he says with a sigh.

'But you got good news. That's exciting!'

'It is,' he says, but his tone doesn't match his words.

'I bet your parents were thrilled. Their son making partner at a fancy law firm?'

'Hey! What about me?' Sawyer says. 'I opened a freaking brewery last week.'

'I'm sure they're proud of you too,' I say, leaning up to his seat. 'I heard it's been getting a lot of business.'

'Yeah, the past couple nights it's been packed. This is our first real week of being open. Last week was our soft opening. I didn't really announce it. I wanted to work out the kinks first.'

'Who's running it when you're not there?'

'This guy, Wade. I hired him last week. He used to run a bar in Eau Claire. So far, he's been working out great. The bartender I hired is good too. I need to hire another one if business keeps up like this.'

'It might slow down in a few weeks,' Nick says, 'once everyone's had a chance to check the place out.'

'I'm expecting that, but even if I get half as many people as I have now, I should still be okay.'

'Sorry for the last minute invite,' Nick says, turning toward me. 'I just thought if you weren't busy, you might want to go out.'

'I didn't have plans, so yeah, I'm glad you asked.' I glance down at my baggy shirt. 'I just wished I could've changed clothes.'

'I think you look great,' Nick says, smiling at me.

Is he flirting with me or just giving me a compliment? I'm so confused. Why did he invite me out tonight? And for breakfast tomorrow? Are we just hanging out as friends, or does he want us to be more than that?

We get to the brewery and I see cars lined up all the way down the street.

'You weren't lying,' Nick says to Sawyer as we go inside. 'The place is packed.'

'I gotta help serve,' Sawyer yells above the noise. He hurries off to the bar.

'I don't see anywhere to sit,' Nick says, his hand going to my lower back as he looks around the brewery.

'We could just stand,' I tell him.

'Nick!' someone yells.

We look up and see Jason waving us over. He's at a table with Brody and two girls I don't recognize.

'Looks like we got a seat,' Nick says, keeping his hand on my back as he leads me through the crowded bar.

'I didn't know you guys were going to be here,' Nick says, pulling my chair out for me.

I take a seat at the long, high-top table. Nick sits beside me, across from Jason and one of the girls. The other girl is next to me and Brody's beside her at the end of the table.

'We were supposed to go to a concert,' Jason says, 'but the band cancelled so we decided to come here.' He smiles at me. 'Hey, Lyndsay.'

'Hi.'

He gives Nick a questioning look, like he's wondering why I'm here with him and what it means. I'd like to know that too.

'When are you going back to LA?' Brody asks me.

'Sunday.'

'Are you going to the reunion?'

'Yeah. I wasn't going to, but I figured as long as I'm here, I might as well.'

Jason smiles at Nick. 'I can't believe you're actually going. You said you never would.'

'Yeah, well, it was the only way to get Matt to shut up about it.' He looks at the girl next to Jason. 'Hi, I'm Nick and this is Lyndsay.'

'Oh, shit, sorry,' Jason says. 'I should've done introductions. Nick is my older brother,' he tells the girl. 'He's a lawyer in New York. And Lyndsay lives in LA, but she grew up here.'

'Nice to meet you,' the girl says. 'I'm Beth.'

'And I'm Ainsley,' the girl beside me says.

'They're just here for the summer,' Brody explains. 'They work at the camp.'

'The one Sawyer went to?' Nick asks. 'I didn't think that was still around.'

'It's not the same one,' Beth says. 'It's at the same location, but it's run by a different company. They have them all over.'

Nick turns to me. 'Sawyer begged my parents to let him go to camp when he was seven, but then he got there and hated it and begged them to let him come home.'

'Why didn't he like it?' Ainsley asks. 'Kids usually love camp.'

'He liked all the activities,' Jason says. 'But there was this girl there that kept beating him at all the competitions. Fishing. Canoe races. Archery. He wanted to get out of there before his reputation was destroyed.'

'Sawyer isn't used to losing,' Nick explains. 'He told his camp counselor he was allergic to his tent so he'd be sent home, but they knew it was a lie and told him he had to stay unless Mom and Dad came to get him.'

'Which they didn't,' Brody says, laughing. 'I think he's still mad at them for that.'

'He must be really competitive,' Beth says. 'We try to make it so the kids just have fun without worrying about winning.'

'For Sawyer, it's always about winning,' Nick says. 'He's extremely competitive.'

'You want a drink?' Brody asks, pointing to a pitcher of beer on the table. 'It's pale ale. It's pretty good.'

'I think I'll get something darker,' Nick says, getting up. 'Lyndsay, what can I get you?'

'I'll just have the pale ale,' I say, grabbing one of the extra glasses sitting on the table.

Nick reaches across me for the pitcher and pours some beer in my glass. 'I'll be right back.'

When he's gone, Ainsley turns to me. 'So how does that work? With you in LA and Nick living in New York?'

'I'm not sure what you mean.'

'How do you guys date living in different cities?' Beth asks.

'Oh, we're not dating. We're just friends.'

'Really?' Beth says like she doesn't believe me. 'You guys seem like a couple. I just assumed you were together.'

'Me too,' Ainsley says.

Nick and I seem like a couple? Why? It's not like we're holding hands or kissing.

'Have you guys been talking since he left?' Jason asks.

'Not really. Nick's been busy with work.'

'Are you going to the reunion with him?' Brody asks.

'Yeah, but only as friends.'

Brody glances at Jason, giving him a look like they know something I don't, or maybe I'm just reading something into it.

'Does he have a girlfriend?' Ainsley asks, in a way that makes me think she's interested in him. She better not be. She's on a date with Brody, or at least I think she is given that they're here together. Then again, I'm here with Nick and we're not dating.

'No, he's single,' I tell her.

'Why do you care?' Brody asks Ainsley, sounding annoyed.

'I'm not asking for me,' she says, putting her hand over his. 'I'm asking for my sister. She's around his age and she's moving to New York next month. She got a job there.'

'Nick's not looking to date anyone,' I say, not wanting this girl's sister going out with Nick. I know he's not mine, but I don't like thinking about him with someone else.

He returns to the table with his beer. 'Sawyer's getting slammed. He needs another bartender.'

'He's gonna make a shitload of money tonight,' Jason says, looking around. 'The whole damn town is here.'

'I'm proud of him,' Nick says with pride in his voice. 'I gotta say, when he was talking about doing this,

I didn't think he'd actually follow through, but he did. He actually followed through and did it.'

'Hey, Nick,' Ainsley says, leaning past me to Nick. 'My sister Maddie is moving to New York in a few weeks. Would you mind if I gave her your number? She doesn't know anyone there and I was thinking maybe you could show her around.'

'She's 31 and a pediatrician,' Beth says, like she's trying to sell Nick on this woman.

'This is her,' Ainsley says, pulling up a photo on her phone. She reaches across me to show it to Nick. The woman is gorgeous, with long blonde hair, a beautiful smile, and a great body. The photo was taken on a beach and she's wearing a bikini. She's perfect for Nick. Smart, beautiful, close to his age, and lives in New York.

'I'd love to, but I don't have time,' he says. 'I've got more work than I can handle. I barely have time to sleep.'

'Maybe you could meet her for dinner sometime,' Ainsley says, taking her phone back. 'You have to eat, right?'

She's really pushing this. She's determined to set her sister up with Nick.

'Congrats on making partner,' Jason says to Nick. 'I know I said it on the phone, but now that you're here, we should celebrate.'

'Yeah, beers arc on us tonight,' Brody jokes, knowing they're free since Sawyer owns the bar.

'Thanks,' Nick says, smiling. 'I'll make sure to order a few more.'

'No, really,' Jason says. 'We'll take you out somewhere else. How about tomorrow night?'

'I'll be at the reunion,' Nick says.

'You won't be there all night. We'll go when it's over.'

Nick glances at me, then back at Jason. 'You don't have to take me out. We can celebrate tonight.'

'You got plans tomorrow?' Brody asks, his gaze bouncing from me to Nick.

'I don't know yet. I just don't want to commit to anything right now.'

That seems to be Nick's story for everything. He doesn't want to commit to anything, except maybe his job. That's all he seems sure of, the only thing he seems to want right now. Maybe later he'll want more, like a wife and a family, but I can't wait for him to get there. I want to get married again and have children. I can't put my life on hold for Nick. My head knows that, but my heart doesn't agree with it. It wants Nick.

Chapter 21

Lyndsay

We stay at the brewery until closing time, much later than I thought we'd be there, but the time flew by. I really like Nick's brothers, and I like watching Nick interact with them. As the oldest, he's always looking out for them, like when Brody mentioned hiring some kid to help him mow lawns. Nick jumped in and warned him of all the liability issues and convinced him to hire someone older. He also offered to look over his insurance policy to make sure he was properly covered for accidents.

I'm amazed at how much he knows, and I love that he cares about his brothers so much, and his parents. He'd do anything to help them out. He's so different from Chris, who only cared about himself. When his parents needed help moving to Florida, Chris made up some excuse for why he couldn't do it. He lied to his own parents and spent the week they moved on the couch with his laptop.

'Thanks for inviting me out,' I say as Nick walks me to my door. 'I had a good time.'

'I did too. It was the first time I've had to relax since I left here last week.'

When we reach the door, I stop and turn to Nick. 'What time do you want to go to breakfast?'

'Is eight too early?'

'Kind of,' I say with a laugh. 'It's after two. That's only a few hours away.'

'Right,' he says, nodding. 'So nine?'

'Sure.' I look up at him, wishing he would kiss me.

'I guess I'll be going,' he says, but his eyes remain locked on mine.

Moments pass, and I can feel our attraction to each other heating up the air, the tension between us rising and ready to burst. I can't take this. I need to get inside before I do something stupid like kiss him.

'Nick, I—'

He cuts me off with a kiss as he grabs me around the waist. The kiss is gentle at first, almost hesitant, but then becomes bolder, more aggressive, his tongue going past my lips. My knees are buckling, my body firing up with those tingles I've been longing to feel since he left.

And then, just as suddenly as he kissed me, he ends it. He pulls away, looking at me with what seems like regret.

'I wasn't going to do that,' he says.

'Then why did you?'

'Because it's all I've been thinking about since the last time I saw you.'

'Really?' I ask, wanting him to tell me more.

He pauses a moment, his gaze moving over my face, then says, 'I'll pick you up at nine.'

He's gone before I can ask him anything more. I go inside the house, even more confused about what's going on with him. He kisses me and then doesn't explain why, or what it means? Maybe it didn't mean anything. Maybe he just wanted to kiss me.

* * *

In the morning, Nick arrives five minutes early. I'm still doing my makeup when I hear the doorbell ring and my mom answering the door.

'How's the dishwasher working out?' I hear Nick say as I hurry down the stairs.

'Wonderful!' my mom says. 'It's so nice not to have to wash them by hand. Nick, while you're here, would you mind looking at something for me?'

'Mom, he can't keep fixing stuff for us,' I say, laughing, as I meet up with them in the kitchen.

'I'm not asking him to fix anything,' she says, looking through a folder. 'This is about the land I'm trying to sell.' She looks up at Nick. 'It's only ten acres, but I don't have a reason to keep it. It's in North Dakota and used to belong to my grandfather. I inherited it when he passed and I'd rather not have to deal with it anymore.' She hands Nick a stack of papers. 'This is the contract for the sale. I wondered if you could just take a look at it, make sure everything's good before I sign it.'

'Sure, I can look it over.'

'Nick, you don't have to do that,' I say. 'You're on vacation.'

'It won't take long. Most of these contracts are pretty standard. I'll look through it and have it back to you before I leave.'

'Oh, thank you, Nick,' my mom says. 'It'll save me the time of having to find a lawyer. Since Benny passed, I haven't found someone to take his place.'

'Mr. Graver died?' Nick asks.

She nods. 'About a month ago. Anyway, just let me know if you see anything of concern. I'll pay you for your time.'

'I won't accept money,' he says. 'But I will accept baked goods.'

Her face lights up. 'Certainly! Any requests?'

'Surprise me.' Nick smiles at her as he walks over to me. 'I'll see you later, Mrs. Davis.'

'You two have fun!' she says as we leave.

We go outside and get in the truck.

'That's nice of you to do that,' I say as Nick backs out of the driveway.

'I don't mind helping her out, especially since she's letting me borrow her daughter for the day.'

'The day?' I ask, surprised.

'Unless you have plans.' He glances at me as he drives down the street. 'Do you?'

'I was thinking of going to Diane's house and hanging out with her and the kids,' I say, not wanting him thinking I reserved the whole day for him, because I didn't. He only asked me to go out with him this morning.

'Then I guess I just get you for breakfast.'

I'd like to spend the day with him, but he didn't say why he wants more time with me and what it means. Until I know that, I don't think I should agree to it. It'll just make me want him more, and why would I put myself through that if I can't have him?

He takes me to Maury's Chicken Roost, knowing it's my favorite breakfast place. We order our food, then I ask Nick about his job and his promotion. I'm enjoying listening to him and learning more about what he does, but what I really want to talk about is us. I'm just not sure this is the right time to ask. The restaurant is crowded and loud. I'd rather talk somewhere that's quiet and have it just be the two of us.

As we're waiting for the check, Diane calls.

'Hey, Diane,' I answer. 'I just finished breakfast. What time should I come over?'

'Leah's sick, so I think we'll have to cancel today.'

'Oh, no. What's she sick with?'

'I think it's just a cold, but I'm going to take her to the clinic just to make sure.'

'So you aren't going to the reunion tonight?'

'We'll probably still go. My mom will take care of Leah. She's coming over in a few minutes to stay with Adam while I take Leah to the doctor. Sorry about this. I wanted us to have one last day together before you have to leave.'

'It's okay. I understand. Give Leah a kiss for me and tell her I hope she feels better.'

'I will. I'll let you know later about tonight.'

'Okay, bye.' I look over at Nick. 'Leah, Diane's little girl, is sick so I won't be going over there.'

'Is it serious?' Nick asks, setting money on the table for the check.

'She thinks it's just a cold, but she's taking her to the doctor this morning.'

'Does that mean you're free today?'

'Maybe. What do you have in mind?'

His phone rings and he checks it. 'It's my dad. I'll call him later.'

'Go ahead and answer it.'

'Hey, Dad, what do you need?' Nick listens, nodding. 'Does it have to be done today?' He listens again. 'Yeah, I'm with Lyndsay. Give me a minute and I'll call you back.' He pauses, then smiles. 'I don't think she'd be up for that. Bye, Dad.'

'Up for what?' I ask. 'Were you talking about me?'

'Dad invited you over while I help him fix the tractor.' Nick chuckles. 'Just what you want to do, watch a guy and his dad fix a tractor.'

I shrug. 'I wouldn't mind. I could bring something to read. Or maybe I could do something with your mom while you guys do your work.'

'Are you serious? You really want to come over?'

'Sure. I love it there. If I went home, I'd just be there by myself. My mom's spending the afternoon at the church, getting stuff ready for the rummage sale. That's why I made plans with Diane, but now I can't go over there. It's a beautiful day. It'd be nice to spend it at the orchard.'

'If you're really okay with this, I'll tell my dad. I was going to see if Jason or Brody could help him out, but they're not good at fixing shit. They can do minor stuff, but I'm better at fixing the equipment. I've been helping Dad with repairs for as long as I can remember.'

'Go ahead and call him. Tell him we'll be there in a few minutes.'

Nick smiles at me as he makes the call, like I'm doing him a huge favor. But I don't see it that way. I wasn't lying when I said I like spending time at the orchard. It's beautiful and peaceful, and the perfect place to spend a warm summer day.

We get to the orchard and find Carl, Nick's dad, in the barn, the old one that's only used to store equipment. It's what you'd typically think of when you think of a barn. The new one is more like a nice building that just happens to look like a barn on the outside.

'How much did you have to pay her for this?' Carl asks when he sees us walking in.

'She volunteered,' Nick says. 'Don't ask me why.'

'Wait—I'm not actually helping, am I?'

They both laugh.

'I was talking about you coming over,' his dad says. 'You're welcome to be here. I just didn't think you'd want to, especially here, in this old barn.'

'Is Mom around?' Nick asks.

'She went to town to run some errands. She should be back soon.'

'You could go hang out at the house if you want,' Nick tells me.

'I think I'll just stay here until your mom gets home.' I go over to a folding chair that's next to the workbench and take a seat.

Nick looks back at his dad, who's standing by the tractor. 'So what do you think is the issue?'

'I have some ideas, but I wanted to get your opinion first. I can get the engine going, but then it quits on me. I was going to take it in the fields today, but I didn't want it breaking down on me out there.'

Nick asks him some more questions, then goes over to the engine and checks it out. How does he know this stuff? He's a lawyer, not a mechanic.

He walks over to the workbench that's behind me and takes off his shirt. It's a nice shirt and I'm guessing he doesn't want to get it dirty. But seeing him shirtless is making my thoughts turn dirty, something I don't need when he's only letting us be friends.

My thoughts get even dirtier as I watch Nick work on the engine, bending over it, shirtless, his jeans hanging low. His dad catches me staring and I quickly look away and pretend to swat at a fly.

'He used to love this stuff as a kid,' Carl says, walking over to me. 'Helping me with the repairs.'

'I didn't know that. I always thought he was more into school work than working with his hands.'

'He likes learning how things work. Doesn't matter what it is. He was always that way. He'd follow me around the orchard, asking me about the trees and what makes them grow. He'd be four, five years old, wanting to know this stuff.' Carl laughs. 'Damn kid about drove me crazy with all his questions, but he just wanted to learn.' He lowers his voice. 'Between you and me, he's better at fixing this stuff than I am. If I can't figure out what's wrong, I have to do some research or call someone in to fix it. But Nick just figures it out himself. He's a smart kid.'

'Hey!' Nick says, noticing his dad talking to me. 'What are you doing over there?'

'Just talking to your girl—' He stops himself. 'Lyndsay.'

He almost called me Nick's girlfriend. Is that what he thinks I am? Nick had to have told him we're only friends. He wouldn't tell his parents I'm his girlfriend when I'm not.

'When you're done,' Nick says, 'come over and try starting it. I think I might know what's wrong.'

As Carl goes back over there, Martha appears.

'How's it coming?' she asks.

'We're getting there,' Carl replies.

'Hi, Mrs. Kanfield,' I say, getting up.

'Lyndsay,' she says, smiling. 'I didn't see you there. What are you doing in the barn?'

'My plans for today got cancelled so Nick invited me to come over.'

'And watch him fix the tractor?' She shakes her head. 'Come with me to the house. We'll have some iced tea and sit out on the porch and talk.'

'Just don't talk about me,' Nick says, smiling at me as I follow Martha out of the barn.

'Nick loves that kind of thing,' she says as we walk back to the house. 'Figuring out what's wrong and fixing it. His dad and I used to think he'd be a mechanic, but then he surprised us and went into law.' She goes in the house, to the kitchen. 'He's done well for himself. I'm proud of him.'

'I am too. That's great news about his promotion.'

'It is.' She takes some glasses from the cupboard. 'I just hope he's happy.' She takes the tea from the fridge.

'You don't think he's happy?'

'It's hard to tell with Nick,' she says, filling our glasses with ice. 'He's not real open about his feelings. He's like his dad that way. Even when he's upset about something, it's hard to tell. And Nick doesn't like us worrying about him. If he was unhappy, he'd tell us everything was fine.' She pours the tea in the glasses and hands me one. 'Would you like something to eat?'

'No, thanks. I just had breakfast.'

I follow her to the large wraparound porch that looks out at the orchard and we sit on the white rocking chairs.

'Such a beautiful day,' she says, sipping her tea. 'Supposed to be around 72, cool for this time of year.'

'Yeah, it's nice to be outside.'

'Did Nick tell you we bought the Carson's land?' she asks.

'No. When was that?'

'It's been in the works for awhile now, but last month it was official.'

Dick Carson and his wife lived on the land just west of the Kanfield property. They moved into a retirement home a couple months ago, but I didn't know they sold their house and the land that went with it. I assumed they'd give it to one of their kids.

'Their children didn't want it?' I ask.

'No.' She shakes her head. 'They've all left Wisconsin and don't care to come back. We offered to just buy the land and let them sell the house separately, but they wanted it all to go at once.'

'What are you going to do with the house?'

'Probably tear it down. We thought of renting it out, but it's in rough shape. We'd have to spend a lot of time and money on repairs.'

'It's such a cute little farmhouse. It's a shame it has to be torn down.' I sip my tea. 'Maybe one of your nephews could fix it up. Isn't that what they do? Fix up old houses?'

Her brows rise. 'You know, I hadn't even thought about that. But they'd have to live here while they fix it up and I don't think they'd want to do that, except maybe Nash. He loves being out in the country. But Callie, his fiancé, is in Chicago. He wouldn't want to be away from her for as long as it would take to fix that place up.'

'Yeah, I could see that. How long did it take for them to renovate Sawyer's bar?'

'A few months, but they took turns coming up here. They all stayed with us. It was nice having them here. They're a lot like my boys, hard working, good manners.'

She forgot the part about how good-looking they are, another trait they have in common with her sons. The Wheeler and Kanfield brothers could do one of those hot guy calendars and make a fortune.

'So you're going to use the land to expand the orchard?' I ask.

'Most of it, yes, but we might reserve the pond for weddings or other events.'

'That's right. I forgot about the pond.'

There's a small pond on the property that Mr. Carson would stock with fish. He planted rose bushes around it for his wife and a bench where she could sit while he fished.

'I was thinking it might be nice to add a gazebo there,' Martha says. 'We could clear some space for chairs where guests could sit. We've had several requests to host weddings here, but we really don't have the space for it, other than the barn, but if it were me, I'd rather be married outside with some scenery around me.'

'I think it's a good idea. And if you fixed up the house, maybe the couple could stay there for the night, like a bed-and-breakfast type of thing.'

Martha laughs. 'I think we're getting ahead of ourselves. Carl's trying to keep things simple and just stick to growing apples. He says at our age, we should be slowing down, not making more work for ourselves.'

Martha and I continue to dream up more ideas for the orchard. Even if they never happen, it's still fun to think about. Her comment about slowing down makes me wonder why they bought more land. What will they do with it all when they retire? I think it'd be hard to sell an orchard in a small town, but maybe not. I really don't know how farm real estate works. I've never even owned a house.

At noon, Nick comes out on the porch, his chest glistening with sweat. I try to keep my eyes on his face, but they keep lowering to his body.

'We got it fixed,' Nick says, wiping the sweat from his brow.

'Thank you for helping him with that,' Martha says. 'He's struggled with it all week. He didn't want to ask you to look at it. I had to convince him.'

Nick sighs. 'Why does he get like that? He knows I'd never tell him no.'

'Yes, but he knows how hard you work and he wants you to have some down time when you come home.'

'This isn't work. I like doing that kind of stuff.' Nick looks at me and smiles. 'How's it going? Is my mom telling you all my secrets?'

'None, actually. We didn't really talk about you.'

'I'm gonna go shower, and then I could take you to lunch if you want.'

'Why don't you eat here?' Martha says, getting up. 'I could make you two some sandwiches and you could take them down to the pond, have a little picnic.'

'Thanks, Mom, but I think Lyndsay would rather go out.'

'I'd be up for a picnic,' I say, thinking this will give Nick and me a chance to talk. We'll be alone, with no one bothering us.

'Great!' Martha says. 'I'll go get it ready.'

'I'll help,' I say, getting up. I smile at Nick as I pass him. 'Go clean up! I'm starving.'

He smiles back, but looks confused. 'Um, yeah, I'll be down in a few minutes.'

This is it, my chance to finally get an answer about what's going on between us. If it turns out he has no interest in a relationship with me, then I'll force myself to stop dreaming about what could've been and move on with my life.

Chapter 22

Nick

The picnic was a good idea. We're sitting by the pond, surrounded by trees and prairie grass. It's a beautiful setting and we have the place to ourselves. It's the perfect time to talk to Lyndsay. But now that we're here, just the two of us, I don't know if I can say this, or if I should.

I've thought about this all week, and after talking to Matt, I realized I need to make a decision. I either need to try to make things work with Lyndsay, or let her go. The idea of staying friends just won't work. We both know it. We just don't want to say it. We both have busy lives. We live on different coasts. And if she starts dating someone, he's not going to want her calling up some other guy.

If I want a chance with Lyndsay, I need to tell her that. I can't go back to New York without settling this. I'll just keep thinking about Lyndsay and wondering what might have been. I need to just say this and see what happens. I'd feel like shit if she moved to New York to be with me and it didn't work out, but I thought about it and decided maybe we could do it gradually, just to test the waters before she moves there for good. Like maybe she comes and stays with me for a few weeks. I'm not sure how that would work with her job, though. I don't want her to get fired for taking time off.

There I go again, finding excuses for why this won't work. I can't keep doing that. Like Matt said, I need to stop assuming that what I want isn't what's best for Lyndsay and let her make the decision.

'Lunch was great,' Lyndsay says, putting everything back in the picnic basket. 'It was really nice of your mom to make it for us.'

'Yeah, it was.' I gulp down some water because my throat feels dry.

'It kind of felt like a setup,' Lyndsay says with a nervous laugh. 'The picnic. The romantic setting.'

'Yeah.' I take a deep breath and let it out.

'Nick, I—'

'I need to talk to you,' I blurt out, needing to say this before I change my mind.

'I was going to say the same thing.'

'I really need to go first, if you don't mind.'

'Go ahead.' She turns so she's facing me, crossing her legs in front of her.

'I can't keep doing this.'

'Doing what?' she asks, sounding concerned.

'Whatever this is we're doing. Pretending to be friends, but acting like we're more than that.'

Her brows draw together. 'So what are you saying? That we shouldn't be friends anymore?'

'No. I mean, yes, I want to be friends, but I also . . .' I take another breath. 'I want more than that. I can't just be friends with you.'

Her face softens and a slight smile appears. 'When you say you want more, what exactly does that mean?'

I move closer to her and take her hand. 'It means I want to date you, for real, not this fake dating shit we were pretending to do. I don't want to help you find someone else. I want you to be with *me*.' I look into her eyes. 'Last week was pure misery. You were all I could think about. I'd go home at night and wish you were there. I'd be at work and everything would remind me of you.'

'The same thing happened to me. I couldn't stop thinking about you. But I didn't think you wanted this. You keep saying how work is all you have time for and how you don't want a girlfriend right now.'

'And I'd probably still be saying that if you hadn't come back into my life. But you did, and now I don't want you to go.' I look down at her hand in mine. 'I just don't know how to make this work.'

'But I bet you've thought about it and you have an idea.' She scoots closer to me. 'Nick, just tell me. Tell me what you want.'

I look at her. 'I want you to move to New York. I know it's selfish of me to ask and I'll completely understand if you tell me no, but it's the only way I think this will work. I want us to have a chance, but that won't happen if we're thousands of miles apart.'

'I agree.'

'You what?' I say, thinking I must've heard her wrong. There's no way she'd just agree to it, just like that. It's too easy.

'I agree that I should move to New York.'

'You're serious,' I say, still not believing her. 'You'd really give up your life in LA to move to New York?'

'LA isn't my home. I have some friends there, but I could still talk to them after I move. And as for my job, it's only part-time and I really don't like it there. I was going to start looking for jobs when I got back.'

'What about your other job? Teaching yoga?'

'I could do that anywhere.'

'Lyndsay, I only want you doing this if it's what you want. I don't want you doing this for me.'

'I'm not. This is what I want. It's all I've thought about since you left. There's just something about you, Nick, something that makes me want to be with you. Even in high school I felt something for you, but I wouldn't let myself go there because of Chris. But when I saw you again at the airport last week, all those feelings came back, except now I could let myself feel them.'

I stare at her, not believing what she's saying. 'If you had feelings for me back in high school, you did a damn good job hiding them.'

'I had to. I was with Chris, and even if I hadn't been, I didn't think you'd ever go out with me.'

'Are you kidding? You were the girl I dreamed about. To say I had a crush on you is an understatement. But you're right. Even if you weren't with Chris, I wouldn't have asked you out. I was a nerd and you were head cheerleader. I wouldn't have asked you out because I knew you'd turn me down.'

'You would've been wrong. And you weren't a nerd. You were smart. And cute. But now . . .' She leans closer. 'You're all grown up and really hot. And I really wish you'd stop talking and kiss me.'

I take her face in my hands and kiss her, still not believing she's actually going to do this, that she's going to move to New York to be with me.

'You have made me so damn happy,' I say over her lips.

She backs away, her eyes on mine. 'It's what I wanted, Nick. I was just waiting for you to ask me.'

She was waiting for me to ask her to move? And here I was thinking she'd say I was a jerk for even suggesting it. If I'd known she wanted this, I would've flown her out last week, had her stay in my apartment, in my bed.

I lower her to the blanket and lay next to her, pinning her leg down with mine as I kiss her. There are so many things I want to do to her right now, things I thought about all week when I was missing her and wanting to be with her, but I don't feel right doing those things out here in the open, where someone might see us. There's little to no chance of that happening, but still, I don't want her to feel uncomfortable.

'Nick,' she whispers, her eyes closed, her head tilting back as I kiss her neck. I run my hand just under her shirt, along her waist. I stay there a moment, then keep going, my hand sliding up to her breast.

Her hips arch up against my leg, her chest rising and falling with each breath. I slide my hand down her flat stomach, under her shorts to her panties. She's soaking wet, which makes my already hard cock feel like a steel rod pressing against my jeans. I shove her panties aside and rub my fingers over her slick center before sliding one inside her, then another as I kiss her.

She softly moans and reaches down to undo my belt. My resolve to not take this farther is instantly broken. She wants to keep going and doesn't seem the least bit concerned that we're out here where someone could see us. But I don't have a condom. I didn't plan on this so I didn't bring one.

'Don't stop,' Lyndsay begs as my fingers pump in and out of her.

I slowly take my hand from her. 'Sit up.'

'What?' Her eyes pop open. 'But I didn't—'

'You will. Trust me.'

She eyes me as she sits up. 'What are you up to?'

I lift up her shirt and toss it aside, then reach behind her and undo her bra.

'You sure you want to do this out here?' she asks, giving me a sexy smile as she lays down. 'I didn't think that was your style.'

'You don't know me as well as you think.' I lower my mouth to her breast, nipping and sucking and making her squirm. 'Hold still,' I command, holding her legs in place.

I hear her laugh. 'You're a bad boy, Nick Kanfield. I never would've guessed.'

'You have no idea,' I say, giving attention to her other breast as I undo her shorts.

She's panting, her body writhing, her hips lifting. She wants this, and wants me, something teenage Nick never would've imagined.

Moving down her body, I leave kisses along her chest, her stomach, slowing my pace as I reach her shorts. Her breath catches as I slide them off, along with her panties.

I pause a moment to look at her, naked before me. It's something I dreamed of, but this is a million times better than my dreams. Lyndsay is everything to me, everything I could ever want. She's kind and loving, beautiful and smart, funny, easy to talk to. She's so much more than I ever imagined I could find in a woman, and I'd do anything in the world to make her mine.

Pulling the blanket over us, I lower down between her legs. I run my tongue over her center, just once as a tease for what's to come. I hear her gasp and feel her muscles tighten beneath my hands as I hold her down. I spread her open for me and settle myself between her legs, pleasuring her, tasting her, devouring her.

'Nick!' She's breathing hard, her body trembling. 'Oh, God! Nick!' she cries out as I send her over the edge.

My cock's begging to be inside her. I'm so damn turned on from doing that to her, touching her, looking at her, running my hands along her soft skin.

She lets out a sigh as I kiss my way back up her body. 'You have no idea how long I've wanted to do that.'

'I wish you'd done it sooner,' she says, still catching her breath. 'That was incredible.'

'I'm glad.' I kiss her cheek, then her forehead, then her mouth.

'Nick.' She holds me back, her hands on my chest, her eyes on mine. 'Don't you want to, you know, continue?'

'I'd love to, but unfortunately, I didn't come prepared.' I kiss her. 'Maybe tonight, after the reunion.'

'I don't think I can wait that long.' She smiles, running her hand down my chest.

I sit up. 'Are you saying you want to . . . without anything?'

She turns on her side, facing me. 'I'm okay with it if you are. I'm on the pill and I haven't been with Chris for over a year.'

A year? Damn, that's a long time. She said their marriage had been bad for a while, but I assumed they were still having sex.

'Nick?' she says, waiting for me to say something. 'If you don't want to do this, we can—'

'I do,' I say. 'Believe me, I want to do this more than anything.'

'So what are you waiting for?' She lays down on her back, giving me a smile, her gaze lowering to my body.

Holy shit, this is really happening. I didn't expect this. I thought we'd just come out here and talk, maybe kiss, but that's it. Did I want to have sex with her? Fuck yeah, but I wasn't going to even try. She just got divorced. I thought she'd want to wait, give herself time, take things slow. I would've given her all the time she needed, but if she's telling me she's ready now, I'm not going to question it.

Within seconds, my clothes are tossed aside and I'm joining her under the blanket, feeling the warmth and softness of her skin against mine. I kiss her mouth, her cheek, then talk in her ear. 'You're absolutely gorgeous.'

'You're not so bad yourself,' she whispers, her hand running up my back. I love her soft touch, the feel of her hand moving over my skin. Everything feels so perfect that I don't want to rush it, but there's a part of me that isn't that patient.

My cock settles between her legs, waiting for what it's been wanting for 15 years. I nudge it inside her, just barely, as I kiss her. She's so wet I could slide right in, but I take my time, excruciating as it is, and slide in a little more. I hear her moan. Shit, that's hot. So much for going slow. I push deep inside her, then pull out and thrust back in.

Her hips start moving, following my rhythm, keeping my pace, which is faster than I wanted but I can't stop now. It's too damn good. The way she feels, the way we fit, and she's so damn tight. I'm pumping in and out of her, loving how she moves with me, how in sync we are. I always imagined us being good together but not this good. I try to slow down, not wanting this to be over, but I can't hold back. It's too late.

Lyndsay grabs hold of me and cries out my name, even louder than before. Her body relaxes and her head falls back as she catches her breath. I keep going, thrusting harder and faster as I feel it rising, the tension building.

'Fuck,' I groan as the feeling rockets through me, more intense than it's ever been. I pull out of her and collapse back on the ground.

Lyndsay rolls on her side, resting her head on my shoulder, her arm on my chest, her leg over mine. 'That was incredible.'

'Yeah.' I blow out a breath. 'I need a minute to recover after that.'

'Did I wear you out?' she asks with a laugh.

'Not at all. It's just never felt that good.'

She lifts up to kiss me. 'Don't take this the wrong way, but I never imagined you being that good.'

'Why is that?'

'You know what people say about the smart, studious type. That you're all shy and reserved and . . .' She lays her head back on my shoulder. 'Never mind. I shouldn't even be bringing that up. It's obviously not true. Not even close.'

'Is that why you never considered dating me? Because you didn't think I'd be good at that?'

'No. It's because I didn't think I was . . .' She pauses. 'It's stupid. I don't want to talk about it.'

'Lyndsay, look at me.' I wait for her to lift her face back to mine. 'Tell me the truth. Why did you pick a guy like Chris over someone like me? You know I would've done anything to make you happy. I would've supported you, cared for you, been there for you no matter what.'

'I know you would've.' She looks down. 'I just didn't think I deserved someone like you back then.'

'What do you mean?'

'I wasn't smart like you. I didn't see myself going anywhere. You were going to college and law school and going to have this exciting career and make a lot of money. I couldn't see myself with someone like you. I didn't think I was good enough.'

'Are you kidding? Lyndsay, I thought you were *too* good for me.' I sit up, so she does the same, lifting the blanket up and wrapping it around her. 'Listen to me.' I take her hand. 'I never once thought you weren't good enough. To me, you were perfect, the girl I always wanted but never thought I could have. You were sweet and beautiful and someone I admired.'

'You admired me?' she asks, sounding shocked. 'Why?'

'Because you still had a smile on your face after everything you'd been through. Your dad dying. Your mom struggling to pay the bills. You somehow managed to see the positive in every situation, and in people, even people like Chris. If anything, that's the one thing that frustrated me about you. Your willingness to forgive Chris for how he treated you.' I rub her hand. 'I hope now that you're older, you realize that you deserve so much better than him. I'm not even sure I'm good enough.' I smile. 'But I'll do my best to try.'

She turns and leans back against my chest. 'You're exactly what I want, Nick. I just wish I'd been able to see that back then.'

I wrap my arms around her and kiss her head. 'This is our chance to start again.'

We look out at the pond, at the ripples forming in the water from the soft summer breeze. We remain there until the clouds roll in, then make our way back to the house.

It was a perfect day, and hopefully the start of even more. It almost scares me how good it felt being with Lyndsay, finding out she wants to be with me as much as I want to be with her. I feel like it's too good to be true, or that I'm dreaming this and about to wake up. Things can't just turn out this well, can they? I made partner and got the girl of my dreams all in the same week? How could I be that lucky?

Chapter 23

Lyndsay

'I can't believe you guys did it!' Diane says, racing into my room and shutting the door.

I smile and lay down on my bed. 'It was so good. I can't even describe how good it was.'

'Really?' she says, like she doesn't believe me. 'Huh.' She sits beside me on the bed. 'I guess I thought Nick would be kind of . . . shy, hesitant, unsure of himself.'

'Not at all. Not even a little. If anything, he made Chris look that way. I always assumed Chris knew what he was doing because he'd been with so many girls before me.'

'And while he was *with* you,' Diane mutters with disgust. Chris cheated on me twice in high school and probably also during our marriage, but I could never prove it.

'But compared to Nick, Chris was like an awkward teenager trying to figure out how to do it. He never even cared if I finished. It was all about him.'

'Then why the hell did you stay with him all those years?'

'Because I didn't want to be divorced. I wanted the fairytale. The happily ever after.'

'With Chris?' she says, scrunching up her nose.

'Hey, I was young.' I sit up, crossing my legs in front of me. 'I didn't know a lot back then. I thought if a guy said he loved me that he really did. I didn't know he'd say it just to have sex with me. I didn't have sisters to talk to, and I wasn't going to talk to my mom about this.' I cringe, just imagining that. My mom and I aren't close that way. We don't talk about sex or dating or guys. She never even gave me the sex talk.

'You had friends to talk to.'

'Who all thought Chris was a god. They didn't care what he did. They would've taken his side and told me I should be grateful to have the guy every girl wanted.'

'Not me. I would've told you to dump his ass.'

'And I did, twice, but he begged me to give him another chance.' I sigh. 'I don't want to talk about Chris. I just want to think about Nick and about our future together.'

'I know Nick is a great guy, but don't you think you're kind of rushing into this?'

'No. He's not some guy I just met. I've known him forever.'

'You knew the Nick from 15 years ago. You're just getting to know adult Nick. People change from high school. Just look at us. I've definitely changed and so have you.'

'Yes, but Nick has changed for the better. He's mature. He has a successful career. He's more confident and bold and definitely better looking.'

'But you still don't really know him. You've only spent a few days with him and you're only seeing what you want. Nobody's perfect. Nick has his flaws like everyone else.'

'Why are you doing this?' I get up from the bed. 'I'm finally happy with a guy and you're telling me to let him go?'

'That's not what I'm saying.' She gets up and stands in front of me. 'I'm glad he makes you happy. I just want you to be careful. You tend to believe what people tell you, even if they're just telling you what you want to hear.'

'So you're saying I'm stupid.' I walk to my closet. 'You know what, Diane? I don't need your help finding something to wear. Despite how stupid I am, I think I got this.' I yank a red dress from the closet.

'Lyndsay, that is not what I said.' She comes over to me and takes the dress, shoving it back in the closet. She faces me, her hands on her hips. 'All I'm saying is that this is moving really fast. Maybe you should give it more time before you move to New York.'

I throw my hands up. 'Would you make up your mind? One minute you're telling me to date him and the next you're telling me to stay away from him!'

'I'm not saying you can't date him. I just don't think you should rush into moving there. Maybe you could just go out there for a few weeks, spend more time with Nick, and decide if this is really something you'd want. Moving across the country is a big deal, especially if it's for a guy you've only been out with a few times.'

'Diane, I know you're only trying to help, but really, I've got this. I know what I want, and I want to be with

Nick. I don't need more time to decide. And really, what's the risk? There's no reason for me to stay in LA. I have no family there. I don't like my job. I'll just be going back to an empty apartment in a place I don't even want to live.'

'You could move here for a few months. You could go see Nick on the weekends, then come back here and have some time for yourself.'

'I don't need time for myself.' I walk away from her. 'Diane, why are you so against me being with Nick?'

'I'm not. But after a long marriage, it's easy to lose yourself. Taking time to get to know yourself again is a good thing. It's healthy. And it keeps you from losing yourself again with Nick.'

'That's not going to happen. Nick isn't Chris. He doesn't tell me what to do or make it all about him. He supports me.'

'By making you give up your life in LA and move across the country to be with him?'

'He didn't force me to do it. I told you how bad he felt asking me to move, and he left it up to me to decide. Now would you stop trying to protect me and let me live my life?'

She nods. 'You're right. It's your life.' She goes back to the closet. 'I don't think I like the red one.' She takes it out and holds it up. 'What do you think?'

'It's too fancy. I want something more fun. Maybe the pink one.'

She finds it and brings it over to me. 'This one would look great with your tan, and I like that it's shorter, not so serious. Try it on!'

And just like that, we're back to being friends. I love Diane because we can argue without staying mad. What I don't love about her is what she said about Nick. She acts like he's just another version of Chris, which isn't even close to the truth. Nick is nothing like Chris, and unlike Chris, I trust Nick. He's not going to hurt me like Chris did. He cares about me. He might even love me.

Diane's just being cautious, but she doesn't know Nick like I do. To her, he's a hot-shot lawyer from New York, not the small-town boy we knew in high school.

'I love it! It's perfect!' Diane gushes as I spin around in the dress.

It's a hot pink, sparkly dress I got for a party years ago. It conforms to my body, has tiny straps at the top, and ends about mid-thigh. I like the dress, but feel like I might be too old to wear it now. That's why it's here at my mom's house, along with some other dresses I never wear and should probably get rid of. I'm storing them here because I don't have much closet space in my apartment and Chris never took me anywhere nice enough for me to wear a dress.

'Are you sure?' I yank the dress down. 'It's kind of tight and really short.'

'On a body like yours? It's perfect. Every guy there's going to be staring at you.'

'I only care about one of them,' I say, smiling as I look at myself in the mirror.

'What about your hair? Are you wearing it down?'

'I think so. And I think I'll straighten it.'

'I think you should wear it like it is. Those natural waves you have are gorgeous. Women pay a fortune to get their hair that way in a salon.'

'I guess I could leave it.'

I'm so used to straightening it because that's how Chris liked it. I rarely wore it natural. But seeing it now, with its loose bouncy waves, I kind of like it like this.

'What about jewelry?' Diane walks over to my dresser where my jewelry is lined up. I didn't bring much, not thinking I'd wear it while I was home. 'Are these real?' She holds up two diamond stud earrings.

'No.' I laugh as I walk over to her. 'Chris and I barely had money for groceries. There's no way we'd spend money on jewelry.' I take the earrings from her and put them on.

'They look great!' Diane says, smiling at me. 'And with the sparkles in that dress, I don't think you need a necklace.'

'I don't think so either. So I guess I'm all set.'

'I need to head out.' She walks to the door. 'I have to make sure Tom showers before he gets dressed. He's been out golfing and getting all sweaty, but for some reason he thinks showers are limited to one a day.' She rolls her eyes. 'Men.'

I laugh. 'Thanks for your help. I'll see you there.'

She leaves, and I take off the dress and go in the bathroom to shower. Nick is picking me up at six and taking me to dinner before the reunion. I'm a little nervous about going with him, knowing people will wonder what we're doing together and why I'm not with Chris.

Just before six, Nick shows up at my door in a light gray suit, white dress shirt, and blue tie, looking sophisticated and hot. I can't believe I'm dating him. There's still that part of me that thinks I'm not good enough, that I don't deserve him. But I *am* good enough, and I *do* deserve him. Nick believes that, and I should too. I just need to keep telling myself that until it sinks in. All my years with Chris had me doubting myself, doubting my self worth, but he's gone now and it's time I let go of those doubts.

'Wow.' Nick's eyes widen as he looks at me in the dress. 'Lyndsay, you look incredible.'

'Thanks!' I reach up and kiss him. 'You look great in that suit.'

'I feel like I'm at work. This is what I wear every day.'

'And you don't have a girlfriend?' I check him out, noticing how perfectly the suit fits him. 'How is that possible?'

'I was holding out for one girl in particular.' He pulls me into his arms. 'But I never in a million years thought she'd actually go out with me.'

'I guess dreams come true sometimes.'

'I guess so.' He takes my hand and leads me over to Sawyer's shiny black convertible.

'We get Sawyer's car?' I ask.

'He loaned it to me. I thought it'd be easier to get into than Dad's truck.' Nick opens the door for me.

'Tell him thanks,' I say as I get into the car. 'This is definitely easier.'

We head to the restaurant, the nice one we went to before. We only had drinks that night, so we decided to go back there for dinner this time.

'When did Sawyer get this?' I ask, running my hands over the soft leather seats.

'A few years ago. He worked two jobs to save up the money.'

'He must've really wanted this car.'

'He did. He has expensive taste. He likes expensive cars, designer clothes. He paid like 300 dollars for those sunglasses he had on the other day.'

'You know, it's funny, but I could see Sawyer living in New York more than I can see you living there.'

'I've thought the same thing. He wouldn't want to live there, but he'd fit in better than I do.' Nick points to his suit. 'He'd actually like wearing this. I only wear it because I have to. I'm more of a jeans and t-shirt type of guy.'

'But you look really good in the suit,' I say, smiling at him.

'Not as good as you look in that dress,' he says, smiling back.

We arrive at the restaurant and are seated at the same table we were at before. The last time we sat here I was heartbroken, thinking I'd never see Nick again. But now I'm elated, my heart filled with joy, knowing Nick and I are a couple.

The dinner is wonderful. The food, the atmosphere, being with Nick. He keeps gazing at me across the table and reaching over to hold my hand. It's nice to be with someone who's affectionate and can't take his eyes off me and gives me compliments. Chris was never like that.

After dinner, we go to the hotel where the reunion is being held. It's a historic hotel near downtown. It's beautiful and has a grand ballroom that's rented out for weddings, but tonight it's reserved for the reunion.

'You ready for this?' Nick asks as we walk up the steps to the hotel.

'Are *you* ready?' I ask. 'You're the one who's been dreading this.'

'I'm not now that I have a gorgeous date.' He leans down to give me a kiss, then opens the door.

Matt's standing in the lobby, wearing a tux, a big grin on his face.

'Hey! You guys look great!'

'Thanks,' Nick says as we walk up to Matt. 'What's with the tux?'

'I thought I should look formal since I'm kind of in charge of this.' He leans in, lowering his voice. 'And Tessa kind of has a thing for tuxes.'

Nick nods, smiling. 'Now it makes sense. Your mom taking the kids for the night?'

'She's staying at the house with them. Tess and I got a room here at the hotel.'

Nick looks at me. 'We should've done that.'

'You still could,' Matt says. 'The manager said there's a couple rooms left.'

'What do you think?' Nick asks me.

'I'd love to stay here. I've always wanted to.'

'Go ahead.' Matt points to the check-in desk. 'Tell them you're with the reunion and you'll get a discount.'

Matt doesn't seem at all surprised that Nick and I are getting a room together. Nick must've told him we're a couple now. After tonight, everyone will know that I'm dating Nick Kanfield, a smart, successful attorney and one of the town's beloved Kanfield brothers. I feel honored to be dating him for that alone. His family is famous in this town. Everyone loves and respects Nick's parents and the job they did raising four good, hard-working men.

'We'd like to get a room for tonight,' Nick tells the guy at the desk. He's young, maybe 22. 'We're with the reunion.'

The guy doesn't look up as he types in his computer. 'And the name?'

'Kanfield. Nick Kanfield.'

The guy looks up. 'As in THE Kanfields? The people who own the orchard?'

Nick smiles. 'You've heard of us, huh?'

'I just moved here, but yeah, you're kind of famous around here.'

'I don't know about that,' Nick says with a laugh.

'My parents used to drive over two hours just so we could go to the fall festival.' He types on the keyboard again. 'My girlfriend's family used to drive up from Chicago for it. It's kind of a big deal.'

'Yeah, my parents are already getting ready for this year's festival and it's not even July yet. It's a lot of work, but they love it.'

'I heard they bought some land to expand the place,' the guy says, continuing to type.

'They did,' Nick says with a sigh. 'I tried to talk them out of it, but my dad really wanted the land.'

'Why'd you want to talk him out of it?' I ask.

'Because he's getting older. The place is already more than he can handle. Adding more acres is just adding more work.'

'He could hire some help.'

'He already has help, but he still does most of the work himself.'

'I got you the suite,' the guy says, handing Nick the key. 'It's our most expensive room so it doesn't get reserved much. I gave it to you at the regular rate.' He smiles. 'I'm sure my manager will be okay with it when he finds out a Kanfield is staying here. Maybe you'd consider putting some of our brochures out during the festival?'

'I'll talk to my dad about it.' Nick hands him his credit card.

The guy runs his card, then hands it back. 'Have a good stay! Let us know if you need anything.'

'Want to go check it out?' Nick asks, holding up the key.

'Okay!' I'm already excited about this. I get a whole night with Nick in a gorgeous hotel. My mom won't approve, but she'll have to get over it. I'm not a teenager anymore. I can spend the night with a guy.

'It's nice,' Nick says as we walk into the room.

'It's better than nice. It's beautiful!' I walk over to the four poster bed, which is covered in a white comforter and piles of white pillows. There's a ruby-colored velvet sofa off to the side with a metal bar cart next to it that has a silver ice bucket and a bottle of champagne.

'What do you think?' Nick asks, coming up behind me and wrapping me in his arms. 'You okay spending the night with me?'

'I can't wait!' I say, spinning around to face him. 'But we don't have a suitcase.'

'I'm sure the front desk has a toothbrush and some toothpaste. We'll ask when we go back down.'

'But what about clothes? I didn't bring anything to sleep in.'

He kisses me, then talks softly in my ear. 'I'm kind of hoping we won't be getting much sleep tonight.' He kisses my neck. 'And if we do, I'd prefer you wear nothing.'

Tingles course through me as his hand cups my ass and he leaves kisses down my neck.

'Nick, we should probably get downstairs.'

'Do we have to? You look so damn good in this dress, I don't think I can wait until later.'

I pull back, smiling at him. 'It'll be worth the wait. I promise. And then we'll have all night together.'

He sighs. 'This better be a quick reunion. How long do these things usually last?'

'I don't know. This is my first one. Probably a few hours?'

He groans and rubs his hand over his jaw, looking like he wants to devour me. 'And you're sure we can't show up late?'

I laugh. 'The sooner we get down there, the sooner we can leave.'

Chapter 24

Lyndsay

Nick and I take the elevator to the main level and go down a long hallway to the ballroom. There's a table set up outside it where a woman checks us in.

'Nick?' She smiles at him. 'I can't believe you came.'

'Kami. Hey.' He smiles back. 'How have you been?'

'Good.' She gets up and goes around the table to give him a hug. Nick dated Kami junior year. They only went out a few times. Back then, she had long dark hair and was skinny with braces. Now her hair is shorter and blonde, and she's wearing glasses. I almost didn't recognize her.

'Is this your wife?' she asks.

'No,' I say, laughing. 'It's Lyndsay. Lyndsay Davis?'

She gasps. 'Oh, Lyndsay, I'm sorry. You look so different with the darker hair.'

'I decided I was tired of being a blonde,' I say, jokingly, but the truth is I felt people didn't take me seriously with my blonde hair so I starting coloring it. I did it a few weeks after I got my associate degree, thinking it might help my chances of getting a bookkeeping job.

'Where's Chris?' Kami asks, looking behind me.

Here we go with the questions about Chris and I'm not even past the door yet.

'Chris didn't come,' I tell her.

'We should get inside,' Nick says, taking my hand.

'Yes, go ahead,' Kami says, going back behind the table. I see her looking at my hand in Nick's. 'Wait, are you two—'

'We are,' Nick says, and leaves it at that as we go into the ballroom.

'Thanks for handling that,' I tell him as we look around for a table.

'You okay?' he asks.

I nod. 'I have to get used to it. It's going to happen a lot tonight.'

'And you're okay with people knowing about us?'

'Of course. I love being here with you.' I reach up and talk in his ear. 'And I can't wait until later when I get you all to myself.'

'Hey. Don't be doing that here.' He glances down at his pants. 'This is a tight suit.'

I laugh as he buttons his jacket, hiding the effect I had on him by saying that.

'You want a drink?' he asks.

'I'd love one.'

As we're walking to the bar, two women race up to me, both very pregnant.

'Lyndsay?' one of them says.

Seeing her face, I instantly recognize her.

'Molly!' I hug her, a distant hug because her belly's so big. 'When are you due?'

'What do you mean?' she asks, sounding hurt as she pulls away.

Is she saying she's not pregnant? She's thin everywhere but her huge belly. She has to be pregnant.

She bursts out laughing. 'I'm kidding! I'm due in August.'

'And I'm due early September,' the other woman says.

'Jane!' I hug her. 'Oh gosh, I need to pay more attention. Everyone looks so different. It hasn't been that long, has it?'

'Fifteen years have not been kind to some of us,' Jane says, laughing. 'Except you.' She looks me up and down. 'You look even better than you did in high school. Do you have kids?'

'No.'

'Well, that explains it,' she says, motioning to Molly. 'We each have two, plus the one on the way. It's impossible to get your body back after having kids.'

Molly looks up at Nick, tilting her head. 'You look familiar. Do I know you?'

'Yeah. Nick. Kanfield.'

She gasps. 'Oh my God, you're right!'

'I hope so,' he says, smiling.

'You got hot,' Jane says, staring at him. She was never one to censor her words, which is one of the reasons I liked her. Jane and Molly were on the cheerleading team with me. We had a really great team. We didn't fight or form cliques or start rumors about each other. As head cheerleader, I didn't put up with that stuff.

I wanted us all to be friends, knowing it would make us a better team.

'*Really* hot,' Molly says, practically drooling over Nick.

'He's an attorney now,' I tell them. 'A very successful one. He just made partner at his firm.'

'I always knew you'd do well,' Jane says to Nick. 'You took all the hardest classes and got straight A's.'

'Where are you living now?' Molly asks him.

'New York.'

'Where in New York?'

'Manhattan.'

'Wow, fancy,' Jane gushes. 'I love New York, but Michael, my husband, hates it. He thinks it's too crowded.'

'Are you married?' Molly asks.

'No. I'm single.' He glances at me. 'Well, actually I'm dating someone.'

'Anyone we know?' Jane asks.

'Me.' I wrap my arm around Nick's. 'Nick and I are dating.'

'Wait—what?' Molly looks at Jane, then back at me. 'What about Chris?'

'We're divorced.'

They both frown.

'But you two were such a cute couple,' Jane says. 'We thought you guys would last forever.'

'It just didn't work out,' I say, not wanting to talk about it.

I knew people would react this way. I knew they'd tell me how Chris was the perfect guy for me and try to convince me I made a huge mistake by leaving him. I wish they knew what he was really like instead of keeping him on the pedestal they put him on back in high school. They only did that because he won us football games, which made him a celebrity in a town this size. But Nick's just as much a celebrity being a Kanfield, so I don't know why people got so crazy about Chris and why they still think he's so great.

'So you guys never had kids?' Molly asks, like she can't believe it.

'They would've had the cutest kids,' Jane adds.

'Chris didn't want kids,' I say, letting them know he was the reason we never had any. 'He forgot to tell me that before we got married,' I say, a hint of anger in my voice.

'Why don't we get some drinks?' Nick says, giving my hand a squeeze. 'It was good seeing you,' he says to Molly and Jane.

'Maybe this was a bad idea,' I say as we walk to the bar. 'I don't know if I can go all night being questioned like that, or having people act like Chris is perfect and I'm the problem.'

'If you want to leave, we'll leave. Just tell me.' Nick stops at the bar.

'I'll be fine.' I turn to the bartender. 'Chardonnay.'

'Whiskey on the rocks,' Nick says, getting his money out.

'How's it going?' someone asks. I turn and see Diane standing next to me, wearing a red dress and heels, her hair in a twisted updo.

'Hey, you look great!' I give her a hug. 'Wait, is this why you told me not to wear the red dress? Because you were wearing red?'

'Maybe,' she says with a guilty smile. 'But the pink still looks better on you.'

'It looks great on her,' Nick says, handing me my wine.

'Hey, Nick.' Diane looks at him in the suit. 'You clean up nice.'

'I'm Tom.' He comes up behind Diane and shakes Nick's hand. 'We haven't had a chance to meet.' He smiles. 'I hear you're one of the famous Kanfield brothers.'

'I wouldn't say famous, but yes, I'm a Kanfield. The oldest.'

'Should we go sit down?' Diane points to a table. 'We're sitting over there.'

We walk over to one of the round tables and take a seat. I'm next to Diane and the guys are sitting on either side of us.

'I really like your brother's new place,' Tom says to Nick. 'The beer's good and I like what he did with the renovations.'

'Our cousins came up from Chicago to do it. They have a construction company. They specialize in restoring old buildings.'

'They did a great job. It feels new, but still has the historic charm of the original building.'

'Tom loves old buildings,' Diane explains. 'Every time we go on a trip he has to look up the history of the buildings.'

'Next time my cousins are in town you should get together with them,' Nick says to Tom. 'They could tell you all about the buildings they've worked on.'

'I'd like that.'

'When do you think you'll be back here?' Diane asks Nick.

'I'm not sure.' Nick glances at me. 'Maybe we should come back for the festival.'

'We should.' I smile at him, loving that he used 'we' to describe us.

'Lyndsay said she's thinking of moving to New York,' Diane says, eyeing Nick like she doesn't trust him. Why is she being like this? She's my friend, not my mom.

'That's the plan,' Nick says. 'We haven't worked out all the details yet.'

'But you're thinking it'll be soon?'

'Why would I wait?' I say to Diane. 'I don't need to stay in LA.'

'Rent in New York is ridiculous,' Tom says. 'You could get a mansion here for what you'd pay there for a studio apartment.'

Oh, great, now Diane's got Tom trying to talk me out of this.

'It might be good to move home for a month or two,' Diane says. 'Save up some money.'

'Would you stop?' I whisper to her, giving her a look that I mean it.

'It's not a bad idea,' Nick says.

I turn to Nick. 'You think I should live here instead of New York?'

'Not permanently. Just until you're ready to make the move.'

'But then we'd be apart.'

'Why don't we talk about this later?' he says, glancing at Diane and Tom.

I let it go, but I'm not happy. Why does Nick want me to wait to move there? Is it because of what Diane said, or is he getting cold feet about having me there? He said he didn't have time for a girlfriend. Is he having second thoughts about us? If he is, we shouldn't be spending the night together.

'Oh, I love this one!' Diane says as a slow, romantic song comes through the speakers. 'Tom, get up. We have to dance.'

He sighs as he stands up. 'Okay, but I'm not doing this all night. You know I hate dancing.'

'And you know if you stop complaining what will happen later.'

A slight grin appears on his face as he follows her to the dance floor.

'Would you like to dance?' Nick asks.

I would, but right now I'm annoyed with him. Why is he siding with Diane, wanting me to wait to move to New York? Does nobody trust me to make my own decisions?

'Could we talk first?'

'Sure.' He turns to me. 'What's going on?'

'What you said just now, about me living here. Did you mean it?'

'It was just an idea. I didn't say it was a good one.'

'Then why did you say it?'

'Because I don't want you feeling like you have to rush into this if you're not ready.' He lowers his voice as people walk past us. 'You just got divorced. You've been through a lot of changes the past year. I'd understand if you need some time before making another big change.'

'But you want this, right? For me to move there? For us to be together? You're not changing your mind?'

'No. Of course not. I can't wait to have you there. But I'm not thinking of just me and what I want. I need you to do what's best for you, and if waiting a few weeks or a few months is what you need, I'll understand. I'll be working a lot anyway so I wouldn't see you much even if you were there. But I could fly you out on weekends, or if you wanted to stay all week, go check out the city while I'm at work, that's an option too.'

I feel better hearing him say that. I'm so used to being with a guy who didn't want to be with me that my mind instantly assumed Nick was the same way when he suggested I stay here instead of going to New York. I need to stop thinking every guy is like Chris.

'I'll take that dance now,' I say, rising up from my chair.

Nick takes my hand and we make our way to the dance floor. I spot Tom and Diane a few feet away. Diane's eyes are closed and there's a dreamy smile on her face as it rests on Tom's chest. He's swaying side-to-side, staring up at the ceiling speaker above him like he's praying for it to stop playing this song so he can go sit down.

'I always wanted to do this,' Nick says, drawing my attention to him as his arm goes around my waist.

'Do what?'

'Dance with you like this.' He moves us along the dance floor like he actually knows what he's doing. He's not at all awkward or uncomfortable like Tom. He seems completely at ease being out here. 'Our senior year prom, I almost asked you to dance, but I knew Chris would throw a fit if I did.'

'You're right. He would have.'

'I should've asked you anyway.' Nick looks into my eyes. 'I have so many regrets from back then.'

'Like what?'

'Like not telling you how I felt. Maybe it wouldn't have made a difference, but at least you would've known.'

'I know now. That's really all that counts.'

The song ends and another one begins. It's another slow one, but I notice Tom and Diane leaving the dance floor. I think Tom needs a break or maybe a stiff drink before being dragged back for another song.

'You're really good at this,' I say to Nick as we reach the edge of the dance floor and he turns us around.

'I've had lessons.'

'You took dance lessons?' I laugh. 'Sorry, I shouldn't laugh, but can I ask why?'

'I've dated some women with money, like a lot of money. From wealthy families. They tend to go to a lot of formal events where you need to know how to dance. Ballroom dance, not country hoedown type of dance.'

I laugh again. 'Yeah, I assumed it'd be ballroom. So you took lessons to impress these women?'

'I took lessons so I'd know what the hell I was doing. I didn't want to try to wing it and accidentally step on her foot or bump into someone.'

'How many of these rich women did you date?'

'I don't know. Three or four?'

'Why did it end?'

'Because I'm a small-town boy from Wisconsin. It doesn't matter where I live now or what I do for a living. Once the girl's parents found out I wasn't one of them, it ended, each and every time. Eventually I stopped dating those women.'

'What was your longest relationship?'

'Lyndsay, I don't want to talk about this. It's the past, and I'm with you, and you're the only woman I want to think about.'

I rest my head on his chest as the song nears the end, closing my eyes as we sway side-to-side.

'Hey, Lyndsay,' a guy says.

I open my eyes and see Chris' friend, Ted, beside us, dancing with a girl I don't recognize. She looks at least ten years younger than him.

'Hey, Ted,' I say, feeling my shoulders tense up and a knot forming in my stomach. I knew Chris' friends would be here, but I was hoping I could avoid them.

'How's it going?' Nick says to him, turning me away from Ted, knowing I don't want to talk to him.

'Nick?' Ted's eyes widen as he looks Nick up and down. 'Shit, you been working out?'

'I spend a little time in the gym,' Nick says, standing up straighter. 'How about you? Still playing football? Hitting the weights every day?'

I try not to laugh. Ted's gained about 50 pounds. He probably hasn't worked out since high school.

'Nah, I don't do that shit anymore. I got a job. A kid to support.'

Ted got a girl pregnant a few years ago. He never even went out with her. He hooked up with her at a bar one night and a few months later found out he was going to be a dad. The little boy is six now and lives with his mom. Ted sees him a few times a month. Sometimes I wonder if Ted's the one who convinced Chris to not have kids. He's always complaining about being a parent.

'So what are you doing with Lyndsay?' Ted laughs. 'Living out your teenage fantasy?'

'We're kind of busy here,' Nick says, his jaw tightening. 'Why don't you move along?'

'I'm just joking around. I didn't mean anything by it.'

'I'm getting a drink,' the girl next to Ted says as she leaves.

I turn toward Ted and put my arm around Nick's. 'Nick and I are dating.'

'Yeah, right,' Ted says, assuming I'm joking.

'We actually are,' Nick says. 'And I'd like to get back to our date, so if you could—'

'Wait—does Chris know this?' Ted directs the question to me.

'Why would I tell Chris? We're divorced.'

'Yeah, I guess. Okay, well, I gotta go find Andrea.' He takes off, then looks back at us and laughs.

'I never liked that guy,' Nick says.

'He was okay back in high school, at least to me. I don't really know him now. He'd call Chris once or twice a year to catch up, but that was it. They didn't really stay friends.'

'You want to go back to the table?' Nick asks as the song ends.

'Yeah.'

We return to our seats.

'Have you recovered?' I say to Tom, kidding with him.

'Barely.' He swigs his drink.

'Hey!' Diane scowls at him. 'I spent an entire day freezing my butt off ice fishing with you last winter. You owe me!'

He turns to her and smiles. 'I promise you, you'll never have to ice fish with me again.'

'Only because you didn't like me being there.' She rolls her eyes. 'He said I talked too much.'

'I miss ice fishing,' Nick says. 'My dad would take us every year. Brody hated it, but the rest of us liked it.'

'Why didn't Brody like it?' I ask.

'Because he's the youngest, so he got stuck doing all the shit work.' Nick looks over at Tom. 'If you ever need someone to go with, let me know. If I'm in town, I'd love to get out there again.'

'Sure, I'll let you know.'

I like that Tom and Nick are getting along. I just wish Diane would stop giving Nick that look like she doesn't trust him.

The night continues and people stop at our table to talk to Diane, not recognizing Nick and me until we introduce ourselves. A few people asked about Chris, but not as many as I thought would. I'm guessing word got around about the divorce and me being with Nick, which shut down any need to ask questions.

'How about another dance?' I ask Nick, feeling tipsy from all the wine I've had. I go to kiss him but miss his lips and get his cheek.

He laughs a little. 'I think I need to get you up to bed.'

'I feel fine.' I stand up. 'C'mon. I want to dance again.'

As he gets up, I feel Diane grabbing my hand. 'Lyndsay.'

'What?'

'Nick's right. You should get to bed.'

'Why would I go to bed? It's only ten o'clock. It's still early and I really like this song.'

'It's not that great,' she rushes to say, glancing behind me. 'And you look really tired. You should go.'

'I'm not tired. I'm just relaxed from all the wine.'

'Fuck,' Nick mutters.

'What's wrong?' I ask.

I look at Diane, then Nick, and see both of them looking back at the door.

'What are you guys—' I stop when I see him.

It's Chris.

Chapter 25

Nick

My blood's boiling seeing Chris here, knowing what an ass he was to Lyndsay and knowing he's hurting her, showing up like this. She came here to get away from him, and then he shows up, without even telling her.

He looks like shit, like an older, fatter version of himself. Girls used to think he was hot, but they wouldn't now. How'd he let himself go like that? He used to be an athlete. He worked out all the time and had the muscles to prove it. Now he looks like a tired old man with a swollen face and a huge gut. And I think he's losing his hair. It looks a lot thinner on top.

'I thought you said he wasn't coming,' Diane says to Lyndsay.

'He told me he wasn't.'

'Let's get out of here.' I take Lyndsay's hand and pull on her to move.

'No. I'm not leaving because of him.'

'You really want to stay? You know he's going to come over here.'

'Yeah? So let him come over. I'm not afraid of him.' She sticks her chest out and holds her head up higher. She's drunk, which isn't a good frame of mind to be in when confronting her ex-husband.

'Shit, he saw us,' Diane says.

We all watch as Chris makes his way over to us. Nobody else seems to notice him. I don't think they recognize him. I wouldn't have if I hadn't seen Diane staring at him. I could tell by the look on her face it was him.

He smiles as he approaches our table. 'How's everyone doing?'

'Great, until you showed up,' Diane mutters.

'Hey, Chris.' I turn to him. 'It's been awhile.'

He looks at me, squinting a little. 'Do I know you?'

'Nick. Nick Kanfield.'

'No shit?' He stands back, looking me up and down. 'Damn, I never would've guessed. You were so scrawny back in high school.'

'He wasn't scrawny,' Lyndsay says, putting her arm around mine. 'He just didn't have all these muscles back then.' She smiles at me.

Is she trying to piss off Chris? I don't care if he knows I'm dating Lyndsay, but I'm not going to rub it in his face. I'm not looking to get into a fight tonight, but if I did fight him, I'd definitely win. I'm taller than him and I've got a lot more strength. He's so fat and flabby, it wouldn't even be a fair fight. Why didn't Lyndsay tell me he looked like this? Was she too embarrassed?

'What's going on here?' Chris says to Lyndsay. 'You trying to get with Nick? You really that desperate?'

Okay, that's it. I was trying to be nice, trying to remain calm, trying to be a gentleman, but I'm not letting him insult me.

I take my arm from Lyndsay's and step up to Chris. 'You want to say that again or should we step outside?'

'Nick, don't,' Lyndsay says, coming up behind me. 'Let's just go.'

'You two are leaving together?' Chris looks past me to Diane. 'Help me out here, Diane. Tell me why the fuck my wife is with Nick.'

Diane gets up. 'She's not your wife anymore, and what she does or who she does it with is none of your business.'

'Like hell it isn't!' Chris looks at Lyndsay. 'We got divorced last week, and you're telling me you're already with someone else?' He points to me. 'Have you been fucking him behind my back? Is that why you asked for a divorce?'

'No! You really think I'd cheat on you?'

'Okay, this is getting out of hand,' Tom says, coming around the table to Chris. 'Why don't we go get a drink? What do you like?'

Chris rears back. 'Who the fuck are you?'

'He's my husband,' Diane says. 'And he was trying to be nice, but obviously, that doesn't work with you. Just get out of here, Chris.'

'I'm not leaving until I know what's going on here. Why is Kanfield with my wife?'

'She's not your wife,' I say. 'And if you don't—'

'Nick and I are dating,' Lyndsay blurts out. She steps up to Chris. 'You and I are divorced. It's final. I can be with whoever I want.'

'And you're choosing *him*? Kanfield? The nerd who tutored you in math? Seriously?'

'I am, and I don't care what you think of him. It doesn't matter. You don't get to have a say in my life anymore. We're over, and I'm asking you to please, just leave me alone.'

Chris looks at me, then back at Lyndsay. 'I don't even know who the fuck you are anymore.' He storms off to the bar to get a drink.

'Are you okay?' Diane asks, holding Lyndsay's arm.

'I'm fine. I just can't believe he showed up.'

'We should go.' I take Lyndsay's hand. 'He's just going to cause more problems.'

'I agree,' Diane says to Lyndsay. 'Why don't we call it a night? It's getting late and we've already talked to everyone we wanted to talk to.'

'I don't like giving Chris that much power,' Lyndsay says. 'He shows up and we all leave? Why are we letting him tell us what to do?'

'We're not,' I say. 'We're making the decision ourselves. We weren't planning on staying that much longer anyway.' I get in front of her. 'We had a good night. We had some drinks, danced, caught up with old friends. Why don't we just end on a high note and get out of here?'

She nods. 'Okay.'

'You'll call me tomorrow before you leave?' Diane says to Lyndsay.

'Yeah, or maybe I'll stop by. I'll let you know in the morning.'

My phone rings. I check it, then silence it.

'Work again?' Lyndsay asks.

'Yeah, I'm just gonna ignore it. I should be able to have the damn weekend off.'

Doug, a lawyer at my firm, has been calling me all night. We're working on a divorce case together, but I told him not to bother me this weekend. He can handle whatever it is or wait until I'm back on Monday. I'm really sick of people at work thinking I'm on call all hours of the day. I need to have a talk with my boss when I get back.

'Oh! I forgot to talk to Marie!' Diane waves at her, then says to Tom, 'I'll just be a minute. Could you get the car? I'll meet you out front.'

'Okay.' He smiles at us as he leaves. 'Have a good night.'

'See ya, Tom,' I tell him. He seems like a nice guy. I could see us being friends if I lived here.

Diane turns back to Lyndsay. 'Get some rest and forget about you-know-who.'

'I will. Bye!'

Diane races off to talk to her friend while Lyndsay and I head out of the ballroom.

My phone rings. It's Doug again.

'You need to answer it?' Lyndsay asks as we wait for the elevator.

'I don't want to, but I probably should so he'll stop calling. Go ahead and go up to the room. I'll deal with this and be up there in a minute.' I give her a kiss as the elevator doors open.

'I'll be waiting,' she says, smiling as she gets on the elevator.

I can't believe I get a whole night with her, just the two of us. The hotel room was a great idea. I'm glad Matt suggested it. Lyndsay and I need some alone time together, and not just in bed, but to talk about the future and where we go from here. I'm thrilled she's moving to New York, but I do have concerns. I want to make sure she's ready for this and not rushing into it. And I want her to live with me, not get her own place. Rent prices in New York are outrageous and if she's spending all her time at my apartment, she might as well live there. I'm just not sure we're ready for that. We just started dating. Moving in together is a big step.

'Nick,' Doug says when he picks up. 'I've been calling you all night.'

'I told you I wouldn't be around this weekend. Can't this wait until Monday?'

'No. Iris is going fucking crazy and refuses to talk to anyone but you.'

Iris is a woman in her seventies who's divorcing her cheating husband, a wealthy businessman. I've been working on the divorce for over a year and it still isn't settled because Iris and her husband refuse to agree on anything.

I let out a frustrated sigh. 'What's wrong now?'

'Donald took his mistress to the house in the Hamptons, which Iris is claiming is hers.'

'Nothing's hers until the divorce is final. I told her that.'

'She's not accepting what you told her. She wants you to get a judge to order her husband and his mistress out of there.'

'That's not happening. You know that. Why didn't you tell her that?'

'I did, but she won't listen to me. She said I'm too young to know what I'm talking about. She wants you to handle it.'

Doug is fresh out of law school. My boss assigned him to work with me since he's new and doesn't have much experience yet.

'I'll deal with her on Monday.'

'It can't wait. Nick, she's hysterical. You should've heard her. You have to talk to her.'

'Fine. I'll call her right now.'

'Thanks. I'll see you Monday.'

I end the call and scroll through my client list until I find Iris. I go outside to the front of the hotel and call her.

'Nick! Finally! You wouldn't believe what Don has done now! He's with that whore at the beach house in the Hamptons!'

'Yes, I heard. I got your message.'

'What are you going to do? He can't be there! It's mine!'

'Not yet. Not until we've made everything final. Iris, we've been over this.'

'He can't stay there! God only knows what they're doing in there! I'll have to destroy all the furniture!'

'There's nothing you can do. It technically still belongs to both of you.'

'Nick, please. I can't allow this. You have to do something!'

'I can't. I'm out of town right now. I'll see what I can do when I get back on Monday.'

'Monday? I'm paying you a fortune! I demand that you get back here right now and do something!'

This is one of those times I hate my job. Clients like Iris calling me on a Saturday night, demanding I deal with their drama.

I try to remain calm as I think of how to respond to her.

'Iris, I wish I could be there, but I can't. You'll just have to wait.'

'Don't you care about me and what I'm going through?' she says, pretending to cry. She does this all the time. She fake cries, hoping it'll make me do what she wants or talk to her for hours. She thinks I'm her therapist and is willing to pay the firm's huge hourly fees just to have someone listen to her. She can easily afford the bills, but I'm not a counselor and shouldn't have to pretend to be one. I'm only going along with it because my boss told me I had to so we can keep billing her. It feels unethical, and is another reason I'm unhappy with my job.

'Of course I care about you,' I tell her. 'But I can't be with you right now. We'll talk when I get back to New York.'

'Can we meet in person?' she asks, sounding desperate. 'I don't want to talk on the phone. It's so impersonal and I need to get out of the house.'

I sigh, not wanting to do this but knowing my boss will make me. 'I'll see if we can meet for dinner next week, but I might have someone coming into town. I'll let you know if I can get away.'

'Oh, Nick, thank you! I'm so relieved. When I kept getting that boy, Doug, on the phone, I thought it meant our relationship was ending and I just couldn't accept it,' she says dramatically.

'Our relationship is not ending,' I assure her. 'I just had somewhere to be this weekend. But when I'm back, we'll resume where we left off. Iris, I know you think I'm not giving you all that you expect from me, but I'm doing my best. And I can't be with you all the time.'

'I know that, Nick, and I'm sorry to be so demanding,' she says, her angry tone turning sweeter now that I've agreed to have dinner with her. 'You're a good young man. I'm so fortunate to be working with you. So where is it you are right now? Doug didn't say.'

'I'm home, visiting my family,' I tell her, not wanting her to know too much about my personal life. I like to keep my personal and work life separate.

'You're up rather late for a Saturday night. Are you out with a girl?'

'I'm not with a girl,' I lie, knowing she'd ask me more questions if I told her the truth. 'I'm at my parents' house. Iris, I really need to go. I promise we'll talk when I get back.'

'And we'll go to dinner?'

'Yes, I will take you to dinner. We'll go to your favorite place that makes those soufflés you like.'

'Oh, that would be wonderful!'

'I need to go. I'll call you when I'm back in New York.' I end the call before she starts talking again. I feel bad for her. She's a lonely old lady who's so desperate for attention that she's paying her lawyer to talk to her and take her out.

'Hey, Nick,' a guy says.

I look up and see Chris coming down the stairs from the hotel.

'What do you want, Chris?' I say in an angry tone.

'Sorry about earlier. I was just surprised seeing you with Lyndsay.' He extends his hand to me. 'Are we good?'

'Yeah. Sure.' I shake his hand, just to end this so he'll go away.

'You going back to the reunion?'

'No, I'm done for the night.'

He nods. 'Well, it was good seeing you.' He goes back up the stairs and into the hotel.

A car pulls up and Diane races over to it. Where did she come from? Has she been waiting here the whole time? The sidewalk is dark, so maybe I just didn't see her.

'Bye, Diane!' I tell her.

She must not have heard me because she doesn't look back. She gets in the car and it drives off.

Going back inside, my anger about work quickly disappears as I think about what's waiting for me upstairs. When I get to the room, I find Lyndsay on the bed wearing only a towel, a glass of champagne in her hand.

'What took you so long?' she asks.

'It doesn't matter,' I say, taking my tie off. 'I'm here now.' I lean down to give her a kiss.

'Why don't you take the rest of those clothes off?' she whispers over my lips.

They're off within seconds and I join her on the bed.

'Want some champagne?' She turns to me and offers me her glass.

'I'd rather have you.' I take the glass from her and set it on the nightstand, then I kiss her as I undo the towel that's around her. I lay her back on the bed, then kiss every inch of her, from her head to her toes, paying extra attention to her most sensitive areas.

'Nick.' She breathes out my name, her chest heaving, her hips rising, as I make my way back up her body. I've got her right where I want her, worked up to the point she can't wait any longer.

I position myself over her and push inside her. I kiss her neck, then her cheek, then her mouth, while moving in and out of her at a slow, steady pace. I'm forcing myself not to rush this, wanting to remember this when we're apart. I'm hoping we won't be apart for too long, but I really don't know how long it'll be. That's something we need to talk about.

'Nick,' she whispers.

I open my eyes and look at her, feeling the connection between us, the one I felt all those years ago but wasn't sure was real. Now I know it is, and I know it's not just me. Lyndsay feels it too, which makes me believe we can make this work. Whatever obstacles are ahead, we can work through them if it means we'll be together in the end.

Our eyes remain locked as I pick up my pace, sensing she's close. I lean down to kiss her, then speed up even faster. Her breaths become ragged and her body trembles as her fingers rake down my back.

'Oh God!' she screams.

I'm right there with her, the sight of her coming sending me over the edge. I pause a moment to catch my breath, then slowly pull out of her and collapse back on the bed.

'I'll take that champagne now,' I say.

She laughs and reaches across me to the nightstand to get it. She takes a sip, then offers me some.

'I was kidding, but okay.' I sit up and take the glass from her. I down what's left of it and set the glass aside.

'Thirsty?' she jokes.

'I was.' I pull her into my arms. 'This was a great idea, getting a room for the night.' I kiss her forehead. 'I love being here with you.'

'I wish we didn't have to leave tomorrow.' She rests her head on my shoulder and runs her hand over my chest. 'When will we see each other again?'

'I don't know. We need to talk about that.'

'My lease isn't up until September, but I could try to sublet my place for the rest of the summer.' She looks up at me. 'What do you think I should do?'

'I can't tell you that. You need to decide. I want you to be with me, but I also want to make sure you're ready to leave your old life behind. You've been in LA a long time. Leaving there means leaving your job, your friends.'

She frowns. 'Why do I keep getting the feeling you don't want me to move to New York? Are you having second thoughts?'

'No, of course not. But this is moving really fast. We just started dating. We might need more time before you decide to move your entire life across the country.'

'I don't need more time. I know what I want. I think *you* might be the one who needs more time.'

'Lyndsay, I want us to be together. I just don't want you having any regrets.'

She lays her head back on my shoulder and gets quiet.

I feel like we should talk more, but I don't know what to say. I want to be with her, but I admit I'm worried we're moving too fast. I don't want her moving to New York, then saying I work too much and wanting to leave. My job is a major concern when it comes to us. I don't want to be one of those couples that doesn't spend time together, but how do I make time for her when my job keeps piling work on me?

She falls asleep in my arms. I watch her sleep until I fall asleep myself. In the middle of the night, I wake up to her kissing me, which leads to us making love again. Afterward, we fall asleep and don't wake up until morning.

'It's after nine,' Lyndsay says, racing out of bed. 'I'm going to be late!'

'Your plane doesn't leave until noon. You have plenty of time.'

'If I was going straight to the airport, yes, but I still have to go home and pack.' She hurries to get dressed.

'What can I do to help?' I ask, yanking my pants on.

'Can you check the bathroom? See if I left anything?'

I go in there and look around. 'I don't see anything.' I return to the bedroom and finish getting dressed. 'I guess we should've got up earlier. I was hoping we could have breakfast in bed.'

'Maybe next time.' She smiles at me as she tugs her dress into place. 'Ready to go?'

'Not really, but if we have to.' I gather up my keys and wallet and we head downstairs to check out.

On the drive to her house, I already miss her, even though she's sitting right next to me.

'Let's talk when you get back to LA,' I say, reaching over to hold her hand. 'Continue our conversation from last night.'

She nods. 'What time are you back in New York?'

'I think around four. I'll have to check.' I pull into the driveway at her mom's house, feeling a sense of panic at having to say goodbye. It's too rushed, and something feels off. We should've kept talking last night. We should've figured out what to do next, but because we didn't, things feel awkward between us, and unfinished. I feel like Lyndsay is angry at me, or frustrated. I was just trying to do what's best for her, but I think I screwed up.

'Bye, Nick,' she says, stopping me at the door. She gives me a kiss, but it's quick.

'Hey, are you okay?' I ask, holding her arm as she turns to the door.

'I'm fine. I just need to hurry or I'll miss my flight.'

'I'm sorry if I didn't say the right thing last night. This is all just happening really fast and I don't know what the right answers are or how to do this so we don't mess it up.'

She gives me the same frustrated look she gave me last night. 'You think too much, Nick.'

'What does that mean?'

'It means sometimes you need to tell your mind to be quiet and let your heart make the decision.' She gives me another kiss. 'I have to go. I'll talk to you later.'

She goes in the house, leaving me standing on the porch, confused by what she meant. Let my heart make the decision? What decision? The one about her moving to New York? That's not my decision to make. It's hers. I already told her I want her to move there, but I'm not going to force her to.

I don't like leaving things this way. Something doesn't feel right.

Chapter 26

Lyndsay

'Hey,' I say, answering Diane's call. 'I'm at the airport. My mom just left.' I laugh. 'She was so nervous driving here and there wasn't even any traffic.'

'Did you see my texts?' she asks in a urgent tone.

'Yes, but not until this morning. I overslept and didn't have a chance to call you. What's going on? You sound worried.'

'Did you spend the night with Nick?'

'Yeah, at the hotel. Why?'

She sighs. 'I heard something.'

'About what?'

'I'm not sure, but it didn't sound good.'

'What are you talking about?'

'Last night after we left the reunion I was outside waiting for Tom to get the car and I heard Nick talking on the phone. It was dark so I don't think he saw me.'

'Yeah? So?'

'He was talking to some woman.'

'It was for work. He'd been getting calls all night from work and wanted to deal with it before he went up to the room.'

'This didn't sound like a work call.'

'Why do you say that?'

'The way he was talking to this woman, it kind of sounded like he might be dating her.'

'Diane, you know Nick would never do that. He's like the nicest guy ever. He'd never do that to me.'

'He might if he's not sure about you or not sure if you're serious about moving there.'

'What exactly did you hear him say?'

'He was telling her that he wished he could be with her and that he cares about her, and then he told her he'd take her to dinner next week.'

That doesn't sound like a work call, but who knows? Maybe it was. I can't imagine Nick cheating. He's not that type of guy.

'He said he might have someone coming to town next week,' Diane says, 'and that he'd let her know if he could get away. I'm guessing that someone is you. Did you tell him you'd be there next week?'

'No,' I say, my stomach knotting. 'What else did he say?'

'That their relationship isn't ending and that when he gets back, they'll resume where they left off. And then she must've asked him where he was or who he was with because he lied and told her he's at his parents' house and that he wasn't with a girl.'

Why would he say that? Why would he lie about me?

'Maybe I'm reading something into it,' Diane says, 'but it sure didn't sound good.'

'No, it doesn't,' I say, that knot in my stomach growing.

'What did he say last night when you were up in the room? Did he talk about you moving there?'

'A little, but I felt like he was trying to talk me into not doing it. He kept saying I should wait, and that he doesn't want me to have regrets. What if he was saying that because he's trying to decide who he wants to be with, me or that other woman? Maybe he wants to date us both until he figures it out, which is why he wants me to stay here instead of moving there to be with him.'

'It's possible. Lyndsay, I'm sorry I had to tell you this. I went back and forth all night trying to decide what to do. Tom said I should stay out of it, but if it were me I'd want to know. I'd want you to tell me.'

'It's not what I want to hear, but I'm glad you told me. I just can't believe he'd do this. It's so unlike him.'

'Maybe it's not true. Maybe it's some kind of misunderstanding.'

'It doesn't sound like it is. What you described doesn't sound like a conversation you'd have with a coworker or a client.'

'That's what I thought.'

An announcement comes over the speaker, saying my flight will be boarding soon.

'Diane, I need to go. My flight's about to board.'

'Call me when you get home.'

'I will. Bye.'

I'm feeling sick after hearing that stuff about Nick, but I'm still not sure I believe it. Diane only heard part of what he said, and maybe she thought she heard something she didn't.

'Are they boarding yet?'

I look over and see Chris taking the seat next to me. He's on my flight? That's just great. Just what I need when I'm already feeling sick.

'They're boarding in a few minutes,' I tell him, getting up. I'm not waiting here with him. I was hoping I'd never see him again.

'I'm surprised you're leaving this early. I thought you'd want more time with Nick.'

'I need to get back to LA. Is your stuff out of the apartment?'

'Not all of it. I have to get a truck for the big stuff.'

I sigh. 'Chris, you promised me you'd be out by this weekend.'

'That was before I decided to go to the reunion.'

He always does this. He says he'll do something, then doesn't, finding some excuse for why he couldn't. I should just move out and give him the apartment. I could stay with a friend until I figure out what to do.

'What about San Diego?' I say. 'You were supposed to meet that guy there this weekend.'

'Yeah, that didn't work out.'

Of course it didn't. It never does. Our whole marriage Chris kept investing our money in businesses that turned out to be scams, each time saying he was going to make us rich but instead leaving us with barely enough money to pay rent.

'I'm going to go wait in line,' I say, pulling the handle up on my suitcase.

'Hey, before you go, I have something to show you.' He gets out his phone.

'I don't want to see it. I need to go.'

He glances behind him. 'They're not even boarding yet.' He turns back to me. 'I wasn't going to record this, but I knew if I didn't you wouldn't believe me.'

'Whatever it is, I don't want to see it.'

'You sure?' He holds his phone out to me and I see Nick on the screen, standing in front of the hotel, talking on his phone.

'You recorded Nick?' I huff. 'You're spying on him now?'

'I went outside to look for Ted. I didn't even know Nick was out there. I heard him talking to some woman and, well . . .' He offers me his phone. 'You might want to hear this.'

I reluctantly take his phone and walk over to the window, watching the airport workers load the luggage on the plane. I start the recording and put the phone to my ear.

'Of course I care about you,' Nick says to whoever he's talking to, 'but I can't be with you right now. We'll talk when I get back to New York.' I look at the screen, making sure it's really him. I hear his voice again and put the phone to my ear. 'I'll see if we can meet for dinner next week, but I might have someone coming into town. I'll let you know if I can get away.' He listens, then says, 'Our relationship is not ending. I just had somewhere to be this weekend. But when I'm back, we'll resume where we left off. Iris, I know you think I'm not giving you all that you expect from me, but I'm doing my best. And I can't be with you all the time.'

It's just like Diane said, almost word-for-word. I want to believe it doesn't mean what I'm thinking, but it sure sounds like it.

'I'm home, visiting my family,' he says, then, 'I'm not with a girl. I'm at my parents' house. Iris, I really need to go. I promise we'll talk when I get back.'

He lied to her. He didn't want her knowing about me.

The video ends and I walk back to Chris and give him his phone. 'I'm getting in line.'

'What'd you think?' he asks with a smug grin.

I shrug. 'He was talking to a client. I don't know why you recorded that.'

'That was not a client,' he says, following me to the boarding line. 'Nick's messing around on you.'

I ignore him and turn my back to him, praying he doesn't have the seat next to me on the plane.

'You know he wanted you in high school, right?'

I turn back to Chris. 'Would you please just shut up? I don't want to talk to you.' I face forward again, noticing the line is finally moving.

'He was using you,' Chris says, ignoring my request for him to be quiet. 'Living out his teenage fantasies. A nerd like him never had a chance with you in high school, but now he's got some fancy job and money to take you out. He was playing you, Lyndsay. Trying to get you to sleep with him. Make his fantasy come true.

That's all it was. You didn't really think he was serious about you, did you?'

I don't answer him. Tears sting my eyes and I feel a lump in my throat. I shouldn't be listening to Chris, but what if he's right? What if Nick was using me to live out some teenage fantasy? He kept telling me how much he liked me back then and how much he wanted to date me. Now he has, so is he done with me? Was this all just a fling and he never had any intention of us having a relationship? I can't believe he'd do something like that. I don't want to believe it.

'Miss? Your ticket?' the lady asks, waiting to check me in.

'Oh. Sorry.' I get out my phone and hurry to find my boarding pass. She scans it and I continue to the plane. I sigh in relief when I see two people already seated in my row. I take the aisle seat, then see Chris coming toward me. He smiles at me, then sits in the seat behind me.

'I'm right here, babe,' he says, leaning forward and rubbing my arm.

'Would you and your husband like to sit together?' the man next to me asks.

'No.' I grit my teeth. 'And he's not my husband.'

Chris laughs. I want to reach back and strangle him. But instead, I put my earbuds in and look through my phone. Nick hasn't texted me. I thought he might send me one before I left, but if he's done with me, it would make sense that he didn't.

I still don't think it's true. Even after seeing that video, I don't believe it, or maybe I just don't want to. Either way,

I'm calling him when I get back to LA and I'm going to ask him if he has someone else. Maybe he really was just living out his teenage fantasy. Maybe I've been doing it too, living out my fantasy of dating my math tutor, a guy I thought was too smart to be interested in someone like me.

The entire flight I think about that, wondering if this whole time Nick and I have just been reliving the past, playing out scenes we wished would've happened back in high school. But if that were true, I wouldn't have all these feelings for him. The feelings never felt fake, like they were just part of some role I was playing. They felt real. I felt like I was falling in love with him.

When I get to LA, I go to my apartment and see Chris' stuff is still there, not just the big stuff but all of it. He's such an ass. He promised me it'd be gone. I should've known he was lying. His promises are worthless. At least he's staying with a friend and not here.

Checking my phone, I still don't see any texts from Nick. He should be in New York by now, but he just landed. He's probably still on the plane.

I call his phone. It rings and rings, then goes to voicemail.

As I set my phone down, it rings. I grab it and answer it. 'Nick?

'It's Diane.'

'Oh. Hey.'

'Did you talk to Nick?'

'No, I just called him. I thought he was calling me back. His plane just landed. He might still be on it.'

'Are you going to ask him about what I told you?'

'Yes. I need to know the truth.'

'Lyndsay, maybe I was wrong. I was talking to Tom some more and he thinks I might've misinterpreted the whole thing. Or maybe I heard him wrong. I was standing a few feet away and cars were going by. It's possible what I heard isn't what he really said.'

'It was. Chris showed me the video.'

'Chris did what?'

I tell her about the video and what I heard Nick say on it.

'It still doesn't prove anything,' Diane says, trying to make me feel better. 'But it does make you wonder.'

'Which is why I have to talk to him. I'm going to try him again. He should be off the plane by now.'

'Okay, let me know what happens.'

I call Nick's phone and get his voicemail again. I wait a few minutes and call back. It rings and rings, then goes to voicemail.

Why isn't he picking up? Why hasn't he texted me?

I don't want to assume the worst, but my mind keeps going there. After being cheated on by Chris, there's a part of me that worries it'll happen again. The signs are there, but I don't want to believe it.

Chapter 27

Nick

'Hey, I just got off the plane,' I say, answering Sawyer's call as I walk through the airport terminal. It's crowded and loud and hard to hear.

'You need to get back here.'

'What was that?' I hold the phone closer to my ear. 'It sounded like you said I need to get back there.'

'I did. You need to get back here. Now.'

'Why?' I stop. 'What's going on?'

'Move out of the way!' a guy yells at me as he goes around me.

I step to the side, dragging my suitcase with me.

'It's Dad.'

'What about him?' I feel my pulse racing, hearing the serious tone of Sawyer's voice.

'Dad had a heart attack.'

'Wait—what? Is he okay?'

'We don't know yet. He was having chest pains and trouble breathing so Mom called for an ambulance. He just got to the hospital. The paramedics think it was a heart attack, but we need a doctor to tell us for sure.'

'Fuck.' I rub my jaw, a thing I do when I'm trying to think. 'I'll see if I can get a flight. I'll get the next one out.'

'Let me know when it gets in and I'll meet you at the airport.'

'I'll have Matt get me. You need to be at the hospital with Mom. Are you there now?'

'Yeah, I'm outside the ER. Mom's in there filling out paperwork.'

'Where's Jason and Brody?'

'They're on their way.'

'Go be with Mom. She'll tell you she's fine, but you and I both know she's freaking out.'

'Yeah, I'm heading in there now.'

'I'll be there as soon as I can.' I end the call and race through the airport to one of the ticket counters. 'I need a flight to Haydon Falls, Wisconsin.'

The woman types on her computer for what seems like forever. 'I'm sorry, sir, but I don't think they have an airport.'

'You're right. Sorry. I'm not thinking straight. I meant Madison.'

She types some more, then nods. 'I have one leaving tomorrow morning at five.'

'I need to be there tonight. Try Milwaukee.'

After what seems like an hour of her typing, she shakes her head. 'Everything's booked. The soonest I could get you a seat would be tomorrow morning.'

Shit. I can't get there tomorrow. Dad could be dead by then. He better not fucking die. I'm not ready to lose my dad. I need more time with him.

'What about Chicago?' the woman asks. 'I have a seat open on a flight that leaves in an hour.'

'Yes. I'll take it.' I give her my credit card. The ticket will probably cost me a few thousand dollars, but I don't care. I have to get home.

Ten minutes later, I've got my boarding pass and am heading to the gate, trying to calculate when I'll get there. Chicago's at least a two-hour drive from Haydon Falls, more with traffic, and I'll have to rent a car.

I text Sawyer and tell him I'm flying into Chicago and give him an estimate of when I'll be there.

Call Uncle Mitch, he texts back. *Mom was just on the phone with him. He'll give you a ride.*

I'm so out of it I wasn't even thinking of my uncle. He lives in Chicago and wouldn't think twice about picking me up and driving me to Haydon Falls. He's probably going there anyway to be with my mom.

I call him up, but his phone goes straight to voicemail. I call his home number, knowing he still has a landline.

'Hello?' It sounds like Nash answering, not Uncle Mitch.

'Hey, it's Nick. Is this Nash?'

'Yeah, hey, I just heard about your dad. We're heading up there soon.'

'All of you?'

'Yeah. Dad's at the gas station, filling up the truck. I'll follow behind him in mine. Bryce and Austin are going with Jake.'

It must be serious if they're all going. I'm afraid to call my mom to find out.

'Hey, could one of you stick around and give me a ride? I'm taking the next flight out to Chicago. I couldn't get anything closer.'

'Yeah, of course. I'll stay behind. It'll give me a chance to check on our job sites before I go.'

'Thanks. I'll send you the flight information.'

'Did you just get back to New York?'

'Yeah, I'm still at the airport. I was getting off the plane when Sawyer called. I haven't talked to my mom yet. I'm kind of afraid to.'

'Dad talked to her a few minutes ago.'

'Did she say how my dad's doing?'

'She said they haven't told her anything yet.'

I blow out a breath. 'I'm fucking scared, Nash. I'm not ready for this. I'm not ready to lose him.'

'Hey, don't be thinking like that. You gotta try to stay positive. Your dad isn't that old and he's been healthy up until now. He could make it through this.'

'I keep telling myself that, but look what happened to your mom. Aunt Barb was younger than my dad.'

Nash's mom died of a heart attack a few years ago. We were all shocked when it happened. I still can't believe she's gone. She and my mom were close, more like real sisters than sister-in-laws. When I was growing up, Aunt Barb and Uncle Mitch would drive up with their boys to see us several times a year. We'd drive down to Chicago to see them too, but it was more fun for them to come to the orchard where all us boys could run around outside.

'You can't compare the two,' Nash says. 'You don't know what's going on with your dad. You need to wait to hear from the doctor.'

'Yeah, you're right.'

'What time does your flight leave?'

'Less than an hour. We should be boarding soon.'

'You want me to stay on the phone with you?'

'No, I'll be okay. I need to make some calls. Thanks for doing this. I'll see you soon.'

'Nick, we're family. You don't have to thank me. Whatever you need, just ask.'

An announcement blares from the speaker above me.

'Sounds like we're boarding now. I just sent you the flight info.'

'Got it. See ya, Nick.'

It's good I'll be riding home with Nash. I like talking to him, and he's been through this with his mom so he understands how I'm feeling.

As I get in line to board the plane, I check my phone and see that Lyndsay called a few times but didn't leave a message. She's probably wondering why she hasn't heard from me. I was going to call her when I got off the plane, but then Sawyer called and everything went to hell.

I call her, but her phone goes straight to voicemail. I leave a message. 'Hey, it's Nick. I need to talk to you. Call me when you get this.'

I don't want to tell her about my dad over the phone, especially when I don't know what's going on. Maybe it wasn't a heart attack. Maybe it was just chest pain caused by stress or indigestion. I hope that's all it was, but I'm worried it's more serious than that.

Knowing I can't keep avoiding it, I call my mom, telling myself to be strong for her and stay positive.

'Hey, Nick,' Jason answers.

'What are you doing with Mom's phone?'

'She gave it to me in case someone called. She's in the hospital talking to the nurse. We're not supposed to use cell phones in there.'

'Any word on Dad?'

'Not yet, but from what the nurse said, it sounds like a heart attack.'

'But we don't know how bad?'

'No. Hey, when are you getting here? I know we're all grown now, but we all kind of look to you to take over when shit like this happens. Sawyer's already freaking out about who's going to take care of the orchard.'

'Can Brody help?'

'Yeah, but this is his busiest time of year. He'll have to either cancel on people or try to hire some help really fast.'

'And I'm guessing you can't get out of your teaching contract.'

'I could, but I don't know who they'd get to replace me. And at night I have to coach, but I could try to get out of that.'

'Don't do anything yet. Give me some time to think. We'll figure something out. Tell Mom I'll be there later tonight. I could only get a flight into Chicago. Nash is driving me up.'

'Okay. I need to get back in there. We'll let you know if we have any updates.'

He ends the call and I scroll through my phone to my boss' number. I don't like calling him on the weekend, but he wouldn't think twice about calling me, so I shouldn't feel bad about it.

'Nick,' he answers. 'This is a surprise. I thought you were on the farm this weekend.' He laughs. He thinks it's funny I grew up on an orchard. He makes fun of me for it, even going so far as calling me Farmer Nick when he introduces me to new people joining the firm.

'I'm in New York now, but I'm heading back. My father had a heart attack.'

'Oh. I'm sorry to hear that.'

'I need to take some time off. Probably all of next week, depending on how things turn out with my dad.'

'Nick, you just made partner. You can't take a week off. You have responsibilities, and you're already behind on your work. I'm still waiting for you to give me the Feinstein contract to review.'

'I'll do what I can while I'm gone, but I can't promise you anything. My first priority is my dad and my family.'

'Your father will be fine. Men have heart attacks all the time. My father's had two and the old man's still around. Don't you have all those brothers? Why can't they be with him?'

I'm furious that he's acting like this isn't serious or important. My father is sick. He could be dying. At a time like this, I don't care about my stupid job.

'I need to be there,' I tell him.

'Then I expect you to still do your work. I need that contract done by tomorrow.'

'It's not going to happen. It's only partially done and I need more than a few hours to finish it. You'll just have to get it when it's ready. I'm sorry, but that's the best I can do.'

He clears his throat. 'Perhaps it was a mistake making you a partner. You don't seem ready for the job.'

'I'm more than capable of doing the job, but I'm not choosing work over my family at a time when they need me. I'm sorry if you don't agree with that, but this is what I have to do. I'll do what I can on the contract and send it to you when it's ready. Enjoy the rest of your evening.' I end the call before he can fire me. I don't think he will, but he might if I don't get back there soon.

I'm so damn stressed I feel like I can't breathe. My chest is tight. My head is pounding. How am I supposed to work and also be there for my family? What Jason said is true. As the oldest I'm expected to take over for Dad, be the rock of the family and hold us all together. I know more about running the orchard than any of my brothers. They'll look to me to figure out how to keep it going. Even if Dad's okay, he won't be able to work. He may not be able to work for months, and we're going into fall, our busiest season.

Thinking about that is making even more stressed. I call up Lyndsay, knowing she'll be able to calm me down. Just hearing her soft, sweet voice will make me feel better.

Her phone goes to voicemail and I leave another message. 'Lyndsay, it's me. I really need you to call me back.'

The speaker above me blares with another announcement so I end the call.

A few minutes later, I board the plane. As soon as I'm in my seat, I go to check my phone but can't find it. I search my pockets and all around my seat, but it's not there. Did I lose it in the airport? I had it with me right before I got on the plane. I remember setting it down to get out my boarding pass. Maybe I forgot to pick it up.

'Excuse me,' I say, stopping one of the flight attendants. 'I think I left my phone in the terminal. I need to go check.'

'Sorry, but the doors just closed. We're taking off soon. If you give me your information, I'll let you know if we find it.'

I give her my name and Sawyer's number since I don't have my phone. I can't believe I lost it, but I've got a lot on my mind right now. It's hard to keep track of everything.

Hours later, I arrive in Chicago and go outside to look for Nash. I see his truck and wave at him. He gets out and comes up to me and gives me a hug, and not his usual quick guy hug, but an actual hug.

'How are you doing?' he asks, letting me go.

'Not great. And I somehow managed to lose my phone. Do you have any updates on my dad?'

Nash nods. 'They're running tests on him. They don't have all the results back yet, but the doctor said it was definitely a heart attack.'

'I was hoping that wasn't the case,' I say with a sigh.

'Let's get out of here,' he says as a car honks at us to get moving.

As we drive away from the airport, I'm already feeling better than I did in New York. Being with family, back in the Midwest, I feel like I'm back where I should be.

'What else did you find out?' I ask.

'It sounds like he has more than one blockage to his heart. They're considering doing bypass surgery, although that could change depending on what they find out from the tests. That's all I know. Dad called right before you came out. He and my brothers are already at the hospital.'

'Did he say how my mom's doing?'

'She's like she always is.' He glances at me.

'Pretending everything's going to be fine.'

'Yeah,' he mutters.

That's my mom, not wanting to worry us. Even when her parents died, she acted like she was fine. Her mom died of cancer, and a year later her father had a massive stroke, but my mom stayed strong through all of it, explaining that death is a part of life.

'Did you talk to your girlfriend?' Nash asks.

'I haven't been able to reach her. I called her before I got on the plane, but she hasn't called back. Or maybe she did. I don't have my phone so I don't know.'

'Here.' He unlocks his phone and hands it to me.

I call her and get her voicemail. 'She's not picking up. She almost always picks up. I hope she's okay.'

'Did you guys have a fight?'

'No. We went to our high school reunion last night and had a really good time. We ended up staying at the hotel where they had the reunion. She seemed kind of off when I told her goodbye this morning, but I think she was just stressed because she was worried she'd miss her flight.' I look at Nash. 'Why'd you call her my girlfriend? Last time we talked I wasn't even dating her.'

'But I could tell you wanted to. I was thinking maybe you two had gotten together by now. So how's that going to work? Is she moving, or are you?'

'She wants to move to New York, but I think it's too soon. We've only been on a few dates.'

'But you've known her forever. It's not like you just met.'

'But we're older now. We're different than we were in high school, and she just got out of her marriage.'

'Sounds like you've got a lot of excuses for why you two can't be together.'

'They aren't excuses. They're facts. I don't want her moving to New York and then regretting it.'

'Are you sure *you're* not the one feeling that way?'

'I want her to move there. I asked her to.'

'But you probably thought she'd tell you no.'

'I did, but I'm happy she wants to do it.'

'Are you?'

'Yes. What are you getting at?'

'I'm just thinking, you've been living alone since college. It's a huge change to have your girlfriend move in. Even if she gets her own place, she'll be over all the time. Maybe you're not ready to give up the bachelor life.'

'It's not that. I mean, yes, I'll need to adjust to having someone around all the time, but I don't think that's what's worrying me.'

'Then what is it?'

'I don't know, maybe thinking it won't work out? I've wanted to be with Lyndsay since high school but never thought it would actually happen. Now that it has, I'm afraid of losing her. Afraid she'll move to New York, find out I'm not the guy for her, and leave.'

'Do you love her?'

I don't answer him.

'Do you or not?'

'Yeah,' I mutter.

'Why didn't you answer me the first time?'

'Because I'm embarrassed to admit it. I just started seeing her. How the hell could I love her?'

'Sounds like you loved her back in high school.'

'I don't know. Maybe.'

'So now you're going to push her away because you're afraid it might not work out?' He nods. 'That's logical.'

I laugh. 'What the hell?'

'Hey, I just tell it like it is.'

'You're worse than my brothers. They just hint at my stupidity.'

'I'm not saying you're stupid. I'm saying you're afraid, and I get it. You made up this dream in your head of what it'd be like if you two were together. If it doesn't work out, that dream is gone.'

'There might be some truth to that,' I mutter, annoyed that he knows me so well.

'What if it *did* work out? You really want to give up the chance of that happening to avoid any risk of it not?'

I shake my head. 'I just can't figure out how Lyndsay and I could make this work. I'm in the office until eight or nine at night. When would I even see her?'

'You're making more excuses.'

'It's not an excuse. I seriously have to work that many hours just to keep up.'

'Then maybe that's not the job for you.'

'You're telling me I shouldn't be a lawyer? You know how much money I spent on law school? And all the hours I've spent at work trying to make partner? I'm not giving that up.'

He shrugs. 'It's just something to think about. I'm not saying you give up your career. Maybe just work for a place that doesn't make you put in all those hours.'

'So where's Callie?' I ask, changing the subject. 'Did she ride up with your dad?'

'No, she wasn't feeling well. She stayed home with Jen, Bryce's girlfriend.'

'Did she go to a doctor?'

'Yeah. A couple weeks ago.'

'She's been sick for two weeks?'

He glances at me. 'If I tell you this, you need to keep it a secret. We haven't told anyone yet.'

'Yeah, go ahead.'

'Callie's pregnant,' he says, a huge smile filling his face.

'Nash, that's great! Congratulations!'

'Thanks. It wasn't planned. She was on the pill, but I guess it's not a hundred percent because she's definitely pregnant. The doctor confirmed it.'

'How's Callie feeling about it?'

'She freaked out a little when she found out, but now she's excited about the baby. We both are.' He laughs a little. 'I can't believe I'm gonna be a dad. I'm still in shock that she's pregnant. I didn't expect this to happen for another few years.'

'But you seem really happy about it.'

'I'm more than happy,' he says, still smiling. 'I can't fucking wait to hold that baby in my arms.'

I'm a little envious he's got his life all planned out at 27, and I'm 33 and still figuring out where my life is going.

'So does this change your wedding plans?'

'Yeah, Callie wants to get married this fall, but I don't know if we can pull it together that fast. All the event spaces in Chicago fill up a year in advance.'

'What about having it outside?'

'We'd be open to that. What are you thinking?'

'The orchard. You could get married outside and have the reception in the barn where we had my mom's party. The place is beautiful in the fall, overlooking the countryside with the changing leaves.'

'That's actually a really good idea. I'll talk to Callie about it.'

'When are you going to tell the family about the baby?'

'We were going to tell them tonight at family dinner, but then we heard about your dad.'

'You're still doing those Sunday dinners?'

'Every week. My dad insists, and you know my dad. He doesn't take no for an answer. We'll see how things go with Uncle Carl. If he's doing okay, we'll tell everyone next week.'

'Maybe you should just tell them now. We could use some good news.'

'I would, but Callie wants to be there when we tell everyone.'

'Yeah, that makes sense.' I go to take my phone from my pocket, then realize I don't have it.

'You want to try her again?' Nash asks, handing me his phone.

'Yeah, I just realized she might not have answered because she doesn't recognize the number.' I call her again and get her voicemail. I leave another message. 'Hey, it's me again. I forgot to tell you I lost my phone. I'm using Nash's. I really need to talk to you. It's important. Call me back at this number when you get this.' I give Nash his phone. 'I don't know why she's not answering. It's really starting to worry me.'

'Maybe she left her phone somewhere. I'm sure she'll call when she's able to.'

This isn't like her. Lyndsay always calls me back. It's possible she lost her phone, but I get the feeling something else is going on. I just don't know what it would be to make her not call me.

I really need to talk to her. Going through this thing with my dad I'm realizing how much I need someone in my life, someone who will be by my side during times like this. I want that someone to be Lyndsay. I know that now more than ever and I need to tell her that. I need her to call me back.

Chapter 28

Lyndsay

Nick has been leaving messages on my phone for hours now, but I haven't listened to them and I haven't called him back. I'm not sure I will after getting that call from Iris, confirming what I didn't want to believe was true.

A few hours ago I got a call from a woman who said her name was Iris, the same name as the woman Nick was talking to on the phone last night. She asked if I was Lyndsay, and when I told her yes, she started yelling at me to leave Nick alone, saying he was hers and calling me a cheap whore. I was so shocked I almost dropped the phone. I didn't want to believe Nick had a girlfriend, but that call confirmed it. I don't know how she got my number. She must've seen it pop up on Nick's phone.

I don't know if I should call Nick back and tell him I know he's been lying to me or just ignore him and never speak to him again. My heart is completely broken, knowing he did this to me. I trusted him, believed he was different than Chris, but clearly I was wrong. Why do I keep falling for guys who cheat on me?

It's after six here, which is after nine in New York. Nick just called again, but he didn't leave a message and he called from a different number. I wonder if his girlfriend knows he's calling me. Is that why he's using someone else's phone? So she won't find out?

I was falling in love with him. I saw us having a future together, getting married, having kids. What is wrong with me? I barely know the guy. Like Diane said, knowing him in high school isn't the same as knowing him now. People change. Nick definitely did, or the real Nick did. The Nick I was falling for, the one he pretended to be, was the same kind, considerate guy I knew from high school.

I haven't told Diane yet. I'm not ready to hear her tell me she told me so and that I was moving too fast with Nick. I haven't told my mom either. I've just been lying on my bed, staring at the ceiling, wondering how this could've happened and why I didn't figure it out before now.

My phone rings. I check it but don't recognize the number. It's the area code for Haydon Falls but not someone in my contact list. Maybe it's one of Nick's brothers. Maybe he told them to call me and convince me to talk to him.

I almost don't answer, but then I do, curious who it might be. 'Hello?'

'Lyndsay, it's Matt,' he says, sounding relieved. 'Are you okay?'

'Yeah. Why?'

'Nick said he's been calling you but you haven't picked up.'

'Because I don't want to talk to him. I know what's going on, Matt. Iris called me, so you can just tell Nick to—'

'Iris? Who the hell is Iris?'

'Nick's girlfriend in New York,' I say, hearing the anger in my voice. I keep alternating between sad and angry, but I'm mostly sad. I really thought Nick and I had something together.

'What are you talking about? Nick doesn't have a girlfriend in New York.'

'I guess he hasn't told you about her. He called her last night after I went up to the room. Diane heard him talking to her. So did Chris. She must've found out about Nick being with me because she called me today and told me to leave him alone.'

'I don't know who the hell that was, but Nick is not dating her. He hasn't gone out with anyone for like a year, except you.'

'That's just what he told you. Apparently, he's a really good liar.'

'Lyndsay, I swear to you, he is not seeing someone else. Hey, I don't have much time. I just called to let you know Nick's dad had a heart attack. The doctors said it was—'

'Wait!' I jump up from the bed. 'Nick's dad had a heart attack? Is he okay?'

'He's in the hospital, recovering. It sounds like he's going to need bypass surgery.'

'Oh my God.' I pace the floor. 'That's why Nick was calling? Because of his dad?'

'Yeah. He really needs to talk to you. He's got his brothers here and his cousins, but it's not the same, you know? It's like when my sister was sick. You know she had cancer, right?'

'No. When was this?'

'A few years ago. She's okay now, thank God, but when it happened, I needed Tessa more than my parents. They were great, but there's just something about having your partner beside you that—well, you know what I mean.'

Is he saying Nick thinks of me that way? Like I'm his partner?

I don't understand this. I don't know who's telling the truth, who's lying, or who to believe. All I know is I need to get back there, back to Nick and his family. Even if Nick did cheat on me, which I'm starting to think he didn't, I need to be there as his friend and to show my support to his family. I love his family, especially his mom. She'll need all the help and support she can get right now.

'I'll try to get a flight out first thing tomorrow.'

'You sure that's a good idea? I mean, it's great you want to come here, but you sound pretty pissed off at Nick and I don't think now's the time to—'

'I'm not going to fight with him. This isn't about us and our relationship. This is about me helping out a friend. I've been through this, Matt. I lost my dad. If anyone knows what Nick's going through, it's me.'

'Yeah, you're right. You should be here. You want me to tell Nick?'

'No, I'll talk to him.'

'Visiting hours end in ten minutes. Try him then.'

'Okay. Bye, Matt.' I end the call and toss my phone on the bed, then race around my room, grabbing clothes to pack. I throw them in the suitcase I just emptied, then get my laptop and start searching for flights. I find one that leaves in the morning, getting to Wisconsin just before noon. I start to put my credit card number in, then remember the gift card Nick gave me for the airline. My heart melts, remembering the night he gave it to me. He said he wanted me to be able to go home whenever I needed to. A guy who would do something like that wouldn't cheat on me. But then who is Iris and why is she claiming to be his girlfriend?

I hear the front door open and Chris' loud, annoying voice. 'Lyndsay! You home?'

'What do you want?' I go in the living room and see him there with a girl. She's short and skinny with long black hair. She doesn't look older than 20 or 21.

'I need to get my leather jacket,' he says, opening the hall closet. He looks at the girl. 'There should be beer in the fridge. Go grab me one.'

'Don't!' I yell as she goes to the fridge. 'Those are mine. I paid for them.' I storm up to Chris. 'You can't just come in here and take stuff. I'm changing the locks. If you want your stuff, you'll have to make an appointment with me to get it.'

He looks over at the girl, who didn't listen to me and took a beer from the fridge. 'See why I divorced her?'

'Get out!' I yell, pointing at the door.

He finds his jacket and puts it on. 'What do you think?' he asks the girl as she walks over to us. 'Should I wear it tonight?'

'Yeah, babe, you look great.' She smiles and hands him his beer.

I stare at her, feeling like I know her somehow. 'Have we met?'

'No,' she says, looking me up and down and making a face. 'Do you always dress like that?'

I'm wearing a long baggy t-shirt and sweats. I just threw them on after my shower because I wanted something comfortable.

'When I'm alone in my apartment? Yes. I wasn't expecting company.' I glare at Chris.

'We're heading out,' Chris says, putting his arm around the girl and taking a drink of his beer.

'Have fun being alone in your apartment,' the girl says, smirking at me. She has this whiny, high-pitched voice that I swear I've heard before.

Chris swigs the rest of his beer, then holds the bottle out to me. 'Toss it for me, babe.'

'I'm not your babe. Toss it out yourself.'

'Bitch,' he mutters, setting the bottle on the floor.

'Let's go,' the girl whines. 'This is taking forever.'

As they walk to the door, I realize how I know her, or how I think I know her. I run in front of her. 'Did you call me today?'

'No.' She laughs. 'Why would I call you?'

It's her. It has to be her.

I look at Chris. 'Do you really hate me that much?'

'I don't know what you're talking about.' He tries to go past me to the door, but I stand in front of it. 'Lyndsay, get out of the way. I'm serious.'

'So am I. Tell me why you did it. Because you don't want me to be happy, or don't want me being happy with Nick?'

'What the fuck are you talking about?'

'Just tell her so we can go,' the girl says, rolling her eyes.

'Shut the fuck up!' he says to her.

She shoves away from him. 'You can't talk to me that way!'

'Just admit it,' I say to Chris. 'You told this girl to call me and pretend to be Iris, who, by the way, is not Nick's girlfriend.'

'Yeah, that's why he called her and said all that shit,' he huffs. 'Are you really that stupid?'

'I was when I married you.' I step up to him. 'But I'm not now. I know Nick wouldn't cheat on me. I don't know who Iris is, but she's not his girlfriend. And having some girl call me up pretending to be Iris so I won't go out with Nick just tells me you're not over me.'

'Yeah, right.' He rolls his eyes. 'Like I really want you back.'

'It's over, Chris. I don't want to see you or talk to you anymore. If your stuff's not out of here by tomorrow, I'm throwing it out.'

'You do, and I'll call the cops. I gave you the fucking apartment and most of the furniture. The least you could do is give me time to get my stuff.'

I glance around the apartment, realizing everything here reminds me of him and our life together. I don't need that reminder. I want a fresh start.

'You really want it?' I look at Chris. 'You can have it. You can have the apartment too. I'm leaving. I'm moving back home.'

'Are you serious?' He laughs. 'You really want to go back to that shitty town?'

'I like Haydon Falls. I always have. I never wanted to leave. I only did because of you, because I wanted to make you happy. But now I'm making myself happy and going back to where I wanted to be all along. My flight leaves in the morning. I'll take what I want. The rest is yours.' I open the door. 'Bye, Chris. Have a nice life.'

He's looking at me like he's trying to figure out if I'm serious or just said that out of anger.

'Let's go,' the girl says, tugging on him. 'What are you waiting for?'

Chris keeps his eyes on me as he leaves, like he doesn't really believe this is goodbye. But it is. I don't want to be here anymore. I have no reason to stay. This isn't my home. It's not where I want to be.

I shut and lock the door, then call up my mom.

'Lyndsay, did you hear about Carl?'

'Yeah. I'm coming home tomorrow to be with Nick.'

'That's good, honey. He needs you right now. Do you need help paying for the flight?'

'No, I'm good. Hey, Mom, is it okay if I stay with you for a few months?'

'Of course. But why? Did something happen?'

'I decided LA just isn't for me. I want to move back home for a while and figure out what to do next.'

'That's wonderful! I'd love to have you here. But what about Nick? You two will be so far apart.'

'I don't know yet. We'll work it out.' I'm not going to tell her what's going on with Nick and me. I want to talk to him first. 'Mom, I need to go pack. Can you get me at the airport tomorrow?'

'Yes, of course. Just tell me what time.'

'I'll text it to you. See you tomorrow.'

As I'm packing up everything I want in the apartment, which isn't much, other than my clothes, I hear my phone ringing from the kitchen counter. I race over to grab it and see Matt's number on the screen.

'Hey, Matt.'

'It's me. Nick.'

My pulse races, hearing his voice. 'Hey. I was going to call you but Matt said you were with your dad.'

'Yeah, I just left his room.'

'Nick, I'm so sorry.'

'He'll be okay, at least that's what we're hoping. He's having surgery later this week.'

Nick sounds exhausted, more tired than I've ever heard him. He must've got to New York, found out about his dad, and had to fly back.

'I'm sorry I didn't return your calls. I didn't know what happened until I talked to Matt.'

'Why didn't you answer your phone? I was worried. I thought something happened to you.'

'I just um . . . I heard something, something I wasn't sure was true, but given what happened before, with Chris, I thought it might be. But I might've overreacted.'

'What did you hear?'

'Do you know some woman named Iris?'

'Yeah, she's my client. She's going through a divorce. She's the reason I kept getting those calls from work last night. She's old and lonely, so she makes up excuses to call me. I feel more like her therapist than her lawyer.' He pauses. 'How do you know Iris?'

'It's a long story,' I say, sighing as I realize what Diane and Chris heard was not even close to what they assumed they heard.

'Let me hear it. What's the story?'

'I'm too embarrassed to tell you.'

'Lyndsay, it's me. You don't need to be embarrassed. I need to know what's going on.'

I tell him what happened, first with Diane, then with Chris and the video, then the phone call I got from the fake Iris.

'You really thought I'd cheat on you?' Nick asks.

'I didn't at first, but then I got that phone call and thought it must be true. Nick, you have to understand that I was with someone I couldn't trust for years, since high school. It's going to take some time for me to learn to trust someone again. I didn't think you would cheat on me, but there's a part of me that wasn't sure.'

'I would never do that to you, Lyndsay. It's just not who I am.'

'Are you mad at me?'

'No, but I wish you had talked to me instead of making assumptions that aren't true.'

'So what does this mean for us?'

'Mom, just a minute. I'm on the phone.'

'Do you need to go?'

'Yeah, sorry. Can we talk tomorrow?'

'Yeah. Actually, I'm going to—'

'The doctor's here to talk to us. I need to go. Bye.'

I didn't get to tell him I was coming there. Maybe it's better if I don't. I'll get there, go to the hospital, and if he tells me to leave, I will. I don't want to add to his stress. I'll do whatever he needs me to.

I really messed this up, all because I didn't trust him. I thought I'd moved on from Chris, and I have, but the trust issues that came from being with him are still there, and if I don't deal with them, I'll lose Nick.

Chapter 29

Nick

'You can go see him now,' the nurse tells us as we sit in the waiting room.

It's nine the next morning, but I feel like it's still yesterday. I was up all night, worried about my dad and thinking about Lyndsay. It really bothers me that she doesn't trust me. I know Chris cheated on her, but I'm not him and I don't want to have to keep proving that to her. If she can't see that I'm different than him, then I don't know how we can make this work.

'You boys go ahead,' Mom says to my brothers. 'I want to talk to Nick.'

Sawyer, Brody, and Jason all get up and head to my dad's room.

'What is it, Mom?'

She sighs. 'Your father's been asking me about the orchard. He's going to ask me again today and I don't know what to tell him.'

'About who's going to take care of it? Tell him we'll hire more help.'

'We're going to need more than a few extra hands trimming branches and spraying for pests. We need someone to take charge, to manage it. You know how much work it is. You were your father's shadow all those years. You know more about the orchard than anyone, even me.'

'So what are you saying?'

'I don't know. I guess I'm just asking for some advice.' She pauses. 'Your father mentioned something yesterday. I don't think he meant it, but maybe he did. After something like this happens, you reevaluate your life. You see things differently.'

'What did he say?'

'He brought up the idea of selling the orchard.'

My heart nearly stops, then races really fast. I'm panicking, but I don't know why. I always knew it was possible he'd sell the orchard someday, but I didn't think it would actually happen. Dad's never even talked about it.

'He actually said that?' I ask. 'That he wants to sell it?'

'He doesn't want to, but he may not have a choice. After the surgery he'll be recovering for months, and when he's better, the doctor said he needs to slow down. He said it's good for him to be active, but he was doing too much, working too many hours.' She puts her hand over mine. 'You know how your father is. Even if he hired someone to replace him, he wouldn't trust him to do it right. Soon he'd be back out there, doing all the work and running himself ragged. The only way he'll slow down is if he's forced to.'

'Mom, you can't sell the place. You two built it from nothing. And you love it. You both do.'

'Nothing lasts forever.' She smiles, but she can't hide the sadness in her eyes. 'Maybe we'll get a little house in town. Something that's easier to take care of.'

'Dad would hate that. So would you. You guys love living in the country, having all that land.'

'I need to do what's best for your father. As much as I hate to do it, I think we need to seriously consider putting it up for sale.'

'You don't need to be deciding that now. Why don't you wait and see how Dad's surgery goes?'

'It won't change anything. Your father needs to slow down regardless of how well the surgery goes. I don't know what we're going to do this fall. Your brothers can help, but they can't replace your father. The only person who could is . . .' She looks down.

'Mom, I can't. I have a job. A life in New York.'

She nods. 'I know, which is why I didn't even want to ask.' She stands up. 'Let's go see him.'

My stomach's in knots and every muscle in my body is tight. I feel like everything's falling to pieces and it's happening too damn fast. They can't sell the orchard. It's my home, the place I go to connect with my past and find myself when I'm feeling lost in the city and need to get away.

'Nick.' My dad smiles as I approach him. He looks so weak in that bed and in that hospital gown. Until now, my dad seemed like the strongest person in the world. It's how I've always seen him—strong and invincible.

But now I'm realizing that's only how I've chosen to see him. The reality is he's getting old, and tired, and his body isn't what it used to be.

'Hey, Dad.' I stand by his bed. 'How are you feeling today?'

'Like shit.' He laughs.

That's Dad, always trying to lighten a dark moment.

'We're going to go find something to eat,' Sawyer says to Mom.

She nods as my brothers leave.

'You seem to have more energy today,' Mom says, smiling as she smooths out Dad's blanket.

'Leave it, Martha,' he tells her. 'It'll just get wrinkled again.'

'Just let me get this tucked in,' she says, struggling to get the sheet under the bed.

'Dammit, Martha!' Dad yells. 'Stop tidying up! It's not gonna make it better!'

'I have to do something!' she yells back. 'I can't just sit here and watch you—' She covers her mouth as tears stream down her face.

'Mom.' I race over to her and hug her.

'Nick, I need to talk to your father.' She pulls away, wiping her eyes and smiling. 'Go ahead.' She shoos me away.

Leaving the room, I go down the hall, then decide to go back. I wait outside Dad's room and try to listen in. I'm not one to eavesdrop, but after that talk Mom had with me about selling the orchard, I feel like I need to hear this.

'Nick thinks we should wait,' Mom says. 'Give it some more time.'

'Time for what? If you and these doctors are going to tell me I can't work, then what's the point of keeping it?'

'You can still be in charge. You just won't be doing as much as you used to.'

'You really think I can stand around, watching some other man do my job?' Dad says. 'I'd rather sell the damn thing than put myself through that. It'd be like watching someone else raise your child.'

'You just need to find the right person to take over.'

'And you think that'll be easy?' he huffs. 'The only person I'd trust to run that orchard doesn't have any interest in it, and I don't blame him. It's a lot of damn work and a lot of responsibility. The whole damn town depends on us.'

Is he talking about me? I don't know who else it could be. He taught me everything he knows, and then I left and went to college. I didn't want that life.

'You could ask him,' Mom says in a hesitant tone.

'I am not asking him, and neither are you,' Dad says, raising his voice. The room gets quiet, then I hear Dad again. 'You didn't say anything to him, did you?'

'I might've brought it up,' Mom says in a soft voice.

'Martha! You know how I feel about this! The boys deserve to have their own lives, not inherit the one their father had. We agreed on that long ago. Nick's a smart boy. He's not going to waste those smarts working on an orchard. His life is in New York and I'm damn proud of what he's done for himself. I wouldn't even think of asking him to give it all up for his old man.'

'Fine. I won't mention it to him again.'

'Why don't you call up our lawyer? See what we'd need to do if we sold the place.'

'We could ask Nick. He might be able to help.'

'I want to keep Nick out of this, and the other boys.'

'But I can tell them, right? I don't see any reason to keep it a secret.'

'We should tell them together. But not now. I'm too tired.'

'You go ahead and rest. We'll talk to them later.'

I hurry down the hall so Mom doesn't see me when she leaves his room.

'What's the rush?' Uncle Mitch says, smiling at me, a cup of coffee in his hand.

'I just walk fast,' I say, slowing down. 'It's a New York thing. Everyone's in a hurry.'

'It's the same way in Chicago.' He looks behind me. 'How's your mom doing?'

'She's worried.' I turn back and see her going into the restroom.

'Let's go sit down.' Uncle Mitch motions me to follow him to the waiting area. 'Your brothers are in the cafeteria with my boys.'

We take a seat. I still feel sick about my dad selling the orchard. I can't imagine coming back here and having it belong to someone else, having strangers living in our house and running the place. What if a corporation bought it, one of those big ag companies that buy up small farms and turn them into production facilities? My dad would hate that. So would I. The whole town would.

'Nash tells me you got a new girl,' Uncle Mitch says.

'Lyndsay. We just started dating. I'm not sure it's going to work out.'

'Love isn't easy, is it?' He leans back and sips his coffee. 'When Nash's mom took off, I didn't think I could ever trust a woman again.'

Nash's birth mother had Nash, then disappeared. Uncle Mitch was left to raise Nash on his own, until he married Barb, Nash's stepmom.

'What did Aunt Barb do to make you change your mind?'

'She gave me time to work through it. It was my problem, not hers. I had to learn to trust that she'd stick around. I think what made me really fall for Barb is that she never judged me for it. She never told me to just get over it or that I was stupid for feeling that way.' He pauses. 'She was a good woman. I miss her every day.'

'I miss her too. And I know Mom does, especially during times like this.'

He nods. 'Those two were quite a pair, cackling away in the kitchen all hours of the night. I miss that, all of us getting together as a family. The boys and I need to get up here more. Nash was just mentioning he was thinking of having his wedding up here. I hadn't thought about having it at the orchard, but it's a good idea. It's such a beautiful place.'

'Yeah, it is.' But it may not be ours for much longer. I turn to Uncle Mitch. 'Can I ask you something about your company?'

'Go ahead.'

'What would you do with it if your sons had decided to do something else? If they didn't want to work construction?'

'I'd let them do what they want. I couldn't force them into it. Nash fought it for years, doing all kinds of jobs that didn't suit him. I think he was just trying to prove that he was different than me. He didn't want to be a version of his old man. The thing he didn't get is that construction is what we do, not who we are. He can do construction and be nothing like me.' He chuckles. 'He actually is a lot like me, but I don't point it out.'

'If none of your boys wanted the company, would you sell it?'

'Probably. I can't do this forever. My body's already showing wear and tear from years of working construction.'

Mom walks up to us, talking to Uncle Mitch. 'Where are your boys?'

'In the cafeteria.' He gets up and puts his arm around her. 'Let's go down there and join them. I'll buy you some lunch.'

'I'm really not hungry.'

'Then your big brother will buy you a cup of coffee.' He forces her to walk with him. 'You coming, Nick?'

'No, I think I'll stay here.'

They continue down the hall to the elevator. I remain in the waiting area and think about what I should do, weighing the pros and cons, calculating the risks. Then I think about what Lyndsay said, about how I think too much and how I should listen to what my heart is telling me.

'Why am I making this so hard?' I mutter to myself as I get up.

It's not hard. This is the easiest decision I've ever made.

As I walk into Dad's room, he hears me and opens his eyes. 'What are you doing back?'

'I came to make you an offer.'

'An offer? For what?'

I grab a chair and pull it up next to his bed. 'I'd like to apply for the job.'

'What job?'

'Taking your place on the orchard until you're better, or until you think I'm ready to take it over for good.'

'Nick, if your mother put you up to this—'

'She didn't. This is what I want. It just took me until now to figure it out.'

'No.' He shakes his head. 'I'm not letting you do this. You didn't spend all that time and money going to school to be a farmer. Your life is in New York and that's where you're going to stay.'

'I don't want that life. I'm tired of it. The only time I'm happy is when I come home, when I'm out working in the orchard, breathing the fresh air. You taught me everything I know, and if I forgot anything, you'll be there to help me.' I look him in the eye. 'I want to do this, Dad. And I'm not doing it because you can't. I'm doing it because this is what I want.'

His brows furrow. 'Are you sure about this?'

'A hundred percent.' I stand up. 'I can send you a resume and we can schedule a formal interview if you have other candidates you need to consider.'

He smiles a little. 'How much do you expect to get paid?'

'We can settle that later. For now I need to know if you'll consider me.'

He looks up at the ceiling, a trick he uses to keep himself from crying.

'You sure you can handle the job?' he asks, still staring at the ceiling. 'It's a lot of hard, physical labor.'

'I'm looking forward to it. It'll save me from paying for a gym membership.'

He clears his throat and extends his hand to me. 'Congratulations. You're hired.'

I smile. 'You won't regret it.'

'I better not,' he says, trying to hide his smile.

'There you are,' Sawyer says, coming into the room. 'We couldn't find you.'

My brothers walk in, along with Mom and Uncle Mitch.

'I had an interview,' I say, laughing a little.

'For what?' Brody asks, sitting down in the chair.

'I'm officially the new manager of Kanfield Orchard.'

'You're *what*?' Sawyer asks.

Mom gasps and looks at Dad.

'What could I say?' he says to Mom. 'The kid wanted it. I couldn't really tell him no.'

'Holy shit.' Sawyer walks up to me. 'You're moving back?'

'I have to. I can't run the place from New York.'

'Oh, Nick!' My mom races up to me and hugs me. 'Thank you.'

'I should be thanking you. I get a job where I get to be outside all day instead of stuck in an office.'

'You're really doing this?' Jason asks. 'You're giving up being a lawyer?'

'He's not giving it up,' Sawyer says, smiling at me. 'I need a lawyer. You think you could look over some vendor contracts for me?'

'Only if I get free beer.'

'You can have all you want.'

'Hey, Nick,' Nash says, standing at the door.

'Yeah?'

'There's someone out here that needs to talk to you.'

'Who?'

'Just get out here,' he says, cracking a smile.

I walk out to the hall and see Lyndsay standing there, wearing jeans and the Kanfield Orchard t-shirt my mom gave her the day Lyndsay helped clean up after the party.

'Hey, Nick.' Her eyes lock on mine and I feel like all those pieces that were falling apart are starting to come back together. I don't know why she's here and what this means, but having her here feels as right as telling my dad I want the orchard.

'I'll leave you two alone,' Nash says, going in Dad's room.

'Lyndsay, what are you doing here?'

'I wanted to be here for you.' She steps up to me. 'As a friend, or whatever we are now.' She glances at my dad's room. 'How's he doing?'

'Better. He's tired, but the doctor said that's normal after a heart attack.'

'Is he still having surgery?'

'Yeah, later this week. How long are you staying?'

'Actually, I live here now.'

'What are you talking about?'

'I decided I don't want to be in LA anymore. So I packed up my stuff and left.'

'To come here,' I confirm. 'To Haydon Falls.'

'Yeah. I'm going to live with my mom, get a job, save up some money. I thought about what you said, Nick, and you were right. We were moving too fast. I'm not ready to move to New York with you. I'm still working through all the issues I had with Chris. I need to learn to trust again. I can't be accusing you of things you didn't do.'

I step aside as a nurse goes by us, pushing a guy in a wheelchair.

'Let's go outside,' I say to Lyndsay. 'I don't want to talk in here.'

Taking her hand, I lead her down the hall and out the doors to the front of the hospital. I spot a bench and we walk down there and take a seat.

'I understand you need time to work through stuff,' I say, turning to her. 'But I'd still like to see you.'

'I'd like to see you too, but how are we going to do this? You can't fly home every weekend.'

'I don't need to.'

'What do you mean?'

'I'm already home. I live here. Well, I don't have a place yet, but I'll work on that next week.'

'I don't get it. What do you mean you live here?'

'I'm taking over the orchard for my dad. He'll still be there, but I'll be the one running the place and doing the work.'

'What about your job in New York?'

'I'm quitting. I don't want that life anymore. I want to be here, with my family.' I take her hand. 'And with you.'

Her face lights up. 'Is this really happening? You're seriously moving here?'

'It's really happening. I already talked to my dad.'

'Nick, that's great!' She hugs me, then lets me go. 'This is really what you want to do?'

'It is. It just took me 15 years to figure it out. What about you? Is this really what you want? To live here again?'

'Yes. I love it here. And I love being able to see my mom, and Diane and Tom. This feels like home. LA never did.'

'What about dating a farmer? You okay with that?'

'Only if it's you.' She smiles. 'I love watching you work in the fields, shirtless and sweaty. It turns me on.'

'Good, because you're going to be seeing that a lot more, assuming you come over.' I pause, getting an idea. 'Did my mom tell you that Cheryl quit?'

'Who's Cheryl?'

'Their bookkeeper. She retired last month. They haven't hired a replacement yet. If you're interested, I might be able to get you the job.'

'Nick, if you're serious, I'll take it!'

'I'll talk to my dad, but I'm guessing it's yours if you want it. We could go ask him right now.'

'Okay.' She gets up.

'Hey.' I stand up. 'Before we go in . . .'

'Yeah?'

I hold her face in my hands and kiss her, getting that feeling again that the pieces are coming together, that things are finally the way they should be.

I've been searching for this feeling for years, but I was looking in all the wrong places. It turns out it was here all along. I just didn't see it until now.

Chapter 30

Two Months Later

Nick

'The baskets go over there,' Jason says to Brody, pointing to the table where people line up for the tractor ride that takes them to the orchard. 'It's been that way forever.'

'Yeah? So why can't we change it?'

Those two have been arguing all day, just like they did when we were kids.

'Nick, where do you want them?' Brody asks, holding a stack of the red-and-white woven baskets we give to people who want to pick their own apples.

'Put them in both places this year. It'll keep the lines from getting too long.'

'That's a good idea,' Dad says. 'I should've thought of that a long time ago.' He comes over and pats me on the back. 'You're pretty good at this, Kanfield.'

'My dad was a good teacher.'

He smiles and continues over to Mom, who's setting up the tables where she'll put out the apple fritters, apple pies, caramel apples, and all the other apple treats we sell.

We're all in the barn, getting it ready for our opening on Saturday. Opening day is always crazy, and it doesn't slow down much after that. Dad was right. The orchard is a lot of work, but I love it. Moving here and taking over for my dad was the right decision. I haven't had a single moment of regret.

'Hey,' Lyndsay says, coming up behind me. 'Want to take a break?'

'I could use a break.' I turn to her and give her a kiss. She's wearing a red Kanfield tank top and denim shorts, her hair in two loose braids around her shoulders. She looks like a sexy farm girl ready for a roll in the hay.

'You make it really difficult to get any work done,' I say once we're outside and alone.

'Why is that?'

'Because you're so damn hot.' I kiss her. 'You need to come over tonight.'

'I was planning on it.'

'I mean the whole night, not just a few hours.'

'Okay. I just need to let my mom know.'

Last month I moved into an apartment. It's just a six-month lease until I find something I like better. I love my parents, but I couldn't keep living with them. I needed my own place where I could be alone with Lyndsay.

She laughs. 'I feel like a kid whenever I say that.'

'Say what?'

'That I have to let my mom know. It's like I'm a teen-ager again.'

'Maybe it's time to move out.'

'And go where? I haven't saved up enough money to get my own place.'

'I know a guy who'd let you stay with him. He might even beg you to if that's what it took.'

She smiles. 'Are you asking me to move in with you?'

'What would you say if I did?'

'Yes!' she squeals.

'Well, that was easy.' I laugh. 'How about tonight? Is that too soon?'

'I think I could make that work if some big strong guy helped me move my stuff.'

'You mean Brody? Sure, I can get him to do that.'

'Nick! You can't make him do that.'

'Sure I can. He's my little brother. He has to listen to me. And I have to stay here and get ready for the opening.'

'I should wait. We have too much to do. I'll move in next week.'

'I don't want to wait that long. You don't have that much stuff. Brody can fit it all in his truck.'

'Okay, but I'm buying him pizza.' Her face lights up and she claps her hands. 'I'm so excited we're moving in together!'

I smile, watching her. She used to get excited like that back in high school, clapping her hands, jumping up and down. And then she married Chris and her joyful, carefree spirit faded away. It's back now, along with the other parts of herself she lost being with him. She even let her hair go back to its natural blonde.

I grab her and lift her up in the air.

'Nick, put me down!' she says, laughing.

'Not until you kiss me.' She does, and I slowly set her down. 'I love you.'

'I love you too.'

We go back inside and I hear Sawyer ranting about something to Brody and Jason.

'What's going on?' I ask, walking up to Sawyer.

'You know the new brewery that's opening?'

'What about it?'

'I just heard the owner is Gina.'

'Yeah? Who's that?'

'Gina Slater!' he says, throwing his hands up.

'The girl from camp,' Jason explains.

'Really?' I look back at Sawyer. 'She's not even from here, is she?'

'No, but apparently her grandfather owned that building and left it to her in his will and she decided to turn it into a brewery. Who the hell does she think she is? She can't open a brewery! In my town!'

'You don't own the town,' I say. 'And why can't she open a brewery?'

'What the hell does a girl know about making beer?'

'Hey!' Lyndsay says. 'Why can't girls make beer? You just follow a recipe.'

'It's more complicated than that,' Sawyer mutters.

'He's just pissed because his competition is a girl,' I say, laughing. 'A girl who beat him at everything at camp.'

'She didn't beat me at *everything*,' he clarifies. 'I won the spitball competition.'

'You and your friends made up that competition,' Jason says. 'It wasn't part of the camp.'

'Who the hell cares? It was still a competition, and I won.'

'Enough of this,' I tell him. 'Get back to work.'

'Sorry, but I gotta go,' Sawyer says. 'I need to get to the brewery and work on my hard cider. There's no way she's going to win that competition. She better not even enter it.'

He's talking about the hard cider competition the orchard has been doing for the past five years. We get people from all over entering it, and this year, since Sawyer's entering, we're hiring judges instead of doing it ourselves.

'He's really angry,' Lyndsay says as we walk through the barn.

'I know.' I laugh. 'I think he might've met his match.'

'What do you mean?'

'This girl. The one who's opening the brewery. She sounds just as competitive as Sawyer.'

'I hope they don't end up fighting.'

'That might be a good thing. Sawyer needs that type of girl, someone who will keep him in line.'

Lyndsay smiles. 'Do I do that to you? Keep you in line?'

'You keep me happy.' I pull her into my arms. 'And calm when we're about to open for the season and I don't feel like we're even close to being ready.'

'We're ready. It's going to be a great season!'

I look at her. 'You just said "we", like you're a Kanfield.'

'Oh, I meant "we" like the business, you know, because I work here.'

'You are, you know.'

'Are what?'

'A Kanfield. You're part of the family.'

She smiles. 'I feel like it sometimes, I'm here so much.'

'You are. It's just not official yet.'

She gets that excited look again but doesn't say anything. She knows it's true. We haven't talked about getting married, but we know it'll happen. Maybe next fall, here on the orchard.

Nash and Callie decided to get married here. Their wedding's in October. Helping them plan it will be good practice for my own.

I'm going to marry Lyndsay Davis, my high school crush, head cheerleader, and the girl of my dreams. And we're going to run an orchard. Everything I thought would never happen actually did.

When I was younger, I ran from this place, ran from this town, never realizing that what I was running from is what I really wanted. A small town. My family. And settling down with the girl I love.

About the Author

Allie Everhart writes swoony, heartfelt, spicy romances that whisk readers away on an unforgettable emotional journey. With over 40 books published, including small-town romances, sports romances, and romantic comedies, Allie's stories are always full of passion, heart, and a dash of humor.

When she's not writing, Allie enjoys long walks, cozy cafés, and baking up delicious treats. Her love for food, holidays, and nature often makes its way into her books.

If you're ready for a romance that will make you laugh, cry, and swoon, you can explore all of Allie's books at www.allieeverhart.com.

About the Author

Allie [illegible] heartfelt, [illegible] romances that [illegible] emotional journey. With over 40 books published, including [illegible] romances, [illegible] and romantic [illegible]. Allie's stories are always full of passion, heart, and a dash of humour.

When she's not writing, Allie enjoys [illegible]

If you're ready for a romance that will [illegible] you can explore all of Allie's books at [illegible]

About Embla Books

Embla Books is a digital-first publisher of standout commercial adult fiction. Passionate about storytelling, the team at Embla believe our lives are built on stories – and publish books that will make you 'laugh, love, look over your shoulder and lose sleep'. Launched by Bonnier Books UK in 2021, the imprint is named after the first woman from the creation myth in Norse mythology. Embla was carved by the gods from a tree trunk found on the seashore; an image of the kind of creative work and crafting that writers do, and a symbol of how stories shape our lives.

Find out about some of our other books and stay in touch:

X, Facebook, Instagram: @emblabooks
Newsletter: https://bit.ly/emblanewsletter